T0008335

INTERGALACTIC EXTERMINATORS, INC

ASH BISHOP

INTERGALACTIC EXTERMINATORS, INC

CamCat Publishing, LLC
Ft. Collins, Colorado 80524
camcatpublishing.com

Hardcover ISBN 9780744305616
Paperback ISBN 9780744305821
Large-Print Paperback ISBN 9780744305869
eBook ISBN 9780744305791
Audiobook ISBN 9780744305845

Library of Congress Control Number: 2022933555

Book and cover design by Maryann Appel

5 3 1 2 4

Dedicated to:

Ash
Sue
Carrie
Anika
Ashton
And especially to Jen.

1

RUSS

RUSS WOKE UP LYING flat on the ground, his mind foggy as hell. He could smell blood. When he reached forward as gingerly as possible, his muscles screamed at the movement.

He was on his back. The forest trees waved down at him, blocking out the faint moonlight. He took a couple of deep breaths and reached forward again, groping around in the darkness. His hand came back slick with blood and fur and leaves.

And then he heard voices.

". . . do you want to do this, then?"

"I just wouldn't call this tracking, is all. The blood trail's three feet across. A tiny baby could follow this trail."

"Show me that baby."

"Shhh. Both of you, quiet. Something's registering on the heat index."

The confusion and pain made it hard to think. *Are these locals . . .?* he thought. He fumbled in his pocket, looking for his flashlight but also testing for further damage. His hand found the light. It illuminated the small clearing.

The deer's corpse was just a few feet away, right where he'd shot it, but it wasn't whole. Something had torn off its back legs, shearing straight through the muscle and bone.

Russ took a deep breath but didn't let his body or mind react to the sight of the carnage.

Seconds later, the strangers' flashlights found him.

"He's over here. To our left."

Russ heard three or four people hurrying through the brush. A woman in all black stepped into the clearing. Her brown hair was tied back in a bun, and she had a long steel shotgun in her hands. An odd earring twinkled in her ear.

"You okay, son?" she asked, crouching down to place her hands on his chest. She stared into his eyes, examining him. "Looks like you're going into shock. Just stay on your back and concentrate on breathing."

A man followed shortly after her. He glanced around, holding up a funny-looking flashlight to cast out the darkness. "He's alone," the man confirmed. "Are you from around here?" he asked Russ.

"I'm from California," Russ groaned.

"I don't know what that means," the man said.

"Just hold still," the woman said. She pulled a gadget from her pack. The end telescoped out like an antenna.

Russ watched as an aqua blue light shone down from the device, running across his entire body. He flinched as it reached his face, and even that small movement caused his lungs to burst with pain.

"He's got four broken ribs, a hairline fracture in the left wrist and a torn hamstring. Did you see what hit you?" the woman asked him.

Russ tried to think. "No." The word was as much a groan as anything else.

"Tell us what you remember."

Russ rolled over onto his side. It hurt badly. Now that she'd pointed out the injuries, everything was localized. His ribs throbbed. His wrist felt hollow. His left leg was pierced with pain.

"I was driving down Route 89, and a deer . . ." Russ pointed to the half deer corpse beside him. ". . . this deer dashed in front of my car. I knew I'd injured it by the sound it made when it hit the bumper, but I didn't think I'd have to chase it this far into the woods to put it out of its misery."

Russ took a moment to swallow. "After I shot it, I—I was kneeling, jacking out the leftover rifle shells. But then . . . I was flipping through the air. I think I hit that tree right behind me."

The woman looked back at the tree. "It's pretty splintered up."

"I was flying upside down. Backwards."

"Can you walk?" the man asked.

Two more women, dressed in the same black combat gear, entered the clearing. They both had long rifles slung over their backs.

Russ glanced at the newcomers, his eyes lingering on the guns. They weren't locals. He could tell that much. "Who are you guys?"

"Just local hunters," one of the newcomers said.

"Sure," Russ said.

"Tell me what hit you," the first woman said firmly.

"I don't know. A meteor? A buffalo? Maybe . . . a . . . rig?"

The woman pulled a roll of pills from a MOLLE strap on her backpack. "Swallow two of these. They're going to kill the pain."

Russ chewed the pills. Their chalky taste filled his mouth and crept up his nose.

"They won't cure any of the damage. You're going to feel fine, but you're not fine. Move carefully until you can get proper medical treatment. The road is two miles north. Can you reach it without help?"

Russ nodded. Whatever she gave him was blazing through his bloodstream, kicking the fog and ache off every organ that it passed.

"What'd I just eat?"

"Two miles north. Don't stop for any reason."

One of the newcomers, a well-muscled young woman with close-cropped brown hair, glanced at the half deer corpse lying next to Russ. Its blood had sprayed a pattern across the splintered tree. "Look at the animal, Kendren," she said.

The guy, Kendren, shone his flashlight over the deer corpse. "Whoa," he said. "We definitely found what we're looking for."

"You really chummed the water with this stag," the short-haired woman told Russ.

"Kendren, Starland, mouths shut," the first woman said, making a slashing gesture. She pulled Russ to his feet. He gritted his teeth against the pain, but it was gone.

Kendren and Starland stayed huddled around the deer, crouched low, inspecting where the hindquarters had been sheared off the bone. Kendren looked at the deer's head and saw where Russ had shot it.

"You make this shot?" he asked Russ. "In the dark?"

"Yeah."

"Was the deer already dead? Were you a foot away? Point blank?"

"No. I was up on a ledge over by the river. Forty feet in that direction." Russ pointed up the gradual incline.

Kendren was still looking at the dead deer. "You shot it between the eyes, from forty feet, in the dark?"

"Yeah. I guess."

"Head on back to the highway," the woman said firmly. "You should start now. It might be dangerous to stay here."

The way she was looking at him, Russ kind of figured she meant that she was what was dangerous.

If he didn't do what she said.

"I just need to find my grandpa's rifle first," Russ told her.

She grabbed him by the arm. Her grip was incredibly strong. In the light from her flashlight her eyes seemed almost purple. "Start walking toward—"

Before she could finish her sentence, the third woman, who'd melted back into the darkness, stepped forward again. "Cut the light," she hissed. "It's here."

Something came crashing through the brush, making a howling sound. It wasn't a sound Russ had ever heard before. It was a deep rumbling growl, followed by a pitched screech that made the hair on his arms stand up. Branches were snapping, and he could hear claws scraping on rock. It was still thirty feet south, but it scared the hell out of him.

"'El Toreador.' You're up," the woman hissed.

The girl they called El Toreador had been on lookout. She was far enough into the darkness that Russ could barely see her, just a wisp of thick brown hair bobbing in the darkness—that is, until she pounded her chest with her fist. The vest lit up red, casting shadows across the trees. "My real name's Atara," she told Russ quickly. Then: "Don't look so worried. We're professionals."

"Starland, hit her with the hormone."

"The vest is enough," Atara growled.

Starland slipped back into the light. She was carrying some kind of tube. It looked like a pool toy. She pushed hard against the end, blasting thick goo all over the other woman.

"Hurry up. It's almost here."

Russ was scrambling around in the brush, looking everywhere for his rifle when the creature burst through the perimeter glow of his tiny flashlight. Atara's vest reflected off its face, bathing it in red light. It was all fangs and claws, huge, twice the size of a grizzly bear and full of rippling muscles stretched out in terrifying feline grace. It leaped at Atara, but midflight it caught the scent of the goo and reoriented to the left, bumping her off her feet but not harming her.

The huge cat-thing landed softly, immediately turning toward the fallen woman, sniffing the air, growling, and bobbing its head.

"It's got the scent. The big kitty's feeling amorous," Kendren yelled. He, Starland, and the other woman all had their rifles raised.

They were tracking the cat, ready to fire. Atara looked pissed, sprawled on the ground with her legs splayed.

"Knock it down. We're authorized for lethal. What are you waiting for?" she shouted.

The creature was fully in the light now. It looked a lot like a tiger, but it was at least six times the size, with wavy, shaggy hair.

"What the hell is it?" Russ shouted.

The feline was practically straddling Atara. "I don't like how it's looking at me. Come on, shoot!" she demanded.

The creature batted a paw, claws extended, and tore the glowing vest off her chest. It drew the vest up to its nose, sniffed, and started to growl again.

Then the huge beast paused, slowly turning away from Atara. It sniffed the air, shoulders hunched, fur on the scruff of its neck rising. As it turned, its deep onyx eyes looked squarely at Russ.

It growled and took a step toward him.

Russ thought his heart had been beating hard before, but as the huge cat glided toward him, the thudding in his chest was so loud it drowned out every other sound. He didn't even hear the discharge of Starland's shotgun, two feet away from the monster.

The wad of pellets sprayed against the creature's flank and it howled, tearing away into the darkness so fast Russ didn't even see it move.

Atara scrambled to her feet and dropped her rifle. "Did you see that? A direct hit and no penetration. I told you Earth tech was garbage. What is this? The thirteenth century? I'm powering up."

The first woman—the one with the purple eyes—glanced at Russ. She was short, wiry, with the powerful shoulders of a linebacker. Russ realized she was the leader of . . . whoever these people were.

"When are you going to learn to keep your mouth shut?" she barked at Atara.

"You already used the CRC wand on him."

"Two hours of mandatory training videos. The second this is over."

"I'd rather be cat food than watch those again," Atara said.

"You skip the videos and I'll send you back through CERT training."

Atara wasn't really listening. She crashed off through the brush in the direction of the big cat.

Nodding toward Russ, the woman shouted, "Kendren, you've got containment." Then she disappeared into the darkness. Starland drew a pistol from her belt and followed.

"Containment? More like babysitting," Kendren grumbled. "I should be the one doing the good stuff." He glanced in the direction they'd gone. Russ kind of agreed. Kendren was huge, at least six-five, and covered from head to toe with what Russ's cousin had always called beach muscles. He had thick, wavy hair down to his shoulders.

Out in the darkness, Russ could see the others' flashlights bobbing up and down. They were headed up an incline, probably straight toward the bank of the river.

"Was it my imagination, or was the cat more interested in you than the vest covered in mating hormone?" Kendren asked.

At first, Russ didn't answer. Finally, he said, "What would make it do that?"

"No idea. It's supposed to follow the hormone. What's better than sex?" Kendren shook his head, seemingly unable to answer his own question. He frowned slightly. "The only thing I've seen them more interested in is an Obinz stone. You ever seen an Obinz stone? They're about this big"—Kendren held his hands six inches apart—"usually green, with yellow veins running all along the edges? I don't think they're native to . . . this area." Kendren looked around in distaste. "But I've seen these cats jump planets just to get near one if it's in an unrefined state. An Obinz stone is basically intergalactic catnip."

"I've never seen one," Russ told him. His voice wavered slightly, but Kendren didn't seem to notice.

"Then we better shut this vest down," Kendren said. He stepped up onto a boulder and reached high into a tree, grabbing the vest from where the cat had tossed it. He folded the vest up and tucked it under his arm. "I'm not even sure how to turn it off," he said.

"That was a saber-toothed tiger, right? You guys cloning stuff? Is this Jurassic World or something?" Russ rubbed his temple. His questions were coming so fast, they were jumbled in his mouth. Kendren had just said intergalactic, and something about jumping planets, but here in the dark Wyoming forest, six miles from his grandmother's house, he wasn't yet ready to face those pieces of information.

Kendren threw the vest on the ground and raised his rifle, pumping a slug into it. It kept glowing. "Damn. It's pretty important I get this thing turned off."

Starland's discarded shotgun was just a few feet away. While Kendren kicked at the vest with his boot heel, Russ inched toward it.

"Touch the weapon and I'll shoot you in the face," Kendren said. He stomped on the vest again.

The flashlights were way north now, probably on the other side of the river. Russ could hear the distant voices arguing about which way the big cat went.

The voices were so loud, neither Kendren nor Russ heard the cat until it was right in front of them, growling, hissing, and spitting. It stalked into the circumference of the faint red light from the vest.

Kendren was still standing on the vest, his rifle slung over his shoulder. Beside him, the cat was enormous, twice as tall as a man. It crouched down, looking him straight in the eye.

"I'm dead," he said quietly.

The creature coiled back on its powerful flanks and threw itself forward like a bullet. Its wicked claws stretched out, razored edges slashing at Kendren's neck and chest. Russ kicked Starland's gun off the ground, caught it, leveled it, and fired. The bullet split the cat's eye socket, ripping through its optic nerve and straight into its brain.

Momentum carried the dead body forward on its trajectory, smashing into Kendren and pinning him to the earth.

A few moments later, the rest of the team returned, clambering through the thick brush. The leader approached the enormous beast and nudged it with her boot.

"Is it dead, Bah'ren?" Atara asked, her gun still pointed at the fallen creature.

"Sure is," the leader, Bah'ren, responded.

The wind was starting to pick up, blowing the branches of the trees, shaking off a few dead leaves.

"How about Kendren?"

"Negative," Bah'ren said.

"Get it off me," Kendren demanded. "It's gotta weigh nine hundred pounds."

"How many intergalactic laws do you think we've broken here?" Atara asked. She moved next to Bah'ren, looking down at Kendren with an expression that was half pity and half amusement.

He had managed to sit up, but his legs were still wedged under the huge carcass."Including the law about referencing intergalactic law on a tier-nine planet?" Bah'ren asked.

"You guys are being a little careless," Starland said.

"Not our fault this thing was a hundred miles off course. The MUP-map promised there wouldn't be any tier-nine bios in the vicinity."

"What are we supposed to do now?" Atara said, nodding toward Russ.

"Oh, we're conscripting him, for sure." Bah'ren said.

"Really?" Atara said. "We're getting another human?"

"Who? Who do you mean?" Russ asked. He glanced back in the direction of the highway. His eyes were starting to adjust to the dark again, and he could make out a thick copse of trees just a dozen or so yards away.

"Get the huge beast off me," Kendren insisted.

Bah'ren moved to one side of the big cat and dug her powerful shoulders into it. Starland ran over to join her, wedging one arm against the creature's flank, but putting her other arm around the waist of the woman giving the orders. "Atara, come on. You, new guy, we could use your help too. It's heavy as hell."

Russ half ran over to them and dug his side into the creature. Its hairy skin sloshed around against the pressure, but the four of them eventually got it moving.

"Roll it the other way!" Kendren demanded. "Its penis is right next to my face."

They kept rolling, and Kendren kept protesting, as the great shaggy cat slowly grinded over his shoulders and face. Gravity finally caught hold of its weight and the corpse flopped to the ground. The three in black all chuckled as Kendren spit out the taste of cat testicle.

"Oh, that's what you meant. Sorry about that," Starland said, laughing.

Kendren crawled onto his knees, still hacking and spitting. He stopped for a minute and looked at the cat's face, poking a finger in the thing's empty eye socket and wiggling it around. "Another hell of a shot."

"The debriefing wasn't just wrong about location," Atara said. "The creature's fur is like steel mesh. Our bullets were doing jackshit."

Kendren rolled up onto his knees, both hands propped on his thighs. "You saved my life," he told Russ.

"No problem," Russ said.

It was the last thing Russ said before he dropped the rifle and sprinted full speed back toward the safety of the trees. He was running as fast as he could, pumping his arms, banging his shins on rocks, bumping past pines, carelessly plunging through the dark.

He'd only gotten about twenty yards, running full speed, when something metal slapped around his ankle. It tipped him off balance and, for the second time that night, he could feel himself careening head over heels.

He hit a tree, again, then slowly slipped out of consciousness.

2

RUSS

Seventy-two hours previous

IT ALL BEGAN SOMEWHERE in Louisiana. He'd just finished his thirteenth day of working the line on a petrochemical plant in Baton Rouge. Thirteen days of lifting this and pushing that. He'd found that in these kinds of jobs they rarely let the new guy do anything important, which was fine with Russ.

The paycheck was what was important to Russ.

He'd expected Baton Rouge, with its strange cultural mix of French, English, and Spanish, to keep his interest, but he'd soured on it almost immediately. He had hoped for music and lights, dancing and distraction; what he'd found was a tired populace dragging themselves to early-morning factory jobs and spending evenings binge-watching Netflix. It was the same thing he'd found in Shreveport, and Fort Worth before that.

A bank teller had tipped him off to an exotic restaurant south of Lafayette that served alligator-meat burritos, and Russ had found himself headed in that direction, moving aimlessly down Highway 49.

His eyes kept drifting to the dash, hoping *E* didn't really mean empty, when a text from his mother arrived:

> *Your grandfather passed away this morning. I know you cared a lot about Grandpop. You might think about calling Norma or sending a card. The funeral is tomorrow in Evanstown.*

"Cared a lot about Grandpop" was an understatement.

Russ had pulled over to the side of the highway and cried for two minutes. He'd wiped his tears with a napkin that happened to be stuffed into his door handle, and U-turned, pointing the car back Northbound. Then he'd driven twenty-two hours straight, to Evanstown, Wyoming.

On the way he'd drunk fourteen energy drinks and chewed every over-the-counter energy pill he could find. By the last seven hours he was seeing double and only swerving the car a little bit. And he'd learned a hard lesson. The small orange gas station pills called *Stree Overlord* that he'd spent the last of his money on weren't energy pills at all, but rather some kind of Chinese sexual stimulant.

Still, he made it to Evanstown, awake, nearly on time, and with only a mild erection. It was strange, driving down off the overpass back into Evanstown for the first time in over a decade. It didn't seem like much had changed. The topography was the same. A wall of wild lodgepole pines still hid much of the main portion of the town from the interstate. He recognized many of the stores—the hardware store, the post office, even the same cluster of liquor stores—mostly there to serve those sneaking across the border from Utah, desperate for a quick drag of something stronger than 3.2 percent.

There were a lot of empty buildings as well—shells of businesses gone under, their roofs sagging, their windows still promising reduced prices and going-out-of-business liquidations. Russ couldn't remember if there had been that many empty spots the last time he'd cruised into town.

He wouldn't admit it to anyone, but despite caring a great deal for his grandparents, he'd purposely avoided Evanstown during the last few years of his travels.

When he was still a kid, Evanstown had been a safe place for him, a place where his grandma was always able to tolerate his childish hyperactivity. He'd come there a lot during his youth, shipped out east when his mom "had had enough."

Rather than try to control him, his grandma had filled his head with all the possibilities of the future. "I know you'll be someone great someday, Russ," she always told him. "Your restlessness is hiding a true talent for intellectual curiosity. Your grandfather is the same way. When you grow up, you're going to make all the Wesleys proud."

Yet here he was, eight years removed from his last failed effort to go to college, closing in on the tail end of his twenties, and he'd made exactly no one proud. Aside from impressing a few people here and there with his marksmanship, Russ hadn't managed to accomplish much of anything at all. Though she would be the last one to ever verbalize it, Russ knew he had let his grandmother down in some significant but undefinable way.

The graveyard was at the east end of town. He could see a crowd halfway up a fifteen-degree incline, clustered around a modest grave. It seemed about a full tenth of the populace of Evanstown had shown up, roughly five hundred people. They had black cowboy hats, black shirts, jackets, and blouses hanging loose over dirty black jeans, and black cowboy boots. The crowd shifted their feet in the hot August sun, their heads bowed respectfully.

A short bespectacled chaplain stood over the freshly dug grave and, as Russ climbed the small hill to the site, he could see the pallbearers lowering his grandfather's casket into the ground. Russ looked over the pallbearers, then the crowd, but even before he saw the last face, he knew that he was the only California Wesley to make the service.

He refused to acknowledge how light his grandfather's casket looked as they lowered it. His grandpop had been a robust man, just some red hair shy of looking a lot like King Henry the VIII. Russ couldn't imagine that big man, with his even bigger personality, fitting in that coffin, much less being light enough to carry without difficulty.

The chaplain began to talk about Russ's grandfather's time as a navy corpsman and the heroic things he'd done during the Korean War. He talked about his grandfather's travels, how he'd journeyed from one coast to the other, picking up odd antiquities and rare books. How he'd used his knowledge to keep one of Evanstown's last privately owned stores in business—"and a bookstore at that!"

As the chaplain continued, Russ pushed his way to the front and stood quietly next to his grandmother Norma. She turned a tearstained face to his, her eyes widening in surprise. Then she took his hand, cinched herself against his shoulder, and buried her old, frail head in the crook of his arm. Her body shook, and Russ clinched her tighter.

And suddenly his own insecurities, and the drudgery of the twenty-two-hour drive, didn't mean anything at all.

After the service, a smaller group of funeral attendants moved into a temporary annex near the entrance to the graveyard. Inside, a man in an oversized suit sat behind a small desk. Russ recognized him as Norma's lawyer, Mr. Baedeker. His tie was too long, and his suit was too large, but both were clean and wrinkle free. The air conditioner was whirring noisily, but beads of sweat still rolled down Mr. Baedeker's forehead.

Norma had yet to release Russ's arm. She kept saying, "He'd be so happy to know you'd come."

"I won't keep you all very long," Mr. Baedeker told the small crowd. "It's hot, and I know Bibi Nguyen has been kind enough to host an after-service wake at her home, with some of her delicious hors d'oeuvres. I understand she's been working on them throughout the day. It sounds like a party that would have made Clark proud." The man mopped his forehead with a handkerchief.

"I have the pleasure of acting as Clark's testator, and as such, I have been asked to share the details of his final will and testament. Unfortunately, as many of you know, Clark's long illness drained the Wesley family of much of their material possessions. As such, there is almost nothing to announce." The lawyer pointed to a redheaded man in a black vest. "William, he asked that you receive his telescope and all related astronomy *apparati*, including the lenses."

"Swee-eet," William said, letting out a short whistle.

The lawyer pointed to an older woman. She had a shock of curly white hair bound tightly.

"Martha, he said that you should come by his garage and take anything that you can use . . ."

"That's fantastic," Martha said.

". . . except his gun collection."

"Oh," Martha said, visibly disappointed. "Who gets that?"

"He left his gun collection to his grandson, Russell Wesley."

"Oh," Russ said, surprised.

Norma turned and looked at Russ, her red eyes searching his face. "He really wanted you to have them," she whispered.

"Grandma, I . . ."

Norma shushed him with a raised finger. "We both knew you wouldn't have any place to put them all. You can keep them in our garage if you'd like. Or sell them. Or give them to friends. Clark just wanted to make sure you had the guns if you wanted them."

The lawyer interrupted. "The exact words of the will read thus: 'No one has ever made those guns sing the way my grandson can.'"

"He was enormously proud of your marksmanship," Norma told Russ.

Russ marveled at his sudden ownership of a vast expanse of rare guns. He was thinking about the Kar98, and the Merkel 141, and especially the M25 Whitefeather. He had trouble concentrating on anything else as the testator gave away Clark's *Life* magazine collection and his military medals. After the reading was concluded, almost everyone shuffled out of the muggy annex.

Before Russ and his grandma could reach the door, Mr. Baedeker waved Norma over to his desk. "I've got some bad news regarding another matter, I'm afraid," he told her.

"Stay here a moment," Norma told Russ. She walked reluctantly over to the desk, and the two spoke in low whispers. Russ couldn't hear the words, but he saw his grandma's face fall as the lawyer spoke emphatically into her ear.

He wondered what the news was that couldn't wait until a day or two after his grandfather was put in the ground. As Norma shuffled back to his side, he started to ask her, but the depth of sadness in her eyes told him his question could wait for another time.

Tired from the long drive and the heavy emotions, Russ slept on the porch at Bibi Nguyen's, missing out entirely on her delicious hor d'oeuvres. It was Bibi herself who shook him awake. Bibi was a first-generation Filipino immigrant. Norma and Bibi were the same age, but unlike Norma, Bibi dyed her white hair an avian red, and permed it into tight curls. The curls bobbed in Russ's face as she gently shook his shoulder. Also, unlike Norma, Bibi wore a lot of makeup, most noticeably a heavy, light-blue eyeliner.

Despite spending much of the last half century in Evanstown, Bibi still spoke with a distinct Filipino accent. On the other hand, Norma's voice carried the echo of a quite different accent, that of someone born and raised in southern Wyoming. Yet for all their differences, Bibi had been Norma's best friend for as long as Russ could remember. He recognized the concerned expression on Bibi's face as identical to the one he'd seen on Norma's just an hour or two before, when the lawyer had been whispering in her ear.

"Have you been to the bookstore yet?" Bibi asked Russ.

"I drove straight to the funeral," Russ explained.

"You might not want to visit the bookstore," Bibi cautioned him. "Like your Grandpop, it's better to remember things when they were at their best . . ."

Russ sat up, shaking off the cobwebs. Still reeling from the death of his Grandpop, he was nowhere near ready for more bad news—especially if it involved the bookstore. "What exactly is—" he started to say.

"Don't bother the boy with our troubles," Norma interrupted. She was standing at the edge of the porch, nibbling on a deviled egg. "My grandson was the only one of us smart enough to never put down roots. We don't ask him to come around just to share in our burdens. He deserves the happy life of a wanderer. Heaven knows, someone should have it."

"Grandma?" Russ asked. "Tell me what's going on with the bookstore."

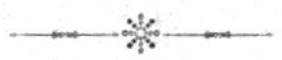

Norma found it easier to show Russ instead.

It didn't take long for them to reach the quaint little cultural center of Evanstown, Wyoming. It was mostly a ranching town, but there was a patchwork golf course, a small community theater, and a few things for people who liked "learnin'," including Russ's grandparents' bookstore. The Walmart Supercenter was just a handful of miles south in the neighboring town of Banville. They approached the front of the store, and Russ could read the old, faded sign: THE MYSTERIOUS UNIVERSE: NEW AND USED BOOKS, ODDITIES, KNICKKNACKS.

"I'm not ready to go home just yet," she told him. "But I'm sure not ready to go in the bookstore either. I'll wait for you outside."

Norma's hands shook as she worked the old key in the lock. True to her word, she didn't follow him inside.

The smell of decaying books was so strong that Russ had to go immediately to the window and wiggle it open. He didn't have to ask his grandma when someone had last been inside. It was clear it had been a while. The "Open" sign wasn't just turned off; it had been taken out of the window and laid across the check-out counter. Above his head, the ceiling was darkened with moisture, clear evidence of a leak, or multiple leaks, in the roof. Someone had nailed a tarp under several of the leaks, but rainwater had just filled it like a balloon and then dribbled over the side. Russ wanted to tell his grandmother, "You've got to put the tarp on top of the leak, not under it," but bit his tongue. His grandfather's illness had taken a lot out of Norma, and he guessed the condition of the bookstore was probably a pretty good metaphor for how she was feeling in general.

Russ explored the small store, moving down the hall to the employee bathroom, the tiny breakroom, and the extended storage room in the back. He reached the other door, which led into an overgrown alley, and he stopped a moment to collect his thoughts.

"It's all right, Russ," he heard his grandmother's frail voice float down the hall. "Everything is finite. Everything ends." Russ turned around to face her words. The way the sound wove through the store, it seemed to be coming directly from the stacks of moldy, unorganized books. "Without your grandfather . . . without your grandfather healthy, this store was too much for me to organize and run on my own anyhow. And so much of it reminds me of him. If I go in there . . . it will be like he's back alive. It has so many memories. Makes the most sense to just let the bank have it. Serves them right anyway. What are they going to do with a bunch of soggy books?"

Russ stuck his head into the storage room. It was where his grandfather had kept all the oddities he collected on his travels. Russ saw a whole cabinet full of neon-colored quartz rocks, three long, carved sticks that looked suspiciously like magic wands, and a Beanie Baby shaped like a minotaur. When he picked it up, he realized it wasn't a Beanie Baby after all. Its skin felt like human flesh.

There were several bins full of more trinkets and oddities. A clump of gray-and-bone-white mush caught his eye. The edges were crusted in red, suggesting it had at one point been actively bleeding. Russ studied it for a moment, trying to decide if it was a dead rodent or a dehydrated flower. When he finally picked it up, it fell apart in his hands, leaving a gory sludge on his fingers.

Norma had always found these things "distasteful and grotesque," and as Russ wiped his hands on his jeans he understood why. A lot of the stuff in the back closet was, at best, unrecognizable, and at worst, borderline occult. Russ knew that his grandfather had established an online portal a few years ago and that the supplemental income from this had saved the store—at least temporarily. Nearly all their online sales had been made from this backroom collection.

Even in this room, which was better insulated from the water, the smell of rot was almost unbearable. Russ walked back to the main portion of the store and picked the "Open" sign up off the counter.

Norma had come to the window and was staring at him, curious. "Now what are you going to do with that?" she asked. When Russ didn't answer, she said, "Do you want it as a keepsake? It's just a silly neon sign. And it doesn't even light up all the way."

"Grandma," Russ said, "I'm putting this sign where it belongs."

"In the trash?"

"In the window." Russ hung the sign up. He grabbed the plug and fished around for the wall socket under the window frame.

"Russ, if you plug in that sign people will think the store is open again."

Russ found the wall socket and the sign lit up: OP_N.

"Or at least they'll think it's op'n," Norma said wryly.

"Well, we don't want to confuse them," Russ told her. "I better get to work so we can get this sucker op'n'd up."

3

RUSS

DESPITE HIS STIRRING ANNOUNCEMENT, Russ didn't immediately get to work. He drove back to his grandma's small home just off the banks of Bear River and crashed on her couch until the following morning. Then he got to work.

He figured it made the most sense to start in the back and move toward the front of the store. The spring rains had come through the damaged roof and wet the books, and now the summer heat was bringing unwelcome life to the pages.

Without any money for cleaning supplies, he had to rely on good old-fashioned elbow grease. Every book that had too much moisture damage went into the dumpster in the alley. He must have thrown out two dozen copies of *Fifty Shades of Grey. Fifty Shades Darker. Fifty Shades Freed. Fifty Shades Even More Darker Still,* he thought.

He wasn't looking forward to moving into the storage room. The fleshy minotaur seemed to follow him with its eyes. Still, if he needed some capital to begin repairs, he knew that selling something from "the back" was his best chance. He held his nose and dug in. The water had only damaged the southern corner of the room, seeping into a collection of Led Zeppelin vinyl records that were now stuck together like a band sandwich. Everything under the records was in sealed plastic bins, which were unharmed. The top bin was full of snakeskins, but their colors were unnatural, swirling hues of blue, purple, and onyx.

The bin under that held only a single item, an enormous crab claw. Russ lifted it out with both hands and raised it up toward the single light bulb dangling from the ceiling. The claw was at least two feet by three feet and weighed close to thirty pounds. He knew it couldn't have come from a real crab. The thing would have had to have been eight or ten feet tall. But as he moved the claw around in the light, he couldn't find how it had been constructed. The parts seemed to fit together organically, like a real exoskeleton.

He was relieved to find the bin in the back corner filled only with books. Of course, when he looked closer, the books appeared slightly misshapen, their covers uneven, the ink dry and brittle. *Now, that's odd.*

He pushed at the topmost book with his finger, and it dissolved into ash beneath his hand. The ash blossomed up his nose, and he went into a fit of sneezing, only stopping long enough to say "Whatinthehell?"

His eyes still fluttering against the sting of the ash, Russ held the bottom of his shirt to his face, waiting, very curious. A portion of the entire book stack had collapsed under the slightest pressure.

Beneath the ash were three more books. Now that he looked at them closer, they seemed to be holding their shape only by force of will. Had somebody tried to fight against the water damage by putting these books in an oven?

He grabbed a ceremonial Aztec knife from one of the boxes and poked at the edges of the burned husk. It collapsed onto itself, falling into a pile of ash. This time the ash didn't plume, and Russ realized that a clump of something was in the middle. Russ crouched over it, looking closely. The object reminded him of a burned chunk of meat.

He tapped it with the knife and another layer of ash shook free. What remained wasn't burned meat, but rather a smooth, oblong stone, about four inches in length. Russ lifted it gingerly, balanced it on the blade of the knife. He blew away the last of the ash that covered it.

"What is this thing?" Russ wondered out loud. For all the oddity of the burned books, the stone itself might have been the weirdest part of the whole enterprise. It was an unnatural lime green, and when Russ tilted it in a certain direction, he could see a network of yellow veins branching in all directions across its face.

A few hours later, he showed his find to his grandma Norma.

"You said it was in the storage room?" Norma asked. They were sitting at the small wooden table in the kitchen of her small wooden home. She peered at the stone in his hand.

"It was under a pile of books. Actually, the books were burned to a crisp, if that seems possible."

"We had a fire?"

"The whole thing was weird, Grandma," Russ admitted. "It didn't seem like a fire. They weren't burned, I guess. More like sucked dry."

Norma tilted her head. "Vampires?"

"No. I mean the books near the rock were burned—literally to a crisp. Some of the others were scattered in a circle around the rock. Like there'd been an explosion."

"Exploding, burning vampires," Norma said.

"I'm glad you can laugh," Russ told her, scratching his cheek.

"I tried to stay out of your grandfather's collection of trinkets. To be honest, they frightened me. Are you sure you want to spend so much time and effort working on all this?"

"What's the name of the guy that owns Ace Hardware, with the beard?" Russ asked.

"Bobby."

"He's a big gun enthusiast, isn't he?"

"He's been after your grandfather's collection for at least a decade. He was respectful enough not to call while your Grandpop was sick, but he really wants to get his hands on them."

"I'm going to see if he'll trade building materials, and one or two roofing lessons, for a few of the guns."

Norma's eyes searched Russ's face. "A new roof is so expensive. We got a few bids, but . . ."

"I can do the work. I did some apprentice roofing in Washington a few years back. I just need the materials, and a little help." Russ bobbed his head. *It could work,* he realized.

"You'll be sticking around that long?"

Russ lifted the rock again, studying its strange network of yellow veins. "I guess I am. It will give me a few days to investigate the rock thing too. Do you mind?"

He watched a slow smile creep across Norma's face. "Do I mind? I'd be delighted."

Russ felt a rush of pride fill his chest. He held up the rock again. "I don't suppose you know any geologists?"

Norma's eyes lit up, now matching her broad smile. The funeral had been so melancholy, but his visit, and his attempts to resurrect the bookstore, seemed to have put a little spring back in her step. Again, involuntarily, he felt a warmth in his chest because he seemed to be making her proud.

"We do have a geologist of sorts in town," Norma said. "You spend enough time in the hospital, you really get to know all the other regulars. There's a fine young lady that lives on the edge of town named Nina Hosseinzadeh. Her father's liver has just about quit, so she was in the hospital with him at least as much as I was with your Grandpop. Heck, she's probably there now." Norma smiled at Russ, and something flickered behind her eyes for just a moment.

Russ couldn't identify it.

His grandma continued, "She's also the smartest woman in all of Evanstown. She's built an electronics lab in an old storage shed at her parents' home, nearly out of scrap, as I understand it. She'd get to telling us about some serious experiment she was trying to run, with all this banged-up, half-cocked equipment, and it would have your grandpa and I hooting with laughter. I'm almost certain she'd be able to tell you a thing or two about your mysterious rock."

Bum's Sam'wich Emporium in Evanstown, Wyoming, wasn't the kind of place you'd expect to find the smartest woman in town. Bum sold seventy-five-cent sandwiches that were exactly as good as they sounded.

Russ pushed his way through Bum's door, a little worried he was walking into an awkward romantic setup. After a little consideration, he'd realized that the look he'd seen flashing across his grandmother's face was what he called her matchmaker expression. His fear had been nearly confirmed when he'd asked how he would recognize Nina and Norma told him, smugly, "Oh, you'll know her when you see her. She's easy to spot."

She was easy to spot. If someone had asked Russ to close his eyes and picture the perfect woman, the image in his head would have been eerily similar to Nina Hosseinzadeh. She had a wild shock of curly black hair that spiraled in every direction, framing her large brown eyes. Her arms and shoulders were lean but curved with muscle. Her mouth was set in a smile, naturally, just by the shape of her lips and her gums. Russ loved women who smiled without smiling.

He could see the intelligence in her bright eyes. She seemed to miss nothing, watching him walk toward her, examining him with careful scrutiny. He immediately regretted not combing his hair, but he knew that if he reached up to pat down his cowlick, it would tell her everything she needed to know about what was going on inside his head.

She was wearing jeans, mismatched socks, and a silk-screened shirt with a rifle diagram on it. She also had huge breasts, though Russ didn't notice them at all. He wasn't the type to notice that kind of thing, he assured himself.

She sat with a book in her lap and her legs tucked under her. As he arrived at her table, she gave him a half-smile and dog-eared the page of her book.

"Are you Russ Wesley?" she asked. "I'm Nina."

Russ shook her hand, still standing awkwardly beside the table.

Nina kicked an unoccupied chair and it skittered to a stop next to him. "Your grandma said you found a weird rock?"

Russ pulled the rock from his pocket and set it down next to her sandwich tray. He took the seat across from her. He had already decided it best to ignore how beautiful she was.

Nina peered down at the rock. Her eyes searched the edges of the stone as her fingers ran along the yellow veins. "I've never seen anything like it," she said.

"Neither have I. Could that color possibly be natural?"

"You found this in the bookstore—"

"It was in the storage area in the back. My grandfather collected odd things, but my grandmother doesn't remember him bringing it home or trying to sell it on the website. Have you been to the store?"

"I've been shopping there my whole life. Norma and I have spent a lot of time together in the hospital, but I've known her for at least a decade. When I was thirteen, I used to ride my bike down to the Mysterious Universe almost every day to look at the weird stuff your grandfather had collected. And to buy romance novels." Nina laughed.

Russ peered over at the book in her lap. It was called *Saving the Rancher's Daughter*.

"I'd love to help out if I could," Nina told him.

"What do you know about exotic alien minerals?" Russ asked, drawing her attention back to the rock.

Nina shook her head. "It's not a mineral. Or at least not a silicate." She looked back at Russ, and for the first time he saw an emotion other than confidence flicker across her face. "I'm actually much more of an expert on electricity. It's what I'm studying at Laramie: electrical engineering. I know quite a bit about magnetics, but aside from that I'm not sure why your grandma thought I could help."

Russ shrugged. "It's okay. You've got to know more than me, which is nothing at all. And worse case, I still get to eat a seventy-five-cent BLT."

"I won't order that. There's almost no bacon."

"These sandwiches suck," Russ agreed.

"To be honest, I think your grandmother was trying to set us up," Nina admitted. She pulled a compass out of her pocket and wiped its small round screen with her shirt.

"I was worried about that too," Russ said.

"This isn't a date, is it?" Nina asked.

"Nope."

"Good."

"I think I'm offended."

"Don't be. You seem cool. I'm just not in the market."

"Fair enough. What's with the compass?"

"It's a simple test. If the rock is magnetic, it'll attract the compass needle." Nina moved the compass around the perimeter of the rock. The needle never stopped pointing north. "And it's not magnetic," Nina concluded. "This is a crude diagnostic, of course, but a rock like this should have some polarity." She turned it over in her hand again. "If you could bring this to my lab, I might be able to run a few more official tests on it."

"I don't have too much else to do."

Nina stood up, carefully placing the rock back into Russ's hand and then wrapping what was left of her sandwich. "My lab is . . . unorthodox. It's on my parents' property. Maybe come by later today?"

"Okay." Russ spotted the silk screen on her shirt again. "Do you hunt? The image on your shirt, that's a diagram for a bolt-action rifle, isn't it?"

"Sort of," she said, looking down at her shirt.

"It's an M24; isn't it? My grandpa has an M25. Or had one. I guess it's mine now."

Nina pointed to her shirt. "This is an M21. And it's not a bolt action. It uses a gas piston." She stretched the image tight and pointed out the piston on the diagram. Nina released her shirt and stuffed the left-over sandwich into the pocket of her pants. "I live out on Old Highway 107. We're the only house on the south side of Country Road." She moved toward the door, pausing to rest her hand on the push bar. "Maybe bring along the M25. I'd love to shoot a Whitefeather."

Russ watched her leave. Beautiful. Smart. Likes to hunt. He tried to be mad at his grandmother for playing matchmaker, but the anger just wouldn't come.

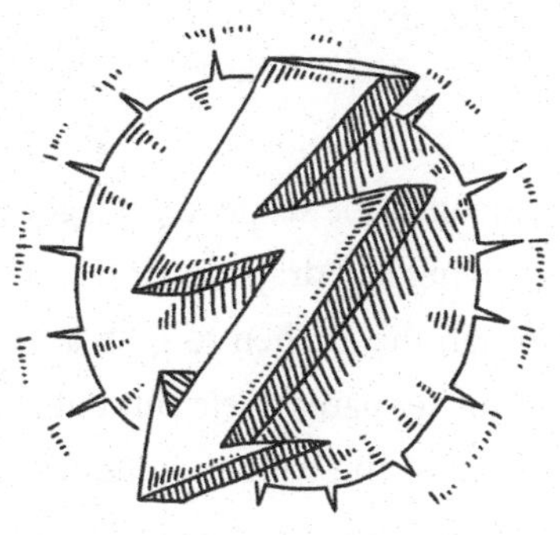

4

NINA

BY 6:30 THAT EVENING, Nina had already finished reading *Saving the Rancher's Daughter*. She'd been trying to decide on her next book, stuck between the equally promising *Having the Frenchman's Baby* and *Shackled to the Sheik*. She didn't want to admit it to herself, but she was excited.

Excited to have a visitor who wasn't one of the same old folks around town. Excited that he was bringing a genuine mystery. Most important, she was excited to get her mind off all the other stuff.

She thought she heard Russ's car in the driveway outside, and she found herself moving quickly to the dirty picture window on the front of her parents' house.

What she saw outside surprised her: a beat-up green sedan peeling away from her property.

Propped against the perimeter fence was a bouquet of red and pink balloons. Nina moved quickly out the front door, grabbing the M21 rifle that she kept in the entryway. She lined the rifle's sight on the fleeing car, flipping open the scope to get a good look at its license plate. Whoever was driving had draped a cloth over it.

Nina passed through the kitchen to grab a pair of scissors, then walked outside, crossing her parents' elegant but extremely run-down front porch. At the base of the balloon bouquet, she found a sealed envelope with her name written across it in a flourish of red ink. "Don't like this," she mumbled to herself.

She was using the scissors to pop the balloons when Russ rolled up her long driveway in a faded maroon Mercury Tracer.

As he climbed out of the car, a rifle in his hand, Nina noticed he'd changed his clothes. They were nicer, apart from a very run-down—she would use the word *bedraggled*—pair of shoes. His hair, which this afternoon had been defiantly unkempt, was now carefully groomed.

He looked handsome, but Nina didn't let herself acknowledge this. She had too many other things on her mind.

"Hello," Nina said, welcoming him.

"This is an incredible house," Russ told her.

"Thanks. When you get closer, you'll see it's pretty run down. My dad's on dialysis, and he wasn't exactly Mr. Fixit before he got sick." Nina gestured to the green fields past the house. "We have ten acres, but that's because nobody else wants the land around here. Actually, my mom listed it on the market three months ago. If you happen to have several hundred thousand dollars lying around, it could be yours."

Russ patted his empty pockets. "I have just enough to afford one more sandwich," he told her. He nodded to the balloons. "Did you guys just have a party?"

"No. It's the weirdest thing. Someone just drove up here and left this."

"That Saturn that passed me headed back to the highway?"

"Yeah. Shit green with oxidized paint? Did you get a look at the driver?"

"No. Sorry. I didn't think it was important. Did you read the card?"

"I'm a little nervous to."

Russ took the card out of her hand. "Looks like it's a romantic gesture? From a secret admirer?" Russ tore open the envelope. He read aloud:

"I dream of being near you every day
I don't care what they say, I cannot stay away.
Every day."

"Oof," Russ said. "Very bad writing."

Nina tried to keep herself from blushing. Not that she was flattered by the romantic gesture. She was upset by it.

"Any idea who left all this?" Russ asked. He looked at the card, the balloons, and the flowers. "You have an obsessive ex-boyfriend or something?"

Nina took the card back and reread the poem. She studied the handwriting. It seemed faintly familiar. "I wish it were that simple," she told Russ. "I think it's my boss."

"What?"

"My fifty-year-old, fat-ass, gropey, married boss. Give me a second to cut up these balloons, then we can go inside, and I'll tell you the whole story." Nina grabbed at one of the pink balloons, lifting the scissors to its neck.

"Wait a sec," Russ told her. "I can think of something better to do with them."

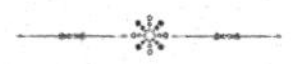

A few minutes later, Nina and Russ were lying side by side on a picnic blanket in her backyard. They were on their stomachs, and she was fiddling with the optics on the Whitefeather. Russ raised a pair of binoculars to his eyes and stared out at the balloon, doing his best to judge the distance.

"It's about thirteen hundred feet," he told her.

"It's not going to matter if I can't get this scope mounted," Nina said. She was attaching her own scope, a Burris XTR, but it was fighting her. When they'd passed the chicken coops, headed into the backyard, she'd picked an actual white feather from the ground, gathered her unruly curls back into a bun, then stuck the feather into it.

Russ's grandfather's gun was a thing of beauty. It was perfectly preserved, all glowing wood and steel. It hadn't been crafted to work with the Burris XTR specifically, but she was managing to wedge it on with a universal adapter.

Russ rolled onto his knees and Nina noticed him catching a quick look at his shoes. She suspected they had been white once, but now they were a combination of brown, tan, and yellow, with the occasional patch of gray fabric insulation poking through.

Trying to be inconspicuous, he slipped them off and tucked them under the edge of the blanket. It was kind of cute.

Nina felt the knobs finally lock into place. "Got it!" she said, raising the rifle to show him she'd mounted the scope. Then she raised the scope to her left eye.

Russ peered through the binoculars at the balloon again. "The wind's running about five miles an hour. I'd go a two-foot lead."

"And you'd miss," Nina told him, pulling the trigger. The gun let out a satisfying thump and they watched the balloon, way in the distance. It stared back at them, unpopped.

"And I'd miss too," Nina said. She handed Russ the gun and took the binoculars from him.

Nina stared through the binoculars. "The wind is picking up. I'd go with a . . ." Before she could finish her sentence, Russ pulled the trigger. The gun thumped, and off in the distance, the balloon snapped out of existence. Nina felt a combination of emotions wash over her.

First was the pleasure of watching the balloon erased. The second was marvel at the perfect shot. "Do it again. Do it again." Nina said.

Russ pulled the trigger. *Thump. Pop.*

"Wow," Nina said.

"It's really my only exceptional quality," Russ told her. Then after a moment, "I can also punch things."

Thump. Pop. Thump. Pop.

A few minutes later, there was only one balloon left. Nina tried again and missed it. She was angry enough about the "romantic gift" that she hadn't yet explained the situation to Russ. She preferred to just erase it. But she could sense his curiosity hanging in the air, like the last remaining unpopped balloon.

"In a way, I'm not supposed to be here right now," she told Russ. "I'm halfway done with the master's electrical engineering program over in Laramie. When my dad got sick, I took a gap year to come back home to help out for a while. He's got stage-four biliary cholangitis, for what it's worth. He's not getting any better, and it's starting to look like it might be more than a year's leave," she said.

"I'm sorry." Russ told her.

"It really sucks to be back," Nina said. "I loved college. I love engineering. But my parents are running out of money, so here I am. To help with the bills, I took a shitty job over at the sporting-goods shop on Main."

"Morty's Sportys," Russ said.

"That's the one. I thought it would just be selling night crawlers to my friends' dads, and at first it was like that. But from the start, the owner, Morty, made me uncomfortable. There was a lot of 'where's my hug' whenever my shifts started and ended—that kind of thing. I didn't like it, but I told myself he was just lonely or whatever. A few weeks ago, he came behind the register to use the fax machine, and I felt his fingers brush against my ass. It's a tight space, so I hoped it was just an accident. But it happened again last weekend. Now the accidents are coming more frequently and more boldly. Two days ago, he reached for a stapler and slid the back of his hand all the way across my left breast."

"And you can't quit? Or sue the fuck out of him?"

"We need the money now, not after some protracted legal battle. I'm afraid to even let him see how gross it's making me feel inside."

"Fuck." Russ said.

"Yeah."

"You've got a sick dad, a family that's going broke, and a pervy, gropey boss."

"Yep. Just eight months ago I was happy and free, learning about all the wonders of electrical science. It's been a precipitous fall."

"Want to help me with my problem?" Russ said, "I found a weird rock." He conjured the yellow and green stone out of his pocket and waved it in the air like a magician.

Nina laughed. "I'd love the distraction of this little mystery. Come on, I'll show you the lab."

They walked together toward the north side of the property. The previous owner had constructed a barn five hundred yards from the back of the house, and next to it, two large six-hundred-square-foot aluminum storage structures. During the summer, the storage units became unbearably warm. In the winter, they were Nina's ad hoc science lab.

Nina held the door open for Russ, leaning over to flip on the lights. She had daisy-chained a series of hanging bulbs to a switch on the wall. The cords ran, unsecured, around the perimeter of the structure, and the bulbs would swing dramatically if she slammed the door too hard. Still, when she threw the switch, the entire lab was illuminated.

Russ entered warily.

He seemed to be afraid to touch the various machines she'd compiled throughout the room. She saw him notice her other Burris XTR scope. A friend had cracked it on a hunting trip they'd taken together years ago. Nina had fished it out of the trash.

Russ moved around the space where the scope was mounted. He stared at it curiously.

"Is there a reason you zip-tied a broken scope to the end of a broken ski pole . . ." Russ crouched on the ground, looking closer at the construct. ". . . held steady by more zip ties, that were . . ." he ran his hand along the bottom. ". . . woven into the leather of a broken beanbag chair?" Russ poked the beanbag carefully with a finger. "Did you take out the beads and fill this full of sand?"

Nina shrugged. "You can't run an electronics lab without optics, can you?"

"I don't know," Russ admitted. He took a step back and accidentally bumped into her toolbox. A multimeter tipped over the edge, but Russ was fast enough to catch it.

Nina cleared a space on one of the tables, packing a loose soldering iron back into its case. She laid down a plastic mat. "The rock?" she said, gesturing to Russ.

Russ placed the green rock into her palm.

She turned it over carefully. She saw that Russ was still holding the multimeter. On a whim, she said, "Let me see that a second."

Nina touched each of the multimeter's pins to the surface of the rock. She flipped the dial to check the AC current, and the needle swung quickly, wedging itself against the maximum readout. She switched the dial to the DC current and the needle did the same thing.

"It's not magnetic, but it's generating power from each current. That shouldn't be possible. Where did you get this again?"

"I found it in my grandma's bookstore. Maybe my grandpop got his hands on it sometime before he died?"

"I think it might be a power source."

"Like a battery?"

"Yeah. Almost exactly, except batteries are generally direct current. By their nature, they can't be both AC and DC, at least not without a converter. This rock is generating power in both currents beyond what my multimeter can track." Nina rubbed her chin thoughtfully. "It's so odd."

She held the rock up to look at it closer, then she carried it over to the Burris scope. She placed the rock on a raised platform in front of the scope, and then stared through the eyepiece, carefully observing the groove patterns in the yellow veins. Still staring through the scope, she pointed to a corner of the shed. "There's an LCR meter on a cart right over there. Could you bring it to me?"

A moment later Nina heard the squeaking of the cart's rusty wheels, and Russ placed the copper probe into her hand. She held the end against the rock and the reading shot up to its maximum of 100 kHz. She tried an oscilloscope next but had already predicted what would happen. The X-Y axes on the meter pinned against their highest point, regardless of which part of the rock she focused on.

"You probably shouldn't be carrying this around in your pocket," Nina told Russ.

"But what is it?" he asked her.

"It's not like anything I've ever seen before. And it's radiating immense power. It doesn't look natural. Come look through the scope."

Russ took Nina's position in front of the scope. She stood behind him, not noticing how good he smelled.

"Look on the left edge," she told him. "See the prominent vein? The darkest one? In the top third?"

"Yeah."

"Notice the pattern? It goes left, right, curl, left, curl . . . something like that?"

"I see it."

"Now look at that same general area on the right side. Curl, left, curl, right, left. It's the same pattern, mirrored. The rock itself is not symmetrical, but the pattern is."

Russ glanced up from the scope to smile at Nina. "That's incredible. How the heck did you notice that?"

She felt a rush of pride, despite herself. "The answers are always in the details."

"And that kind of symmetry can't be common in nature . . ." Russ started to say.

"Bilateral symmetry is fairly common in nature," Nina interrupted gently. She drew a line in the air, from Russ's nose down to his waist. "Including the two halves of your own body."

Russ grinned. Then he admitted: "I'm pretty far from being a scientist,"

"I'm sorry. I shouldn't have corrected you. I am a scientist, but I'm also being a snob."

"You're being a huge help."

"Here's the interesting thing, though. Bilateral symmetry is never found in geological patterns. At least not that I'm aware of. These vein patterns—I think they were inscribed onto the rock."

"It's man-made," Russ said, realizing what she meant.

"You must leave it with me. I have to study it more."

5
RUSS

RUSS LEFT NINA'S LAB feeling lighter than he had in weeks. She really was the smartest person in Evanstown. He reached the fence at the perimeter of her property and snapped the last balloon free from its string, stopping to watch it rise shakily into the breezy Wyoming sky.

He was probably a little heavy on the gas pedal as he zipped down Route 107, then on to old Highway 89. He had cranked his grandma's AM/FM radio so loud that he almost missed Nina's text when it blinked across the face of his phone.

It read:

I'll keep the rock safe and bring it back tmrw. u forgot ur shoes but—"

Russ was still reading the last line, not at all dreaming of Nina's perfect smile, when he looked back out the windshield and caught the spotted, chestnut-colored tail of the deer, crossing right in front of his headlights.

Russ woke up hours later in a pile of bloody leaves, hoping his strange night in the forest had been a dream. When he looked to his left, the head of the deer carcass was staring back at him.

Some joker had taken the time to rest it against the tree, its dead eyes staring deeply into Russ's soul. Russ leaped back, scrambling to his feet too quickly. The rush of blood made his head spin. Remarkably, his body didn't ache.

"Was it a dream? It had to be a dream," he told himself. A panicked look around the clearing revealed no sign of the dead alien cat, or any of the strange hunters who had clamored through the dark. "It was a dream," Russ told himself, but then his eyes settled once more on the shredded deer carcass.

He took a step toward it, and something odd jangled from his left ankle. The thing attached there shined back at him in the soft morning light. He bent down and examined it: a woven metal anklet clasped tightly just above his anklebone. It was made of thin rivets, linked in a masterful weave. To the normal observer, it might have looked like a tasteful piece of jewelry. To Russ, it looked like a handcuff.

There didn't seem to be any way to unclasp it or get it off. His eyes barely registered the large purple bruise on the back of his calf, until the memory flashed through his head of how he'd gotten it. An explosion of fur and claws. His hurtling backwards through the air, smashing into the sapling tree.

It was enough. He wanted out of this magical forest. Now. He barely took the time to search for his grandfather's Whitefeather. The brush was thick and scattered with deer remains.

He hated to leave the gun behind, but his desire to get away was stronger than his desire for the family heirloom. He found the car where he'd left it, parked carefully on the side of Highway 89, its front bumper crushed, bloody.

The note his grandma left him on the kitchen table said the following:

I'm not worried. I know you're a young man capable of staying out all night without telling his dear grandmother where he's gone. Perhaps you've spent the entire night with Nina? I did not think she was the type, but I hardly understand young people these days. I'm out with Bibi, not worrying.

PS Bobby at Ace liked your roofing idea. He said for me to pass along his phone number. We should talk before you make him any kind of deal.

Russ read the note crouching next to the couch, his free hand rolling the anklet up and down the lower part of his leg. He glanced at the device again. It was clearly some kind of woven metal, a quarter of an inch wide and as smooth as sea glass. And there was an energy coming from it. When he pressed his forefinger against the metal he felt a faint pulsing, almost as if the device itself was breathing.

The more he studied it, the more he felt that it wasn't built in America. Or on Earth. Or during the twenty-first century.

A part of him knew that the whole experience in the forest was linked to the discovery of the weird rock. "An Obinz stone is like intergalactic catnip," the man called Kendren had told him.

The rock had drawn the alien cat to the planet. The cat had brought the hunters.

He put the note down and went out the kitchen door into the large double garage. The garage was nearly the size of the house, and it had twenty-nine rare guns hanging on every available bit of wall space. Russ saw the Kar98 and the Merkel 141. As he hurried past, his eyes lingered a moment on the empty space where the Whitefeather usually hung.

Russ found a chisel on his grandpa's workbench and tested the point against the ringlets on the anklet. Next, he found the hammer, but he was nervous enough that it slipped from his hand and bounced twice on the floor with two loud clangs.

"Russ?" He heard a familiar voice outside.

"Nina?"

"Yeah. What are you doing in there?"

"Nothing."

"I've got your rock. And your shoes. You didn't text me back, which, I admit, kind of hurt my feelings, but I thought I'd better bring them by early. I've been out here knocking—"

"Yes. Uh . . . hold on a second. I've got some . . . problems . . . in here."

"What's going on?"

"Just—" Just what? *Just wait while I try to remove a potential alien tracking device from my leg? Just hang out while I come to terms with the idea that I may have run across legit Men in Black and helped them kill a huge alien? And that the alien might have been drawn to Earth by the very same rock you're probably holding in your hand?*

Russ pushed the garage door opener and watched anxiously as the door slowly rose. Nina was wearing black hiking boots, black leggings, and a yellow workout top.

"I need you to come hit me with this hammer," he told her.

"You're an interesting guy, Russ," Nina said, stepping into the garage.

He was holding the chisel to the thing on his ankle.

"Your face is all banged up," she said. "And your chest. Look at that bruise on your leg!"

"Take the hammer," Russ insisted.

Nina ignored the hammer, choosing to kneel on the floor and touch the anklet with her finger. "What is this thing? It doesn't look normal."

Russ lowered the garage door again, then turned her palm upward and put the hammer firmly in it. "Hit the chisel as hard as you can."

"Really?"

"Right now. It's very important you hit it right now."

He cringed, looking at the far wall of the garage as Nina hauled back, hammer cocked over her head. "Most jewelry has some kind of clasp," she said, hammer poised.

"Hit it," Russ commanded.

She brought it down lightly on the top of the chisel. The anklet quivered, sending a volt of electricity through his body. The electricity traveled up the head of the hammer, shocking Nina as well. She let out a short scream and fell onto her backside. Again, the hammer clanged to the floor.

Russ shook his head, grimacing away the pain. "You okay?" he asked.

"Are you okay?" she asked back. Then she crouched on her knees and stared at the device more carefully. "Where did that power come from? Something this small shouldn't be able to generate that many volts." She touched it, carefully. "I don't see a battery pack. Or even a port for charging it. This has something to do with the rock, doesn't it?

"The rock is called an Obinz stone." Russ told her. "And we probably shouldn't hold on to it for too long."

"How do you know its name? What is it?"

"Get the anklet off and I'll tell you everything I know."

Nina was still rubbing her fingertips where the electricity had punched through her body. "Can I have it?" Nina asked, gesturing to the anklet. Her face was flush with excitement.

"You get it off, you can have it," Russ promised her. He put the hammer back in her hand. "Just give me a second," he said. He took a few stabilizing breaths. As he waited for the pain to dull, he glanced around at his grandfather's huge gun collection, but the familiar sight made everything that was happening seem that much weirder.

"Hit it again," Russ told Nina.

"You sure?" she asked. She found a loop of rubber insulation next to the workbench and wrapped it around her hand. Then she raised the hammer again. Nina's face was full of concern, but it didn't keep her from hitting the chisel, harder this time. The electricity shot through Russ's body with so much force he thought he might pass out. Nina dropped the hammer in order to catch his arm and hold him steady.

"What on Earth is going on?" she asked.

"Not Earth, maybe," Russ gasped. "Hit it one more time."

"I won't," Nina insisted.

"Just once more."

"No. Your central nervous system is not made to take repeated blasts of electricity. You could knock your heartbeat off cycle and . . . die."

"Just once more," Russ said, reaching for the hammer with shaking hands. Nina danced away from him. When he stepped toward her, the anklet fired another shock of electricity into his body. It dropped him to his knees. He tried to roll back onto his butt, but the anklet spasmed a fourth time and it laid him flat. He could feel sweat pouring down his forehead and was even faintly worried that he must look like a huge, dead spider, curled up on its back.

"Russ, I'm going to call a doctor. You've probably harmed your heart, and your chest is a mess."

"Put. Your. Phone. Away," Russ panted.

The anklet spasmed a fifth time, with much less juice than the previous four. The jolt was followed by a loud clicking sound. Then Russ felt the device fall away from his ankle. Through ringing ears, he heard the two halves clanking to the floor.

A second later, a mass of black goo spurted out of both halves and sprayed across Russ's leg. He kicked the device away, then rubbed at the goo, trying to get it off. None of it transferred to his hand. It had already hardened into a thick, black shell.

"Is that ink?" Nina asked. "It shot out like a squid." She wiped at the goo with the tip of the rubber insulation. "I tried to steal a dress from a clothing store when I was fifteen. When I broke off the alarm dongle, ink came out, just like that."

"It's not ink," Russ said. With the anklet broken in half, he found himself finally starting to calm down. "But I think you're right. It's some kind of anti-tampering protocol." Russ rubbed his eyes, wondering what the hardened ink could mean.

He paced quickly in a circle.

"Russ, what's happening?"

"Do you have the rock? Give it to me."

Nina handed him the Obinz stone. She had wrapped it in aluminum foil and was carrying it in a canvas sack. "You shouldn't touch it with your hands unless you absolutely have to. I ran tests all night." She yawned. Despite the excitement of the situation, she couldn't seem to stop herself. "I learned a few things, but the results were all over the place. Whatever it is, it's powerful."

"An Obinz stone," Russ said again.

"What does that word mean?" When Russ didn't answer, she said, "Can I take you to the hospital, Russ? The nearest one is in Banville, but I'm sure their ER is open . . ."

Russ sat on the ground again, rubbing at the hardened black goo on his ankle. "No. This isn't a situation for a hospital." He dug at the goo with the chisel, but he could tell that his skin would pull free before the substance ever did.

Nina went over to the two halves of the anklet. She picked them up carefully, holding the anklet away from her body. One end fired a spurt of goo, which landed harmlessly on the ground and hardened immediately.

Nina wrapped both halves of the anklet in the rubber insulation. "Tell me what's going on. Right now."

Russ told her almost everything. He left out the part about the size of the alien creature, because even saying it in his head made him feel like a madman. They had moved into the backyard and were sitting on either side of a picnic table, which Russ's grandma had decorated with a series of small, potted succulents.

Nina had the anklet unwrapped and she was examining it carefully. "You helped a bunch of hunters kill a deranged mountain lion and now you're afraid they want to kidnap you?" she said.

"They used the word *conscript*," Russ explained quietly.

"And the Obinz stone?"

"It attracted the cat. That's what one of the hunters told me. It must have smelled the stone on my clothes. In fact, I know it did, based on the way it stalked me."

"Usually, mountain lions don't like rocks."

"This was a special mountain—" Russ stopped mid-sentence. He wasn't sure how much to say, not because he didn't trust Nina but because he didn't want her to think he was a lunatic.

He was saved from having to answer by a sharp knocking on the front door.

Russ held his finger up to his lips, motioning for Nina to be quiet.

They crept to the end of the cedar fence, and Russ peeked through the gap between two of the slats. He could see portions of the front walkway. They were scrunched so close together that Nina was almost in Russ's lap, but she didn't seem to mind.

The person at the door was partially obscured by the shrubs around the front window, but Russ could tell it wasn't a member of the gang from the night before. It was a man in his late fifties. His hair was gray at the temples, and he was wearing a badly fitting business suit. *If I'm hiding in the backyard from a salesman or an evangelical, I'm going to feel pretty silly,* Russ thought.

They waited silently for the old man to give up and leave. The man knocked again, and Russ could hear him jiggling the knob.

"Is that one of them?" Nina whispered.

"I don't think so. There were four total, a guy and two girls around our age, and a woman closer to mid-thirties."

"And this all happened on the way home from my house last night?"

"Yeah."

"I'm so curious," Nina whispered.

"I would use the word *alarmed*," Russ whispered back.

Russ watched as Nina took one last look at the two pieces of the electrified anklet, then rewrapped them in the rubber insulation. She disengaged from their little huddle and slinked back toward the house.

"Where are you going?"

"They're looking for you, not me. I can be your spy."

She was already across half the yard, too far away to hear a whisper. Russ bugged his eyes and shook his head, slicing his fingers back and forth across his throat. A few moments later he heard the bolt slide back and the front door creak open.

He couldn't hear everything they were saying. The words drifted in and out depending on the tone and volume.

". . . think you have the wrong house . . ."

". . . your name, young person . . ."

". . . Doreena. Don't ask how it's . . ."

". . . a female?"

They lowered their voices too much for Russ to understand, then trailed off into silence. He watched Nina's body language shift, then heard her voice rise in anger. Then the door clicked shut again and he watched Nina through the back windows, coming around to the kitchen. He rubbed his hand unconsciously over his sore ribs. The pain seemed to be returning, slowly trickling back.

Russ turned to see the man leave the porch, slowly, rotating his head back and forth, taking in everything. Russ hoped it was just his imagination, but the man's face looked abnormal. All the pieces were in place, but even from that distance his eyes seemed unnaturally large, and his skin was off color, closer to candle wax than actual flesh. The gaze from those huge eyes lingered for a while on the fence line, and Russ was sure he'd been spotted, but the man kept scanning, finally reluctantly climbing into a gray Ford and turning the ignition.

Russ moved into the kitchen, quietly pulling the door shut. Nina was sitting in one of the dinner-table chairs, looking confused. "I don't think this is going to make you feel any better," she said. "He asked if I was Russell Wesley."

6

RUSS

NINA FIRED UP THE engine and put the truck in drive. Russ had the idea that if the anklet device had been tracking him, like some kind of alien GPS, then the best thing to do was get away from wherever it had sent its last signal. He insisted that Nina throw the remains out the window, but she wouldn't budge. "You promised I could keep it," she reminded him.

"The man asked if you were me?" Russ said for the second time. "Was he blind?"

"Not with those huge eyes. He kept staring, like he was analyzing me. When I said no, of course I wasn't Russell, he asked if I was female gendered. That's when I got kind of mad, because—"

"I knew right away. The first time I saw you."

"—it scared me."

"You got mad, or you got scared?"

"I got mad because I got scared. His weird face was enough to put me on edge, but the questions . . . the whole time he was carefully studying my eyes, trying to make sure I was telling the truth. And his skin—it was too yellow. I mean the whole thing was off. I wish I hadn't answered the door."

"Let's go to the bookstore," Russ said.

"And there was one other freaky detail," Nina added, cranking the wheel to turn onto the onramp for Highway 61. "My cell phone started making all this noise, like interference. The closer he got, the louder the static." Nina made a noise in the back of her throat, mimicking radio static. "That only happens when a nonlinear circuit element comes in contact with a wave pulse. And a cell phone is the one supposed to be sending the waves, not detecting them. It's so curious."

"I'm certain those words mean something to someone . . ." Russ replied.

Nina lapsed into silence. Russ could see her pupils dodging back and forth as she tried to make sense of what was happening.

"He was a robot!" Nina said suddenly, as she pulled the truck to a stop in front of the bookstore. The sign in the window was still blinking: OP_N.

"A robot?"

"That's why my phone was emitting static. He was what was sending the wave pulse. It's probably how he communicates with his creator, or his boss, or whatever. I couldn't get the sight of his skin out of my head, and it just clicked. It was thin, yellow, plasticky. Because he was made of motherfucking plastic. When we broke the anklet, we summoned a Terminator."

"Whew," Russ said.

"What is it?"

"I was worried that you would think I was looney. But you're way crazier than I am."

Nina punched Russ in the arm. "His skin was plasticky. I swear. He was a simulation of a human, probably passable from a distance but not up close. What have you gotten me into? Also—and don't let this detract from how scared I am—I've got to get my hands on that tech."

Nina chewed at her bottom lip. Russ hardly noticed; he was deep in thought: The rock brought the cat. The cat brought the team of hunters. The hunters brought the anklet. The anklet brought the weird dude.

But why? Who sent the guy in the business suit? And why couldn't he tell Nina was female gendered?

Was it possible he really was a robot?

Even in her agitated state, Nina couldn't miss the condition of the bookstore.

"Oh no. What happened to the Mysterious Universe?" she asked.

"Roof leak. Neglect. Terminal illness. I'm going to get it up and running again."

"That's good. Quite a job though." Nina patted her pockets with her open palms.

"There's very stale tea in the break room," Russ promised.

"Simulacra," Nina said absently.

"Huh?"

"The robot. It's called simulacra when something inorganic mimics something organic."

Russ led her into the break room. He wiped down a dusty coffee mug with the end of his shirt, then checked the mug for stains. Finding none, he filled it with the stale tea. "It's cold and we're going to have to share," he told Nina.

She wasn't listening. She had pulled out the two parts of the anklet and put them side by side on the circular break-room table. She analyzed each part, running her fingers over them, even touching her tongue lightly to one of the broken edges. "It's still holding a charge," she said. "This is not any kind of tech I've ever seen. I'm itching to get it back to my lab."

"I haven't told you everything," Russ said. "There's one more important detail."

Nina glanced up from the device, ready to hear more, but Russ had trouble finding the words. "That mountain lion I was telling you about . . . it wasn't normal sized. I mean, it must have weighed at least eight hun—"

And once again, before he could explain the alien nature of his encounter, there was a knock on the front door.

"Shit," Russ said.

"What do we do?"

"We sit here. Very quietly," Russ commanded.

The two of them sat in the stillness of the break room, unwilling to make a sound. They stared at each other, though Nina's gaze darted back and forth between his own and the wall that separated them from the door.

The silence hung heavy. Russ was sure enough time had passed that he could have counted to one hundred, slowly.

Then the knock came again.

"I have to see what's out there," Russ whispered.

"I'm so curious," Nina admitted.

They peered around the corner of the hallway as stealthily as they could. A large shape loomed on the stoop, blocking out the sunlight. It was big, nearly too big to be human. It was also round, carrying a disproportionate amount of its weight in its front midsection, like it had eaten voraciously for a long, long time. It was sweaty.

"Oh no," Nina said, truly terrified. "That's my boss, Morty."

"What in the hell is he doing here?" Russ asked. A second later, Morty knocked again.

It took Russ only a few seconds to cross the small store and wrench open the door.

"We're closed," he told Morty.

Morty looked back at him, a smug look on his broad face. He was a big guy, close to Russ's height but at least 150 pounds heavier, almost all of it in an impressive, gravity-defying beer gut. He was carrying a rolled-up paper bag that said "Daisy's Donuts" across its face. It was spotted with grease. Morty's shirt was equally spotted, but by sweat. Even though it was an unusually temperate day, Russ could see the sweat pooled in small rings around Morty's armpits, and all along where his rib cage would be if you could peel away all the body mass.

"Why's your sign say 'op'n'?" Morty asked.

"It's optimistic," Russ told him.

"Where's Norma?"

"She's home. Her husband just died."

"Yeah, yeah," Morty agreed.

"How about taking off?" Russ suggested.

Morty peered over Russ's shoulder. "I just need a book really quick. It looks like you could use the business."

"We're closed," Russ said again, but Morty wouldn't budge off the stoop.

The two men stared at each other, neither one moving. More sweat was forming on Morty's forehead, the unfortunate side effect of moving around so much weight. It dripped into his eyes, but that didn't stop him from bird-dogging Russ. "If you turned off your sign you wouldn't waste people's time like you've wasted mine," he said finally. "Maybe I should waste your time for a while?" Morty nudged his foot forward, blocking the door from closing.

Russ didn't want to give an inch to this enormous asshole, but he found his mind winding back to the threat of the simulacra. "Will you leave if I grab you what you need?"

"I'm looking for books on poetry," Morty told him.

"Who?" Russ asked. "Whitman? Dickinson?"

"Not that crap," Morty said. His voice dropped to a whisper, as if they were conspiring together about something. "Give me the best poet of all time. Somebody everyone loves," he said. "I need a better understanding of how to write stanzas and all that hoopla."

Russ left Morty on the stoop and retreated to the poetry section. "That's one mystery solved," Russ said to himself while he pulled a used, musty copy of *The Cambridge Shakespeare*, from a shelf.

Nina was peeking out from the hallway, and Russ flashed her a quick look at the book cover. She grimaced.

Russ handed Morty the book, his free hand on the door, already pulling it closed.

Morty stared at the book suspiciously. "How much?"

"It's eleven ninety-nine," Russ told him.

"I've got to get my wallet out of the car." Morty finally shuffled his large body off the stoop.

"Why are you shopping without your wallet?"

"I wasn't sure you were open," Morty called out as he turned the corner to the small parking lot at the side of the bookstore.

"Sonofabitch," Russ mumbled. "Just keep the book," he called. He waited for Morty to respond. Instead, he heard Morty say to someone:

"Sorry friend, they're closed."

"I'm just returning something to the proprietor," a familiar voice responded.

Atara came around the corner from the parking lot wearing a camouflaged hunting backpack and cradling Russ's grandfather's Whitefeather in her hands. Even though Russ hadn't been able to see her very well in the dark forest the night before, it was unmistakably her.

Russ tried to pull the door shut but he hadn't moved from the doorway, so he just ended up banging it against his own toes. Though he was ashamed to admit it, his main thought was *How did I not notice that she was this pretty?*

Atara had close-cropped wavy brown hair and bright blue eyes. She was on the short side, maybe five foot three, but her body was lean and well-muscled. She had a hint of mischief in her eyes that attracted Russ immediately.

She was the one they'd called El Toreador, and it was quickly apparent why. Once she reached the stoop, she moved faster than Russ's eyes could follow. One moment she was in front of him, then she was ducking under his arm, then she was inside the store, standing between him and the hallway, presenting the Whitefeather in outstretched hands.

"Hey, man," Atara said.

"Hey. What's up?" Russ said, taking the rifle and a few steps back. He popped open the receiver and found it unloaded. He leaned the rifle against the wall, his hands raised slightly to show Atara he didn't mean any harm.

"You're pretty fast," Russ said.

"Like a toreador," Atara nodded, rolling her forearm in a toreador's bow. "When they gave me that nickname, most of the crew probably didn't understand it wasn't entirely appropriate for a Jewish girl from New England. But I've been sticking with it. You've had a strange day, I'm guessing?"

"Yeah," Russ confirmed. "A strange twenty-four hours."

Both of them paused as a Ford turned from the street into the parking lot, haphazardly bumping its front right wheel on the curb. Russ recognized the car as the one that had brought the simulacra that morning. He glanced over his shoulder to see if Atara knew what was happening.

She stood behind him, silently listening. They heard the Ford's door open and shut.

"Say partner, do you have eleven ninety-nine I could borrow?" Morty's voice cut in from around the corner.

"Are you Russell Wesley?" the simulacra asked in response.

"No sir. I'm Morty Forte of Morty's Sportys, over on Main."

"Are you male gendered?"

Atara turned her head toward the voice. "Your day is about to get a little stranger." As she spoke, she grabbed Russ's shirt collar and dragged him backward into the store.

The yellowy old man in the oversized business suit turned the corner and took two long paces toward the front stoop.

Russ fumbled the lock closed and then reached up and pulled the string to turn off the "Op'n" sign.

"Is there a back door?" Atara hissed.

He led her quickly down the hall. When they reached the break room, Nina stuck her head out. The two women eyed each other suspiciously.

"Who are you?" Nina said.

"Who are you?" Atara responded.

"The simulacra is outside," Russ told Nina.

"I did not expect to see one of those here," Atara said. "You must have broken the anklet. Did you get the ink anywhere on yourself?"

Russ lifted the leg of his jeans and showed her the ink.

"No sense running then," Atara said. "That's nanotech. Basically, millions and millions of tiny tracking bots. A few have probably burrowed under your skin already."

Russ was alarmed by that idea. "What do we do?"

"We've got to destroy the . . . what did you call it?"

"Simulacra," Nina said.

"We've got to destroy the simulacra. Otherwise, it won't stop coming. They're not fast, but they're relentless. Check this out." Still facing Russ and Nina, Atara kicked the back door open with the heel of her boot. Standing stock-still in the alley behind Norma's store was the old man in the business suit. He stood without expression, staring blankly forward, his arms hanging at attention on either side of his body.

Within seconds of seeing Russ, he came back to life, his eyes narrowing with purpose, his hands reaching. Atara hooked the door with her foot and pulled it closed again.

A moment later the sound of fists pounding on the door filled the small hallway.

"How did he get back there so fast?" Russ asked.

"I've only got nine dollars and twenty-five cents," Morty called from out front. "I figure that ought to be enough."

"Just keep the book!" Russ shouted again.

"What you called simulacra, we call an SAS unit. I think this is one of the earlier models, but it doesn't matter. They're low-cost tech, overused and underfunctional. This one will pathfind through any obstacle, relentlessly following the nanotech. It's hunting you."

"I told you it was a robot!" Nina said, excited.

Atara shook her head. "You shouldn't have broken off the anklet. That's not the best thing to do."

"You guys put it on me!" Russ reminded her.

Morty pounded on the front door. The SAS unit kept pounding on the back.

Atara turned to Russ. "The anklet was a temporary visa. It made you legal, albeit with a limited collection of civic rights. When you broke it, you told the government scanning algorithms that you were trying to stay in UAIB space illegally."

"But I'm not in UAIB space. I don't think. What the hell is UAIB space?"

"All the creature outside knows is that you are behaving like an illegal alien. Everything's systematized, so it doesn't really matter what the truth is." Atara scrunched up her face apologetically. "You're currently on the wrong side of the intergalactic border patrol."

"I didn't ask for this," Russ reminded Atara. "I've got problems of my own." Russ pointed to the roof of the bookstore.

"What does the simulacra want?" Nina asked Atara.

"Earth is considered an undesirable planet. The file on Earthlings says we're violent toward the environment and each other, and that we use a lot of magical thinking. I wish I could disagree. For a planet like this, the Alliance would prefer the inhabitants never learn the greater secrets of the universe. As such, until you're an officially CERTified citizen, the SAS units will do their best to make you forget any and all extraterrestrial experiences."

"What's that mean, make me forget—"

"Its central mission is to perform a street-side mind-wiping procedure. The mind wipe is brutal but effective tech. It attempts to erase so-called undesirable memories by artificially aging your brain. Before you ask, yes, it's extremely painful. And sometimes it goes horribly wrong."

Russ could feel himself grinning, but it was the grin of a ghoul. He still managed to chuckle with his face pinched tight. "That thing outside wants to attack my brain?" Russ asked.

"It wants to wipe away your memory of me, that big cat, the UAIB and the Intergalactic Exterminators, Inc. Basically everything from last night," Atara told him.

The knocking stopped and Russ's cell phone started to crackle, making the same static sound that Nina's had.

"You hear that?" Atara asked, her voice full of excitement. "The SAS unit is powering up to tear down the door."

The noise from Russ's cell phone was growing in pitch and volume. "Maybe you can tell us how we stop the robot?"

"Oh, that's easy," Atara said, drawing a gun from her backpack. "We kill it."

She fished a small suppressor from her pocket and screwed it onto the barrel of the strange-looking pistol. Then she put her hand on the doorknob. "Better if we can back it into the alley. The suppressor makes the gun quieter, but not totally silent. If that fat dude on the front stoop hears anything, he might think we're murdering a real human."

"What should I do?" Nina asked.

"The Whitefeather is by the front door. It's unloaded but there might be some seven point six two behind the counter. Don't let Morty see you," Russ said.

Nina slipped out of the hallway and began to crawl toward the register, staying out of view of the front windows.

"You ready?" Atara asked Russ.

Russ nodded. "I'll knock it off its feet, drive it backwards as far as I can," he whispered. "Once I give the signal that I'm clear, you disable it."

"Okay," Atara said. She threw the door open. The SAS unit was on the other side, its fists glowing electric blue.

Until that moment, Russ had had some trepidation about killing something that he wasn't sure wasn't human, but the glowing blue hands were enough to convince him.

He launched his body toward it, digging his heels in, confident in the physics of two hundred and twenty pounds moving quickly forward. As he lowered his shoulder, he was surprised to find the muscle memory from four years of high-school football helping him along.

He hit the SAS unit with all his force, square in the chest. The simulacra did not budge. It stood its ground spectacularly, and Russ heard the crunching sound of flesh against metal at the same time he felt a burst of tremendous pain from his injuries. He suddenly had a different memory from high school, when in a moment of academic frustration, he'd thrown the skeleton from science class against a brick wall. Only, in this situation, Russ was the skeleton.

He could feel the robot hook its powerful old-man arms under his armpits. Then he felt his feet lift off the ground as it leaned back in a perfect suplex. Russ's shoes peeled off on the top of the door frame, but the rest of him flew through the alley. He landed on a pile of leaves fifteen feet away with another burst of agonizing pain."I'm clear!" he groaned.

The whisper-hiss of three bullets leaving Atara's pistol slipped through the air, and Russ heard the SAS unit collapse to the ground.

Atara sauntered over, kneeled by his side, and grinned at him. "Good teamwork," she said. Then: "You've done some impressive damage to your own body, even since yesterday. Didn't Bah'ren tell you to be careful? That you couldn't feel the damage, but it was still there?"

"Is it dead? . . . and . . . do you have any more of that medicine?" Russ gasped.

"It was never alive, and yep," Atara said. She handed Russ a roll of white pills. "You can dissolve these in liquid or eat them whole."

Still on his back, Russ popped two into his mouth.

"That's the last you're getting until you sign on with the crew," Atara said.

Russ could feel a warm tingling sensation as the medicine swept through his body. It started in his chest, at his heart, and moved outward, evaporating the pain in a blissful wave.

"I never said I was signing with any crew," Russ told her, rolling back to his knees. He stared at the SAS unit, which was lying on its stomach, one leg splayed awkwardly to the side.

"See, that's where your situation gets a little complicated," Atara told him, slipping the pistol into her pocket. She went back to the door and plucked Russ's shoes off the ground, looking at their condition with exaggerated horror. "Also, it looks like you could really use a paycheck."

Atara hooked her free hand around the SAS unit's collar and dragged it deeper into the alley. She hefted it, with some difficulty, and dropped it into the bookstore's dumpster.

"The Alliance isn't a bunch of fascist swine. We've got laws, and civil rights. We don't perform abductions anymore. There's no probing, unless you specifically request it. In fact, we don't employ anyone without their official, signed permission. It's why we tagged your leg instead of just throwing you aboard our ship. We thought a day or two to process what had hap-pened might make you more open to the idea."

Russ climbed to his feet, flexing his arms and shoulders as he joined Atara at the dumpster. "That medicine is fantastic," he said.

Atara withdrew a small piece of paper and began to unfold it. It unpacked into a long legal-sized document. She read from it: "The undersigned agrees to the employ of the Intergalactic Exterminators, Incorporated for a time period beginning upon the act of signing and ending with either termination or death. Early termination, for any reason, shall result in the signee owing the IEI all the costs of CERTifica-tion training and surrendering itself to a mandatory mind cleanse . . ."

Before she finished reading, Russ took the document away from her and folded it back up. It wasn't paper, exactly. It felt like half-liquid goo.

From the back door, he heard Nina gasp. She had the Whitefeather in her hands. "Sign the paper!" she insisted.

Russ held up the folded document. "This contract is for life. I don't know what the job is, what the pay is, who my employer is. I'm going to read it before I sign it."

Nina's eyes narrowed. "He's not going to sign it. You're not going to sign it, are you?"

"I don't think he's going to sign it," Atara said. She glanced over at Nina. "Anyway, it's his decision to make, not yours."

Atara finally handed Russ his ratty, open-tongued shoes. "I'm not going to lie. The job's dangerous as hell, but it pays the equivalent of two grand a week, which it looks like you could really use."

"I probably will sign it," Russ said.

"I'll sign it right now," Nina said. "I need a job worse than anyone has ever needed one. What's the job? And who is this Alliance you keep mentioning?"

Atara took a moment to grab scraps of trash, mostly moldy books, and layer them on top of the SAS's body. Something about Nina seemed to bother her, but she answered the question: "About three-quarters of the cosmos, including the part we're in, is governed by a capitalist collective, the United Alliance of Intelligent Beings, or UAIB. They're a loose conglomerate of seventy-three sentient species. They work like the US federal government, proposing and voting on galactic rule changes and so forth. For our purposes, their most important function is keeping the municipal services up and running. The Galactic Border Patrol"—Atara nodded toward the robot in the dumpster—"Law Enforcement, Infrastructure Maintenance, Transport Security, Refuse Disposal, Ecosystem Preservation, and Emergency Response. The UAIB collects taxes and funds the teams that keep our portion of the universe safe and orderly. Or a close approximation thereof. The job I'm offering Russ is with Ecosystem Preservation. Pest control, mostly."

"You're offering him a job with a government organization in space? For two grand a week?" Nina gave Russ a look like he was crazy for not signing the contract immediately.

"Yes and no. Like all government work in a capitalist collective, there are some hoops to jump through. There's always a push to privatize government systems, save on taxes, that sort of thing. The system, in its current, fragile state is one of freelance workers, fighting for government subsidies. My team, the IEI, is one of a couple dozen different municipal extermination squads, all of us racing around various galaxies trying to get jobs done and keep fuel in the tank."

"Freelance pest control," Nina said. "Based on government commissions." She seemed to have wrapped her head around the idea no matter how ridiculous it sounded to Russ.

"Not pests," Russ explained to her. "Think much larger than that."

"The UAIB qualifies a pest as any species that jumps planets and is identified as invasive to its new environment. You know, like a threat to the ecosystem," Atara explained. "If that big kitty Russ killed last night had stayed on Earth, it could have thrashed all of southwestern Wyoming."

"I want the job," Nina said again.

"And I'm not offering it to you," Atara said firmly. "I'm here speaking for my boss. Last night, Russ happened to catch her eye. It's an uncommon opportunity for an Earthling—trust me on that—and it shouldn't be turned down casually." Atara dropped her backpack at Russ's feet. "Take a day or two to think about it if you want. If you decide to sign, unpack that backpack and wait. We'll do the rest."

"Russ, tell her you'll take the job!"

"What about the nanobots on my leg? How do I get those off?" Russ asked Atara.

"Not with Earth tech," Atara said shrugging. "That's what I meant about your situation being complicated. Since the SAS unit failed, the UAIB's automated systems will send more, maybe two or three at a time. They'll keep coming until you're granted CERTification . . . or they get their fingers into your brain, and you forget any of this ever happened."

"You guys put the anklet on me. You should also be able to call off the SAS."

"Of course, we can." Atara smiled slyly. "But you know governments move slowly. We've got the paperwork to fill out, to notarize; it needs to be filed with the correct bureau. Tomorrow's a galactic holiday, and then there's the weekend . . . Even if we did file the exception right away, it would be three or four days before your record got expunged. That's if we filed it right away," Atara said again, as if the possibility was growing more remote by the second.

"What do I do about the SAS?" Russ demanded.

"Sign the contract," Atara told him, as if the answer were simple. "In the meantime, consider the SAS a free, first lesson in extermination."

7

RUSS

BEHIND THE COUNTER OF the bookstore, Russ unfolded the contract and took another look. The same words jumped off the page: *. . . beginning upon the act of signing and ending with either termination or death . . . surrendering itself to a mandatory mind-cleanse . . .*

He put the contract down and went outside on the front porch. Atara had left, with Nina following closely, still peppering her with questions. Morty's money was still there, a decent amount of it in loose change. Russ crouched over the welcome mat for a few minutes, picking up each coin, his mind lost in space.

He went back into the store and dropped the money into the cash register. "It's a start," he said under his breath. Then he looked at his shoes again.

Simulacra. Alien bug hunters. Intergalactic space travel. It seemed like more than he could have ever dreamed possible. He had been bored exploring New Orleans. He doubted he would have the same problem in UAIB space.

He opened the contract again. Farther down the page he read: "Inability to perform work for any reason will result in a legal forfeiture of all chattels, including, but not limited to, what the UAIB quantifies as grave necessities . . ."

The next section was labeled "Personal risk and injury: if the undersigned requires medical care utilizing nonstandard company resources, the undersigned agrees to perform the job without pay for an entire galactic cycle, or until the cost of recovery is paid in full, whichever is longer . . ."

There were other headings: "Required training gear during probation," "Release of right to sue in the instance of permanent physical damage," "Release of right to sue in the instance of theft, loss and unanticipated death," and finally "Release of right to end employment." He stopped reading about three-quarters of the way down the next page. He shook his head, drumming his fingers on the contract.

Then he folded it carefully closed, slipped it into the backpack, and dropped both of them unceremoniously into the dumpster in the alley.

No text messages, or SAS units, or intergalactic exterminators arrived for the rest of the day. None arrived the next day either. Or the day after that. Each night in the shower Russ scrubbed at the inky mess on his ankle hard enough to leave the skin around it red and raw. The nanobots wouldn't come off.

The following Wednesday evening, he found himself on the roof of the Mysterious Universe working shoulder to shoulder with Bobby, the owner of the local Ace Hardware. The sun was setting and the sky was ablaze in orange.

Bobby was about two decades Russ's senior. Most of his hair had receded away, and what was left was thin and white. It was incongruous with his youngish face, which was still handsome if you ignored the deep worry lines.

When he saw Russ looking at the sunset, he paused a minute to look at it as well. "I've been dreaming of getting my hands on that Merkel since the first time your grandfather showed it to me," he said.

"It's a fine gun," Russ agreed absently.

"It's not the reason I'm up here with you," Bobby said. "The truth is, I can't really afford to give away all this wood, much less help you do the work, even for a special weapon like that." Bobby shook his head. "I wish it weren't so. We all felt awful when this place fell into disrepair, but every business in this town is going to crap, including mine. We're all barely staying above water."

"But you are helping . . ." Russ pointed out.

"Yessir," Bobby said.

Russ waited for him to explain further, but Bobby just started hammering again.

"If you help me get started, I can finish it myself. I worked drywall in Oregon for about six weeks, so I'm somewhat familiar," Russ told him.

"Only six weeks?" Bobby asked.

"It might have been four. But I also did stucco for a month down in Florida. And I did some HVAC and nonunion roofing for a while in Washington State."

"Your grandma told me that you were some kind of drifter."

"That's a good word for it," Russ said. He finally quit looking up at the sky, instead using the claw on his hammer to yank out a ruined board.

"Fuck. I'm jealous," Bobby told him. He opened a can of beer and took a long drink. "Your grandpa was the same way, well into his sixties. Of course, he used this store as an excuse to go out and explore. He came back with quite a few rare books, rare trinkets . . ."

"And rare guns." Russ finished his sentence for him.

"Just like that beautiful Merkel."

"I'm sorry your store is in trouble too," Russ said. "You know, I don't have anything. Just these clothes I'm wearing. My car barely runs. Look at my shoes! I'm not really a person to be jealous of."

"I'm still jealous. I mean, I guess I could just walk away from it all, but there are so many people counting on me now. My wife, my kids, my employees, the church . . ."

"That's how they get you," Russ said

"It wasn't always this stressful," Bobby went on. "But between Amazon and the Home Depot in Banville, I'm slowly going broke."

Russ just shrugged. He knew he should be more sympathetic, but he had no idea how to help. He couldn't force people to stop shopping online any more than Bobby could. And his mind kept drifting to the SAS corpse in the dumpster no less than twenty feet from where they sat. Bobby had problems, sure, but they weren't trying to mind-wipe him.

Norma poked her head up above the roof's overhang. She was standing on the electrical box in the alley, watching Russ and Bobby talk. "How about less chatting and more hammering? I'm getting excited to get this fixed!" she said. She had a laptop in her hands, and she opened it. She looked at Bobby. "Do you think your son would help me get our web portal open again? At least half our sales were online last year, but Clark was the one who handled it all. I just did the shipping. I can't figure out how the stupid thing works."

"Bobby doesn't like online shoppers," Russ told her.

Bobby ignored him. "My son's been struggling with his pepper crop, but I'll ask if he has the time." Then he nodded at Russ. "Why not let this youngster do it?"

Norma cackled at the question, and even Russ had to smile. "We have a family policy to not let Russ anywhere near computers," she explained to Bobby.

"I break them," Russ said. "Sometimes on purpose, usually by accident."

"Russ can break a computer faster than it takes most people just to turn them on."

Russ went back to work ripping out the old roof and letting Bobby replace it with new decking. Bobby ended up staying much longer than he'd agreed to.

When the sun got too low, Norma climbed on the box again and offered them both homemade cookies and lemonade.

The two men sat side by side in the dusk, sipping lemonade. Russ felt his pocket buzz, but he left his phone alone.

"Job well done," Bobby finally said, glancing over their work.

"You did most of it," Russ told him. Russ reached out to shake Bobby's hand, and the pain in his ribs wrenched.

"You okay, son?" Bobby asked.

Russ nodded. He quickly popped the next to last of the pills Atara had given him and the pain disappeared. He didn't really like to think about what would happen when they ran out. It was a mistake to be doing anything other than recuperating in bed. He knew he had more than a few broken bones. He should probably see a doctor, go straight to the ER over in Banville, but he had zero dollars in his pocket, and he couldn't remember the last time he'd had medical insurance. Plus, he didn't like the idea of being in a hospital bed, foggy from painkillers, if another SAS unit arrived to tear apart his brain.

Bobby climbed down from the roof. Then Russ heard him climb back up again. "I'll come back tomorrow and help you lay the felt," he offered.

"Only if you can," Russ told him. "You need an extra hand at Ace, let me know."

"Well, I appreciate that," Bobby said. He stared at Russ a minute, a strange look on his face. "This is a gift, what you're doing to help your grandma. But take my advice: avoid putting down roots as long as you can. Roots are just a fancy word for life-crushing responsibility. I didn't have this gray hair until I had roots."

Russ nodded again, his hand on his ribs. He thought of the draconian contract, still folded up in the dumpster less than a hundred feet away.

Russ's father had given him nearly the same advice when he graduated high school. Of course, Russ's father was better at taking that exact advice than anyone Russ knew. As a consequence, he hadn't been around for most of Russ's life. When he was around, he'd permitted Russ to do whatever he wanted. He'd taught Russ how to gamble, how to pick up girls, and even how to roll a joint, but he'd never cared much how Russ did in school, nor was he willing to help when Russ found himself struggling with homework. In fact, he'd called high school "a waste of good time and energy." Russ stayed in contact with his mom, but his parents had never married, and his life of wandering had separated him semipermanently from any information about his dad.

Yes, he'd given him the same advice, but Russ's dad was a much different kind of man than Bobby.

"See ya tomorrow, Russ," Bobby yelled, waving from the door of his beat-up GMC.

Russ waved back. He watched the entire way as Bobby's truck took its long journey down Main, disappearing behind a copse of trees as it turned in the direction of the highway. He wondered which man he was more like, Bobby or his father.

He was afraid he knew the answer.

He sat on the roof alone for a moment longer, just thinking. Then he pulled the phone from his pocket and read the text. It said:

How do you compare to a nice summer's day?
You are more sexy and more legitimate.
And I get excited to just be around you.

Russ wrote back:

Seems familiar.

Nina: *the Shakespeare book is not helping much. i've got more balloons to pop.*

Russ: *Sorry to hear that.*

Nina: *but I left my scope on the whitefeather.*

Russ: *I can bring it by tonight.*

Nina: *at dialysis with my dad, tomorrow tho*

Nina: *you sign the contract yet?*

Russ: *Maybe pretty soon.*

Nina: . . . *no sign of any simulacrum?*

Russ: *Nothing.*

Nina: *still rather not meet at my house . . . 2 miles north, off route 107?*

Russ: *I'll be there.*

Nina: *4:30 tomorrow. look for my truck*

Russ tried to stop it, but he couldn't keep a smile from creeping across his face.

8

RUSS

RUSS DROVE CAREFULLY DOWN Route 107, making double sure not to hit any deer. He found Nina's truck parked just off the road and climbed slowly out of his grandma's Mercury.

Nina smiled when she saw he'd brought the Whitefeather. She had a picnic blanket tucked under one arm and a six-pack of Coors beer hanging from her other hand.

It was early evening, but the heat was back to being nearly unbearable. Nina was wearing a pair of jean shorts, a button-up shirt, and one of those cowboy hats girls wear, with the brims permanently pointing toward the clouds. Her shirt had a logo on it that read "Morty's Sportys."

"You just get off work?" Russ asked. They began to walk together down a horse trail.

"Best day of work I've ever had," Nina said.

"You tell him to keep his hands to himself?"

Nina's face lit up with a grin. "Not directly," she admitted. "Actually, it has to do with your device. Check this out," Nina raised the side of her shirt so Russ could see the edge of her bra line. Her bra wasn't touching her skin though; she had a heap of layers underneath. Half of the broken anklet was woven into the seam of her bra.

"I've spent the last four days studying it. I had two years in a pretty intensive electrical engineering program in Laramie, but this anklet . . ." Nina trailed off as if words couldn't describe it. "The rock you showed me, that was a power source, like a huge, dense battery. This is totally different but no less amazing. It keeps itself powered, probably through a very advanced manipulation of magnetic waves. And if those waves weaken, it can be recharged by simple contact with any metal. We broke it in half; right? But when it's together in a loop, it appears to trap magnetic waves in an endless cycle, preserving the kinetic energy with far more efficiency than anything I've ever seen. I only tested one half at a time, there doesn't seem to be any way to put them back together, but even so, the energy retention and amplification rates it produced were off the charts. We could solve a lot of the Earth's problems with a few hundred more of these things."

"It's powered by perpetual energy?" Russ asked.

"Almost. And what little power fades can be recharged by tapping it with a metallic compound. The only reason we were able to break it is because we used a metal chisel. We filled it too full of power, which shocked us, and blitzed the device."

"So you put it in your bra?"

"I was solving one of Earth's problems." Nina said, blushing slightly. "I'm actually wearing four layers. A sports bra, a lining of rubber insulation, a thin mesh net, and my actual bra. My boobs are sweating like a pair of atheists at the Pearly Gates, but it was worth it. Whenever Morty would walk behind the counter, I'd slide the anklet forward so it came in contact with the layer of steel mesh, and they would power each other up."

Russ thought for a moment, making sure he followed what she was saying. "You electrified your breasts?" he said.

"Yep." She raised her fist triumphantly. "Do you find that udderly shocking?" she asked.

"Did I hear two *D*s in there?" Russ asked.

"Double *D*s, yes," Nina said.

Russ laughed. Like everyone, he enjoyed a good round of electrified-boob puns. He thought for a moment: "Titty, Titty, Bang, Bang?" he said without much confidence.

"Not terrible," Nina said, nodding.

"What happened to Morty?" Russ asked.

"He brushed his hands against them twice. Once reaching for a stapler, once while finding a 'knot' in my lower shoulder blades that had to be 'massaged.'" Nina laughed. "The first time, he just nicked the electrified net. It zapped him, but probably no more than a normal electrostatic shock. The second time, he really dug his finger in and, well, the shock hit him so hard I believe he may have pooped his pants." She cackled triumphantly. Then she nudged the anklet forward with her elbow, powering it up. "Want to try it out?" she asked Russ mischievously.

With an act of some willpower, he waved off the offer, and continued down the path.

It was funny to be talking about such a personal issue in service of avoiding the real subject, Russ's job offer. He knew she was bursting with curiosity, but the truth was the contract was still folded up neatly in the dumpster.

They crested a second hill. It broke sharply downward, and the view of the entire valley was spectacular. "I usually like to go down the other side," Nina pointed to another path, far more overgrown, which wove down the hill and through some dense trees. "There's a beautiful waterfall less than a quarter mile from here. But I'm already too hot. Let's have a beer."

In that moment together on the hill, Russ finally had a chance to give her the last of the details about the night in the forest.

"Wait, the cat was how big?" Nina asked again.

"About the size of an F250."

"That's why you didn't sign the contract? It's too dangerous?"

Russ shook his head no. He stared out over the tops of the trees. They were waving in the slight wind. Russ couldn't hear any of the normal chirping of birds, or strumming of crickets, or even the crunch of leaves as they journeyed from the tree branches to the ground, surfing along on the gentle breeze. "I know you want to talk about it," he said finally.

"Why didn't you take the job?" Nina sounded agitated.

"It isn't that I don't want to go to space. I want to explore space more than you do."

"Debatable."

"I just know myself. It isn't a good idea to sign a contract for life. I don't have a job. I don't have a mortgage, or even a month-to-month lease. I don't have a credit card. I'm piss-poor at obeying formal authority." Russ held up his flip phone. "I use a burner phone specifically so I can throw it away when too many people get my number. I value my independence, and my freedom." Russ shrugged. "Now that we know what's out there, I'll find a way to get to space, I just don't want to do it as an indentured servant."

"It must be nice," Nina said quietly. Her tone sounded sharper than Russ expected. "To not have any responsibilities. To not have to care about anyone else."

"Well . . ." Russ let himself trail off.

"I can see why your grandma's bookstore is in so much trouble. It would be tough to keep a business going with your husband dying and no loved ones willing to help. I guess that's why you and I never met in the hospital during the last months of your grandfather's stay in the hospital."

"Oof . . ." Russ said, trailing off again. He didn't have a decent response to her accusation. For a moment, he was lost in his own mind, trying not to picture his grandma sitting alone in a cold, hyper-hygienic hospital room, watching the love of her life slowly die.

If Russ had been busy working, going to school, raising kids . . . at least he would have had some kind of excuse. Instead he had just been wandering around the American South, accomplishing nothing.

It was Nina's turn to be silent.

Russ wished she would say something. "I know I should have come sooner," he admitted. "I know it. But I am here now."

"That's true," Nina said. "It's a start, I guess."

Russ stared at Nina. He could see the pain of her own situation just behind her eyes. "Listen, I can't—"

"Shut up," Nina said.

"Hey, I—"

"No, shush." Nina rolled into a crouch. "What do you hear?"

Russ shut up and listened for a moment. Somehow, the forest had become even more quiet. "Nothing," he admitted.

"I've been coming here for years," Nina whispered. "'Nothing' is not normal."

Neither moved. Russ stayed seated and Nina held her crouch. The forest was awash in silence.

It was so quiet out there in the gloaming that the sudden heavy static erupting from both of their cell phones was all the more jarring. Though not quite as jarring as the old, balding guy in a gray business suit, off in the distance, tromping through the mud, pushing his way between the branches toward them.

"We should have locked the lid on that dumpster," Nina whispered, but Russ had rolled to his feet before she even finished her sentence.

He checked the load in the Whitefeather and drew a bead between the SAS unit's eyes through Nina's Burris scope.

"No bullet holes. It's a different unit. They must all look the same."

There was a crunching sound behind them, and Russ swiveled the barrel one hundred and eighty degrees. Behind them stood another SAS, identical in appearance: same bald head, same weak chin, same business suit. He was standing at the bottom of the small hill, staring back up at them.

"Uh-oh," Nina said.

"What do you want?" Russ yelled down at the one closest to them. Holding the gun in his hand gave him a certain confidence.

"Are you Russell Wesley?" the simulacra asked.

"No," Russ told him.

Russ could feel the thing's gaze run along the length of his body. He heard crunching sounds, wingtips on fallen leaves, and realized the other bot was approaching from the back.

"His name is Steven Applebum," Nina said. "We've never heard of Russell Wesley."

Russ risked a quick look at Nina, and she shrugged, like that was the best name she could think of.

"You are Russell Wesley," the one moving in from the trees said. It must have been scanning the inky blot still stuck to his ankle. "Your identity has been confirmed. Please do not attempt any violence. Please do not attempt escape. You are mandated to remain still by the governance of UAIB law."

"I'm just going to move my finger," Russ said, pulling the trigger.

The kneecap of the SAS at the bottom of the hill exploded. The bot collapsed at a funny angle, striking hard against the warm earth. It didn't cry out in pain. It didn't make any sound at all. It just started to zombie-crawl toward Russ and Nina, its hands digging deep into the dirt. Russ jacked a new bullet into the chamber and turned to the guy at the edge of the trees. That robot had covered a lot of distance.

His arms pumped in perfect, mechanical rhythm as he sprinted right at them . . . until Russ gently squeezed the trigger, and that SAS unit's kneecap exploded too.

Russ went back to scanning the trees. Atara had said three units, maybe more, would come after him, but Russ could only see the trees shaking in the gentle wind. Another crunching sound dragged Russ's gaze back to the guy at the base of the hill. Nina stood over him, a huge rock between her hands. The SAS unit's head was squished under the rock.

"It wouldn't stop coming," she cried.

Russ swung the rifle barrel back toward the original SAS unit. Though he knew better, its human appearance made him pause, just for a moment. The rifle site moved back and forth the short distance between the SAS unit's eyes, until Nina let out a short scream.

Russ swung back in the other direction again to see three more men advancing, identical to all the others. They must have come quickly out of the line of trees, because they weren't ten feet from Nina and closing fast. The Whitefeather recoiled, and the closest one spun off its feet, thudding solidly in the dirt. Nina hurled the large rock at one, but it was too heavy to aim properly, and the robot sidestepped it. It closed the gap and grabbed Nina by the arms. The other circled around and scooped up her feet. She struggled hard against the one at her elbows, while trying to kick free from the one holding her legs.

Russ held the rifle steady. He knew he wasn't going to miss. He never did, but she was kicking around so much, he couldn't take the chance.

"Hold still!" he yelled.

"Are you kidding me?" she screamed back.

"Hold still for just one second!" he demanded.

"Don't shoot!' Nina yelled back. "They're . . . too . . . close."

Nina couldn't fight and yell very effectively, and one of the SAS units took the chance to wrench her in more tightly. One held her hips, while the other had its arms wrapped tightly around her upper torso. She started twisting at an odd angle, like a wriggling fish. She was clawing at her own rib cage.

Russ kept the gun trained on the three of them, waiting for anybody to hold still long enough that he could get off a clean shot.

Then Nina did hold still. As the robot leaned over her, there was a tremendous hiss—a long electronic discharge. Russ hadn't fired a shot, but the robot shook for a moment, electricity coursing through its body. Then it fell down and didn't move again.

Nina fell heavily beside it, and Russ saw the anklet, half wrapped in rubber, clutched like a knife in her hand. Grunting, she kicked herself free from the other unit, then delivered two more powerful jabs with the anklet, straight to its chest. The blast loosened the thing's elbow joint, and its left forearm hung limply. She finished it off with another swipe of the anklet, jamming the device against its skull with a resounding POP!

She wanted me to try that, Russ thought as he slid the box magazine out and checked the count. He had two bullets left. He didn't pack expecting to have to repel a wave of android bankers.

Bullet one split the forehead of the first guy on the far side of the hill, who was still dragging himself determinedly toward them.

Russ checked the magazine again, even though he knew there was only one bullet left.

Then three new SAS units emerged from the trees. "Two or three more units, my ass," Russ mumbled.

The new simulacra stood shoulder to shoulder. Confirmation of Russ's identity seemed to have removed the last of their social restraint. Forgoing any semblance of human behavior, they lurched toward him in triple synchronicity, their legs pumping, their arms chopping effortlessly through the thick brush . . .

9

RUSS

. . . AND RUSS AND NINA ran away even faster. It turned out that a mammal feeling real dread can outpace an SAS unit from wherever-the-hell by a pretty safe margin. Nina reached her truck first, got in, and fired the engine. She kicked open the passenger door and yelled out to Russ. "Get in!"

"I'll follow you in my car!" Russ shouted, launching himself into his Grandma's Mercury.

It looked for a moment like Nina was going to climb out of her truck and into his sedan, but the pursuing SAS units reached the edge of the road, and she buried her foot in the gas so hard that her tires kicked a shower of dirt down onto the hood of Russ's car.

He tore across the road onto old Highway 107. He followed Nina for less than a mile, then he wrenched on the e-brake and swerved into a savage U-turn.

There were three reasons why he did it. First, his grandma's car was almost out of gas. He'd been using it instead of his own car specifically because his own car was completely out of gas. Maybe, Russ considered, there was a life out there where he didn't have to always worry about being out of fucking gas.

The second reason was that the run had aggravated his injuries. His ribs, his wrist, his thigh were all throbbing. He had broken bones, maybe a handful of them, but he'd been ignoring them with scarily effective space-age painkillers. The very last pill was buried deep in his pocket, and he managed to slide it into his mouth as the car slid to a stop.

But the biggest reason for his sudden change of direction was that the Evanstown community trash trucks had cruised by his and Nina's fleeing vehicles, headed toward Main Street. It was Wednesday, trash collection day.

Russ wasn't sure if Nina missed his dangerous U-turn, or if she was too scared to stop and turn around herself. Either way, her dusty old pickup kept going, and he saw it turn out of sight in his rearview mirror as he buried the gas pedal in the floor.

It took him twenty minutes to cover the thirty miles back to his grandma's store. The old Mercury was wheezing, popping, and coughing, as he swerved in and out of the lanes, veering around the lumbering trash trucks.

The Mercury ran out of gas just before he reached the alley behind the Mysterious Universe. As Russ climbed from the sedan, his pocket buzzed.

why did we split up?
are you alive?

Russ didn't respond to Nina's texts. He was busy sprinting to the dumpster, then digging around inside, pulling the camouflaged backpack free from where it had gotten tangled with the simulacra's broken right leg. The backpack had a huge peach-colored stain on the bottom, but it seemed to be unopened. There was an envelope taped to the back door of the bookstore, but Russ ignored it, sneaking inside with the backpack on his shoulder. He was sliding the lock on the back entrance shut with adrenaline-charged hands when the first trash truck turned the corner down the alley. He took the backpack to the checkout counter and began to unpack it.

There were twelve metal tubes inside, each emblazoned with a faint series of lines, like machine-etched runes. He studied the pattern, trying to decide if it was bilateral symmetry, then he gave up and lined the tubes up on the counter by size. They weren't all identical; some of the ends were squared and some rounded. In fact, each one would only fit together with the end of one other correspondingly sized tube. He started pushing the tubes together, twisting and locking them. The rune lines matched up, and with each connected pole, the thing grew bigger and bigger. He worked quickly, the faint memory of putting together a model rocket from his childhood flitting across his mind.

Most of the metal tubes telescoped to two or three times their packed height. The structure grew, getting so big Russ worried that people would look in the window and wonder what he was up to.

He gathered up the remaining parts and carried the whole thing down the back hallway toward the storage room, where he'd initially found the Obinz stone. He turned the alien tube structure sideways and guided it through the doorway. He had to lean the structure against the wall to keep it upright.

In the cramped space of the small room, he slid together the last few pieces, then stepped back to look at his work.

The whole thing was about the size and shape of a doorway, maybe seven feet tall by three feet wide. It had tripod legs to keep it stable, and wedged tightly against the wall. It covered roughly a third of the entire south side of the storage room. Unlike the anklet, it didn't look entirely alien. It could have been the ad hoc backdrop of an avant-garde photographer or a madman's lawn sculpture.

Russ waved his hand through the doorway-sized opening between the tubes, and nothing happened. "Unpack that backpack and wait," Atara had said. Russ stood back against the other wall, his hands in his pockets, wondering what would happen next.

When nothing did happen, he went outside to clear his head with some fresh air. The sun was quickly setting, and the streets were deserted except for a few local kids loitering in front of the Laundromat, failing to land kickflips on their skateboards. He didn't know how long he had before the SAS units arrived, but he could feel the precious minutes slipping away.

He turned back to the front door and noticed it also had an envelope taped to it, identical to the one he'd passed on the back door. He grabbed the envelop and, still conscious of the ticking clock, he tore it open.

Dear Mrs. Norma Wesley:

With all due courtesy, we ask that future correspondence be through email or fax, and NOT via handwritten letter. Our client has carefully considered your request to waive the contractually mandated late penalties because of circumstances of "bereavement." While they appreciate you as a long-standing tenant, legally speaking, you'll either have to provide them a portion of the monies owed with consideration toward the penalty-adjusted interest rate or find some other way "to remain close to the memory of your loving husband." Thank you for understanding.

Respectfully,

Logan Trent, Esq.
Trent, Cole, and Kerch

Russ carried the note back to the counter, reading it once more. His grandma's lemonade jug from the day he and Bobby had repaired the roof was still there. She'd washed it carefully and turned it upside down to dry. Next to it was the plate still half full of cookies. Absently, Russ took a cookie and ate it. Then he grabbed a few more and stuffed them in his pocket.

Then he read the letter again.

"I get it, universe," he said to no one in particular. "I'll sign the fucking contract."

The storage room was cramped now, with the giant tube structure inside.

He had sat down on a box of rare Native American curse stones and took a long look at the device. Then he ran his hand along the tubing, gliding the length of the frame. His fingers traced the runes, which now ran along the entire frame.

He mumbled to himself: "I don't care about anyone . . . That's not fair . . . I care about people . . ."

The individual tube sections were now locked into place. There were no knobs, buttons, anything. He had to fight a crazy impulse to search the internet for "how to activate an alien tube structure."

He unfolded the contract. Maybe he needed to sign it before the device would activate. He scratched his finger along the top, and the motion registered as a mark on the document. He hovered the same finger over the signature line and pinched his eyes tightly shut.

From his pocket his phone buzzed faintly. *A nonlinear circuit element coming in contact with a wave pulse.* The SAS units were getting closer.

"Wait just a second," he said to himself. He folded the contract back up and stuffed it into the backpack, unsigned.

His mind made a connection. *Rocks with enough juice to power a city.* That's what Nina had said about the Obinz stone.

He had a rock that generated great power. He had a tube structure with no power. "C'mon Russ, it can't be that simple; can it?" he muttered. He grabbed the Obinz stone from his pocket and thrust it through the opening between the tubes.

Nothing happened.

He tried running the Obinz stone along the structure, while turning it slowly in his hand. He couldn't tell if the veins on the stone were pulsing very faintly or if it was just his imagination.

At seven feet in height, the topmost tube was nearly at the ceiling He slid the stone along its underside. The veins in the stone did seem to glow brighter, though very, very faintly.

In this new, pale light, he could see hundreds, maybe thousands, of shallow, interconnected runes along the bottom half of the topmost tube.

He put the rock back in his pocket and slid his hands along the tube. He could not feel the runes. To the touch, the tubing was just cold, unvarnished lightweight metal.

The feedback from his cell phone was growing louder.

As he continued fumbling with the structure, the topmost tube shifted very slightly.

"Got you, you son of a bitch," he said.

He spun the top tube, slowly at first, then with more force. Only the top half of the tube moved. The bottom stayed in place, revealing a hollow four-inch cradle. There was a mechanical hum, and, suddenly, the rock in his pocket was glowing so much he could see the vein lines through the material of his jeans.

"Progress," he said to himself. "Volatile alien energy that might blow up the store, but also progress."

Russ slipped the Obinz stone out of his pocket again, measuring its size against the open space inside the split tubing. It was a close match. He held his breath and dropped the stone carefully into the cradle. The hum grew louder, and, suddenly, the center of the entire structure lit up a brilliant blue. The color swam in a rolling quantum pattern.

Russ grinned triumphantly.

He squinted his eyes, expecting pain, and slowly reached his fingertips into the pattern. He felt a faint warmth, like reaching into a toaster oven. He pushed his hand through to the wrist, then lost his nerve and pulled it back again.

His cell phone fired another blast of static, this one louder and longer. Russ pushed his arm all the way to the elbow, but all he felt was the back wall of the storage room and the same sensation of faint warmth. Russ reached up and shook the half tube. Maybe the stone wasn't completely set in it.

The stone fell into place with a click. The blue quantum pattern surged, and the light bulb illuminating the storage room over Russ's head burst into a thousand shards. He ducked as glass rained down into his hair. At the same time, he heard the breaker box in the alley outside pop all its circuits simultaneously. Then he heard the skateboarders outside shout as the streetlights burst. He heard other circuit breakers and transformers all along the alley pop. He heard cars screech and honk as they braked suddenly, fenders thumping together in a terrible crunch.

"Whoops," Russ said under his breath. He could see under the crack in the door that the store was nearly dark. It was in sharp contrast to the structure, which now hummed with tremendous light and power.

"Ha! Nina! Told you. Didn't even need to sign the contract," Russ said aloud to no one. Then he reached his hand through one more time, and something yanked hard from the other side.

He found himself surrounded fully by the glowing blue, and goose bumps rose across every inch of his skin; his hair stood on end and his arms and legs tingled, but the goose bumps didn't stop rising. They pulled and pulled, dragging his skin, his muscles, his bones up and away from where he felt his body should be. A deep, warm sensation bloomed inside what was left of his stomach, a yellow sun blossoming there in his gut, so warm that fire shot from his eyeballs and the tips of his toes. It felt surprisingly good, heat exploding out of every nerve. It felt so good, he thought it might tear him in half.

And then his body started to cool. The molecules slowed down their crazy dance. His skin re-contracted, bringing his muscles and bones back in their proper order. His lungs gasped for oxygen, and he realized he was on his knees in hard, gritty white sand. The sky over his head was a deep, cloudless purple.

He took his first breath of stale, thin air, and knew immediately that he'd made a terrible mistake.

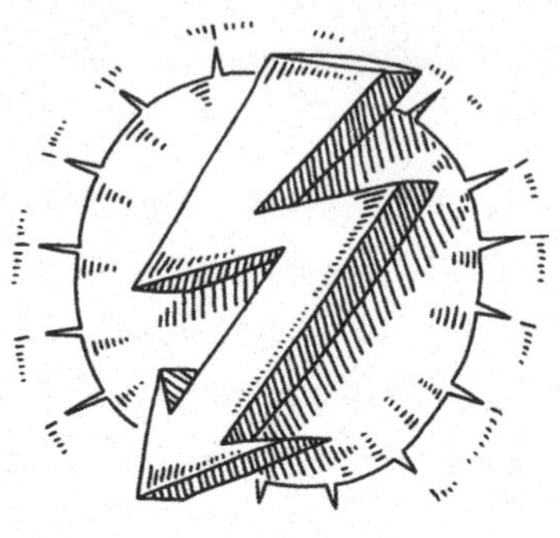

10
NINA

why did we split up?
are you alive?

Nina waited for Russ to respond to her texts. “Sonofabitch,” she said when there was no answer. “I hope he’s not dead.”

“Doreena Thibodeau Hosseinzadeh,” her mother called. “Come down from the loft this instant.”

Nina glanced down through the small square opening in the barn loft at the dirty, hay-covered floor. Her mother stared back at her, her elegant French-Canadian features stitched together in clear annoyance.

“Katherine Francis Hosseinzadeh, what do you need?” Nina asked her mom.

“Do we really have the money to be ordering takeout? I thought you were better than this.” Nina’s mom held a plastic bag in the air. Nina could see the white rice container through the plastic, as well as the outline of a fortune cookie.

Nina reached down through the opening in the loft and snatched the bag away. She set it down next to a lit propane lantern. On the other side of the lantern was a Mauser K98 sniper rifle on a tripod, its nose pointed out the small barn window. Next to that was an open romance novel lying flat on the straw.

Nina waited for a moment, hoping her mom would simply go back inside the house, but her mom stayed on the floor below, tapping her foot and clearing her throat.

Nina glanced through the opening again. "Would you mind going back in the house, locking the door, and turning off all the lights?" Nina asked her.

"I'm not in the mood for your jokes," Katherine said. "Your father isn't either. He could barely eat the meal I fixed tonight. You weren't anywhere to be found, and then Nancy shows up at the door with takeout." She shook her head, at a loss for words. Nina's mom was at a loss for words a lot these days. She was shaking her head a lot too. "Are you wearing a Kevlar vest?"

Nina stared silently at her mom; her mom stared silently back at her. Then, without another word, her mom turned and left the barn, too tired to possibly want to know why Nina would be wearing Kevlar.

Nina moved back to the barn window and raised a pair of night-vision goggles to her eyes. She watched her mom stomp back to the main house. The older woman moved stiffly, her shoulders as tight as a drum.

Nina ran the goggles along the edge of the trees surrounding her property, scanning for robots in business suits. Then she shifted her view back to the main house where she knew her father would be sitting at the window, staring silently out across the dark expanse of the front yard.

Pithyou Firas Hosseinzadeh was always there these days. In the early stages of his illness, he'd been able to work, but he'd gone out on disability just six months after the initial diagnosis. He'd worked as Banville and Evanstown's only commercial real-estate broker, almost entirely on commission, so the disability check sent down from Cheyenne was a lot lower than what anyone would have anticipated.

For a while they'd had a satellite TV package, and he'd sit, coughing, in his easy chair in the living room, watching Persian channels on the Tamashakhane network. Sometimes, when she'd return from college for weekend visits, Nina would watch TV with him. Even though she found the programming corny as hell, it was still fun to see so many other people with thick wavy hair and skin as dark as hers and her father's.

Around fall of last year Nina came to realize she needed to return home full-time and pitch in however she could. The same day she arrived, men from Banville in gray coveralls came and took away the satellite dish. Now her father mostly just sat in the window, his hands folded neatly in his lap.

In the green/gray of the night-vision goggles, Pithyou looked like a ghost. His eyes glowed white, and his skin, grown pasty and covered in dark splotches by the failure of his kidneys and liver, shined back at her against the dark curtains. *I can't let him die,* she thought for the one-thousandth time that week.

Nina watched him until she couldn't bear to anymore. This was usually when a sort of blanket of sadness would settle in over her. But in that moment, she felt something else instead. Sure, the familiar sensations of anxiety and helplessness were there, but they were mixed with a new, less familiar sensation: excitement. Less than an hour ago she had bashed a cyborg into submission with a rock. Two hours before that she had used an alien source of perpetual energy to shock the shit out of Morty. A smile slipped across Nina's face. She might still be broke. Her dad might still be in his sad seat by the window. But so much else had changed since Russ had waltzed into Bum's Sam'wich Emporium, the Obinz stone stuffed in his pocket.

Nina realized she was still holding her phone. She put it down and picked through the plastic bag to open the rice container and the kung pao. She'd managed to fork a flavorless bite into her mouth when she suddenly remembered the sound her cell phone had made when an SAS unit got close. *A nonlinear circuit element coming in contact with a wave pulse.*

She was up in the loft, vigilantly on lookout, and it wasn't necessary. She could use the phone as an early warning device. Heck, if she amplified it, she could use it to scan for the location of active SAS anywhere in the area. All it would need was a big antenna and a continual source of power. Nina shuffled the anklet half out of her pocket and turned it over in her hand. She checked for a text from Russ one last time, then she bagged up the Chinese food, climbed down the wooden staircase and went to work.

Katherine pushed her way into the ad hoc lab just as Nina was building the antenna by fusing together two pieces of metal fencing.

Nina didn't hear her approach.

Ironically, she was in a rush, worried that the arc-welder was making so much noise she wouldn't be able to hear the arrival of the SAS. She finally caught sight of her mom from the corner of her eye, but she couldn't turn around for fear of losing the ground on the welder.

Both her phone and the anklet were on the floor at her feet, attached to a length of copper wire ending in the heads of disassembled jumper cables. Once she finished the antenna, she planned to clip on the power source, strike the anklet lightly with something metal, and the whole device would be ready for what she called a smoke test.

Her mom shuffled across her view. "I'm sorry I yelled at you," she said. "You deserve a takeout meal every night of the week for all that you've done. I've just been so uptight for . . ."

"A year," Nina said, finishing her sentence.

"I know the sacrifice you're making just to be here. If you really do need to go back to Laramie, I—I think you should. I can handle things with your dad. It's really not that bad, and with a little luck . . ."

Nina shut down the arc-welder. The flame snuffed out with a dramatic popping sound. "I would never leave you to do all this on your own, Mom."

Nina's mom brushed the backs of her hands across her right eye. She turned to look at the exit. Then she turned back again. "Well . . . thank you. These came today," her mom said, holding out flowers and candy.

"You can just leave it all on the table. Or throw it in the trash."

"I opened the card . . ." Katherine said.

Nina raised her welding googles. She tried not to let any of the worry she was feeling show on her face.

"What did it say?" she asked.

"It was a poem. A really weird version of Romeo and Juliet in the garden, I think." Katherine looked closer at her daughter's worried face. "Does this bother you? It's poorly written but still sort of romantic. The card wasn't signed. Do you know who left this?"

"I've got an idea."

Katherine stared at her, eyebrows arched.

"I think it's Morty," Nina admitted.

"Morty Forte? Morty Forte, your boss?"

Nina nodded. She tried to restart her welder, but the thing betrayed her, refusing to relight.

"Nina, he's not your boss anymore. Starting this minute. You have to quit."

"I can't, obviously."

"Of course you can. We'll make money some other way."

"How?"

Katherine gestured furtively, her hands moving in small circles.

Nina smiled at her. "It's okay, Mom. I can handle an old guy's attention."

"I'll work for him. I'll take your shifts."

"Do you see that alligator clip on the ground? Could you hand it to me?" Nina asked.

Her mom kneeled and picked up the copper wire leading to the anklet. "Is this going to zap me?"

"Not yet," Nina said. Then she grinned to defuse her mom's newest alarmed expression. "Just hand it to me and hold this antenna for a second. And no, you're not taking my work shifts."

Katherine held out the antennae tentatively.

Nina secured the base she'd created around the bottom of the antenna, allowing it to stand on its own. She adjusted the grip around the base, so the antenna could still swivel in whatever direction she pointed it.

Then she scooped up the alligator clips from the floor and motioned for her mom to step back to the edge of the doorway. "Hand me the hammer, please."

Katherine handed her the rubber mallet, but Nina shook her head. "No. The other one. With the metal head."

"Nina, I'll take the shifts."

"Are you hoping to move in on Morty? You're so pretty, Mom, I do like your chances."

Katherine made fake barfing sounds.

Nina turned back to look at her again. "You already work full-time. You cook. You drive Dad to the hospital every day, help him get dressed, help him use the bathroom. You're not adding another part-time job working for a . . ." Nina tried to think of the right word. If she called Morty a pervert or gropey, her mom would never let her go to work again. And they needed the paycheck. "Working for a lusty old fellow," she said finally.

"What if he tries to kiss you? He's *married*."

Once the clips were in place, and her mom was safely away from the device, Nina drew back the hammer, ready to power up Russ's anklet for the third time in twenty-four hours. "If he does, I'll take care of it," Nina said.

She brought the hammer down hard and the lab went completely dark.

"Wha!" Katherine let out a short gasp. "You really know how to drive home a point."

The sun had dropped behind the mountain range, and no moon shone that evening. Without any ambient light from the city, they were in total darkness. Nina could hear her mom but couldn't see her.

Nina listened for a moment longer. The LED lights she'd installed were silent, but the one old-fashioned incandescent she'd kept for nostalgia, was fizzling—it was the sound of the filament frying itself under tremendously high heat.

"That wasn't me," Nina said. "That was electrical feedback greater than I've ever . . ." She trailed off as the thought occurred to her. Not even a military-grade electromagnetic pulse blast could send electricity into the grid with enough force to slow-fry the filament in a bulb. She only knew one thing that might be capable of that kind of power, and Russ was carrying it around in his pocket.

Nina clutched the hammer as she rushed out to the edge of the property. As she passed her father's window, he looked out at her, his face illuminated in the glow from his cell phone, his eyes still white in the darkness. Nina tried to give him a reassuring smile, but she knew it was too dark for him to see her expression.

She climbed over the fence that ran the length of their house and found herself at the top of a small hill. It was a spot she visited often as a kid to look down on the whole expanse of the tiny city of Evanstown. Right now, all that she could see below her was darkness. A few seconds later, the confused sounds of car horns broke the silence, far in the distance.

Nina peered into the black, right at the point where she knew Norma's bookstore was. *What in the hell is he up to?* she wondered.

11
RUSS

RUSS SUCKED AT THE air, but it felt like he was trying to draw a breath through a long, thin straw. The sickening sound of wheezing filled his ears, and he was startled to realize he was the one making it. With each heavy breath, his lungs ached and his chest shook. His hands, covered in a film of white dust, pounded at his own chest.

Somehow, he was outside, kneeling on a darkened hillside.

Russ grabbed at a nearby boulder to stabilize himself. He closed his eyes and concentrated on the wisps of oxygen that were entering his lungs with each heavy breath. He was still alive, he reminded himself. The oxygen was still eking its way into his bloodstream.

Sparse green brush grew around him. It sparkled with blue and orange blossoms, their bright colors striking against the purple sky.

He climbed shakily to his feet, still sucking at the thin air like a newborn baby. The thing in his grandma's storage room had dragged him through a hole in the universe and spit him out here.

But where was here?

Russ could feel his body weaken with each breath. His eyes searched the sky for a moon, but instead, a field of unfamiliar stars stretched out before him, peppering the dark purple atmosphere with faint light. A stronger illumination came from the device behind him, which hummed softly.

A second later, the humming sputtered to a stop, and the blue light snuffed out.

Russ lurched back through the opening, but instead of being transported away, he landed with a thud on the other side of the rock outcropping. The tube structure had clearly powered down. Russ's breath caught even more in his throat as he realized that his only means of escape had just fizzled away. *I could die here,* he realized. *Soon.* With trembling hands, he fumbled his cell phone out of his pocket and switched on the flashlight.

He heard a noise. Something fairly large dragging itself across a nearby rock. Russ pointed his phone in the direction of the sound. A medium sized creature, maybe forty pounds total, stared back at him with large, dilated eyes. The creature perched on the top of the ridge, blinking hastily and throwing up a claw to ward off the unwelcome light. It opened its mouth and burped out a small screech that was half bird, half rodent. Russ lowered the light, shining it on the deep black granite boulder that the winged creature stood on.

The rat-bird continued to squawk indignantly at Russ.

"Sorry, big guy," Russ gasped. He didn't dare switch off the light completely. He couldn't tell if the bird was predator or prey, and he sure as hell wasn't going to simply hope for the best. As he felt himself easing back into a defensive stance, Russ was hit with a spasm of coughing, the obvious result of the thin air. The creature squawked again.

"Sorry." Russ gasped again. "I won't hurt you, if you promise to keep those claws away from me." He used his most soothing voice.

It seemed to reach the creature. It cocked its head like a bird, staring at him warily from its huge right eye. Russ glanced around, turning slowly in a circle. He was going to need to find more oxygen-rich air, somehow, but without a moon in the sky, everything beyond the light of his cell phone was shaded in a haze of semidarkness.

He turned around to examine the tube structure. He ran his hands over the device, looking for some way to activate it. He found the cradle at the top where the Obinz stone went, but it was empty, and the stone he had had was still in the storage room back on Earth.

Russ heard more scraping, and he swiveled the light in another 180-degree motion.

A second set of huge eyes popped into view. It was another bird-rodent. It shuffled next to the first and they both looked at Russ, their expressions a comic exaggeration of distrust. Russ patted the front of his pants to show them he was unarmed, and he felt the squish of Norma's homemade cookies. He carefully drew one of the cookies out and held it in front of the creatures.

"These are a special recipe," he told the creatures. "Only available in Wyoming." Russ broke off an edge of the cookie and tossed it onto the rock ledge where the birds sat.

Both aliens looked at the crumbs, their eyes wide with fear.

"Maybe you can tell me where civilization is?" Russ asked the creatures. "Buildings? Oxygen?"

Russ saw no sign of intelligence in either animal's eyes. Then the second bird creature craned its face forward and snapped the cookie off the ledge, gobbling it down in a single motion.

Russ was still searching its face. He saw the creature's eyes shift suddenly, from distrust to immediate, clawing hunger. Russ tossed a second part of the cookie, and the creature caught it, its razor-sharp beak slicing through the thin air. Suddenly the other creature was moving closer, its eyes large, appealing. There was a rustling of wings, then a third bird creature appeared. Then a fourth. And a fifth. Russ took a step back, until his shoulders touched the frame of the tube structure. The bird-rodents pressed forward, leaping over and around their granite ledge, cooing in a discordant melody. The one in front had the courage to snatch at what was left of the cookie in Russ's hand, and Russ felt its beak slice into his palm, opening a long cut.

He instinctively jerked the food, and his injured hand, in the other direction. The creature's eyes narrowed, its head bobbing to follow his hand. Its expression said, *You owe me the rest of the cookie. Why aren't you cooperating?* The creatures' cooing brought more scraping and more bird-rats. Russ felt dizzy from the thin air, but he managed to snap the second cookie into ten or so pieces and hurdle them away. The pack of creatures flew after the pieces, smashing against each other, snarling and snapping.

Russ knew instinctively that he only had a few seconds before the creatures would return, demanding more sugary goodness. *This is it,* he thought. *I'm going to die here. Pecked to death by an angry mob of alien scavenger rat-pigeons.*

The creatures finished the last cookie scrap and turned back toward him, hopping in his direction, their eyes bright with vicious hunger.

Russ scooped up a rock from the ground and held it carefully in his closed fist. Before the first creature could reach him, he hauled back and threw the rock as hard as he could. The closest creatures leaped in the air, trying to snatch it from its trajectory, but Russ had applied just enough force to crest the edge of the highest beak.

The bird-rats all scrambled after the rock, hurtling themselves in the direction of its flight, climbing over each other in their haste. Russ understood that the trick wouldn't work twice.

But when they reached the darkness where the rock had landed, the whole pack burst into the air, flapping their wings in a mad rush. They took off with clumsy avian hysteria, feathers exploding in every direction.

From the darkness, a creature of unimaginable horror appeared. It had a bird-rat in its hands, and it was tearing the creature apart as if it was made of paper. It chewed feather, flesh, muscle, and bone with equal enthusiasm. The new beast towered over Russ, at least seventeen or eighteen feet tall, a moving wall of broad shoulders and rippling muscles. As it stepped into the glow of the cell phone, Russ once again instinctively lowered the light, out of perfect, unadulterated fear, layered atop the impulse to hide the creature's indignity, to protect them both from the sheer repulsiveness of its face. The thing only had one eye, and it was glassy and small, almost like a child's marble, barely visible behind puffy pink flesh. It had no ears, not even the genetic memory of ear holes. The side of its face dripped with doughy overlapping folds of skin. Only its nose was prominent, an enormous vacillating vacuole. Its single nose hole climbed upward, searching for Russ's scent. As it smelled the air, it took lumbering steps forward, moving closer and closer to where Russ clung to the powerless tube structure.

The cycloptic creature lumbered right up to Russ, its glassy eye shifting sightlessly in his direction. It leaned over, bringing its nose hole to the top of Russ's six-foot-two-inch frame. As the huge, gnarled nose sniffed at his forehead, Russ knew that he needed to breathe soon or his lungs would collapse. He felt the tickle in his throat grow until it was dry and pounding. His systems were fighting against each other. His lungs told his body, "Breathe deeply or die," but his gut told his body not to make a sound, not to move an inch.

He gasped in a large breath.

The creature flinched, then it flung its powerful arms forward, swinging blindly but still managing to smash them into Russ's chest. The pummeling knocked him completely off his feet. He slid backward on the cold rock. He tried not to cry out, but his old injuries were exploding from pain and he was collecting some impressive new ones as well. The creature was immobilizing him. It would feed next. It stood over him and opened its cavernlike mouth. Russ could see row after row of sharp teeth. He closed his eyes, cursing himself for being so stupid.

Then came the whistling sound.

It was something large, moving through the air very quickly.

When the death blow didn't come, Russ opened his eyes and saw the creature peering upward into the sky, searching for the cause of the sound. The whistling was getting closer with every passing second. It reminded Russ of the sound of a rocket. The oxygen was thinner, and so the friction from the wind produced a much higher pitch. What it really sounded like was a child screaming.

Out of the darkness overhead came two white ships in the shape of eggs plunging through the sky. They were ten feet in radius, and landed heavy side first, as if powered only by inertia and gravity.

When they hit—one on either side of the huge creature—they cracked in half with a thunderous crash.

From inside the ship on the left side, an arm thrust forward, knocking away the cracked pieces of the outer wall. A head followed. It was remarkably like watching something hatch from a giant egg. It didn't hurt that the creature that emerged was covered with tropical-colored feathers and had a broad beak. Its black pupil-less eyes held the intelligence that Russ hadn't been able to find in the eyes of the rat-birds. This new bird fully emerged from the egg, breaking through the last of the thin cracked shell. It was clad in feathers of blue and green, standing seven feet tall on thin, Z-shaped legs. It was smoking a cigarette.

"♏⧫⬧ ♑♏⧫ ⧫♒♓⬧ □❖♏❒ ❑◆♓♍," the giant bird yelled.

Two more creatures broke through the shell of the egg on the right. They weren't birds, but insects. Looking like a pair of twin mantises, they had identical triangular heads and deep black, elongated eyes. Unlike the bird, they were dressed in uniforms—loose fitting orange jumpsuits with patches on the sides. The jumpsuits were roughly cut to allow the free movement of their segmented legs, which had menacing-looking hooks branching inward from the inside of each thigh and calf.

A fraction of a second later, the horrific cyclops sprung toward the bird, howling a primordial yawp. The cigarette fell from the bird's mouth as it yanked a rifle off its back.

It didn't have time to fire.

Fortunately, one of the mantises had yanked a small tube from a fanny pack around its waist and lobbed it at the bird's feet. An acrid yellow smoke rose from the contents of the tube, briefly enveloping the bird and the cyclops. The cyclops, with its enormous nose, took the brunt of the venom, hacking and coughing, its small single puffy eyehole spilling out translucent mucus.

"⌖♒♋⧫ ⧫♒♏ ♐◆♍&!" the bird demanded, its own black eyes raw and puffy.

The mantises didn't respond. They'd both drawn twin clubs from inside their egg. For a moment the clubs seemed like a poor weapon choice against such a massive creature, but as the mantises gripped their hilts, the clubs crackled with lethal electricity, two personal lightning storms against the outline of the dark, moonless night.

The cyclops did not like the electricity. It pounded its chest, once more releasing a savage cry. But it also took a step backward. By now the bird had the rifle raised and steady. A needle projectile buried itself deep in the cyclops's neck.

The cyclops yelped, batting at the needle with its heavy hands. All it managed to do was dig the projectile in deeper. For a moment longer it continued to thrash around, trying to get its meaty fingers around the edge of the needle. But as Russ watched, the beast grew unnaturally weary. Its movements slowed to a near stop, until it was finally, futilely batting at its neck like a tired, angry baby. It let out one more pathetic cry, and then collapsed to the ground.

The bird shuffled forward and fired another needle into the cyclops's neck. It pulled a small tablet from somewhere beneath its feathers and held it up to the monster.

"✡□◆ ♑♏⧫ ♓⧫?" one mantis said.

"⧫⬧ ■□⧫ ♍□■♐♓❒❍♓■♑ ⧫♒♏ □♌," the bird barked back. It looked disappointed about something.

They seemed to be having a conversation. The mantises' voices were more guttural, while the bird's voice danced musically across octaves. They understood each other but seemed to be speaking completely different languages.

Midway through the exchange, the bird grew frustrated. It gestured at Russ with one long wing, then it advanced toward him, its rifle pointed lazily in Russ's direction.

Both mantises turned their elongated faces to look at him. They lifted their clubs and electricity crackled through the air.

"I come in peace," Russ said.

The bird kept advancing, weapon raised.

"I come in peace, motherfucker," Russ said, taking a quick step backward. "If you shoot that thing at me, I'm going to have to take it away from you."

The bird raised its rifle and shot Russ in the neck.

12
RUSS

"THANK GOODNESS WE DIDN'T kill it," Russ heard a voice say.

"The Earth-thing or the Vaqual?" another voice asked.

"The Vaqual, of course. I've never even heard of an Earth-thing."

"I feel like a racist prick. I saw a monster stomping around chewing on that bird, and I figured it had to be our target."

Russ's eyes fluttered open, but his vision was blurry, unfocused. He was lying on a long medical table inside a steel room. He tried to sit up and his head began to spin.

"Take it easy there, friend," a voice said. "We hit you with a pretty heavy sedative."

Russ's vision swam back into focus, and he saw the bird grinning down at him, an odd sight in and of itself because its bottom beak was cupped, and it had no teeth.

"Where am I?" Russ asked.

"You're in the med ward of my ship," the bird told him.

"You speak English?" Russ asked, amazed.

"What the fuck is English?" the bird asked. "You mean how can we understand each other? I gave you a liquid translator while you were out. Makes the whole extradition process easier when the perp can understand me."

"Perp?"

"Do you only know how to ask questions?" the bird snapped.

"Who's asking?"

"We scanned your ankle," a second creature said. It was one of the mantises he'd seen with the electrical clubs. Its voice held more warmth, and Russ thought it might be female—if giant alien mantises were even gendered. "You're Russell Wesley of San Diego, California. You had a conditional work visa for one day, but you cracked it off. You've been on the lam ever since."

"Not exactly," Russ said. "It's kind of a big misunderstanding."

The mantis pushed him back on the table. She retrieved a wand from a nearby cabinet. It looked a lot like the wand the other exterminators had used to check Russ's injuries during what felt like a thousand nights ago in the forest outside Evanstown. The mantis ran the wand along Russ's right ankle, where the nanobots still held fast. Then she read from the small, digitized readout on the wand: "'If this creature is found anywhere in Alliance space, return it, dead or alive, to the nearest immigration outpost.'" The mantis shrugged at Russ. "It's a standard message that triggers anytime a governing ring is popped open. We're legally within our rights to kill you. Hell, it's actually our job."

"You're exterminators."

The mantis shifted to show him the patch on her right shoulder. For a moment, it appeared in alien symbols, but as Russ stared, the letters rearranged themselves until it read "Gas 'em and Trash 'em, Unlimited."

"We specialize in interplanetary swarm migrations, dangerous fungal mass, crop dusting, that sort of thing. Or at least we used to.

Times are tough now, so we try for just about any job that pops up on the MERC board."

"I'm an exterminator too," Russ said.

"You're not," the bird told him. "You are a dangerous species that has illegally jumped ecosystems."

"I am," Russ assured them. "An exterminator, I mean. Or at least I will be soon. I have an offer from Intergalactic Exterminators, Inc?"

"Bah'ren's crew," the bird said, snuffing out his cigarette. "We know them. An okay bunch." His deep black eyes opened in realization. "They have an Earthling on their crew already, don't they? You as fast as the Toreador?"

"Nope," Russ said.

"That's too bad. Can you tell us what you were doing on a demilitarized planet without any credentials, weapons, or survival gear? Or a way home?"

"Another misunderstanding," Russ said.

"You seem to have a lot of those."

Both creatures waited for Russ to explain further. When he didn't, the mantis said, "First time in space?"

"Yeah."

"Welcome to the wider world. Did you pee your pants?"

Russ had, of course, peed his pants, right when the cyclops—the Vaqual—had initially lumbered over to him. "I did," Russ told them both. "And I'm not sorry. That thing was scary as hell."

"Second we exited our EFlyer, I saw it lumbering around and thought it was the job," the bird admitted. "Turns out it's native to the area, and critical to the ecological balance of that hemisphere. Guess it keeps the wild bird population down—the murderous bastard." He shook his bird head disapprovingly. "You were the job. The tiny, scared pink thing clutching the unpowered Waypoint. You humans don't look dangerous, but as a species, it seems you have an abysmal ecological rating. One of the worst I've ever seen. Hell, I've hunted herd animals that fart thunderclouds of methane gas and they still don't destroy planets as fast as a pack of Earthlings apparently can."

"Seems fair," Russ agreed. "So, what happens to me?"

"We follow protocol," the mantis told him. "Take you to the immigration outpost orbiting Galliopia."

"And I hate fucking immigration outposts," the bird grumbled. "No offense, but you're barely worth the peanuts we're making for bringing you in." The bird grinned at Russ but spoke to the mantis. "Maybe we should just leave him where we found him?"

"We're not doing that," the mantis assured Russ. "I'm Alaniea. The other Kruxfas you saw was my sister, Nulinea. You can call us Lanie and Linnie if it's easier. This big tropical brute is named Tyrano."

"Call me Ty," the bird said gruffly. "Come on. I guess we can make a quick trip to the land of the robots."

From the tip of the nose of the ship, Russ watched a sky bridge unfurl and attach to an orbiting satellite. The satellite didn't stop spinning, and the starship had to punch its thrusters every few seconds to keep pace with it. Lanie watched Russ watch the bridge and correctly guessed his worry. "It's all automated," she assured him. "The ship and the satellite are linked by a paralleling program. Just hold on to the handrails tightly and you'll be fine. And wear this. It's called a rebreather."

Lanie was a good foot taller than Russ, so she lowered the rebreather over his mouth with ease and locked it in place with a twist. The device was similar to a gas mask. It covered his face, from the bridge of his nose to the underside of his chin. Around the mouth was a ventilated cannister about the size of a soup can. When he reflexively took a deep breath, he could feel the cannister rumbling softly. Lanie worked at the buckles of two adjustable straps that wrapped around the back of his head to hold it in place. Russ felt like a little kid being dressed by his insect mother.

She handed him four long sleeves of dense polymer.

He heard her voice over a speaker hidden inside the straps of the rebreather: "Compression gear. Put these over your legs and arms or you'll freeze to death. They'll cinch tight once you have them on. I know this is a pain in the ass, but immigration outposts are under municipal jurisdiction, and everybody gets pissed when we use taxes to modernize them. Worse yet, since they're classified as 'homeland security,' we don't have access to their incoming Waypoint coordinates, which is why we have to do this the old-fashioned way."

Lanie pulled a release valve. A series of small tubes along the wall sprayed a gooey substance into the air. Russ watched as the substance solidified into a thin translucent membrane. A light switched on on the other side of the membrane and the starship door began to lift open. Russ pulled the compression gear over his arms and legs. The right leg sleeve was long enough that he kept pulling it, stretching it over his crotch, his belly, and his chest. It hooked over his shoulders and cinched tight.

Lanie checked his helmet one more time, then pushed him through the membrane. Russ felt it stretch thin, tearing involuntarily against his weight, and reforming almost instantaneously behind him. The whole of the dark, shining universe appeared before him.

Lanie continued to talk to him through the helmet's comm system. "Just last year, these outposts would have been manned by organics, but the UAIB found a cheaper way to keep them running. Aside from the medical staff, they're now completely operated by SAS units which—"

"I'm familiar with SAS units," Russ told her. "How is a fully functioning robot cheaper than a person?"

"No health insurance. No disability pay. No time off. No sick days. No retirement. No meals. No bathrooms. Think of the savings on plumbing alone. The upfront cost is more, but the long term is much less expensive."

Then she continued: "First thing the border patrol is going to do is quarantine you and run you through a cleanse to remove any bacteria, parasites, and toxins from your body. It's a diverse urban ecosystem, so we've got to keep out the bad germs. Unfortunately, the process flushes all medication, and most of your helpful probiotics. If you end up with any memory of this conversation . . . you'll want to eat a lot of yogurt."

The spacebridge was a far-in-the-future descendent of a handmade rope bridge. Taut, thin metal handrails were the only visible thing keeping Russ from drifting into space, and they were only waist-high.

Lanie kept talking but Russ didn't hear another word. He had stepped off the deck of Tyrano's ship. They'd lost gravity when they slipped through the membrane, and Russ had to concentrate to get his feet to fall in the right place. It was like walking through marshmallows. On every side a million stars twinkled back at him. Without the buffering of an atmosphere, each star was an explosion of energy, a thousand, blazing points of light.

There was a planet to Russ's left that the satellite outpost was using to guide its slow rotation. The planet loomed just below Russ's eye level, a giant purple god of swirling gas and fire.

For a moment, the satellite, the starship, and the open-faced bridge that Russ stood on danced slowly together in a circle, moving in perfect synchronicity, the starship letting out little puffs of propulsion to keep the balance. Russ held on to the railing, in the direct center of the dance, watching in awe as the entire, vast universe spun around him. It was the greatest moment of his life.

". . . and that's when they'll send you home," Lanie concluded.

Russ reached the entrance to the satellite and once more pushed through a gooey membrane. He snapped back into normal movement, fighting through the last suck of the membrane and into normalized gravity. The journey across the spacebridge had taken less than five minutes, but his feet and legs felt like they were draped in weights.

Lanie followed. "Do you have any questions?" she asked. "I know Tyrano's itching to get us back to work."

"You're not coming with me?"

"We already tagged you in the system. No matter what, we'll get our commission now that you're here. I just came across to get the rebreather and sleeves back. They're not free, you know?"

"Oh," Russ said, peeling off the compression gear. "Thanks for the lift anyway." He looked into Lanie's deep, black insect eyes, for a hint of what emotion might be hidden there. She just nodded her triangular head. A strange look passed over her eyes. "We kind of just fucked you over, Russ. I'm not sure you understand that."

"By rescuing me from certain doom?"

"No, by bringing you here. It's our job, but that doesn't make it the right thing to do. If the SAS want to mind-wipe you, you won't have much chance to avoid it."

"They're going to try and mind-wipe me. That's what they've been trying to do since I met them."

"There's nothing worse that could happen to you. The UAIB likes to say a mind wipe is more humane than murder, but it's not. Maybe if it worked like it was supposed to, but the science is unreliable and the doctors aren't doctors, they're poorly educated med techs, fresh out of CERT school."

"So how do I get off this satellite with my brain intact?"

"Don't let them get you to the med ward. Like all computers, the SAS are imperfect. They glitch. They blitz. They crash. Best way to make that happen is to try and get their basic functions working against each other. My rich aunt has a domestic SAS that cleans her house. Fucking thing can factor pi to the one-thousandth, but it always gets stuck on the rocking chair. Always."

"I'm surprised your aunt has a rocking chair," Russ told her.

"Don't let them mind-wipe you," she said. "People are never the same after." Her large, oval eyes drooped.

"Don't be so worried," Russ said. "I'll be fine."

Lanie nodded. "Maybe I'll see you on the job," she said, giving him a small, sad smile like she didn't believe a word coming out of her own mouth.

13
RUSS

AFTER SHE LEFT, RUSS stayed at the membrane a moment longer, staring out into space. He was in a tough spot, but it didn't stop him from lingering over the awesome experience of the spacewalk. He watched as Tyrano's ship blasted away so fast it almost left skid marks.

Russ was worried, but he knew something about himself that Lanie didn't. He could break computers better than anyone else on Earth. He could disable a PC in two minutes, just by trying to use it. He once broke a girlfriend's phone while holding it long enough for her to use the restroom at a movie theater.

On the other side of the spacebridge dock was a small, unadorned room, maybe thirty by thirty feet. Faceless robot men sat at computer consoles along every wall.

They weren't the poorly disguised "human" simulacra he'd tangled with on Earth. These looked like highly functional units with absolutely no resources devoted to aesthetics: intricate, articulating fingers attached to thin, symmetrical arms, with thin, symmetrical legs and clubfeet. Their faces had no discernable features, just a mouth and eyes cut hastily into bland, tan wax.

Instead of hunting him, they ignored him.

In the direct center of the room there was a tubelike chamber made of thick, translucent plastic. It was empty, but footprints of brownish goo led to and from its sealed door.

Other SAS units dressed in simple uniforms zipped by in every direction. They must have had small wheels on the bottoms of their clubfeet. They expertly maneuvered around him without saying a word. One finally came to a stop before him and scanned his ankle.

"Prisoner Russell Wesley, you are not permitted to be off your origin planet." The SAS told him.

"Yeah." Russ agreed.

"Please proceed to the decontamination tube for further processing."

"What happens in the tube?"

"Illegal biological entities are not allowed to ask questions except as they relate to that entity's immigration status."

"I'm not an immigrant," Russ told the robot. "I'm an emigrant."

"You are an illegal biological entity. If you wish, you may formally appeal that status. Take warning: You are allowed one appeal, and failing that appeal, you forfeit your right to cranial reorientation and instead qualify for immediate termination."

"Let me think about it in the decontamination tube," Russ said.

With the SAS unit nipping at his heels, Russ climbed into the large plastic tube. Once he stood in the center of it, the SAS instructed him to spread his arms and legs apart. Blobs of thick brown goo were ejaculated onto him from every angle. The goo splattered against Russ's chest, face, and back, and then dripped down his legs to slough across the floor. Just like Lanie had said, the decontamination purged the medication from his system. For a while he'd been feeling tingling pain in his ribs, wrist, and leg, but after decontamination, everything throbbed. Thankfully, the ache of his torn hamstring was less obvious, already healed down to a faint pulling sensation.

He had to think fast to get out of this situation, but the pain was so sharp it was tough to concentrate on anything else. If he appealed, he'd face "termination." Was it possible that word meant something else to a robot other than death? Maybe they'd try to power him down and sit him in a closet somewhere?

Dragging his wounded body out of the plastic tube, he looked at his ankle and was happy to see that the brown goo had damaged the nanobots stuck there. They remained half in place, a thin membrane of black gunk.

The SAS robot that had forced him into the tube sprayed a foam on his ankle and then brushed away what was left.

"Thank you . . ." Russ started to say, but then he realized the tracker was being removed because he was caught. He was already Russell Wesley, prisoner. It was slipping a dog off a leash just before leading it into its permanent metal crate.

"I wish to formally appeal my status as an illegal biological entity," Russ told the robot.

The room went silent. All the other robots stopped tapping at their various computer screens and swiveled their wax heads to look directly at him.

"The penalty of losing the appeal is the forfeit of your life. Do you acknowledge this?" the robot asked.

"I do."

There was a series of clicking sounds, like each robot had been momentarily recording Russ's response and was logging it with some central database. After they confirmed his official answer, they all returned to their duties.

"Please proceed to window eleven."

Russ found window eleven, one in a line along a countertop, each window with a different, nearly identical, SAS standing patiently behind it. At the robot's request, he signed a series of digital forms with the tip of his finger.

"I will be administering your appeal," the unit said.

"Just you?" Russ asked. "No judge or jury or appeals court?"

"Those things are not necessary," the SAS promised him. "We have an honesty protocol. It's a system of ensuring you're telling the truth. Once the truth is established, only the facts matter. As such, I am a technologically perfect judge."

"What's your system?" Russ asked.

The SAS shone a light directly from its own pupil into Russ's. Russ blinked, expecting it to be blinding, but the light was soft. It occupied the entirety of the visual field of his right eye.

"I will study the contractions of your iris to ensure you aren't lying. If you are in UAIB space legitimately, simply answer my questions with the truth and you will be freed. If you are here illegally, or you display any evidence of lying, I will commence your immediate termination." The robot's eyes went lax for a moment. "We will continue your appeal shortly. I am currently downloading the associated file on Earthling optical biology."

"You don't need it," Russ told the robot. "I do plan to lie."

The robot studied the iris in Russ's right eye. It was clearly running a recording of his response through a database of Earthling tells. "That is not a lie," it concluded.

"It's not," Russ assured the robot. "So, no termination necessary."

The robot twitched slightly, just a small shift of its waxlike jaw a quarter of an inch to the right. It realigned its face and continued. "Your answer has qualified you as a flight threat." It reached across the counter and wrapped its long, articulating fingers around Russ's wrist. "The appeal process requires strict honesty. Consider this your only warning: Evidence of lying immediately invalidates your appeal."

"I didn't lie. I plan to lie," Russ said.

"That is . . ." the robot began, then it trailed off. The light dimmed in its eyes, then came back with a sudden surge. "We cannot continue the appeal process until the truth is established." The robot held Russ tight. Its fingers were thin but as strong as any metal Russ had ever encountered. "I will try again with simpler words. Lying will cause your immediate death. Do you understand?"

"I do, but I can't help it," Russ told the robot. "I'm a compulsive liar; even this sentence is a lie."

The robot stared into Russ's eyes, processing what Russ had just said.

Russ grinned back at it. "Take your time," he told it.

The robot did take its time, staring at him, trying very hard to quantify what he'd said through its adaptive programming code. Russ knew the problem it was having. If his last sentence had been a lie, then it wasn't a lie. If the sentence wasn't a lie, then the sentence was a lie. It couldn't be both; it couldn't be neither. A classmate had tricked him with the same paradox during an agonizing school field trip back in 1999.

The robot continued to stare at him, its face now visibly twitching. He felt its grip loosen, then tighten. It began to emit a whirring sound, as if it had an old-school magnetic hard drive. The robot powered down, then immediately powered back on. The sound got louder, and louder; there was a clicking, then the light faded from the robot's eyes.

That was fast even for me, Russ thought, as he peeled the dead robot's fingers from his wrist.

Russ wandered away from window eleven. The other SAS units tapped away at their screens, ignoring him. "I'm going to find the bathroom real quick," Russ said, mostly to himself.

He walked swiftly down the hall, glancing back to see if any of them were following him. The coast seemed clear, but he still opened the first door he came across and ducked inside.

Two creatures in medical robes stood with their backs to him. They were leaning over a table. For a moment, he was happy to see organics, until he realized they were hunched over a third body.

The third was somewhat human shaped. It was secured onto the table by neck, wrist, and ankle restraints, splayed out, its head held steady between the forearms of one of the creatures. The other creature had a scalpel and while Russ watched, he carved a slice out of the restrained creature's brain. Light orange blood sprayed where the scalpel cut, and both of the restrained man's legs twitched involuntarily.

"Nicked the oblongata," the creature with the scalpel grunted. "That's going to be a problem."

Russ snuck out the door and quietly backed away. Then he moved farther down the hall.

On the flight over, Tyrano had complained that the immigration outposts wouldn't let them use their Waypoints. Waypoints, Russ understood, were what they called the Obinz stone-powered transportation devices like the one he had hidden in the bookstore. He figured if he could find a Waypoint, he could get the fuck off this satellite of sadness.

He headed down a long unadorned hallway. At the end were a series of signs, all in alien Kanji. He now knew to stare at them a few seconds and the nanotransbots would shift the words into English. He followed the sign labeled "Transfers and Exchanges."

The SAS Waypoint didn't look much different from the others he'd seen, but the robot guarding it did. This SAS had male facial features, a full head of combed steel wire for hair, and oversized eyes that locked on Russ when he entered. It had tightly coiled steel muscles and skin of gleaming chrome. If the other SAS were budget sedans, this guy looked like a classic muscle car.

Russ approached warily. The fancy SAS acknowledged him with a mechanized nod.

"Russell Wesley, headed for Evanstown, Wyoming, 82997," Russ said. "There's a Waypoint in a bookstore on Main Street, if that kind of targeting is possible?"

The robot studied him for a moment. When it leveled its gaze, it seemed to be carefully considering Russ's presence, but Russ now understood that the machine was simply in the process of downloading, fetching his file from a consolidated brain on some UAIB server planet somewhere.

"Why have you paused your appeal process?" the SAS asked him.

"The unit at window eleven malfunctioned," Russ said.

"That is unlikely," the robot informed him. "That unit is a Tech11, manufactured in Divian year 20,20.01. It has been updated and regularly maintenanced."

"Go figure," Russ said.

"You are to remain under the supervision of an official SAS immigration unit until you have completed your appeals process. Or you may submit voluntarily to a mind-cleansing process."

"I prefer my oblongata un-nicked," Russ told the robot. He studied the SAS. It was clearly a more advanced unit, which made military sense. Put your best guy guarding your biggest resource.

The machine leveled its gaze. It was downloading again. "The unit at window eleven did malfunction. That is highly improbable. Only point-zero-one-two percent of units are incapable of performing their mandated duties, and only point-zero-four percent ever fail in instances of simple improvisation."

"How'd you end up here?" Russ asked it. "Why do you look different from the other units?"

The robot studied its own arm. It gleamed chrome. "Illegal biological entities are not allowed to ask questions except as they relate to that entity's immigration status."

"You don't know the answer, huh? Maybe you had your own mind cleanse?" Russ suggested.

The robot paused again. It was downloading. "According to my file, I have been reformatted. I am a factory-refurbished prototype."

"They went a different direction?"

The robot paused a moment. It twitched its chin. "I had a critical design flaw . . . however, you do not need to be concerned," the SAS continued. "My operating system has been recoded, so I am capable of any of the same standard features as my fellow SAS units. I am able to continue your appeal." The soft light shone from its eye right into Russ's.

Russ blinked it away.

The robot shined the light again. Russ waved through it with his left hand but finally allowed it to lock onto his iris.

"I don't trust a rebuilt prototype," he told the robot. "Even the regular guy blew a fuse."

"That is the truth," the unit confirmed.

Russ looked down at the watch on his wrist. It was a worn-out Casio that he'd had since high school. During that time, his friends had stopped wearing watches, then started again with nerdy Apple Watches. Meanwhile, the Casio just kept ticking.

It gave Russ an idea. "How about using this watch to supervise my appeal?"

"No." The robot said without downloading.

"It's never needed reformatting. Or new firmware," Russ said. "In a way it's kind of better . . ."

The robot twitched slightly. Not because it was confused, Russ realized, because it was offended. "You believe you are telling the truth. That is highly incorrect. A simple timekeeper is not better than a specialty prototype Tech12 with fully updated firmware."

"And yet . . ." Russ said, drawing out each word, "this watch has a long battery life. It never crashes. It's got multiple simultaneous functions, a stopwatch *and* a timer: it can count down at the same time as it counts up."

"Those are not the only parameters to judge inorganic life," the SAS unit explained calmly. "I am capable of over 100,000 advanced logistical—"

"What time is it?" Russ interrupted.

"Please indicate specifically which planet and which portion of that planet you are requ—"

Russ checked his watch. "Six-oh-five," he told the robot.

The robot stood before the Waypoint quietly, its head slightly downturned. Russ couldn't be certain, but it appeared to be pouting.

"I never crash either," the SAS said, finally.

"Still . . ." Russ took the watch off his wrist. He wound it carefully around the SAS unit's thick, steel wrist. "Let's make a deal. If you can outperform the watch, I'll trust you to administer my appeal. How long do you go between charges?"

"I am recharged with kinetic motion," the robot told him. "I never need to be plugged in."

"Watch versus robot, round one. You claim you never need a charge. I believe the watch will outlast you. Prove to me you're right, I'll submit to a mind cleanse immediately. No appeal necessary."

The robot's eyes went lax, lit up again, and then went lax again. The Tech12 was likely downloading various protocols to attempt to answer Russ's challenge in the appropriate, legal manner. After a moment, it switched off the light shining in Russ's left eye. Then the Tech12 sat, legs folded on the floor. He raised the watch to its face and studied it.

Russ waited. He waited a little bit longer. The robot continued to stare at the face of the watch.

"Here's the problem," Russ said. "While you try to defeat the watch, there's nothing else you can do. The watch, meanwhile, continues to tell the time. It even has a daily alarm function that I can't figure out how to turn off."

"I can outlast the watch and simultaneously perform any and all standard duties," the robot insisted.

"We'll have to find someone new to run the Waypoint," Russ said.

"Incorrect."

"Evanstown, Wyoming, 82997," Russ said.

The robot shook his head. "I believe you are trying to trick me, and so I remind you that you must remain under the auspices of an immigration official until you have completed your appeal."

"How are you going to prove you can run the Waypoint unless I leave?"

The robot was silent.

"I can't trust you to administer the appeal unless you run the Waypoint. You won't let me use the Waypoint unless I finish my appeal. We're trapped in a paradox."

"One moment while I access my improvisation protocol," it said.

Russ watched the robot carefully. This was the moment when the last SAS shut down, but Russ could tell that this one was different somehow. Smarter.

The SAS reached a conclusion, though Russ could only guess what it was. Suddenly its chrome fingers wrapped around Russ's wrist. With a single arm, it lifted Russ completely off the ground.

"That kind of hurts," Russ grunted. "What's the plan here?"

"I'm resolving the paradox," the Tech12 said.

The Tech12 gathered Russ up like a newborn and carried him through the Waypoint.

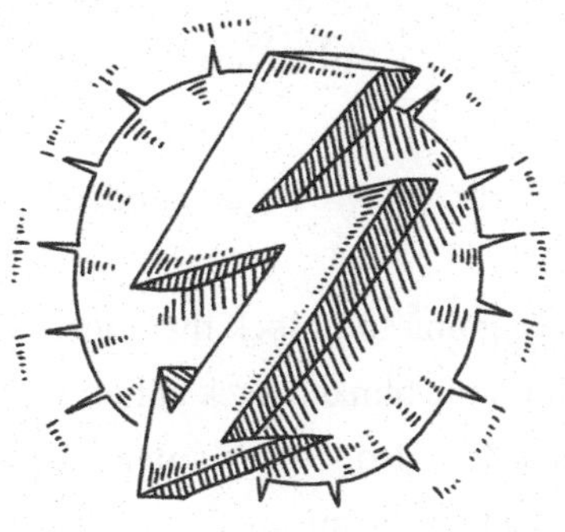

14
NINA

IT TURNED OUT THAT when you attach a cell phone to an infinite power source, then to a giant antenna, it makes a lot of noise when it rings. Russ's call was so loud, it knocked Nina off her feet backward. She landed hard on her butt in the thin hay of the loft. Her butt was sore from the number of times she'd fallen on it lately.

"Who still calls?" she demanded, when she finally fumbled the phone open and shut off its screeching ring. The resulting static electricity set her curly hair on end.

There was a long groan on the other end.

"Russ? You okay?"

"I need your help," Russ said. The cellular connection was tenuous at best. Russ's voice kept fading in and out. He was also grunting, or maybe panting. It was the sort of call she expected from Morty, not him.

"Where are you?"

"I'm at the bookstore. In the storage closet. Come here right now."

"I shouldn't drive in a power outage. Evanstown's small, but we—"

"Come. Here. Right. Now," he demanded. "Key . . . under the dumpster . . . alley."

"You're not even going to unlock the door? Is everything okay?" Nina asked, but her phone blinked back at her: *Call dropped.*

The second the call ended, Nina's antenna contraption blasted a warning, a wave of feedback so strong that she yanked the whole thing apart just so it would shut up. When it finally quieted, she was half covered in straw, huffing.

"They're here. The SAS are back in Evanstown," Nina said aloud. Her voice echoed eerily in the darkness. She powered on her phone's flashlight, then gathered up all the antennae parts and carried them carefully down the barn stairs.

The drive to the bookstore wasn't particularly dangerous. Most of Evanstown had the smarts to stay off the road. In fact, it seemed like everyone had taken the power outage as an excuse to be out walking around. Kids holding candles ran in circles in front yards. Adults chatted with neighbors, their faces half cloaked in shadow.

When Nina pulled into the alley, she spotted Russ's car, parked at a slant, as if he'd jumped out in a hurry. Or maybe run out of gas. She gathered the antenna contraption from the bed of her truck. Once she'd figured out what Russ needed, she'd hook it back up and try to determine where the next SAS attack would be coming from.

She followed the weak light of her phone's LED to the dumpster, then fumbled around in a small space underneath. It was disgusting down there, a foul mixture of rotting food and mildew, but she found an envelope taped to the bottom.

The envelope had a key, the key unlocked the door, the door opened to the completely dark hallway.

Everything was going as she expected until she opened the door to the storage room. Inside was a huge machine, alive with power, crackling and glowing blue. Before the machine stood a robot at least seven feet tall. Its gleaming chrome skin appeared ocean blue in the other machine's light. It stood erect, its arm held above its head, Russ dangling from its arm.

"Holy fuck," Nina said.

"A little help?" Russ asked her.

Nina grabbed a stack of books and slid them under Russ's feet. Once he could stand, he exhaled deeply. "My arm's completely numb," he told her. "The blood is all pooled in my feet. You just saved my ass. It was really starting to hurt." Russ looked at Nina, who had not yet spoken a word other than her initial, blasphemous reaction. "What's with the antenna?" he asked her.

"T-there are SAS in Evanstown." Nina stuttered.

"No kidding?" Russ said. He turned to the robot. He couldn't really look it in the eye because of the angle at which it was holding his shoulder. "I think she's talking about you, big guy."

"I am not an ordinary SAS," the robot said. "I am a repurposed prototype with a fatal flaw."

"It's having an existential crisis," Russ said.

"Is it dangerous?" Nina asked.

"All intellectual crises are dangerous in their own way."

"Not . . . I mean . . . why is it holding you off the ground?" Nina asked.

"It is necessary to immobilize him until he has concluded his appeal process," the Tech12 explained. "It was also necessary to prove to him the superiority in my coding."

Nina carefully laid the antenna on the ground. She went outside to the main portion of the bookstore. She found an empty lemonade jar, an empty cookie plate, and a loaded tool belt, likely used to repair the roof. She selected a hammer from the tools, then picked up a roll of ceiling insulation. She returned to the supply closet, taking a moment to disentangle the anklet fragment she'd been using as a power source.

"Can I approach you?" she asked the robot.

"Of course. Every Tech12 is built with the latest safety protocols and unable to harm nonviolent organics that are currently in compliance with all UAIB behavioral codes."

"Cool," she said. She approached the SAS unit, then put the anklet fragment against its clubfoot. She saw Russ register the hammer in her hand. She saw his gaze drift to the insulation, which she'd wrapped around her entire arm.

"Are you sure?" he asked, as she stuffed the insulation between him and as much of the robot as she could. "This thing looks really metal-y. I mean, pretty conductant."

Nina grimaced back at him. She threw in a shrug for good measure. It said, Not sure what else to do.

"Tech12?" she asked. "Would you mind grabbing ahold of the light above you? The one with the broken bulb?"

"Like this?" the robot asked helpfully.

"Almost. Actually, push one of your fingers inside it. Until you're touching the ground wire."

"Like this?" the robot asked again.

In answer, Nina brought the hammer down hard on the anklet.

The outflow of power fired upward, exploding down the ground wire, but also back into the electrical grid. It was so much juice that for a moment, the lights in the bookstore surged back on, as did the lights in the donut shop next door. There was the distant chunk-chunk as the machines in the Laundromat down the street did several rotations. The power traveled all the way to Morty's Sportys, lighting enough of his sign to read MOR_ SPOR_.

For that brief moment, the people outside in the streets, chatting with their neighbors, holding flashlights and cell-phone lights, stopped what they were doing and cheered.

Neither Nina, Russ, nor the Tech12 heard the cheer. They were lying on the floor of the storage room, in a heap.

15

RUSS

RUSS DIDN'T WANT TO move. Nina was snuggled against him, her head on his shoulder, her cheek pressed against his upper chest. He raised a hand to his own heart, making sure the electricity wasn't still coursing through his body. It kind of felt like it was. He wasn't sure why any of them were still alive.

Nina was snoring softly, her feet resting across the legs of the SAS unit. Russ carefully extracted himself from her grip and slid out to the back alley. Not knowing what else to do, he pushed his grandma's car against the fence. It gave him a chance to collect his thoughts.

It was morning, and a pair of electricians from Banville were working out of the back of a van, scratching their heads and studying the electrical boxes.

Rubbing his wrist where the SAS had held him in the air, Russ slipped through the bookstore's back door. He had his hand on the knob to the storage room when he heard a knocking on the front door.

Norma was on the front stoop, both her hands cupped against the window, peering around inside. Morty leaned next to her, sweat pooling on his forehead, his beady eyes searching the store. Standing side by side, with his mass and Norma's frail, thin body, they looked like the number ten.

Warily, Russ opened the door.

Morty stared at him with disapproval. "Left your grandmother to walk the side of the highway by herself, did you?"

"Not on purpose."

"You have her car!" Morty insisted. "How else can she get around?"

Russ nodded. "The car is in the alley, Grandma, but, uh . . . it's out of gas."

"Unbelievable," Morty huffed. "If I hadn't been headed in this direction, she'd still be walking."

"It was very kind of Morty to stop and pick me up," Norma said. "Are you okay, Russ? You look frazzled. What on Earth did you do to make your hair stick up like that? And why didn't you come home again last night? I've started to get used to it, but it still worries me."

"Are you going to step aside and let your grandmother into her own store?" Morty asked.

Before Russ could answer, Norma said, "It's okay, Morty. I went inside yesterday, but . . . yesterday, repairing the store seemed a lot more possible." Norma's face drooped. She unfolded a letter from her pocket. Russ recognized it. It was another copy of the rent notice from the lawyer trio of Trent, Cole, and Kerch. "I—I found this taped to the door of the house this morning. I can't pay what they're asking. I knew I'd better hurry here and warn you not to work on the roof anymore. There's no sense in repairing everything if the business isn't sustainable. Mr. Baedeker cautioned me about this, the day of your grandfather's funeral. I knew it was coming, I just wasn't quite ready to lose the store."

"I'm still going to fix it up, Grandma."

"Russ, why?"

"I think we can still save it. We just need to start generating a little income. We've got, what, five days before their deadline? And the world is better with the Mysterious Universe in it."

"I don't know, Russ." She shook the letter with her hand. "This isn't the only bad news. Bobby can't help you finish the roof. His son owns all those sweet pepper crops that you can see east of the highway. The heat"—Norma fanned herself—"the heat is so bad they've got to harvest early. They worked late into the night last night—at least, until the blackout hit. And they're doing it again tonight. Even with Bobby's help they'll lose a good portion of their yield. I thought if you were to stop working on the store, maybe you could lend a hand there instead?"

"I've got a lot going on," Russ told his grandma.

"Which is why you haven't been coming home at night?"

"I fell asleep here, working. When the blackout hit, I figured it wasn't a good idea to drive home." Russ was amazed at how quickly the lie came spilling out of him. He was getting a little cocky, what with how much sense he was making.

"That's fine, dear. It was an unusual night."

"Yeah," Russ agreed, and he imagined an SAS unit somewhere (maybe the one behind him in the storage room) nodding and registering, "not a lie."

"If I could get my book?" Morty asked.

"We're closed," Russ told him. "I even took the sign down."

"He drove me all the way here. We should get him a book, at a discount. The problem is, he won't tell me what the book is."

"I don't have a specific title in mind," Morty insisted. "And it's kind of private . . ."

Norma looked a little surprised. "Boy talk? Okay. I'll be across the street getting coffee. Maybe Morty can give us a ride to get gas next?"

"I would," Morty said with false earnestness. "But I have to open my own store. The girl that runs my cash register didn't show up this morning. No call, no excuse. She must be in league with your grandson." Morty chuckled. "And now she might be looking for a new job."

Norma walked across the street to the donut shop after urging Morty to give the young lady another chance. Especially if he was talking about that lovely Nina.

"What do you need?" Russ asked him, once she was out of earshot.

"Reference books." Morty said.

"My grandma hasn't carried many of those since people started using the internet," Russ said. "In 1997."

"I couldn't find what I was looking for on the internet." Morty said stubbornly. "I need reference books"—his voice dropped to a whisper—"about magic."

"Magic?"

"Witches."

"I think you want the internet," Russ told him.

Morty shook his head. "The internet is full of made-up nonsense. But I've experienced something real."

Russ arched an eyebrow at Morty. He wondered, for a moment, if Morty had had some kind of alien encounter. It didn't seem farfetched these days.

Morty was adamant. "It doesn't have to be magic. It could be science. What I need to know is this: Is it possible for a person to become electrified?" The question rushed out of Morty, the words sped forward by shame and curiosity. "Can a part of someone's body become loaded with electric current?"

"That's udderly ridiculous," Russ told him.

After passing Morty copies of *The Encyclopedia of Things that Never Were*, and *Electricity for Dummies*, Russ stuffed Morty's twenty-dollar bill in the cash register and carefully locked the front door. He could see his grandmother through the window of the donut shop, talking to the owner and nodding her head. He rushed back to the storage room.

He heard Nina's voice through the door. She was speaking carefully, in a soothing tone. "It's all right," she said. "We'll get you fixed up in no time."

As he entered the storage room, the Tech12 was responding. "All my offline functions are registering completely normal, but my online diagnostics keep failing. Statistically speaking, there's only a point-zero-zero-two percent chance that this could be happening."

"How's that watch doing?" Russ asked, peering at the watch he'd left on the robot's wrist.

The Tech12's eyes dimmed, then lit up again. He was trying to reboot his system. "I—I think my safety protocols have been erased."

Nina turned to Russ and leaned close. She whispered into his ear. "Its wireless radio is fried. It can't download. It must rely on a persistent Wi-Fi-type connection to some sort of central server. But the connection's severed. It also seems to have forgotten who it is. The electricity fired up its spine, traveling along some kind of neural network, probably popping the circuits on the way. It's why we're not both dead." She leaned out again, then leaned back in quickly. "I must study it."

"This is most distressing," the Tech12 said. "Only three percent of my memory code is uncorrupted. I'm lucky to still possess language."

"Why does it speak English?" Nina whispered.

"What's English?" the robot asked.

"You're a Waypoint guardian," Russ told the Tech12.

The robot glanced at the Waypoint. "That . . . syncs with what remains of my memory code," he admitted. "And my job is here? In this small space?"

"It is," Russ told him. "Though sometimes you are asked to perform other duties as well. Mostly maintenance."

The robot's chin twitched to the side. Then it said, "The Tech12 is capable of a number of focused jobs. But—I feel compelled to stare at this watch." The Tech12 kneeled on the floor near the Waypoint and began to stare at the face of the watch.

"Your name is Steven Applebum," Russ told the robot. He was really starting to enjoy his new gift for lying.

Nina shook her head no. "We'll remember you a better name than that," she told the Tech12.

"What are we going to do?" she asked Russ.

"Leave him in here, I guess. The watch won't run out of batteries for another year or so."

The SAS seemed to sense something. He stood up again and touched the Waypoint, then held the left tube tightly, studying it.

"What's up?" Russ asked him.

"Incoming traveler from Waypoint 7102.1233.3," the Tech12 said.

"Incoming . . . to here?" Russ asked.

"Please step back from the Waypoint to avoid molecular collision," he instructed.

Russ and Nina looked at each other, then they stepped back to the far wall. The swirling blue face of the Waypoint churned noisily. Though the color didn't change, there was a shift in the atmosphere, the sudden presence of electrified molecules.

Russ could feel the energy dancing like butterfly wings against his cheeks. The hair on his arms stood straight up.

It was happening, he realized. He'd put the tube structure together and the Intergalactic Exterminators were handling the rest, just like they promised.

There was a loud popping sound, and a figure formed in front of the three of them. It started as swirling light, almost indistinguishable from the gate's normal energy, then shifted, hardened. An old man appeared. Then, layer by layer, the details emerged: pale skin, thin white hair, oversized nose.

He was wearing a large backpack that somehow was still packed to the brim. He must have been strong, despite his advanced age, to not topple over from the weight of the thing.

The old man belched. Russ smelled heavy alcohol on his breath. "Oh shit. Earth," he said, looking around the tiny room. "It's smaller than I remember. You Russell Wesley?"

Russ nodded. "You were sent by the Intergalactic Exterminators?"

"I was." The old man pulled a fresh copy of the contract from his backpack and unfolded it. "First things first," he said.

Russ took the contract from him and stuffed it into his pocket. The old man narrowed his eyes, but then something else caught his attention.

"Where is your governing ring?" he asked, gesturing at Russ's ankle.

"I broke it off, by accident."

The old man's eyes shifted quickly to the Tech12. "Is that why he's here?"

"In a manner of speaking," Russ said.

"I'm Doreena Hosseinzadeh," Nina told the old man.

"Pleasure to meet you," he said. "I'm the CERT trainer. The name's Ensine. Major Rufus Ensine."

He broke his gaze and turned from Nina back to Russ. He took a deep, dramatic breath, launching into a speech he must have given dozens of times before: "I'd like to say I'm here to train you in the art of ecosystem preservation, a noble job with a vast history. But what I'm really going to do is put you through a series of job-related challenges. It's dangerous work, and the CERT trainer's main function is to weed out the weaklings. No matter what you think of a mind wipe, it's better than being shredded to pieces on a remote planet in the jaws of an apex predator. You prove you can handle the job, you'll get your papers. You fail"—the old man looked at the Tech12 again—"well, you can expect to see a lot more of these big guys in your near future."

"Okay," Russ said.

"You can train me too?" Nina asked, hopefully.

"Only if you're Russ Wesley," Ensine told her.

"I'm not," Nina admitted. "But I would like CERTification. I want to be trained."

"Though my services are priced in the, shall we say, budget portion of the CERTification pricing spectrum, they are still far more costly than anyone from a shithole planet like Earth would be able to afford. I'm very sorry, young lady. You seem a bright and motivated pupil."

"I need a job," Nina told him. Then she put her hands directly through her curly black hair. "My job! Shit!"

The SAS had returned to looking at the watch. Nina grabbed the Tech12's wrist to check the time. "Sonofabitch!" she said. "Gotta go." She pointed her finger at Ensine. "I'll be back immediately after my shift, and I want to talk numbers. Costs. I want the damn job. I'm probably about to lose my current one."

"Morty just left," Russ told her. "Take the back way and you might be able to beat him to the door."

Nina nodded hastily. She took one last, long look at Ensine and the Tech12, then she forced herself out the door and into the alley behind the bookstore.

Russ addressed the Tech12: "You are not to move from this spot. If anyone other than me, or Nina—"

"Or me," Ensine corrected him.

"If anyone other than the three of us tries to come through this wooden door, prevent it from happening without revealing yourself."

The Tech12 nodded.

"If anyone else comes through the Waypoint, keep them here until I return. Do not let them outside."

As Russ closed and locked the door to the storage room, he could hear the SAS still responding. "Without my safety protocols, I'm not sure what you expect . . ."

"My grandma is on the other side of this wall," Russ told Ensine. "I'm going to tell her you're an old friend, here to help me repair this bookstore."

"Son," Ensine said, "I don't really care what you tell—" he was in mid-sentence as he and Russ rounded the hallway corner—"who is that luminous creature?"

Norma was back at the front door, peering inside. She seemed to be studying the work Russ and Bobby had done on the roof.

"Where?" Russ asked. As he turned to the old man, he saw a terrifying change come over Rufus Ensine. His features softened. His eyes widened. His old, cracked lips pushed up into a loopy smile.

Ensine pulled the front door open wide. He did a short bow in front of Norma and said, "Major Rufus Ensine, late of the 4029th Naval Command. How may I be of service to you?"

"Naval command," Norma said. "Are you a friend of Russ's?"

"This is my grandmother Norma," Russ interjected. "The Major was stationed in San Diego. That's where we met. Uh . . ." Russ's recent gift for lying seemed to have abandoned him. "We met in San Diego."

The three of them just stared at each other, Norma blinking, Ensine beaming, Russ grasping for words.

"Do you know my daughter Becca? Russ's mom?"

"I do not," Ensine said. "If she is as beautiful as you though, I would be interested to meet her."

Norma covered her mouth and chuckled. "Your friend is very bold," she told Russ. Then to Ensine: "Did you just arrive? Are you planning to stay long?"

"Originally? Only a few days. But I may extend my visit." Ensine patted at his head, moving his thin hair around a little bit.

"Any friend of Russ's is welcome here in Evanstown," Norma said.

It seemed to Russ that they had forgotten he was there.

"Do you have a place to sleep, while you're in town?" Norma asked.

"I'm always looking for something soft to rest my head against," Ensine said.

Norma's eyes widened. She covered her mouth again, but this time she giggled. Russ hadn't known she could still giggle. "There's only one hotel—" she said.

"But they always have a vacancy," Russ finished. "Evanstown is not exactly a vacation destination. Grandma, we were just leaving, is that okay?"

"There is absolutely no hurry," Ensine said.

Norma held up a bag full of donuts. "You can't leave on an empty stomach," she said firmly.

By the time Russ got back from exchanging Morty's twenty dollars for a jerrican full of gas, Norma and Ensine were chatting like teenagers. Russ grew increasingly uncomfortable with how energized they seemed to be by each other's company. It was a relief to get the car running again and finally drop Norma off at her house.

"Your grandmother is delightful," Ensine told Russ as they drove Norma's beat-up old Mercury back toward the highway. He paused a moment, his nose tilted slightly out the open window. "There's a river nearby," he declared.

"The Bear River," Russ told him. "It's less than half a mile south of my grandma's house."

"She's so fit for a woman her age." Ensine said, jumping back onto his original line of thought.

Russ just grunted, displeased. "My grandfather passed away very recently," he said.

"So, she is not currently espoused?" Ensine asked.

Russ ignored the question. "Do you really need the hotel? Where are we going?" They were back in Evanstown's main commercial "district," just a loose collection of freestanding buildings. They passed the bowling alley, Robinson's lumberyard, and Morty's Sportys.

Ensine started to answer, but he was interrupted by a fit of coughing. It was a deep cough, and wet, as if the old man had a respiratory infection. When he finally caught a quick gasp of breath he said, "Stop! Stop right here." Russ swerved the Mercury to the curb, glancing at his rearview mirror. No cars approached, and the sidewalk was as empty as a ghost town.

Ensine coughed again. "Of course, I don't need a hotel. I assume you have some isolated bodies of water around here. Preferably brackish?" Ensine reached up to his ear. He had a small metal device clasped at the top of his right lobe. He fiddled it free and completely transformed.

One second he was an unremarkable, old Caucasian dude, and the next he was an amphibian. He still stood on two legs, but that was about the only thing that wasn't different. His skin was blue green, covered in scales, with a spectral shine like abalone. He had a pair of arms, but also a pair of fins, folded carefully down over the backside of each bicep. His eyes were large, without lid or brow, and they bulged from his head. Along his jawline was a matching set of gills. He was missing a few scales on his shoulders and chest, likely the signs of his advanced age. His fish eyes stared back at Russ unblinking. "If I'm going to stay on this planet, I have certain physical requirements," he told Russ. His hands were clasped in his lap, but his fins fluttered with emphasis when he spoke.

He coughed again, then he climbed out of the car and stood on the sidewalk. His appearance, out in the open, in the center of town, was alarming.

"Put the metal thing back," Russ said, gesturing to his own ear. He glanced in all directions. It was a quiet day—all days in Evanstown were quiet days—but that didn't mean Ensine should be walking around looking like a bipedal six-foot-tall sparkling albacore.

Mercifully, Ensine reaffixed the metal device. The vision of the old man shimmered across his features, then locked itself back in place.

"I've got to go there," Ensine said. Over his left shoulder was an empty building that had once been the town's video-game arcade. Russ had loved it when he was little.

Over Ensine's right shoulder was a liquor store. Russ realized that was where he was pointing. "Give me some money," Ensine said.

Russ had almost two dollars in change in his pocket. He passed it to Ensine. Ensine glanced at it distastefully. "When I get back, that contract had better be signed. This job is already costing me money," he said. Then he disappeared into the liquor store.

Russ unfolded the contract and looked at it again. "Inability to perform work for any reason will result in a legal forfeiture of all chattels, including, but not limited to, what the UAIB quantifies as grave necessities . . ." it read. He poised his finger above the dotted line and signed a name: "Steven Applebum."

Ensine came out of the liquor store a few moments later, still coughing, two lottery tickets and a case of Budweiser in his arms. The coughing continued until he had wrestled a can free, popped the top, and guzzled the entire beer. Finally, with a few last violent hacks, he got his breath back. "Forever tied to water," Ensine said, holding the empty beer can aloft. "A genetic gift from my ancestors."

"That's not water," Russ said as Ensine popped and guzzled another beer.

As he drank a third, then a fourth beer, Russ noticed the stress lines disappear from Ensine's face. "Son," Ensine said, "you Earthlings can be proud of two things: your libations and your women. Aside from that, this place is a deserty shit-planet. But those two things . . ."

Russ waited patiently, his hand on the roof of Norma's car, while Ensine drank a fifth and sixth beer. He watched the man's face soften again. It seemed the right time to slip him the contract. Russ passed it to Ensine over the hood of the car and then watched with relief as Ensine stuffed it into his backpack without examining it.

"You want to find out if you have what it takes to be an Intergalactic Exterminator?" Ensine asked him. "Take me somewhere with a body of water, and plenty of privacy."

"I know just the place," Russ said.

16
RUSS

FOR THE SECOND TIME in as many days, Russ found himself parking the Mercury at the edge of the trail leading up to Nina's favorite hunting spot.

Russ led Ensine away from the path, toward where Nina had indicated there was a waterfall. He wasn't disappointed. After a few hundred yards of thick brush, they could hear the steady thrum of water falling on rocks.

A hundred yards farther, and the brush cleared to reveal a beautiful swimming hole, fed by a tall waterfall. The water looked ice cold and crystal clear.

Ensine slipped out of his shirt, shoes, and socks, and immediately dove in. He slid through the water like a porpoise, kicking from his waist, his mouth agape as he drank in long, powerful gulps. He surfaced at the edge, his gray hair plastered against his face. "Not brackish, but it will do," he said. "Dig into my bag. There is a set of small metal discs in there. Pick out your favorite."

Russ pulled open Ensine's backpack. It was threadbare and faded by the sun. Inside were a series of boxes, equally old, damaged by both sun and water. The first box was half open and Russ could see the small discs stacked inside. There were about thirty total, and each had writing on the top, like an old-school music CD. Russ glanced at the first one. It read: "Tharcus—whose skin is without weakness."

"What's this?" Russ asked.

"A series of adversarial training programs," Ensine explained.

Russ flipped to the second disc. It read: "Dreadwalker—whose grip is mighty." The one after that read "Buuffaaffaa—whose enemy is left flattened."

"Do you have any for 'Swedish girl—whose breasts are soft like pillows?'" Russ asked.

Ensine ignored the question.

"What are we going to do with them?"

"What better way to get used to fighting monsters than fighting monsters?" Ensine asked.

"But where are the monsters?"

"I will be the monster. That's what it means to be a CERT instructor. I know the tendencies and fighting styles of every creature on those discs. With a few physical alterations, I will disappear into the role completely."

"We're going to fight each other?"

"Yes. Live combat. Being a budget trainer, I can only afford to license safety protocols for myself. For you, the dangers will be real. I thought I'd at least let you choose your own ass kicking." Ensine climbed back onto the shore. He popped a beer and drank it. "We need a twenty-foot square, without obstacles. If you're not going to be safe you should at least have space to move. While you're clearing away these rocks and brush, we can take care of some the required, boring crap."

Most of the rocks that littered the area around the swimming hole were roughly the size of Russ's head. He lifted them with some difficulty, and after a few minutes of work, the sweat started to build up on his chest and back.

"You're moving like you're injured, son."

"I'm fine," Russ insisted. He paused a minute to take off his shirt and splash fresh water on his face. He was back hefting rocks when he noticed Ensine's eyes running the length of his body. "You're really hurt badly," Ensine said.

"Do you have any of those pain pills?" Russ asked.

Instead of answering, Ensine said, gruffly: "There are several universal rules that all municipal employees must adhere to. Think of them like the four commandments, if that helps. They're called the SSCs, or shared system of civics. If you violate any one of them, you'll be fired, deCERTified, and your citizenship will be revoked." Ensine ticked off each SSC on his fingers. "A municipal employee must protect the anonymity and reticence of the United Alliance of Intelligent Beings. A municipal employee must do no permanent harm to any planet's natural ecological balance. A municipal employee must not remove a planet's natural resources for his or her own benefit. A municipal employee must not be the direct cause of death for a civilian belonging to any of the sixty-seven certified UAIB population groups."

"Does that include Earthlings?" Russ asked, dropping a heavy rock into the swimming hole.

"The inhabitants of Earth are not a recognized civilization according to the UAIB." Ensine said. "It's no problem if you accidentally kill one."

"Fantastic," Russ said.

Russ handed Ensine a disc marked "Grendo-Fend—who moves with the grace of the wind." It seemed a peaceful-enough description.

Ensine handed him a roll of pain pills, then walked to the center of the cleared space. He dug around in his backpack before finding something that looked like a miniature 1980s-era boom box. He slid the disc into the box and then removed the transformer from his ear. He was immediately a tall, two-legged fish once again. "I find it's best if I don't speak during these lessons," Ensine explained. "It helps preserve the illusion." He held the transformer close to the boom box. "I'm reconfiguring my transformer to replicate a Grendo-Fend," Ensine said. "I will be accurately mimicking its predatory patterns. Try your best to keep me from killing you."

"With my bare hands?" Russ asked, munching on a pill.

"Use the environment to your advantage." Ensine gestured around the small clearing with one of his fins. He pulled two final items from his backpack, a pair of handheld grips, each six inches long. He held them in front of himself like the twin handles of a jetpack. He tested one lightly, and a small burst of fire exploded from the bottom. It was a powerful enough propulsion to momentarily lift him six inches in the air. Satisfied, he moved the transformer away from the boom box and reattached it to his ear.

Russ took a step back as a new image shimmered over Ensine's features. Where the man had had a split-fingered hand, he now had six sharp talons. Where he'd had diaphanous fins, several yards of extra skin now sprouted, hanging from his armpits like a sheet, so thin as to be translucent. Where Ensine had had a gaping fish mouth, he now had a beak of white bone, its tip bearing sharp four-inch incisors. The illusion crept across his entire form, until the flaps of extra skin grew to fasten between his sixth long talon and his ankle bones. Ensine preened in a small circle, extending his arms, showing how the skin had formed effective wings, not the kind that stretch out from shoulder blades, but rather the fixed wings of a mutant pterodactyl.

A gust of wind picked up and Ensine extended his flesh-wings, catching the thermal, his body lifting into the air as smooth as a kite.

"Who moves with the grace of the wind," Russ said under his breath. "It's not a metaphor. This beast actually rides the wind."

Ensine as a Grendo-Fend rode the thermal peacefully, climbing higher and higher. Russ watched as it disappeared into the glare of the sun. It was only a last-minute glimpse of its wings pulling tight against its body that allowed him to realize it was hiding in the sun's glare in order to tuck itself into a steep dive. "Coming right at me," Russ realized as he splayed his feet. He shuffled away from the spot, managing to look past the glare and see the Grendo-Fend's body barreling toward him.

He knew that if he moved too soon, the bird would be able to correct its approach and still hit him. He had to wait until the last possible second. Russ held his breath as the beast hurtled toward his chest, a deadly spear of feathers, leather, and bone. Seconds before it reached him, Russ dove recklessly forward. He felt the wind of the Grendo-Fend's descent, felt the feathery touch of its skin, and heard the resounding crack of its beak striking hard against the ground.

"Hey, asshole. That would have killed me," Russ told Ensine. He scrambled to his feet, dancing over to the shore to scoop up a large rock. The Grendo-Fend was back preening again, high stepping in a small circle, extending its rear end in the air. It shook its wings at Russ mockingly.

Russ hurled the rock at its head. The Grendo-Fend dodged, but not quickly enough. It had been too caught up in its own dance. The rock glanced off its shoulder. The bird squawked mightily. Russ paused a minute to admire Ensine's dedication to his character.

The wind came up, and once again the Grendo-Fend caught it, drifting into the sky, hovering thirty feet above Russ's head.

It did a slow barrel roll, Ensine still showing off his mastery of the creature's physicality.

The creature had three sharp points, its beak and its two claws. Russ knew he had to stay clear of each. As it rolled through the air a second time, Russ noticed its back was smooth. A creature of the air wouldn't need to evolve many natural defenses on its top side.

Russ moved toward the swimming hole. He didn't want to be a stationary target. He kept his eyes upturned but it was difficult with the heavy glare of the midday Wyoming sun. When he reached the river, he danced down the muddy bank until he could feel the cool water gather around his ankles. From this position, the sun was tucked behind one of the sparse clouds. The mud slowed Russ's movements, but it was worth it to gain visibility.

"Hey bird breath, you smell like rotten eggs and seagull poop," he called.

The Grendo-Fend immediately folded its wings and dove again. Russ ignored the impulse to dive for cover. He waited until the creature was less than a yard above him, then he flung his body in an arc to the left, trying to catch the underside of one of its wings.

He'd made the play too early. He realized that he didn't yet have a good-enough sense of how fast the bird was. The Grendo-Fend shifted quickly, its wing slipping away from Russ's grip. It twisted its body again, and Russ was suddenly staring into its beady eyes, its sharp beak inches from his chest.

Ensine twisted his false Fend head away at the very last second—so he wouldn't impale Russ, but they still collided with all the force of Ensine's sky fall. They toppled together into the deep water. There was sudden bloody thrashing, the Grendo-Fend throwing its talons in every direction. Russ punched and kicked at the creature, feeling the incongruous sensation of Ensine's scales beneath his fists. It was all at odds with what he could see, which was a violent, wet bird in distress.

He finally pried himself free and tried to kick to the surface, but he felt Ensine's webbed hands wrapping around his ankles.

The other man's voice echoed up through the cold, deep water, filling Russ's ears: "You only get to overestimate the enemy once. After that, you're dead."

17
RUSS

"DID YOU ASK ENSINE? About CERTifying me?" Nina's voice sounded hopeful. She was standing by the cash register, and her posture seemed almost shy. As Russ walked toward her, he realized it wasn't shyness he was reading in her body language. It was anxiety.

Russ shook his head. "I asked. He gave the same answer."

Nina hung her head. It was cruel, Russ realized, to have this adventure without her. He wanted to save the bookstore. She wanted to save her father's life.

"Maybe you could take my place?"

"He won't allow that," Nina said. "They paid for you. They want someone who can shoot like you can."

Russ looked around at the bookstore. It needed a lot of work and a lot of money to facilitate that work. He looked down at his own shoes, horribly worn and holey. Not knowing what else to say, he just looked at Nina.

"How are *you* at roofing?" Russ asked her.

She shook her head.

He moved back into the storage room where the robot was sitting by the Waypoint, staring at Russ's watch on its wrist. "How are you at roofing?" he asked the Tech12.

"I am unfamiliar with that phrase. One moment." The robot's eyes went dim. It was trying to download, but Russ could see that nothing was happening. "I'm sorry," the robot said. "I will try again in a few minutes."

"Don't bother," Russ told it. "I have a better idea." He went to the reference section and found a book titled *101 Tricks of the Amateur DIYer*. He carried it back to the storage room and handed it to the SAS. "This is a book. It's how humans download. How fast can you read?"

"The Tech12 unit is equipped with a state-of-the-art processor capable of .02 S-THz response times, including ocular rendering to the one thousandth—"

"Read that," Russ interrupted.

"I cannot," the Tech12 told him.

"Why?"

"It—I believe it is against my core programming. Manufacturing a robot capable of reading is a violation of inorganic protocols, section . . . *bzzzt* . . ." the unit's eyes dimmed as it rebooted. "Protocols," the unit tried again, "section one twenty-nine *bzzzt* . . ."

"I'm familiar with protocol section one twenty-nine *bzzt*," Russ told him. "And you're remembering it wrong. There's nothing bad about reading. Everyone should do it, even robots. Open the book and use your ocular rendering to digest that fucker. I'm giving you a direct order."

Russ watched the Tech12 try to reboot again. He clenched his fist and shook it at the book. "And you're not just a Tech12. Your name is Steven Applebum."

The robot finally lowered its eyes and began to study the pages. It took a moment for it to get through the first page but then it began to flip pages at a rate of about one per second. *Was it reading that quickly?*

Russ went back to the reference section.

Nina had moved to the corner, and her back was turned. The main portion of the bookstore was almost completely dark, with just the light from the streetlight filtering in through the window. In the shadows, she struck a particularly sad figure.

So many people around here need help, he thought to himself.

In a way it was reassuring. Russ had spent the last five years drifting, but it didn't come without a cost. He hadn't been able to shake the notion that he wasn't making progress in his life in any definable way—and, even worse, that he fundamentally didn't matter. The moment he'd drifted into Evanstown, that had changed.

"You know you're wrong about me?" he asked Nina.

"In what way?"

"When you said I lived my life the way I do so I wouldn't ever have to help people."

"I know that's not your main reason, but it's a consequence."

"I live the way I do because I like to have new experiences. But the thing about not helping people? The real consequence of my lifestyle is that I have no obligations."

"Which is the same as—"

"And having no obligations leaves me free to help people," Russ finished.

He left her by the cash register and went to the reference section to find a new book. When he got back inside the storage room, Applebum was on the last third of the one Russ had just given him.

"These techniques are rudimentary but fascinating," the Tech12 said. "I believe I am ready to 'roof' now."

"Soon," Russ promised him. He dropped the new book in Applebum's lap.

The robot read the cover: "*From Seed to Harvest*?"

"Learn everything you can about harvesting sweet peppers," Russ commanded.

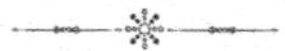

The next morning, Russ found Ensine asleep in close to the same spot he left him, curled under a moss-covered log at the bottom of the riverbed. Beer cans floated everywhere on the surface.

Russ tried to call out to him, but when he opened his mouth, a yawn pried its way out. He'd been on his feet all night. He had a thumping in his head and in his body where his injuries were lingering.

At first, Russ and Nina had just watched the SAS work, as it moved efficiently from sweet pepper to sweet pepper, in ordered, mechanical patterns. There wasn't much of a moon in the sky, but still the robot's skin reflected bright chrome. Russ wondered if the occasional car passing by on the highway could see what was going on, but he figured if they did catch the reflection, they would think someone just left a machine parked among the crops. When they'd watched enough to learn the harvesting process themselves, they worked alongside Applebum, though at about one-tenth the pace. The three of them had kept at it, pulling the remaining peppers, slicing them from the plant, wrapping them, and stacking them in neat piles atop the tractor trailer, moving from row to row, all the way until the first rays of sunshine spilled over the horizon. They'd harvested about 70 percent of the yield when Russ decided it was too light to keep the gleaming silver Tech12 outside.

Nina had gone home, likely to collapse exhausted into her bed. Russ had returned the robot to the storage room, his hands full of callouses, his ribs aching. And now it was time to start training again.

Ensine was gesturing to the large waterfall that fed the riverbed. He'd been talking though Russ was too fatigued to fully listen. ". . . and that rock is the perfect place to continue your training. Take off all your clothes and sit on it, until I say otherwise."

"All my clothes?" Russ asked.

"Naked."

"This is some Weinstein shit."

"Don't make me say it again," Ensine told him.

A few minutes later, Russ found himself buck-ass naked on a rock directly in the center of the waterfall. He clutched a beer in his hand, his other arm held outstretched for balance.

At first, the water was so cold it took his breath away, but as his skin numbed, the thrum of the water across his head and shoulders became a pleasant sensation, waking him up, making him forget his fatigue and his pain. He sat crossed-legged, with his arms folded in his lap.

Russ wasn't bothered by the nudity or the cold. Nudity felt more natural than shameful, and besides, Ensine had removed his transformer again, and Russ figured if someone wandered into the clearing, they'd be more interested in the human-sized, two-legged, drunk fish flipping playfully about in the water than Russ's lack of clothing.

After a while, Ensine stopped enjoying the water and scrambled up on the rock next to Russ. "Essential to being a successful exterminator is learning to control your own shock reflex," Ensine instructed. Somehow, Russ could hear Ensine's voice clear as day, despite the sound of falling water. As with the previous day when he and Ensine were fighting at the bottom of the swimming hole, it was almost as if the water itself was amplifying the words, echoing them from every direction.

Ensine continued: "One of the few qualities that unites every species, regardless of origin planet, is the warring impulses of fight or flight. No species successfully evolves without both impulses, but if you lean too far in either direction, bam, that'll be the end of your genetic line. Over the course of the job, you will encounter creatures that are the stuff of your wildest, darkest nightmare . . ."

Russ nodded, the vivid memory of the Vaqual still in his mind.

". . . if you choose poorly, flee when you should fight, or fight when you should flee, you die. Controlling your shock reflex, learning to live with a clear head even when your mind is screaming at you to panic, that's how you make the best possible decisions. You did not flee from the Grendo-Fend. That was the proper decision. A creature with the Fend's speed could follow and you'd be fighting it from an indefensible position. Today, when you face the Jinxden, you may want to consider a different tactic."

Russ nodded.

"Do you know how to shoot a gun?"

"Yeah." He took another long drink of the beer, though it was becoming very watery. With each second under the freezing waterfall, he could feel the numbness in his body giving way to a deeper level of cold, but he held himself steady, refusing to allow his body to shiver.

Ensine slid off the rock, disappearing under the water, but firing up out of it seconds later on the far side of the swimming hole. He landed gracefully on his feet next to where he'd left his backpack. Russ watched Ensine root through the backpack until he finally withdrew a small drone—no bigger than eight inches in length—and a snub-nosed firearm.

"This is the worst gun in the universe," Ensine said. He tossed the snub-nose to Russ, an impressive throw from the bank all the way across the water. Russ caught it in the air, rising into a standing position. He inspected the gun as best he could, with the water pounding down on his head. Despite its alien craftsmanship, it looked a little like a snub-nosed .38 revolver. The barrel was barely three inches long, and the whole gun was small enough that he could hide it in a clenched fist. It was a weapon built for emergencies when you had no other choice.

The barrel was so short, you wouldn't want to use it if you had to aim more than five feet in front of you.

Ensine held up the drone. "I can replicate many creatures, but not the all-too-common tiny pests which are nonetheless dangerous. This drone was built to fly and fight just like a Jinxden. It's capable of tremendously fast starts and stops, can move instantly in any direction with equal force, and it spits a small projectile, roughly the size of a sewing needle. If you were to stumble onto a nest of these creatures and piss them off, you'd die painfully.

"I'll be piloting the drone and using its projectiles to harass you and to wound you—don't worry, I have pain pills I'll share at the end of the exercise."

Pain pills, Russ thought hungrily.

"I've had students hit by over a hundred projectiles before they learned how to move quick enough to escape its sting. Remember, these travel in packs of hundreds. This lesson is as much to teach you how to pick your battles and how to survive long enough to escape." Ensine detached a small electrical device from the drone and gripped it in his hand, his thumb covering the end like a joystick. "The snub-nose gun is meant to give you false confidence. You must not be fooled into a sense of your own power. If a creature is too dangerous, or you lack the proper equipment to fight it, you must evade. Use the rocks and water for cover. Dodge as many projectiles as you can. When you get outside the perimeter of the water, I'll consider the evasion complete."

The drone spun into the air, bobbing, weaving, and dipping in frantic bursts. It zigged one way then immediately zagged back the other. It was moving so fast, Russ had trouble focusing on it. It was like trying to see the wings of a hummingbird. The water still beating against him, he glanced down at his naked body and the pathetic weapon in his hand. The drone buzzed close to the waterfall, spitting a small metal needle at Russ.

It stuck in his chest, digging into his skin like the bite of a horsefly. "This will not be a pleasant experience," Ensine promised. "But when your squad Waypoints to a remote island on planet Nustrix, and you find yourself surrounded by a hundred of these, you'll thank me."

Russ closed his left eye to help him focus on the herky-jerky movements of the tiny drone. He watched for a moment, as the drone dipped and dashed. Russ barely registered the sensation as it spit a new needle deep into his right shoulder.

"You need to surrender your pride. You need to know when to run," Ensine urged.

Russ raised the tiny pistol and took aim.

Ensine saw him aim, fired one more projectile into Russ's chest, them dogged the drone away, zipping it across the water, as far from Russ's weapon as possible.

It had almost reached the edge of the bank when it exploded into a hundred pieces.

Ensine's mouth gaped open like he'd gotten ahold of the business end of a fishhook. "Holy shit." he said. "What a lucky shot."

He dug into his backpack again, removing another drone. "Good thing your cut-rate instructor isn't too cut-rate. I packed another of these in case that one ran out of batteries before you managed to escape. No one's ever made the first shot before. You should feel like you just landed a one-in-a-million jackpo—" Ensine wasn't able to finish his sentence.

The second drone had barely risen above his two-fingered hand when Russ shot it out of the air. Ensine hurled himself backward with a startled cry.

"What. The. Fuck." Ensine said, shaking his hand and inspecting his two fingers for damage. His eyes moved to the drone pieces, which were now littered all around him.

"I've never seen anything—" "Twenty long cycles I've been doing—" "I don't even know what to—"

Ensine couldn't finish any of his sentences.

His eyes drifted back to where Russ was standing in the middle of the waterfall, the gun still extended in his hand.

"Let's have another beer," Russ shouted.

"You've always been able to shoot like that?" Ensine asked. Russ had slipped back into his jeans, and they were sitting together at the shoreline.

"As long as I can remember," Russ said.

"I didn't think humans possessed that kind of dexterity. But then"—Ensine glanced around—"Earth has changed a lot since I first started coming here."

"When was that?"

"It's been eighty life cycles, close to a hundred Earth years. My first visit was in 1915, and it was wartime. Folks were still splitting uranium atoms to power their ships, so the UAIB set up observation outposts on uranium-rich planets. I was stationed just off the coast of Namibia, over in Africa. All galactic tech has moved beyond using uranium these days, but at the time the UAIB thought Earth might become a resource-rich battleground planet." Ensine's eyes became wistful. "It was there that I learned to love your women. And your beer." Ensine lifted the Budweiser to his lips.

"Was that the 4029th Naval Command?"

Ensine nodded. "I became something of a war hero half a decade later." He chuckled at the memory.

Russ stared at the fish man, his faded and wrinkled clothes, his old threadbare training backpack.

Ensine rose to his feet, stuffing the shattered pieces of drone into his bag. "I guess we can skip the other lessons on ranged weapons?"

Russ nodded.

"How are you with martial weapons?"

"Meek like a child," Russ admitted.

"Hmm . . . I might have made a poor choice for opponents then." Ensine held up a new disc. It read "Beuala—who snaps the necks of his enemies." "Let's practice a few rounds before you meet Beuala." He withdrew a small steel pole and snapped it forward. In a rush of clanging metal, it telescoped out to three times its original length. Ensine clutched the handle, and the metal came alive with buzzing electricity.

Russ had seen this weapon before, in the hands of Lanie and Linnie.

"Anything you don't have in that backpack?" Russ asked, just as the older man leaped forward and brought the metal pole winging in an arc toward his head.

"Watch it!" Russ yelled, but Ensine was already on the attack.

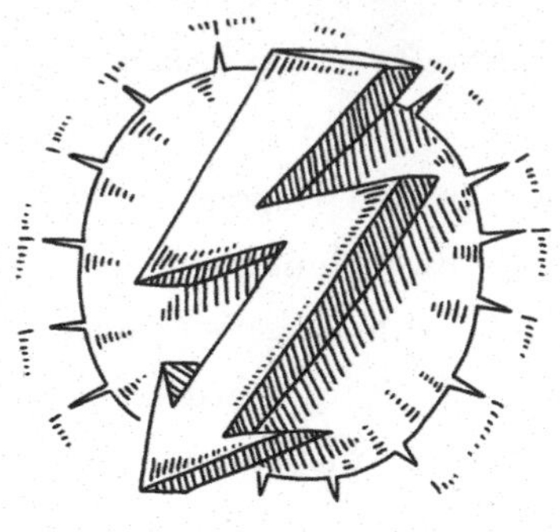

18

NINA

NINA'S HANDS WERE COVERED in callouses. She rubbed them nervously as Pithyou's doctor finally made it into the hospital room. He was carrying a stack of papers and his expression was grave.

"Are those test results?" Katherine asked anxiously.

The doctor shook his head, and for a minute looked embarrassed. "No. Sorry. The floor manager passed these to me on the way in. I don't think he wanted to bring them himself." The doctor handed the stack to Nina's mom sheepishly. "I only glanced at them, but I'm afraid they're bills. For the various tests and procedures from the last few months—"

Katherine flipped through the bills. In his bed, her dad looked pained. They had just removed a portion of his liver for an updated biopsy, and he was still shaking off the effects of the anesthesia.

"We've received most of these same bills in the mail," Katherine said, flipping page to page.

"The bills have been paid?" the doctor asked.

Katherine put the bills aside. "Very soon," she promised.

"The hospital has been reviewing your situation for some time," the doctor said.

"We know. We're very thankful for everything you've done," Nina said, chiming in.

"Administration has asked that we carefully consider any new testing as long as the bills remain unresolved," the doctor told them.

"Carefully consider?" Nina said. "What does that mean?"

"Who said that?" Katherine said, her voice climbing. "Wayne and Suzanne?" She got to her feet, the bills spilling onto the floor. "They were too cowardly to come tell us in person?"

The doctor's face colored. He didn't seem to want any part of the situation, and even through her anger and fear, Nina could see how unhappy he was to find himself in the middle of it. A part of her relished his pain and wanted it to be worse.

"What are we supposed to do?"

"Let's wait on the results of the new biopsy. Depending on what they show, it may be appropriate for him to continue his care in Laramie. They have a larger facility, and much more access to the appropriate equipment. They also have policies in place that prevent them from refusing care in situations like—"

"*Bullhonkey!*" Katherine interrupted the doctor.

Nina had risen to her feet and moved to the door as her mom began to inform the doctor, loudly, of all the problems with continuing care in Laramie, including the family's inability to actually reach Laramie, much less stay there, or even visit it every few days for dialysis.

Looking for a distraction, anything to keep herself from crying, Nina glanced down at her phone.

Depressingly, there was a text from Morty:

Need you for the evening shift tonight. Wear the new uniform this time. It's not too small. It looks great.

"Where are you going?" Katherine called as Nina swept out of the room. She didn't answer because she knew her mom would be upset to learn she was headed back to Morty's Sportys. As she closed the door behind her, she could hear her mom immediately restart her verbal attacks on the doctor. Nina felt bad for the doctor, and for her mom, and for everyone. On the way out, she spotted Wayne Perkinsky, one of the hospital administrators. He was hiding in a corner, making himself as small as possible. She breezed past him without saying a word.

The truth was they couldn't expect free health care, not under the current system anyway. Being in the wrong didn't make the situation any better though; it made it worse.

She reached her truck and dug around in the backseat for her Morty's Sportys uniform. Morty had gotten her the right size pants, but the shirt was at least a size too small.

Nina climbed into the cab and stripped off her T-shirt. She picked up the uniform and eyed it again, disgusted. "No, truly fuck it," she said to herself, shrugging back into her own shirt. She put her car into drive and buried her foot on the accelerator.

She discovered Russ a hundred yards down the trail, lying in a clearing, surrounded by a lot of empty beer cans. "He's really training hard," she mumbled. She glanced around for Ensine, but there was no sign of him.

As she got closer, she saw the most peculiar thing lying a few feet away from Russ. Nina had to shield her eyes from the light reflecting off its scales. It was the biggest fish she'd ever seen. Did Russ pass out fighting it to the shore? Had that huge fish been in the water where Nina liked to swim? How had she missed it over the years? It was going to break a hell of a lot of records.

She was still thirty or so feet away, and at that distance, the two prone bodies looked like drunken puddles of flesh and scales. It was even more shocking when she reached the pair of them and the fish sat up, recognition alight in its eyes.

It shook its head at her. "Doreena Hosseinzadeh," it said. "You're here for training, I assume?"

Nina nodded, her eyes blinking in disbelief as the fish stared back at her.

"I'm sorry, young lady, but every new CERT costs resources, drones, wear and tear on my body. . . If you had some money, perhaps I could give you a discount, but even a sentimental old fool like me knows better than to work for a negative balance."

"Ensine?"

The fish lifted a small box out of his backpack and fiddled with a metal clasp in his ear. A moment later, he looked like the old man she'd met in the bookstore. The only difference was, he wasn't bald. He had a thick crop of wavy white hair on his head. As she looked closer, she realized his chin was stronger too, and his eyes were deep and bright.

He still wasn't wearing a shirt, and where he'd had a small, paunchy beer belly, now he had six tight abdominal muscles. He had been meddling with the illusion of himself, Nina realized.

"I—I want to make a deal," Nina said, pushing past her disbelief. "What if I had something else to offer you?"

"What did you have in mind?" Ensine said.

"I was thinking maybe this?" Nina said. She reached into her pocket and held out the Obinz stone. The yellow veins along the surface of the rock pulsed lightly.

Russ's eyes fluttered open. "S'that mine?" he asked.

Ensine considered it. "That is an unrefined stone," he said. "You shouldn't have it. It's very dangerous, for many reasons."

"What's it worth?" Nina asked.

"Worth?" Ensine asked, incredulous. "It's illegal. As a CERTified civil servant, I am mandated to remove it from your possession." Ensine reached for the stone, but Nina snatched it away.

"No chance," she said.

"You could be exposing all of us to dangerous levels of isotopic diffraction. Worse yet, those things can attract all kinds of different creatures."

"Truth," Russ said.

"An unrefined stone has no preset destination. If you put that in a Waypoint, you'd be playing a dangerous game of chance."

"Truth," Russ said again.

"And yet . . ." Nina said, letting the end of her sentence trail off.

"And yet they're very valuable," Ensine admitted. "A stone that size would fetch a significant amount on the galactic black market."

Nina's eyes lit up.

Ensine could not help but grin at her expression. He stepped forward to snatch it out of her hand again and this time she let him take it. He hustled it over to his backpack and removed something square and white like a first-aid kit. He drew a plastic bag from the kit, tore it open and retrieved a folded foil sack from the bag. He wrapped the Obinz stone carefully in the foil sack, put the foil in the bag and zipped it tight.

Ensine slipped the bag into his backpack and set the backpack down carefully, as if it might explode. Then he turned to Nina. "You'll have to come early tomorrow to make up for lost time." He flashed a lizard's smile. "I'll make sure to bring the pain pills."

19

RUSS

WHEN RUSS ARRIVED THE next day, Nina's truck was already parked along the hidden trail. He put his palm on the hood and found that the engine was cold. How long had she already been there?

He could hear the cries of martial combat even before he rounded the last corner. He spotted Ensine first, soaring twenty feet in the air disguised as the Grendo-Fend. Nina had moved to a spot away from the water, between two large rock outcroppings. It was an easier spot to defend than the swimming hole, which had been Russ's choice.

He watched from a distance as the Grendo-Fend repeatedly tucked into a dive and fell through the sky, its sharp beak pointed toward Nina. Each time he got close, Nina ducked behind the rocks, positioning them between herself and Ensine's attack. He didn't manage to lay a single feather on her.

By the time Russ reached the clearing, Ensine had landed and removed the transformer. He had his hands on his hips.

"It's a little easier with more clouds in the sky," Russ suggested.

Ensine held a single finger in the air, gesturing for Russ to wait while he took a few deep breaths. "She's not as good a shot as you, but man, is she hard to hit," he said finally. He was still short of breath from his unsuccessful attacks. "And, she's already memorized all her SSCs."

"Those are easy," Russ said.

"Name one."

"Uh . . . don't steal valuable shit from other planets."

"Not the exact words of the textbook, but . . . good," Ensine said, nodding.

"Like an Obinz stone," Russ said looking at Nina. "Don't break into a friend's bookstore storage room and take his Obinz stone without asking."

"That's not one of the SSCs," Ensine said.

"A municipal employee must be conscious to protect the anonymity and reticence of the United Alliance of Intelligent Beings. A municipal employee must do no permanent harm to any planet's natural ecological balance. A municipal employee must not remove a planet's natural resources for his or her own benefit. A municipal employee must not be the direct cause of death for a civilian belonging to any of the sixty-seven certified UAIB population groups," Nina said, counting off each one on her fingers. She had a broad grin on her face, and Russ realized it was the first time he'd seen her with a full, genuine smile.

"Words to live by," Ensine said.

Something occurred to Russ, and his gaze shot over to the rock directly beneath the waterfall. Had Nina sat there completely naked, just as Russ had done on his second day?

When he looked back at Ensine, he was pretty sure he'd gotten his answer. Ensine was giving him two enthusiastic thumbs-up.

"As I promised, today we will be drilling unarmed combat. I will be teaching you multiple stances from the Lama'Pai school of martial arts. It is a school of combat originating on this very planet, so I thought it appropriate. Meet me in the clearing in two minutes." Ensine walked toward the clearing, dug into his backpack, and returned with a disc that was probably labeled something like "Super Beast—who will bite your leg off with a single chomp."

"The training is only four days," Nina whispered.

"What's that?"

"We're heading to space soon."

"There's only three days left? We haven't learned that much," Russ admitted.

"After this we have some kind of residency in space. Ensine said it's dangerous. He told me that the percentage of people that survive the whole process is very low." Nina's face clouded, and she studied Russ for a moment. If he wasn't mistaken, she seemed to be deciding how she'd feel if he died. "Do you know what kind of workers only get four days of training before they start a dangerous job?"

"The kind no one expects to last very long," Russ answered, and he knew the second he said it that he was right. Ensine was only covering the basics of space combat. It was like those corporate safety videos he would have to watch before starting a warehouse job. They didn't make you any safer, but they checked a box on someone's liability worksheet somewhere. "Maybe they expect us to learn more during the space residency?" Russ suggested, not really believing himself.

"That's just free labor. We'll be doing the job, but not yet CERTified. If we die during the residency, they'll have gained two temporary employees for just the cost of Ensine's modest services."

"This is why I don't sign contracts," Russ reminded her.

Ensine snapped his fingers between them, breaking up their whispering.

"Follow me and do exactly as I do," the no-longer-old man said. He moved to the middle of the clearing and relaxed his posture, bending slightly at the knees, his fists bunched at his sides. "The first stance is called the cat stance. I assume you humans haven't messed up this planet so bad that you no longer have cats?"

"We've got them still," Russ grumbled.

Following him to the center of the clearing, Russ and Nina did their best to mimic Ensine's movements, both knees slightly bent, fists open now, palms forward and flat. At Russ's elbow, Nina looked lithe and dangerous. She seemed to be picking up the instructions effortlessly. Her curly black hair had worked itself free from its bun and it was cascading down her shoulders.

Despite her natural poise, Ensine called out small shifts in her body position. "Bend your left knee more. Back straight. Your weight should be on your heels," he barked. "Unarmed combat is not about something as primitive as swinging a stick or squeezing a trigger. It's about poise, balance, strength, and the more important laws of physics."

Russ balled his fists on either side of his hips, trying his best to hold the cat stance.

"Not terrible!" Ensine barked. "But can you move smoothly to crane?" Ensine whipped his hands around in a semicircle, raising them up into the crane position. Russ tried to follow suit.

"Now heron!" Ensine barked, modeling the heron stance. "Now hourglass! Now square!" Ensine thrust his fists forward.

They worked until the sun began to dip behind the trees, swinging between stances and varying strikes, thrusts, hooks, and sweeps. All the while, Ensine shouted for simple changes in their body positions. Russ had never had any formal fighting lessons. He found when he followed Ensine's directions, his body moved more fluidly. He understood that if he could master the balance, every stance could blend perfectly into the next stance and the next attack, like a beautifully executed dance. "Now strike from square . . . now hook from square . . . now strike from heron!"

Surprisingly, it was Nina who lost her balance first.

Ensine was switching rapidly back and forth between positions, and she landed on her ankle wrong, crumpling to the ground. It was likely exhaustion as much as anything else.

"You fall on your ass a lot," Russ told her. He tried to help her back to her feet, but she shrugged him off.

"I need a minute to load up the combat program," Ensine said. "While I do, practice on each other. Hooking sweep from crane."

Nina scrambled to her feet and dropped back into the bow stance, then quickly realized her mistake and moved to crane. She flicked her hair from her eyes and smiled humorlessly at Russ. It was an effective strategy because he was briefly distracted by her perfect beauty. Then she struck, moving extremely fast. She hit Russ twice, once in the shoulder, once in the chest. Then she scampered forward, sweeping at his leg with her own.

Russ leaped over it effortlessly. He hadn't consciously registered her attack. His instincts just moved his body where it needed to be. He landed, balanced, and swept her legs out from under her. She tipped onto her backside but was back up on her feet immediately. She launched her shoulder into his chest with unchecked malice.

It was the beginning of what would be several days of violent, merciless unarmed combat. Sometimes Russ fought Nina, sometimes he fought young Ensine, sometimes Nina and Russ fought "Buuff-aaffaa—whose enemy is left flattened." Despite his pessimism, Russ could feel some improvement. They were both moving with more confidence and grace.

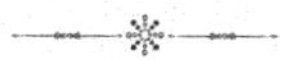

On the evening of their final day of training, Russ decided to work through the night, finalizing repairs on the bookstore with Applebum. The ceiling was sparkling with a fresh coat of lacquer. Applebum had proven both an adept sander and painter. He'd stripped all the shelves down to their base and stained them as well. If they didn't move quickly, the bookstore was going to look mighty fine, practically brand new, when they had to hand it over to the bank.

Russ had taped newspaper over all the windows so they didn't have to work in the dark. Applebum diligently ran an orbital sander across the shelves in the travel section. He had kind of a faraway look in his eyes, which was an odd expression to see on a mechanical man. When he saw Russ staring, he powered down the sander and asked, "Would I be considered a muggle?"

Russ just shrugged. The Tech12 had read every book in the bookstore, and he seemed to be hungering for more. The problem was, there wasn't another bookstore for a hundred miles, and Russ lacked the address, smartphone, credit card, and soullessness to order any online. He didn't dare introduce the robot to the internet anyway.

Applebum kept talking and he kept sanding. He said something about being "definitely Ravenclaw," but the sander was too loud, and Russ was too lost in thought to hear him.

Russ had only been in Evanstown for a few weeks now, but his mind was already tired of the same trees, the same river, the same everything. Considering that they would be jumping to space the next day, loose in the mysterious universe for the first time, legally—well, he figured his need to travel would be sated soon enough.

He decided that his stomach wasn't fluttering. That was too wimpish. It wasn't butterflies. His stomach was surging with excited expectation.

20

NINA & RUSS

NINA HAD A SMALL headache at the top of her spine. She had worn herself out, training harder than she ever had in her life, and every muscle was sore. Despite that, she hadn't slept a wink. Russ had given her copies of *You Took my Heart, Dr. Garth* and *Beloved Tyrant/Dear Tyrant* from the bookstore, but she hadn't been able to read either. She'd spent most of the night rolling around, hoping that lying in bed with your eyes closed was the same as actually being asleep.

It didn't help to hear her parents arguing faintly in the kitchen. First thing in the morning she tried to sneak into the shower, but the floorboards were in such bad condition that they creaked with every careful step. It took only seconds for her mom to be looming in her door arch, an unrecognizable expression on her face.

"Did you quit your job yet?" her mom asked. "At Morty's Sportys?"

"Not yet, Mom."

"You need to quit. Right away. But also, do you have your latest paycheck? We're"—Katherine shifted her weight from one foot to the other—"we're a little light this month. On the bills. The house bills. Don't even get me started on the hospital bills. I should just change my name to Bill," she said. "But you do need to quit your job."

"I haven't quit yet, Mom. I missed a day, but I don't think Morty will fire me."

"I don't think he will," Katherine agreed. "So, you just need to—"

"I'll quit when I find a new job," Nina promised.

Her mom's expression said it all. "Where on Earth could you find a new job?"

Maybe not Earth, Nina thought.

For Russ, the morning seemed to begin like most others. He had some steel-cut oats at the small, round wooden breakfast table while his grandma read the paper.

Norma shook the paper, like she always did when she was trying to straighten a crease. Then she stopped reading, folded the paper neatly, and laid it down next to her plate. She looked Russ in the eye. "You're not twitching today," she told him. "I suppose that means I'll be saying good-bye soon?"

"What do you mean?"

Norma's face fell. "How long have I known you?"

"My whole life?"

"Yep. And I've gotten pretty good at recognizing when you get all wound up and restless. You don't twitch exactly, but that's how I think of it. You move all around the room. You pace. You can't get comfortable, no matter where you sit. You have trouble concentrating enough to answer my questions. It always happens right before you hit the road again and disappear. Your grandfather was exactly the same way." Norma put her hand on Russ's. "I noticed it starting earlier in the week. It's okay if you can't finish the bookstore. I know how you are with your need to keep moving. And I treat every minute of your visits as special, because I only have you for a finite amount of time."

"I wasn't planning on leaving," Russ told her. "And I'm sorry I wasn't around sooner. To help you with Grandpop."

Norma was silent a moment and Russ could tell he'd screwed up. Not in this moment, but in the long year that his grandfather had been dying. Norma had wanted Russ here, he realized. She had needed his help. And he had been off chasing gator burritos in Louisiana.

"There's nothing anyone could have done," she said finally.

Russ remained silent. He could see his grandma was deep in thought.

"Your grandfather was so stubborn. He always had to do things his way. Even dying!" she said.

Russ scrunched up his eyebrows. "What do you mean?" he asked.

"You know your grandfather. We were only in the hospital a few months before he started to fight with all the doctors. He just couldn't stand to be trapped in the same bed day after day. He questioned the medical staff's judgment, refused treatments, eventually checked himself out completely. 'Against medical advice,' they called it. And then he started taking these long walks, out into the forest. He was frail and tired, but he still wanted to walk by himself—he insisted on it. He kept saying that nature was the best medicine. A few times I even woke up in the middle of the night totally alone in bed. He was nowhere to be found."

"I'm sorry he was so stubborn. It's a family trait. Those were precious moments with him that you lost—" Russ started to say.

"And I don't want to talk about it," Norma interrupted. "Give me a little more time. The two of you have always been my restless, wandering Wesleys. This is usually about the time I come home to find the trunk of your car open, with a packed-up suitcase inside." Norma's eyes brightened. "Wait a second! Are you in love? With Nina?"

Russ looked away. "Definitely not."

Outside there was a honking horn. Norma glanced out the kitchen window. Bibi was standing next to her car, waving.

"It's one miracle after another this morning," Norma said. "My grandson is sticking around a little while longer. That's the first miracle, but listen to this: remember how I told you yesterday that Bibi's car broke down, that she had to cancel our plans together because she couldn't afford to get it fixed? She called at eight a.m. and told me that when her husband went out to check on it, the thing started right up."

"That's great," Russ said, yawning.

"But her husband knows cars, Russ. He claims the entire carburetor was rebuilt, during the night! How could that be possible? And remember what I told you about Bobby's son's farm? How they couldn't harvest the sweet peppers quickly enough? Bobby told me that when he woke up on Wednesday, all the sweet peppers had been harvested. They were picked, wrapped and loaded on the trailer, ready for market."

"It's really great," Russ said.

"I get the feeling that when church starts Sunday morning there will be a lot more people there than usual," Norma said. "If your grandfather was still around, he would have loved this. Nothing he liked more than the weird and the unexplained."

Bibi honked her horn again, so Norma rose slowly.

She studied Russ's face. "Bobby brought us these," she said, lifting a huge basket of sweet peppers off the kitchen counter.

Russ would have rather died than touch another sweet pepper.

"Those look delicious," he said.

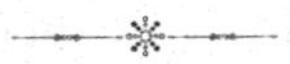

When Nina arrived in the alley behind the bookstore, Russ was waiting patiently, leaning against the wall.

He was wearing a sharply cut suit, with a matching orange tie. "Am I underdressed?" she asked.

Russ shook his head. "My clothes are too rundown. I got into my grandpop's closet but he was a big guy. This was the only thing I wasn't swimming in."

Nina took a moment to straighten his necktie, then stepped back to look him over again. "It actually fits you well," she admitted.

They snuck together through the back entrance to the Mysterious Universe, and Applebum let them into the storage room.

Nina saw a thick brown book in his hand. "Going through the classics again?" She asked.

Applebum showed her the cover. It was Dickens' *Tale of Two Cities*. "I have read this novel three times, but the message still confuses me," he told her. "It recommends violence as the answer to inequity, and then it condemns that same violence. How can it be the right answer and the wrong answer?"

"Life's complicated," Russ said, shrugging.

Applebum leveled his gaze at Russ, then went back to reading.

Nina moved to the Waypoint and stared at the exotic rune patterns all along the piping. She watched the swirling quantum pattern in the opening. "All I have to do is touch it? That's all it takes?" she asked.

"Not touch as much as kind of fall through," Russ said.

"So excited." Nina grinned.

"You want to go first?"

Nina gave him a half smile, as if to say, "Are you kidding?" then she launched herself headfirst through the Waypoint.

The sensation was like lying face down on the hot concrete at the end of an afternoon playing in the pool. Only the concrete was moving in slow rhythmic patterns, massaging her belly, her legs, her chest, her spine, and the insides of her eyeballs. Nina felt her body pulled away, sliding her free from existence. *I could do this part all day, every day,* she thought. But then her body reformed, like she was being birthed out of the warm fire into cold reality. She found her footing and stood up in a crowded causeway. A part of her wanted to jump immediately back into the Waypoint, but then she looked around at where she was.

Nina's eyes bulged at every tentacle, every third and fourth eye, every bit of thick scale and thick fur and paw, claw, and hand. Aliens filed past on every side, making their way to other Waypoint jumps which would take them to work, or perhaps on a holiday to see family. She felt Russ come through a moment later. He smacked right into her because she was too overwhelmed to move.

"Didn't really expect it to be real," she whispered. "Didn't expect this. Didn't expect . . . I mean, I know we trained with a fish. . ." She trailed off as a two-legged six-foot-tall praying mantis walked past.

"I-It has antennae," she stuttered.

Across the causeway, a huge picture window stared down at an alien city. Down wasn't quite the right word. The cityscape was covered in tremendously tall megatowers, and the transportation hub wasn't on the ground, but rather suspended in air, built onto the connecting points of three different towers. Nina couldn't see how far the ground was below, because it was masked by a thick layer of smog.

The air above was somehow crystal clear, but she couldn't see the top of the megatowers either. They stretched on and on, upward into the clouds. Along the way there were hundreds, maybe even thousands, of walkways, greenbelts, and intersecting bridges.

Nina remained facing the terminal window, watching silently, counting her breaths. Aliens outside moved around in their crowded world.

Her trance was broken by someone making a coughing noise. Ten yards to her right, a uniformed creature waited behind a large desk. It looked at her expectantly. It had a flat face like a bulldog, but the back of its head was long with a bulbed end. The way it sat at the desk reminded Nina of a clerk, or ombudsman. It also looked a little bit like a flower. It was so strange Nina could have watched it for an hour.

Instead, she approached it tentatively.

"Could you help me?" she asked it.

"I am a spaceclerk," the creature told her. "Do you need a spaceclerk?"

"Definitely possibly maybe," Nina said. "Where is the municipal wing?"

"You are a CERTified employee of the UAIB?" it asked.

"Almost," she said. "We're in phase two."

The creature's eyes softened, and it seemed to see her for the first time. "Well, it's good to have a job anyway," it said. "What you want is the 'no pay' dock. It's three hallways in that direction, then take a hard left when you pass the indoor garden. You'll know it because—"

The spaceclerk's directions were lost as noise erupted from all around Nina. It was the crowd of travelers, reacting to some spectacle. Nina turned in the direction they were all looking and found Russ, still standing at the Waypoint.

He was getting punched in the face.

Aliens were passing Russ in every direction, speaking in alien tongues, just fragmented enough to challenge his nanotranslator. Some were seven feet tall; some were no larger than eighteen inches. Some were covered in fur, others in feathers, others in lizard scale or razor-sharp yellowed bone.

Beside his Waypoint, there was another, identical Waypoint. Beside that was another, and another, all the way down the line. He was in some sort of transportation hub. While he watched, breathless, a small alien materialized beside the framed structure next to him. It let out a squeak of surprise to see Russ blocking the path to the main intersection. Russ quickly danced out of the way to avoid the rush of other alien creatures. They were all passing across a commuter thoroughfare. There were so many disparate noises, clucking tongues, honking, voices rolling up and down the musical spectrum that Russ felt like he was moving, even though he was pressed against the thick plastic of a huge picture window.

Along the hall to the west, five men walked in perfect synchronicity. SAS units, Russ realized. They were gleaming chrome like Applebum, but they were also dressed in matching uniforms with badges that read "IBED." They reached the end of the long passageway, still moving in lockstep.

"Wonder where they're going," Russ whispered. He was so engrossed, he didn't notice that Nina had gone up ahead. Nor did he sense the next traveler materializing through a Waypoint behind him.

Until: "Stand aside," that creature demanded.

Russ swiveled in a circle to face the newcomer. He was a small guy, maybe five feet tall. He appeared somewhat human, except his skin was faintly purple, and, as he stared malevolently at Russ, Russ noticed his eyes were a mixture of many neon colors, bright blue, yellow, green, and even gold.

He had a badge on the shoulder of his pressed cotton jacket. It was a red swoosh against a white background. In the center of the swoosh was an alien-looking golden key.

The creature bobbed his head at Russ angrily. "This is why I generally only use privatized Waypoints," the alien whined.

"I'm sorry, I—" Russ started to say, then he stopped himself. This guy was obviously an asshole.

"Get clear," the little purple alien commanded. "The rest of my team is coming through."

Reluctantly, Russ moved aside. One by one, more aliens began to pop through the Waypoint. They looked like a squadron, with their matching orange jumpsuits. Each had the same badge, the red swoosh against the white background. Finally, a rock creature, thick and round and looking a hell of a lot like The Thing from Fantastic

Four, arrived. It barely fit through the Waypoint, and it had so much mass and momentum that Russ had to take a few more steps back, or he would have been knocked over like a bowling alley pin.

"You guys all on the same team?" Russ asked them.

The purple man with the neon eyes grunted and pushed Russ out of his way.

Russ watched the other jumpsuited aliens shuffle past. He was determined to make a good impression even if these aliens reminded him of a pack of middle-school bullies. The rock creature was last, and it glanced at Russ out of the corner of its eye.

Russ nodded to it.

The giant rock creature stopped and turned to face Russ. It put its huge stone mitts on Russ's shoulder. "What are you?" it asked him, its voice a deep rumble.

"I'm Russ. An Earthling."

The rock creature swiveled its head around to examine Russ.

"You are small and weak. And I don't see any natural defenses. Why do you have eggshells on either side of your head?" the creature asked, reaching out.

"These are my ears," Russ explained, knocking the creature's huge fingers away from his ears.

The creature continued to size Russ up. "No exoskeleton. No scales. No wings. No fangs or claws. No sharp points of any kind. Based on your muscle structure, you're clearly not built for speed." The rock creature flexed its shoulder, and the motion rippled down to its huge bicep. "Not built for power either, I don't think. You've even lost much of your body hair. How do your foundlings stay warm?"

"Baby Gap," Russ told it.

"Come on, Lenus," the purple man demanded. "Stop playing with the little hairless monkey."

"Seriously, tiny fellow, with your obvious genetic limitations, how do you intend to survive in space? Much less make a living?"

Russ was getting annoyed. There were creatures all around them smaller than Russ, some of which were diaphanous, petite, fragile. The rock thing was just being a dick, but as Russ looked back at the bully, it loomed over him, seven-feet tall and probably close to four tons, roughly twice the weight of his grandmother's car. Russ decided to keep his anger to himself.

The purple man returned to join the fun. "Why don't you stop distracting my crew and hop on back to whatever shithole you just popped out of?" he suggested. He was a good foot and a half shorter than Russ, but he had chosen his friends well.

The rock creature grinned.

Russ glanced at Nina. She was talking to someone on the other side of the hall. He took a step toward her, but something made him stop and turn back to the two assholes. "I'm here for a job," Russ said. He spoke out of the side of his mouth. For some reason it helped keep the anger out of his voice.

"Better hope its mechanized," the rock creature grunted.

"It's extermination," Russ told them.

The moment he said it, he knew he'd made a mistake. Russ was good at recognizing his mistakes, just after making them.

The rest of the crew had walked a little way down the hallway, but when they heard his words, they moseyed back. There were seven of them now, all wearing the same jumpsuits, all grinning the same bully's grin. They stood around Russ in a loose semicircle.

"Extermination?" The purple man said, savoring each syllable as they slowly slid out of his mouth. "Which crew would that be?"

"The Intergalactic Exterminators."

The purple man nodded, a look of fake deference dancing across his face. "That is impressive. It's a tough job, exterminating, and we ought to know." The man's voice dripped with malice. He continued: "We're SOL Pest Control. We're in the same business. Do you know what that makes us?"

"Colleagues?" Russ ventured.

"Sure," the purple man drawled. "Colleagues. Lenus, how about you extend a warm SOL welcome to our new colleague?"

Lenus nodded. Then it swung its huge, granite fist directly into Russ's jaw.

Russ heard the stone fist connect with his chin a split-second before he felt the pain. *Somebody firing a gun?* he wondered to himself.

Then a whole grand finale's worth of fireworks exploded behind his eyes.

"Already making friends?" Nina asked as she lifted Russ back to his feet. The small purple man and his gang strutted away, too important to stop despite the spaceclerk's command to halt and complete an official incident report.

"Nice suit," the clerk told Russ. "Are you okay?"

"He hits like a baby," Russ said, but blood was pooling beneath his nose, and his eyes were glazed.

"You shouldn't mess with a Divian," the space clerk cautioned him.

"That the one covered in rocks?"

"No, the other one."

"The little purple guy?"

"What makes him so special?" Nina asked.

"Political connections," the spaceclerk said. He moved efficiently back to his desk and sat down.

Russ spit a bloody loogie onto the floor.

"I got the directions," Nina said. She pulled a napkin out of her pocket and dabbed at the blood from Russ's nose. "Can you walk?"

"Walk? Let's run after the Divian so I can stuff his rock-shaped friend up his ass."

They did not run, but Nina noticed Russ glancing around for the little purple man each time they reached a new hallway. As they moved farther from the main hub, the crowd got thinner and thinner. They passed star freights that looked like big rigs, with weary aliens loading and unloading goods. Other aliens sat in small batches with splayed legs against various walls. One held a sign that said "Immunized, with updated transpods."

Nina guided Russ out of the way as a squad of silver-colored SAS marched past wearing "IBED" badges. The robots lined up at the end of the causeway, clearly preparing for their morning deployment.

As they watched, one of the units malfunctioned, sputtering the same repetitive salute. "Ready for—" it said, saluting. Then: "Ready for—; ready for—; ready for—"

"What you deserve!" one of the seated aliens shouted.

The nearest SAS unit in the line turned to the malfunctioning unit and put its hand on its shoulder. "I'm sorry friend, you seem to have lost your network connection. I'm going to attempt to refresh your authorization codes," it said.

Russ and Nina's path eventually circled around to a long platform, built straight out of the side of an abandoned part of the hub. Two ships were docked there, both clunky, heavy metallic behemoths, constructed with function in mind, regardless of form. The closer ship had the words "Southland Demolitions and Refuse Removal" emblazed in garish yellow. Russ pointed at the ship beside it.

"That's got to be Bah'ren's," he told Nina. He was rubbing his chin, where a shallow purple bruise was forming.

"Who's Bah'ren?"

"Our new boss."

The second ship looked like a huge garbage truck surrounded by jet engines. It was almost all a single, long square shaft, with four fifteen by fifteen-foot thrusters on the bottom. The ship was painted a faded cherry red, except for a blue bar with the words "Intergalactic Exterminators, Inc" along the inside.

"I hope the insides are more impressive than the outsides," Nina said. "It looks like it goes zero to sixty in just about an hour."

They entered through a door at the base of the main shaft.

No one was waiting for them inside.

Nina and Russ looked at each other and shrugged. She used her napkin to dab at the blood under his nose again.

"Wonder what we're supposed to do next—" Russ started to ask.

He was interrupted by the piercing shriek of someone dying violently.

21
RUSS

SCREAMS OF BLOODY TERROR erupted from deeper in the ship.

"It's coming from this way," Russ told Nina.

He could feel her right at his heels as he ran down a twisting corridor. He came to a fork in the corridor with a door headed left and another headed right. He didn't have to wait long before there was another strangled cry. Russ followed the sound to the right.

"Be careful," Nina said, huffing behind him. "Could be a creature got loose, wiped out the crew."

By Russ's best guess, they had made it halfway through the long ship without seeing anyone. He came to a stop again when they heard the cry once more. It was a death cry. It was human, and whoever was making it wheezed, their voice climbing to a dying pitch before the rattle and gurgle of lungs flooded with blood choked out the last of the sound.

Russ realized it was coming from the right, but there was no door, and no discernible openings. He approached that portion of the curved metal corridor warily. Even though he was certain they were too late, he pushed around for a latch or button that might get them access to whatever was going on. Finally, he found what he was looking for, a small switch etched into the top half of the metal.

He threw it and the entire wall began to split into smaller ten-foot sections. The sections lowered seamlessly into the bottom half of the corridor wall, revealing an enormous viewing window into a large room. The dead body was just on the other side of the window. It was definitely human. Despite the badly burned skin and the twisted bones, Russ could see what was left of a fair skinned woman in her late twenties. She looked dignified, even in death. Russ could see her features, her thick hair and high cheekbones, beneath all the blood and even with the damaged flesh.

Nina gasped, recognizing her at the same moment Russ did.

Russ pounded his fists against the window. "Atara!" he shouted. "ATARA!"

"What? What do you need?" Atara asked. She had materialized beside Russ and Nina. She glanced through the window at her own dead body and shook her head. "I'm just going to say it. I look gorgeous, even dead. Kind of scary to stare straight into the eyes of the reaper, though. Not that I don't deserve it, with the performance I put on. The others will be out in a minute."

Russ stared at dead Atara and alive Atara. "Out of where?" he asked, trying to pretend like what was happening made sense.

"The virtual training room. Technically, it exists to refine our combat skills, but we use it every day because it's fun as hell, like a huge, badass video game. Welcome aboard the *Flashaway*," she said as an afterthought.

Behind her, her other body, the dead one, dissolved into a swirl of zeros and ones. The corridor faded away, leaving a large, empty white room with padded walls. Two other aliens kneeled in a small rectangle on the floor in the middle of the room.

"Starland, Kendren, quit playing games and come say hi to the new CERTies."

The aliens stood up and crossed the room toward them. As they approached, lights on the viewing window shifted from red to green, and the entire wall rose up into the ceiling.

Russ knew he'd met Starland and Kendren in the forest of Wyoming, but they looked different now. Starland had no hair on the top of her head, only a thin layer of scales. The same scales, though smaller and less densely packed, covered her arms and the backs of her hands. She had no chest or hips, just a long, smooth torso stretching up from the ends of her legs to the start of her neck.

The man, Kendren, was the one who'd had cat penis rolled across his mouth. He looked relatively human, certainly primate-based, but his homeworld must have been more hostile than Earth's, with a more powerful sun. His muscles rippled under his jumpsuit. Coarse hair covered his forearms, neck, and the top of his head. He looked like a human would if humans hit a second, more advanced stage of puberty sometime in their twenties: bigger, stronger, handsomer, hairier.

Behind them, an enormous beast dug its way out of the floor. It clambered onto its four pincered feet. Russ recognized it immediately from a lesson with Ensine: "Safrurn—who tears his enemies into very small portions." It skittered toward Kendren and snapped its huge claws around his waist.

Russ saw Nina flinch. Kendren didn't react at all.

"The illusion can't hurt you unless you're in the box," Kendren said, nodding to the rectangle in the center. He waved at the Safrurn, which was still jabbing at him with its claws. "VTR: Cancel all simulations," he called out, and the giant beast disappeared.

"Who are you?" Kendren asked. He took a step closer to Nina and pushed his palms together, flexing his shoulders. They were massive, and the muscles strained against his tight orange jumpsuit. He looked, to Russ, like the professional wrestlers of the WWE had when Russ was a teenager: huge, hypermasculine, impossibly strong, slightly ridiculous. He was either sizing Nina up or flirting, maybe both.

"My name is Nina. It's nice to meet you," Nina told him.

"We getting two new CERTS?" Starland asked. "I thought we only had the budget for one."

"Bah'ren's probably not going to want to pay for two," Atara admitted.

"What do you mean?" Russ asked, but before anyone could answer, a device on all three exterminators' wrists blinked red.

"Look at that," Kendren said. "It's time to go kill something real."

"Tell Bah'ren we'll be a little late," Starland said. "I'm going to get the rookies set up with their training gear."

"Poor little CERTies," Atara said, ruffling Russ's hair.

"You two need to follow me," Starland told Russ and Nina.

"Did she say only one of us was getting the job?" Russ whispered to Nina.

"I think so." She turned and stared at Russ, her eyes studying his. "What do you think of that?"

"Something we should probably talk about."

"Come on, CERTies!" Starland called.

Russ stood aside, letting Nina walk the narrow corridor ahead of him.

They followed Starland down another long hallway, passing sleeping quarters and a centralized living space replete with a pair of couches and a minifridge. A deck of alien playing cards was spilled across the coffee table in the center. Russ stooped to pick one up, but Starland grabbed him by the arm and led him down another hallway and into something that resembled a med ward. Inside, a row of steel sanitized tables were set up under heavy, hanging fluorescent-type lights.

"Take a seat," Starland told Russ.

Nina was still standing by the door, her eyes scanning over the heavy equipment lined along the far wall. One machine looked big enough to envelop an entire person, a great big, bulbous iron lung. Russ hoped he never had to use it.

"Is this going to be invasive?" Nina asked.

Starland pulled open a drawer and removed a pair of watches. "Only if you find wearing wristwatches invasive."

"You have one of those blinking red on your wrist," Russ said.

"They're called transponders. One item, many, many functions," Starland told him. She swiped her finger across the face of her transponder and its screen expanded to cover a portion of her forearm. It buzzed for a moment and the flashing red signal disappeared. "Check this out," she said.

She tapped the transponder, and Russ saw a yellow energy pulse fire from the watch, flowing outward in an ever-expanding circle. As the pulse traveled, the watch screen populated various locations. There was a vivid white blip where Nina and Russ stood. A few rooms away, they could see more white blips, likely the rest of the team beginning their mission briefing.

"Is that a heat index?" Nina asked.

Starland nodded. "It will help you find nearby organics, which is very useful for hunting. And if you get separated from the group, you can track us by following our unique heat signatures. You have to push here to send off the pulse," Starland tapped at the watch screen, and another pulse blazed through the room, disappearing into the steel walls. "It sends the heat information back to itself as it travels. The farther you are from your target, the longer it will take the pulse to reach them and retrieve their location."

"You're not on the heat index," Russ pointed out.

"TEN-awtch are ectothermic," she told him, running her hand over the scales along her scalp. "Make sure this thing stays on your wrist, because if you get lost, you'll be able to use it to find us. This watch will be one of your best friends . . . and one of your worst enemies."

"Why's that?" Nina asked.

"Yours are loaded with the CERT probational training software. The watch will be analyzing every move you make, every decision in the field and in the training room, every expenditure of resources, from actual physical resources like bullets, to the more ethereal, like the way you spend your time while on the clock. Do not violate any of the shared system of civics, even if you see another member of the crew do so. It's an auto-fail."

"Don't steal shit from other planets," Nina reminded Russ.

"That's a big one. Don't even put a leaf in your pocket. The transponder will see it and flunk you. It will also be examining your heartbeat and your twitch reflexes, analyzing how you perform under pressure. At the conclusion of each of your probational missions, if your RQ score falls below one thousand, you will be removed from CERTification eligibility and returned to your origin planet. If your RQ score stays above a thousand for all of the required training hours, you will be advanced to CERTified status, and you can start making money. A little bit of money."

"That's the goal," Nina told her.

"Right or left?" Starland asked.

Russ rolled up the sleeves of his orange suit jacket and Starland strapped the transponder onto his wrist; the screen expanded and cinched against his forearm. "This seems like fancy tech," he said.

Starland went over to Nina and strapped the watch on her left wrist. Nina tapped its face, and a yellow pulse burst from the device, zipping quickly through the room.

"Everything in this room is fancy tech, and most of it is off limits," Starland explained. "It's no small thing to run an exterminator squad. The margins are low, and the overhead is very high. Bah'ren takes her finances very seriously. I love her, but if you need a Kruxfasian seed nut cracked, shove it up her ass and ask her for a raise. The seed nut will shatter into a hundred pieces."

"She's a tightwad," Russ concluded.

His watch vibrated. *"Slandering an administrator. Your RQ score has been lowered 10 points, to 2,140,"* it said. Its voice was smooth, mechanical.

"Dang," Russ said.

"Welcome to the grind," Starland told him. "I hear it's going to be a weird one."

Starland showed them their lockers and handed each an orange jumpsuit with "Intergalactic Exterminators, Inc" stitched on the lapel. Russ reluctantly changed out of his snazzy suit.

In a medium-sized room near the center of the ship, a woman was already there, waiting for them, seated on the arm of one of the easy chairs in front of Kendren and Atara. Her skin was light blue, with what looked like sporadic birthmarks of a much deeper blue. Russ was surprised to see that the blotches were moving. Maybe exploding was a better word: they blossomed on her skin, then faded away, only to blossom again in another shape and location, like a hyper, ever-shifting Rorschach test.

She was less than four feet tall. Even on the arm of a low chair her toes barely touched the ground.

She nodded as they arrived.

But then he saw her purple eyes and Russ realized who it was: Bah'ren, the tightwad. The members of the IEI appeared quite different without their transformers.

"Welcome to your first mission," she told Russ. "You must be Doreena Hosseinzadeh," she said to Nina in greeting. "Mr. Ensine spoke very highly of your skills and convinced us we should give you a chance."

"Thank you," Nina said.

"It's fair to tell you both that I am not budgeted for more than four employees," Bah'ren said.

"I'll make it worth your while," Nina promised. "I really need this job."

Bah'ren nodded. "I'll always accept free labor."

Bah'ren spoke in quick, curt phrases, cutting through any small talk and getting down to business, so it wasn't until they'd moved toward their seat that Russ finally comprehended what Bah'ren had just said. She'd told Nina she didn't actually have a job. "If you're only budgeted for four," Russ said, "what happens when we finish our training hours?"

"Assuming everyone else on the team is still alive?" Bah'ren said. "I'll take whichever of you finishes with the higher RQ score."

"And what will happen to the other one?"

"If you pass CERTification, you'll have the opportunity take up with a different company, assuming they're hiring. If you fail, you won't have the necessary credentials to remain within the boundaries of UAIB space. You'll be returned to Earth none the wiser."

Russ considered what she was saying. They had to compete against each other. Worse yet, they were both at risk of getting mind-wiped—removed from this fantastic experience and given a little extra brain damage as a bonus prize.

Nina's jaw was set in determination, but she didn't say anything. Russ knew what she was thinking, whatever stood between her and rescuing her dad would need to be overcome. Even if it was Russ and his dream of saving his grandma's bookstore.

They joined Atara on a long microfiber-covered couch that seemed to have come from IKEA. Nina sat perfectly still, deep in thought. Russ moved a little bit away from her, inching down the Finnala. He watched her carefully while sorting through his own emotions. Nina had stolen his Obinz stone. Would his job be next? What else was she capable of?

Once Starland had taken her seat, Bah'ren said, "You missed most of the briefing, so I'll recap quickly." She removed a rectangular device the size of a smartphone from her pocket. She tapped on it and a light projected from the end, shining on the wall.

"You bloodthirsty savages will be sad to know that we're not going to kill anything today, for a change."

"Boooo," Starland and Kendren called out simultaneously.

"This is a Ryncyn." Bah'ren clicked the device and projected an image on the wall. It was a large flying mammal that looked like a cross between an orca and a pterodactyl. "This escaped from an unlicensed Awtchian traveling zoo and found enough resources on one of the fringe planets in the Proxima Imperatus cluster to survive. For the past three days it has been devouring the local argon-producing flora, doing enough damage to set off the UAIB's environmental alarms, which generated our automatic work order. The plan is simple. We secure the Ryncyn, return it to an immigration satellite, and get paid."

"It looks like a big space whale," Atara said.

"Is it dangerous?" Nina asked. The image of the creature was still projected on the wall, and the longer Russ stared at it, the more benign it appeared. It didn't seem to have any noticeable natural defenses.

Bah'ren shook her head no, then she reconsidered. "It was in a zoo for a reason. The creature is a universal curiosity because it generates a strong magnetic field. Its skin will attract and repel certain metallic compounds. Evolutionarily, it's a big disadvantage, which is why the Ryncyn is federally protected. It's also nonviolent. We're not supposed to kill it. We can't kill it. I suggest you select nonlethal weapons made from polymer, graphene, or other nonmagnetic composition." She turned toward the three humans on the IKEA couch. "I'll fill you in on everything else you missed after launch."

"What about SOL Pest Control?" Starland asked as everybody stood up and began to file out of the small room.

"We already talked about it. While you were putting transponders on the CERTies."

"Who are they?" Nina said, stopping at the door.

"Cheap-shot artists," Russ said, rubbing his sore jaw.

"And what are we going to do if it happens again?" Starland asked, ignoring Nina's question and Russ's answer.

Bah'ren shook her head. "It won't happen to us this time."

Nina and Russ stared at each other, confused.

"Others are having the same issue," Starland said. "At least three groups posted on the MERC board that it happened to them. Recent posts. SOL isn't just running their own claims, they've been showing up everywhere. They're openly trying to muscle out the smaller organizations."

"Time's wasting," Bah'ren said firmly. "Let's get weaponed up!"

22

RUSS

"THE UNIVERSE IS SO incredible!" Nina yelled, her hair whipping every which way and dancing around her rebreather. They were disengaging their two-seater flying canoe—Bah'ren had called it a Stinger—from the dock of the *Flashaway*. It unlatched, fired its own thrusters, and suddenly they were hanging in the sky eight miles above Qello.

Russ tested the steering mechanism gingerly, and the Stinger reacted, pivoting, its nose pointed toward terra firma. Using short propulsion bursts, Russ humped the Stinger clear of the docking gear. All he'd gotten for flight instructions was a terrifyingly brief tutorial from Atara as they'd assigned drivers for the small convertible craft.

Mounted all along the Stinger's bottom were hundreds, maybe a thousand, miniature thrusters. By sliding his hand across a touch screen, he could adjust each thruster individually or in groups. In theory the system created precise, tactical control of direction and speed, though Russ had only a small notion of where to start.

He was seated on a long, cushioned bench, with his legs wrapped around a lock bar at its base. With no top on the Stinger, the lock bar was the only thing keeping him from flying out of the craft and plunging to his death on the ground many miles below.

"Please keep your hands and arms inside the vehicle at all times," he told Nina. *"Permanese sentados, por favor."*

Planet Qello was the fifth planet from the large Proxima Imperatus sun. They were far from cold, but every bit of the wind produced from their flight was whipping around them, tearing at their compression gear. Nina was in the backseat, making joyful screams like it was a carnival ride. She kept shaking Russ's shoulders to point at everything, including the lush, mostly tropical biomes below. Qello was a small planet; Russ guessed it was about a sixteenth the size of Earth.

He could hear Bah'ren through the comm on his rebreather, her voice deep and clear despite the wind. "The Ryncyn eats a flora called luchen. Last time this planet was updated on the MUPmap, about five years ago, luchen was mostly blossoming in two locations, the deep south, at the base of a dormant volcano, and just east of that great lake. Go easy on the thrusters, or your Stinger won't have enough battery to investigate both."

"We may not have to," Russ said. "Look." He pointed to a large object far below. Around it, colors shifted in the sky, blue, yellow, then green, like the aurora borealis.

Atara and Starland were together in another Stinger, hovering beside Russ and Nina. Starland was in the driver's seat, Atara on the bench seat behind her. Atara saw Russ pointing and gestured to Starland, "There! Go there!"

As Atara and Starland dove forward, their Stinger let out a plume of gray smoke, like the emissions from a diesel engine. Russ noted it briefly, but it had a natural-enough appearance that he didn't linger too long on the incongruity of diesel smoke coming from a battery-powered craft. They were about a mile above the beast when

Bah'ren piped up again over the comm. She and Kendren were in the third craft, hovering behind Russ and the others in a line. They had separated out by weight to keep the Stingers from straining under too large a load. It was a strategy Russ would have approved of if he'd had even a smidgen of experience as a starcraft pilot. He looked over at the diminutive Bah'ren as she perched behind the incredible bulk that was Kendren. She was lecturing them through her comm. "According to UAIB planetary archives, Qello has a hostile classification: lethal bacteria, fauna, flora, and fungi. There is no apex predator in the skies, but on land it's a carnivorous, highly territorial, four-legged Ophidian. The archives also mention sporadic, unpredictable tremors, often followed by volcanic eruptions and tsunami."

"Is that all?" Nina shouted.

"Must be why the MUPmap had a little skull and crossbones on it," Starland said. Her Stinger was suddenly back beside Nina and Russ, and she piloted it with an expert hand, gliding in and out of the thin clouds. Atara waved from behind Starland, her other hand holding tight to the side of the ship.

"We should stay off the surface," Kendren suggested.

"This job is high pay because Planet Qello qualifies as extremely hostile. Take the necessary precautions," Bah'ren said.

"Don't land," Starland translated. Then she pitched her Stinger's nose down and raced toward the planet far below.

Russ and Nina followed. The wind whipped through their hair. Russ put his hand up to his rebreather, sensing the wind was strong enough to tear it free.

The wall projection in the briefing room hadn't prepared them for the Ryncyn's size. It was at least ten thousand pounds, bobbing in the air like a lead balloon. Its enormous wings beat hard against the sky to keep it afloat. The wings were unexpectedly fragile, almost diaphanous. They stretched outward from its white and black body. The creature was covered in a fine, green dust that Russ hadn't remembered seeing during the briefing. As they approached, a medium-sized rock, maybe fifty pounds, began to drift up from the ground far beneath the Ryncyn.

It was exhausted, its enormous wings beating out a tired rhythm. It seemed aware of the large rock as it rose up from below. It tried to fly higher, but its heavy body wouldn't let it.

Bah'ren's voice came over the comm, "Let's triangulate, see if we can pinch him between us."

They followed Bah'ren's suggestion, carefully positioning their crafts in a triangle shape around the creature, one above, two below. Starland had to pivot her Stinger to avoid the rock as it rose through the air.

"Floating rocks? What's with this antigravity shit?" Atara demanded. "There was nothing in the mission briefing about floating rocks."

As the rock finally reached the Ryncyn, the creature darted toward it, and the rock exploded in a burst of fine-grain dust. The dust rained down on the Ryncyn and Starland and Atara.

"What does the MUPmap say about the geography here?" Nina asked. "What are these rocks made of?"

"Why does that matter?" Bah'ren barked. "They shouldn't be floating." She had to pitch her Stinger left to avoid two new rocks that were now rising from the landscape far below.

"It matters," Nina said.

There was a moment of silence on the comm. "Jadeite," Bah'ren said, finally. "The MUPmap says jadeite."

"Is that magnetic?"

"Probably?"

"It must be," Nina said. "The rocks are caught in the creature's magnetic pull. It's not attracting them on purpose."

"Clearly," Starland said.

The creature flapped to the left, tiredly trying to escape another floating rock.

"But why are they exploding?" Nina asked herself. Before anyone could answer, she spoke again. "The Ryncyn must be bursting them with some kind of supercharged magnetic pulse. It's a natural defense mechanism."

Russ looked at the creature, bobbing, weaving, and squawking as a third rock rose to meet it. The Ryncyn was clearly out of place on Qello. Whatever miracle of evolution had given it its magnetic composition hadn't intended it to live on a planet with equally magnetic rock formations.

"I'd bet it hasn't had a chance to land or rest since it got loose," Nina added. "We need to be gentle with this guy. He must be exhausted."

"We can't get too close. If it can do that to the rocks, it can do that to our Stingers," Russ pointed out. And he knew immediately he was right. Though he hadn't been conscious of it until now, there was a definite magnetic pull coming from the Ryncyn. He'd naturally compensated with the thrusters, knowing by instinct not to get too close.

The three ships edged farther away from the creature, each rotating slightly to preserve a loose triangle pattern around it.

"What do we do?" Russ asked.

"We throw a big fucking net on it," Kendren barked over the comm. "Keep the thing pinched between us."

Kendren let Bah'ren take the controls of his Stinger. He stood in the back of the craft and began to unravel a long net. It seemed perilous to be standing up on a topless craft in the strong wind, but Kendren handled it with a dexterity that belied his large size. The net unrolled, then unrolled further. Soon it was hanging below the relatively small Stinger, fifty feet of loose, woven polymer. Kendren hooked one side to some pegs on the top of the Stinger; the other side continued to unfurl, far below.

"Our Stingers aren't strong enough to carry this thing. We've got to wrap it up and then initiate a controlled descent." Kendren cautioned them.

"I thought we were supposed to stay off the ground?" Nina reminded them.

Before anyone could answer, there was a long, smooth sliding sound, like a gigantic cardboard box shifting around in the back of an equally gigantic pickup truck.

A ship appeared above them in the sky. It didn't look anything like the *Flashaway*. It was all curved contours and shining chrome. It had an enormous swoosh logo along the side, and stenciled inside the swoosh was the outline of a key and the words "SOL Pest Control."

"We already claimed the job, assholes," Bah'ren shouted.

Obviously, they didn't hear her. Men climbed out of access hatches and into smaller ships mounted all around the edge of the larger one. They moved in synchronously, untethering and blasting down toward the Ryncyn and where Bah'ren's ragtag crew were working.

"We've got to secure the payload," Bah'ren shouted, sounding scared for the first time. "Attach the net!" she screamed at Starland. "The other side of the net!"

Russ watched the arrival of the new exterminator team warily. It wasn't really a team; it was more like an army. The Stingers they drove were brand-new, unblemished, lacquered in a fresh coat of paint, and not belching out gray smoke.

The people inside were strapped in with safe-looking harnesses and protective roll bars. As they grew closer, Russ watched for the two he'd tussled with at the Waypoint hub: the little purple guy and the big rock creature.

But the squad coming toward them weren't people at all, Russ realized. He'd had enough experience to recognize the Tech12 model, even from that distance. This was one of the private businesses participating in the pilot program to employ inorganics.

"We've got to secure the payload!" Bah'ren was still shouting.

Nina's hand was on Russ's shoulder again, drawing him back into the situation. "The creature is electromagnetic," Nina told him.

"Is that supposed to mean something to me?" Russ asked her. He glanced again to the sky above. The SAS units in their fancy aircraft were drawing closer.

"The Ryncyn is reversing its own magnetic field," Nina explained. "Like a physical EMP blast. We shouldn't get any closer in this damn metal canoe."

As if they heard her declaration, the SAS units from SOL Pest Control halted their arrival, hovering their Stingers just outside the perimeter of Russ, Starland, and Bah'ren's smaller, more pathetic craft. Russ pushed his own Stinger backward, creating a sizeable cushion between themselves and the creature.

Bah'ren fiddled with her rebreather. When she spoke, her voice projected outward in the direction of the SAS, loud against the wind. "We've claimed this contract. You are required to back the fuck off, according to the auspices of the MERC board and all applicable contract laws of the United Alliance of Intelligent Beings."

The robots stayed, hovering just beyond the perimeter, their faces set in passive, emotionless masks.

Bah'ren switched back to the comm. "I'm going to file a fucking grievance," she said. "Let's move quickly; we still have the jump on them."

Atara and Starland hurriedly lined up their Stinger alongside the lower edge of the net. Atara took the free side and looped it onto the pegs on her own ship.

The ships leveled out, rising above the creature and angling inward until the net, stretched tight between two Stingers, was only a handful of yards from the tail of the Ryncyn. They intended to scoop it straight out of the air like a fish from a fish tank.

"I don't think this is a good idea," Nina cautioned them.

The creature hovered a moment, seemingly unaware—until it wasn't. The second it sensed the net descending over its enormous, whalelike cranium, it darted—fast as a rocket—in the direction of the two Stingers. It was the movement of scared prey, spending its one trick in defending itself: the rattlesnake's strike, or the cat's quick claw.

Atara and Starland were closest. Seeing the huge whale charging in her direction, Atara dropped to the floor of her craft, falling onto her stomach and grabbing hard to the lock bar. Starland did the same. The decision probably saved their lives.

With the Ryncyn atop them, their Stinger trembled. The colors of the sky shifted, and then all three Stingers were thrust backward by a powerful magnetic force. Russ lost sight of the other two for a moment as his ship went wholly vertical, the nose pointed sunward, only his feet around the lock bar keeping him onboard.

He tipped backward, releasing the controls, and banged into the front of Nina, who was leaning forward with all her strength. His blood was pulsing so much he could see the veins surging in his forearms as he dragged himself back into position.

When he righted the ship again, he saw that the magnetic blast had even scattered the Tech12s' Stingers.

It had hit the rest of the Intergalactic Exterminators with much more force.

Starland and Atara's craft was hurtling toward the trees far below. For a second Russ thought they would plunge all the way out of sight, but just as they reached the treetops, the Stinger leveled off, righted itself, and let out a tremendous crackle of magnetic energy. The same diesel smoke he'd seen earlier began to pour out of a handful of the thrusters.

"Having some trouble here," he heard Starland say through the comm, and then her ship fell through the trees.

Kendren and Bah'ren had reestablished control of their Stinger some fifty yards away.

They slid through the sky until they were back alongside Russ and Nina, the long net fluttering between the two craft.

"Permission to go after them? They might be hurt," Russ shouted. "Atara? Starland? Can you hear us?"

"We've got to secure the payload," Bah'ren snapped. The SAS units had already regrouped above. They had deployed their own nets, at least six of them and their ships were rotating slowly in a predatory pattern.

Russ ignored Bah'ren, sliding his hand across the touchscreen and pivoting his ship in the direction he'd last seen Atara's. He was about to fire the thrusters forward when his watch vibrated menacingly. *"Manual adjustment; disobeying a direct order. Your RQ score has been lowered 100 points, to 2,040."* He heard Nina's echo the same message a split-second later in the same smooth, mechanized voice.

"No one cares about their safety more than me," Bah'ren said. "But we need to finish the job."

Russ felt Nina's hand on his shoulder, but she didn't say anything. "It's too late," she said finally. "Look."

Russ looked to the sky, and he could see the SOL Pest Control Stingers closing in, their own nets crackling with electricity. Each net stretched between four different ships, so long and large Russ and Bah'ren had no choice but to pivot away from the Ryncyn or be caught up in the wash themselves. The nets had long swooshes in the center, painted in matching red and chrome.

The Ryncyn's eye widened as the robot men descended onto it. Hit 'em with the EMP, Russ thought. In that moment he found himself identifying with the enormous, exhausted whale-beast far more than the robots that hunted it.

It never had a chance.

It must have needed time to recharge the EMP. Once the electrified net touched its skin, there was a powerful crackling in the atmosphere. A new set of rocks, which had been gingerly floating skyward, raced up at the creature, its natural magnetic draw supercharged by the added electricity. Russ's Stinger was yanked hard toward the beast as well and he had to slide every thruster in the other direction just to slow it down.

The creature struggled against the net, which hadn't stop shocking it. Its tail and its dorsal fins thrashed ineffectively. It was blowing air frantically out of its blowhole, which created a high-pitched whine that sounded a lot like crying.

"This is terrible," Nina said.

The Ryncyn kept squirming as the SAS units rolled their Stingers through the sky, wrapping the net tighter and tighter. Each new layer of net sent a new shock to the creature. The floating rocks pounded against its flanks, its chest, its neck. Soon it was oozing blood from multiple wounds.

And then SOL Pest Control secured the payload. They sped upward, their top-of-the-line Stingers more than capable of lifting the heavy creature. Russ watched the Ryncyn grow smaller as it was drawn farther away. It still emitted its whistling moan, clusters of rocks cinched against its skin.

"Fuuuuuuckkk!" Bah'ren screamed as the sliding sound returned and the SOL ship blasted away, passing through the Kármán line and out into space.

23

RUSS

THE GROUND WAS RUMBLING slightly as the *Flashaway* touched down on a patch of green brush surrounded on all sides by tall, alien trees. The ruined Stinger was belching out so much smoke it hadn't been hard to find Starland and Atara's crash site.

Bah'ren was the first one out of the ship, bounding off the loading dock and up to the edge of the crumpled remains even before Russ had fully exited the main hatch. She'd seemed full of confidence ten minutes before, but the sight of the crashed, empty Stinger had a profound effect on her. Worry stitched hard lines across her brow.

A pulse fired out of her transponder. She was studying the screen intently when Russ arrived by her side.

"Something took them," Bah'ren grunted. "Something really big." She nodded toward large footprints in the brush. The prints alone were six feet across.

Russ was scanning the edge of the Stinger and the surrounding forest for blood, but he didn't see any. Bah'ren had already climbed into one of the remaining Stingers and was yanking a long cord of graphene out of its backside. She attached the cord to the second working Stinger and fired up the engine.

"You have fifty-one percent of your battery remaining," the machine told her.

"Atara's heat signature is about a quarter mile south, but it's moving," Bah'ren said. "Ophidians eat in their burrows. I think I can catch up to them. If I can't, well . . ." A grim looked passed over Bah'ren's face. ". . . at least both you and Nina will make the team."

"Let me come with you," Russ said.

"There's not enough battery to tow the second ship and support our weight," she told Russ. "Get your range shit loaded up and give me supporting fire when I'm on my way back."

By the time Nina had joined them, Bah'ren was already lifting above the treetops. The chain between the two Stingers groaned from the load it carried.

Nina watched Bah'ren fly out of sight. Russ could tell she was anxious, but she wasn't saying anything. Out of the corner of his eye Russ saw her start to poke around the crumpled Stinger.

"There's no blood," Russ said. "I think the thing dragged them away without hurting them."

"Nature isn't usually that forgiving," Nina said.

Russ continued to investigate the spot where Starland and Atara had crash-landed their Stinger. The ring of trees that surrounded the wreck had appeared green from the sky, but as he moved closer, he realized their green branches were mixed with layers of deep purple. Wholly alien insects jumped from branch to branch and buzzed around Russ's ears.

There was barely any breeze. The heat, combined with the residual effect of the magnetic blasts, was making him nauseous. Russ rotated his arms; he could still see the blood pulsing in his veins like it was attached to a metronome. He checked the settings on his rebreather, but they were correct. He put his hand on the lowest branch of one of the purple trees and leaned his head forward, taking a series of deep breaths.

"You okay?" Nina asked. She was still poking at the downed Stinger.

"It's hot as shit," Russ said. He found himself unzipping his jumpsuit, pulling it down to his waist. The faint breeze against his skin didn't help much.

He turned around to see that Nina was slipping out of her compression gear, sliding off one arm at a time. Wisps of her thick, curly hair were standing on end from the electromagnetic energy. Russ rubbed his temple for a moment and looked away. Then his eyes drifted back again.

She had somehow managed to disengage an access panel from the port side of the Stinger, and she buried her face in the complex chain of wires and circuit boards. "This is really something," Russ heard her say under her breath. Then to him: "You sure it's safe to be half naked? With these alien bugs buzzing around?"

"It's hot," Russ said, shaking his head. He pulsed his transponder, noting that Bah'ren and Atara's heat signatures where now only about five hundred yards apart. He already regretted not forcing her to let him come along. *How did she plan to get the other two free from the jaws of the Ophidian anyway?*

"You going to be able to do anything with that?" Russ asked Nina, nodding to the Stinger.

In answer, she yanked out a wire, and the smoke trickled to a stop.

"No kidding?" he said.

"There's something happening here with quantum physics and a really weird set of force carriers," Nina told him. She gestured to several large wires coiling through the guts of the ship. "I don't understand it. I certainly couldn't replicate it, but I can see how it's traveling."

Russ leaned in close to watch what she was doing. A little too close, actually. He was suddenly aware of his bare, sweat-dripping skin being inches from her arm and shoulder.

Nina flinched, just perceptibly, but it was enough for Russ to remember the problems she was having with her boss. He backed away as casually as possible.

"Well, that was a shit show," Kendren said, and they both jumped at the sound of his voice. He was strolling down the lowered ramp from the ship, a backpack strapped to his back. "Bah'ren must be furious. They just snagged a million credits out of the air in front of us. A million we desperately need. Doubt we'll be able to recoup though. Too many powerful people in SOL's pocket." Kendren looked down at Russ. "Were you two about to kiss?" he asked.

"Definitely not," Russ said.

Kendren shrugged. "I'm going to go on a quick treasure hunt. I won't be more than a couple minutes, but watch the ship for me, and don't tell Bah'ren I left, okay?"

"Okay," Russ said.

"Fair warning, I'm pretty sure your transponders will dock you points if you start making out."

Nina grunted her disapproval, her head still buried in the access hatch of the Stinger.

Bah'ren's voice came in over the comm. "I'm almost to the heat signature. There are things moving in the trees all around me. Really big things."

"The Ophidians," Russ said.

"Battery is reading low. I shouldn't have tried to tow the second ship."

"We'll be ready to go when you arrive," Russ promised her.

"Back in a minute," Kendren grunted. He walked briskly to the edge of the clearing, his backpack chugging with each long stride. Then he disappeared into the brush.

"Is it safe to leave the landing zone?" Russ called after him.

In an ominous answer, the ground began a low, prolonged tremor. The planet itself seemed to be barely holding back its own violence.

After the tremor subsided, a howling cry ripped through the trees. It was echoed by more howling, farther away, in multiple locations.

"That sounded close," Russ said, more to himself than to anyone on the comm. He looked in the direction Kendren had gone. "This is nuts."

He climbed up the launch ramp until he was at the entrance to the ship. The ramp was more than twenty-feet tall, and from that vantage he was just high enough to see over the tops of the trees, where creatures moved, out in the perimeter around the *Flashaway*. The things were just tall enough that Russ could see the occasional crest of an enormous scale-covered lizard skull.

Russ activated the comm and whispered, "Bah'ren, the faster the better. Those Ophidians are starting to gather around us too."

". . . ucking battery is already low . . . cheap as . . ." Bah'ren's voice came back through the comm, the signal cutting in and out.

"Have you found Atara and Starland?"

There was a short blast of static, and then the comm was silent.

Russ went back into the cargo bay and climbed up the ladder to reach the ship's weapons closet. He looked through the guns lined up along the wall. It reminded him of his grandfather's garage, a few hundred years in the future.

He yanked down a gun labeled "RNO-Tech 5790 range rifle." As he went back through the cargo bay to the launch ramp, he unfolded its tactical stock, feeling the way the gun fit naturally against his shoulder.

He didn't like waiting. He tried to keep himself busy by adjusting the scope on the 5790, but found it focused naturally, even zooming in on whatever he was looking at.

". . . found . . . und . . . route . . . urry . . . gerous," Bah'ren's voice crackled over the comm.

Russ banged his palm against the edge of the rebreather where he imagined the comm speaker was stored. "Repeat that, Bah'ren. Say it again, please."

". . . route . . . danger . . . ast . . ."

"I do not copy. Are you close?"

". . . zard . . . hasing . . . urry!" Bah'ren said.

Russ fired the pulse on his transponder, waiting impatiently for it to reach Bah'ren's position. Nina's heat signature populated first, then Kendren's, about thirty yards to the south. Bah'ren and Atara appeared later, roughly half a mile farther west. They were together now, but they seemed to be moving farther from the ship.

Russ scanned the skies to the west. "I don't see you. Why aren't you flying above the tree line?" There was no answer, but just as he asked it, a large dinosaur-shaped head crested the trees and swiveled its eyes to look at him. "Kendren, wherever the hell you went, it's almost time to leave," he called out. "Nina, you better get back on the ship too."

"Just a second," Nina said, and the engine on the damaged Stinger began to hum. There was a long, high-pitched beep, and the ship rose into the air on its thrusters.

Nina's watch said, *"Major repairs in the field. Your RQ score has risen 150 points, to 2,190."*

She hopped into the controller's seat, wrapped her legs around the lock bar, and piloted the not-quite-as-broken Stinger up the launch ramp into the cargo bay.

Russ watched as she disappeared into the hull of the ship, feeling for the first time that he might not actually get the job.

The comm crackled to life again. Bah'ren's voice boomed: ". . . ing chased by a huge lizard. Get your weapons ready! Russ, can you hear me? Get your range shit loaded up."

Russ fit his eye tight against the RNO-Tech scope. He already had his range shit loaded up.

In the distance, Bah'ren rose into view. She was puttering toward the *Flashaway*, her Stinger a few feet above the treetops. The battery must have been too low to fly higher. Starland was in the weapons seat, but her head was lolling to the side, and she was not conscious.

They were towing Atara, who was strapped by rope to the lock bar of the second Stinger. A thin length of powerful graphene separated the two vehicles.

Neither woman had been in shape to fly back. Bah'ren was on her own. And she was being followed. Behind Atara's Stinger, the biggest lizard Russ had ever seen was running full tilt after them, whipping its thick tail and sticking out its forked tongue. It was about twice the size of a school bus and looked like a monitor lizard. The kind that can run, swim, and climb faster than you can.

Russ held the rifle tight against his shoulder, keeping it focused on the Ophidian.

"Kendren, now or never," he shouted into the comm. Through the scope, he could see the expression of sheer terror on Bah'ren's face. She was seconds away from being swallowed by a sixty-foot-long lizard.

Russ waited for the perfect shot, willing Bah'ren to drive faster. When the monitor got close enough, he gently squeezed the trigger, exhaling. The round ricocheted off the monster's temple, six or more inches to the left of its eye.

His watch vibrated. *"Poor marksmanship. Your RQ score has been lowered 5 points, to 2,035."*

He'd missed the shot. He sat for a moment is shock. Later, in reflection, he would convince himself that perfect marksmanship needs a quiet mind, and with the suffocating heat, Kendren lost, and the ground trembling, he knew his was nowhere close. The transponder didn't help.

The huge monitor howled, a few paces behind Atara's small craft. Two more monitors stuck their heads above the tree line and howled a response. Their black lizard eyes stared back at Russ from a distance of five hundred yards, then all three bore down on Bah'ren's convoy in giant leaping strides.

"Shoot them, Russ; why aren't you shooting them?" Bah'ren's voice poured through the comm, desperate.

Russ looked. He waited. He breathed. He fired. The round struck the closest monitor through the left pupil.

It screamed with a new, furious energy, twisting its body and disappearing, temporarily, beneath the treetops. The other two were still coming, but they were far-enough back that Bah'ren would just make it.

Russ folded up the tac stock. "We need to go now," he said through the comm. "Would be great if someone that knew how to fly the ship was on board."

Kendren came tearing out through the trees, a baby lizard snapping at his heels. The baby was about the size of a great dane.

Kendren wasn't going very fast because he was cradling a huge chunk of jadeite in his arms. As he ran up the launch ramp, small multicolored crystals fell from an open pocket in his backpack. "Shoot the baby!" he shouted. "Shoot it!"

Russ didn't bother to unfold the tac stock. He fired from the hip, slicing the bullet through the lizard's cold nose. It howled and peeled away.

After what seemed like an eternity, Bah'ren drove the twin Stingers right up the side of the ship, expertly mooring them against the hull. She stood up, but Russ shouted, "Stay in there."

He could see the fear in her eyes.

At his words, she quickly crouched back down, one hand gripping Starland, the other wrapped around the lock bar.

Kendren fired up the secondary thrusters, and the *Flashaway* screeched into the air, lopsided, burning a twenty-foot concentric circle in the ground below.

The closest monitor wasn't ready to give up and it leaped after them, catching one of the tailfins in its mouth.

The *Flashaway* continued its trajectory upward, blasting past where they'd tried to capture the Ryncyn, then past where they'd last seen the sleek SOL Pest Control ship. It surged upward so fast, the Ophidian didn't realize it was a good idea to let go until they were several thousand feet in the sky.

Its scales glistened in the warm Proxima Imperatus sun as it fell.

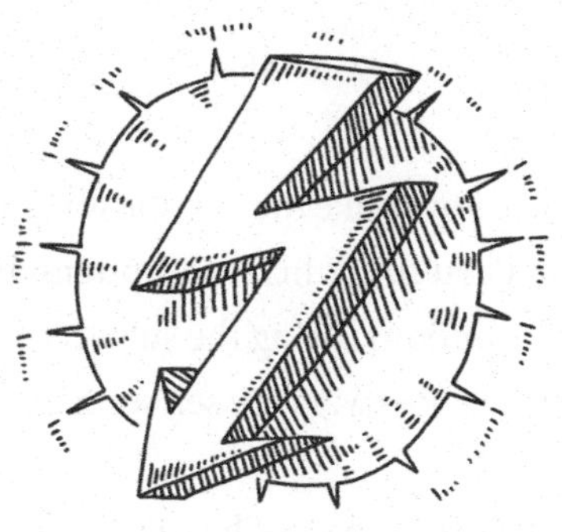

24
NINA

NINA REGRETTED FLINCHING. THEY were competing for a job, exploring space, almost rescuing magnetic whales, but in this moment, standing in the hallway at the back of the Mysterious Universe, her and Russ's weird encounter over the control panel of the Stinger was foremost in her mind. She had flinched when he'd gotten too close, and he'd noticed, respectfully moving away.

And that was the way she wanted it; right? Russ squarely in the friend zone? He was her competitor for a job she desperately needed. As cruel as it sounded, Russ was just an obstacle between her and saving her dad. She definitely hadn't noticed his weathered, natural muscles, the lean, tight body from a life lived outdoors doing physical labor. She certainly hadn't caught herself sneaking quick glances away from the incredible Stinger technology, just because he's taken his shirt off. She hadn't. Right?

It had been a long time since Nina last had sex. In fact, her sexual history was pretty limited, more often than not only existing within the pages of a romance novel, like the one she was currently cradling in her left hand. It wasn't that she didn't have options. Part of the problem was she had too many options. Being the subject of the relentless male gaze, pretty much since puberty, made sex seem cheap, unwanted, and impersonal.

She recognized that some part of her liked sex, a lot, and she knew it was important not to let men like Morty dictate her opportunities for happiness. It was something she always promised herself she'd work on . . . later.

Nina leaned against the wall and studied the cover of the novel in her hand. A cowboy in tight Wrangler jeans looked back at her, his shirt misplaced, his skin glistening with nonspecific lubricant. The cowboy was smiling, in much the same way Russ smiled.

She put the novel quickly back on the shelf.

To distract herself, she watched Norma fussing around the store's countertop making last minute adjustments. Nina was exhausted, but she was glad she'd managed to stay awake long enough to be a part of the grand reopening of the Mysterious Universe.

Russ and Applebum had done an incredible job restoring the inside of the store. Nina couldn't help appreciating the way the shelves had been sanded down and stained a rich maple color. The ceiling had been repaired, improved even. Russ had stripped away the office-style panels and raised the ceiling up to a line of beautiful oak. Because of all the water damage, there wasn't as much product as the shelf space allowed, but they'd turned many of the surviving books face forward, and their colorful covers beckoned to Nina from every shelf, with the promise of a thousand equally colorful worlds waiting to be explored.

Norma craned her neck to smile at Nina. "It's happening! It's really happening!" she cheered, tapping her finger against the face of her watch. "And we're open!"

Norma threw open the deadbolt lock and began to enthusiastically greet the first few customers.

Two were strangers, likely tourists passing through town delighted to see an actual bookstore still in business. The third was Norma's friend Bibi.

"I'm going to buy so many books right now," Bibi promised.

A guy Nina didn't recognize followed. "Ron Griese. I traveled all the way here from Lakewater," he said, introducing himself to Norma. "I've been waiting for you guys to reopen for weeks. I can't tell you how disappointed I was when the store closed."

"What can we get you?" Norma asked. "Cookbooks? Spiritual guidebooks? Maybe your life needs a little more romance . . . novels?"

Nina hadn't really considered Norma a close friend until they'd spent so much time together in the hospital, but she easily recognized the charismatic saleswoman from her youth.

"You have a cat skeleton with three eye sockets?" Ron said nervously. "Several months ago, it was featured on your website for one hundred and twenty-five dollars. I finally convinced my wife to let me buy it the very same day your online portal went dark. Feels like I've been waiting forever to get my hands on it."

"I know that cat. It's always bothered the heck out of me," Norma admitted, "and I'd be happy to remit him over to your ownership. Sadly, the price on that type of item has risen somewhat in the past few months . . ."

Norma led Ron toward the back of the store, where Russ and Applebum had built a display to showcase some of Russ's grandfather's more unusual finds.

"It's really happening," Russ said as he approached from the alley, where he liked to park Norma's car.

He sounded very satisfied.

Nina went to the window to see if anyone else was waiting outside, and sure enough, there was a man standing awkwardly on the curb. He had thin red hair and pale freckled skin. He was wearing a brown business suit and holding a briefcase. Nina didn't recognize him.

"Howdy." Russ greeted the man as he walked in, passing the bright neon "Op_n" sign. Russ had moved behind the counter, a big smile on his face and a brand-new Mysterious Universe apron hanging around his neck.

"Come in, sir. Welcome to the grand reopening," said Norma.

The man walked inside warily. He looked around at Nina, Bibi, Russ, and Norma, all staring at him, and an expression of embarrassment flashed briefly across his face. Then, in businesslike, almost robotic, fashion, he laid his briefcase on the counter and popped it open.

"Which one of you is Norma Wesley?" he asked.

"I am," Norma said.

He removed a document from his briefcase. "I'm David Cornelia, from the law firm of Trent, Cole, and Kerch." Cornelia took a moment to remove a handkerchief from his pocket and wipe it across his pale skin. "We have thrice warned you that if you can't pay the balance of rent owed by August 28, we will begin the formal eviction process. Today is August 25, and my firm has asked me to personally travel up here from Salt Lake, at the firm's own cost, to give you one last warning."

A grave expression had descended upon Norma's face. She wasn't looking at Cornelia, however. She was looking past him, over Nina's shoulder where Russ was still standing behind the counter. "Don't," she warned Russ. "Killing him will only attract more lawyers."

Nina and Cornelia turned at the same time to stare at Russ. He was jacking the ammo out of the Whitefeather and lowering it back down behind the counter.

Cornelia turned to Norma, shifting nervously from foot to foot. "Are you prepared to pay the balance due?"

"We don't have it yet," Norma said quietly. "We have about a sixth of it."

"Why don't you give them another week?" Nina asked. "They just got the store back open. Today."

Cornelia turned to Nina, fiddling with his tie. "My firm is acting under the direction of the SDLE commercial real-estate conglomerate. They set these deadlines by strict policy, with no exception, and all such policies obey the proper, legal grace periods for debts traded and owed. We are confident we have given them ample opportunities." The red-haired man paused a moment, his eyes registering the sorrow on Norma's face.

Nina didn't think it possible, but Cornelia looked even less comfortable.

"It's completely out of my hands," he said. "To be honest, I've never been asked to collect in person before. I suspect, because of your circumstances, the recent death of your spouse, they fear some sort of public relations . . ." Cornelia trailed off.

Nina thought he was worried he'd said too much, but his eyes were back on Russ. She didn't have to turn around to know Russ had picked up the Whitefeather again.

"Anyhow," Cornelia said quickly. "If you could just sign this paper indicating that we visited in person and gave you one last chance to balance your . . ." He trailed off again.

Nina recognized the sound of a bullet sliding back into the Whitefeather's chamber.

"Actually, the paper is just a formality," Cornelia said, closing his briefcase. "Just a formality." He moved quickly out the door and down the block.

Norma turned to face Nina, Bibi and Russ. "Thank you for fixing up the bookstore," she said sadly. "Thank you all for being here. For trying." Norma's shoulders sagged. She was a woman of great vitality, but in that moment, it was slipping right out of her. She seemed suddenly frail, even ill. "Clark would have been very proud of how the store looks today," she managed to say.

It was the perfect time for another customer to come inside, maybe to make a big purchase, but the sidewalk outside remained empty.

Norma quietly rolled Ron's three-eyed cat skeleton into bubble wrap and taped it closed.

"It's not over yet," Nina told her. "We've still got three days."

"What would you always tell me in high school when I failed a math quiz?" Russ asked his grandma.

"No giving up," Norma reminded herself.

"Maybe the Chrome Man will save us," Bibi said suddenly.

"Who?" Russ asked.

"The Chrome Man."

"I don't know who that is," Russ told her, but Nina sensed an extra degree of interest in his voice.

Bibi cocked her head. "Have you not spoken to anyone in town in the last two weeks?"

"Maybe," Russ said.

"All anyone is talking about is the Chrome Man." Bibi stared at Russ, but he just shook his head.

"I've heard of the Chrome Man, and I live in Lakewater," Ron said. "Do you, by chance, sell any Chrome Man paraphernalia?"

"Not yet," Norma told him, handing him the cat. "But check in again in a few days."

Bibi continued: "Nancy was the first one to see him. She'd gotten drunk at the Koo Koo Club in Banville. Like an idiot she tried to drive home and ended up sliding into one of the maples up on the 105. Thank God she only drives five miles an hour or we'd be having another funeral.

"She was stuck there for an hour, yelling for help and switching her phone in and out of airplane mode to try and get a signal.

"And then the Chrome Man appeared, arriving out of the darkness, her headlights gleaming off his skin. She said he was shaped like a human, but his entire body was made of metal. She said he moved the car with his bare hands, just wrenched it free from the tree as easily as shuffling a deck of cards."

"That just sounds like one of Nancy's crazy stories," Nina said, trying not to glance nervously at Russ.

Bibi continued: "Of course we all thought it was just Nancy being Nancy. But when Smokey arrived the next day with his tow truck, he verified the story. He said the car had all sorts of driver-side damage, but it was moved a solid two feet away from the tree and the door had been ripped off its hinges. Ripped outward!"

There was silence in the room. Norma was nodding. Nina finally turned to glance at Russ. He was a little bit pale.

"June's farm was having a hell of a time with coyotes," Norma said suddenly, life creeping back into her voice. "The heat keeps driving the packs up into the mountains. Her husband has been trying to hunt them, but he's not as young as he used to be, and he had to let his farmhand go back in February, so he's tired all the time. June said a pack was howling right outside her coop, they'd gotten so bold. The chickens were losing their minds. And then the Chrome Man showed up. Like with Nancy, he just stepped right out of the shadows. It was dark, but the coyotes were howling and snarling and snapping at his skin and he paid them no mind. She said she heard popping sounds, but she was too scared to get any closer and see what was happening. The next day she came out at first light and found six dead coyotes piled beside her chicken coop, each of their necks broken."

"First of all, that's a crazy story," Russ said. "Those are both crazy stories and not at all sensible."

"Desperate people need something to believe in," Norma told him.

"How's this Chrome Man going to save us from lawyers? And debt?"

"They're saying he rescued Robert's yield of sweet peppers. Saved him a bundle. Nobody saw the Chrome Man do it, but who else could it be?" Bibi said.

Nina looked down at the callouses on her hands.

"He fixed Bibi's car!" Norma said. "It must have been him."

"Customer!" Bibi said suddenly. "Another customer!" Then she added, "It's Morty!"

Nina was saved from the Morty experience by her phone's buzzing. She was down the hall and out the back into the alley before Morty could wedge himself through the front door.

"Hey, Mom," she said into her phone.

"Where are you?" Katherine asked.

"I'm at Norma's bookstore. It's the grand reopening, but there aren't too many people here. Maybe Dad needs a book?"

"Nina . . . I'm calling about your dad."

"Is something wrong?"

"Just another bad day. The worst yet. He can't even get down the porch stairs and into the car for his dialysis. His face is ashen."

"He needs real care," Nina admitted. "He needs a real hospital, like St. Michaels down in Laramie. I'm pretty sure my old truck could get us down there."

"And stay where? How would we pay?"

Nina's voice was flat, matter-of-fact: "We haven't paid the hospital in Banville for four months. They can't turn us away, legally."

"Are we going to sleep in the hospital too? We can't afford rent, unless you have some money secretly saved. I can't bear the thought of leaving him there and"—Katherine's voice caught in her throat—"and maybe never seeing him again. Your dad needs dialysis, not once, not twice, but for the rest of his life. And these complications. He's not doing well, Nina. Something needs to change, soon."

Frustrated, Nina ended the call. She went back into the bookstore and found Russ and Ensine in the storeroom.

"Hullo!" Ensine said. "I didn't want to miss the grand opening."

"Did you hear what I just said?" Russ asked Ensine. "We need the stone back. Or we need some of the money from its sale. My grandma's going to lose the store. Nina's dad needs help. We can't earn a penny until we're CERTified."

Ensine was dressed very dapperly in pressed slacks and a button-down shirt. He was old again, but his chin was still strong and his eyes still fierce. "I spent it," he told them.

"All of it?"

"Almost all of it. Touch my chest," he said.

"What?" Russ was too flustered to want to put his hand on Ensine's chest.

Nina put hers there instead. His chest felt weirdly normal. "Your skin. It's human skin." she said. "There's no scales."

Ensine tapped the transformer attached to the top of his ear. It had a ruby stone set in the middle. "I upgraded to a hard-light transformer," he told them both. "A more advanced form of illusion. It doesn't just cast an image over my existing body. It uses hard-light technology to shape that image into something that mimics flesh. When you touch me now, I'll feel human." Then he added: "Technically they're illegal, but when you're selling a black-market Obinz stone, sometimes you buy a black-market transformer with the money you've made."

"Why do you care about feeling human to the touch?" Russ asked. "What difference does it make?"

"I've found all the books you requested!" Norma chimed in from the end of the hallway. She had eight books clutched vertically between her two hands. She also had the spring back in her step. "I went with the Kellermans. I thought you'd like them best."

Nina watched Ensine look at Norma. She saw his posture straighten just slightly and his hand run quickly through his hair. In that moment she knew the answer to Russ's question about the hard-light transformer.

"He doesn't just want the Kellermans," Russ told his grandmother. "Get him Patterson too."

"All Patterson or just the ones he actually wrote?" Norma asked Ensine.

"He wants every book with James Patterson's name on it," Russ said.

"Oh my!" Norma said. "That will take a moment." She handed the Kellermans to Ensine and hurried away.

"Did I forget to mention I'm broke?" Ensine hissed.

"You want to keep hanging around my grandma, you buy her books," Russ said.

Ensine shrugged and then carried his Kellermans back into the main portion of the store.

The bell above the door jingled, and Nina heard Norma cry out: "Welcome to the Mysterious Universe!"

Russ sagged against the wall. "I'm exhausted."

Nina nodded, but there was something still on her mind. "I'm sorry I stole your Obinz stone."

Russ was about to say something but for whatever reason he held back. He seemed genuinely upset at what she'd done. All he did was grunt and say: "Doesn't matter now."

"We haven't talked about the exterminators' only having one job," she reminded him.

"We both try our best. I sure as hell aren't going to work against you. Whoever is the most qualified gets the job, and the other guy can find work with a different company."

Other guy? Nina thought.

Somewhere in the front of the store she heard Morty chuckling.

"We've got enough enemies without making more out of each other, don't we?" Nina said.

Russ nodded.

She put her hand on his shoulder as if to say, "You've got a deal." Nina was sympathetic to Russ's attempts to save Norma's bookstore, but it was nowhere near as important as saving her father's life. She hoped she wasn't making a mistake in this idealistic—almost naïve—declaration they were making to play fair with each other. Worse yet, she wasn't sure she knew Russ well enough to trust he'd keep his end of the bargain.

She realized Russ was staring at her. He seemed to register something in her eyes. For a moment he looked down and away from her, the top of his uncombed hair almost brushing her forehead. He was standing very close. Nina pressed her back to the storage-room wall and watched him curiously.

When Russ raised his head again, they just stared at each other. He had a lot happening behind his own eyes: exhaustion, worry, anger, hope, and that wasn't all. Nina saw something else, and she recognized it more easily than any of the other emotions. Men had been staring at her like that since she'd hit puberty.

Her palms began to sweat. She half consciously wiped them against the storeroom door.

"The Chrome Man," Nina said finally, breaking the spell.

Russ remained quiet, as if he wanted to linger longer in the moment she'd just interrupted.

Then he gave her a sideways grin. "We're so absolutely fucked," he told her.

25

RUSS

AFTER THE GRAND REOPENING, Russ ducked quickly into the storage room. Applebum was not there.

Applebum wasn't there the next day either when Russ snuck in to teleport to work. A renegade SAS unit was loose somewhere in Evanstown. That was a problem. But even getting into the closet was harder now, with the store open. Bibi and Norma were chatting away at the counter, not twenty feet from Russ as he hastily opened the padlock he had affixed to the outside of the storeroom door.

Russ was kneeling on the floor in front of the Waypoint, rifling through Applebum's stack of books, when Nina snuck in behind him.

"He's not here?" Nina said.

"Nope. I have no idea where he's gone."

"Did it scare you at all that he snapped those coyotes' necks?"

"Yes ma'am."

"What's he reading?" she whispered. "Maybe it's a clue to where he's gone."

"I hope it's not a clue," Russ told her. He held up three of the books, showing her their spines. "Sun Tzu's *The Art of War*. Machiavelli's *The Prince*. The Anarchist's Cookbook." Russ nudged a graphic novel with his toe. "Alan Moore's *V for Vendetta*."

"No matter what, do not let him learn about the internet," Nina told Russ.

"We can't even find him."

Nina sighed deeply. "That's a problem for another day. We've got to get to work," she reminded Russ.

Russ still wasn't fully used to the warm feeling of the Waypoint jump, or the hustle of the alien crowd on the other side.

Nina seemed to be having no problem finding her way back to the *Flashaway's* docking position.

Russ followed, watching the strange world move all around him.

He was marveling at an alien with four arms, when he saw the rock creature again. It bobbed through the crowd, shouldering aside anyone who got in its way. Russ followed the creature with his eyes until it cleared the "riffraff" and its small purple companion stepped into view.

They were all there, a large team dressed in white jumpsuits with the red swoosh on the breast.

"SOL Pest Control," Russ said, more to himself than Nina. "What do you suppose they do when they get to work, since the robots are performing all the actual labor?"

"That little purple guy is the one who stole our Ryncyn?" Nina asked. "He looks pretty harmless."

"I don't think he is," Russ told her. "I wonder if Bah'ren had any luck filing a complaint."

“Thus far,” Bah’ren was telling them, “we haven’t heard from any of the proper channels about SOL Pest Control stealing our contract. I called Civics and Standards, and they basically hung up on me, which is alarming. I also contacted the Municipal Workers Union but that’s always a crapshoot. Maybe they’ll ignore us, maybe they’ll help, maybe they’ll make things worse. Meanwhile, there are no jobs on the MERC board, and the *Flashaway’s* down to half a tank of gas.”

“We’ve been in worse spots,” Starland said reassuringly. She was relaxing on the IKEA couch next to Russ. Bah’ren stood in her characteristic spot at the front of the room, her small projector in her hand.

“We’ve never been in a worse spot that this,” Bah’ren admitted. “It’s not that there are no jobs. There are the same number of jobs. SOL Pest Control is just grabbing them all. By my count they’ve got at least six ships in service at all times, day and night, none of them manned by organics. Even when they don’t get a proper claim in on time . . . well, we know what happens with those jobs. They come for them anyway. We can’t compete with an ever-expanding inorganic work force.”

“Times are desperate,” Bah’ren continued. “Desperate enough that we’ve got to do a little out-of-the-box thinking. Today we’re running a gig off the board for the yellow suits.”

“Who are the yellow suits?” Russ asked.

Atara poked her head inside the briefing room. She was out in the hall doing something or other. “Yellow suits are the nickname for Infrastructure Facilities workers. They’re space janitors, basically,” she told him.

“Glad to see you’re okay,” Russ told her.

“Thanks!” she said, smiling.

“So, we’re going to be space janitors?” Nina asked.

"Something like that, yes," Bah'ren said. "It's far less likely SOL Pest Control will be trolling this listing since thus far they've been focused solely on driving other exterminators out of business."

"Have we considered getting our own robots?" Nina asked.

Russ knew what she was thinking about, the night in the field with Applebum harvesting sweet peppers. He'd worked tirelessly, and far more effectively than Russ or Nina.

"It's always been against the law to employ inorganics for anything other than immigration work, and during wartime."

"But . . ."

". . . until recently." Bah'ren continued. "A fringe movement in the UAIB high council convinced the rest to greenlight a pilot program that would allow a 'randomly selected' business to employ the Tech12 in the commercial workforce, at their full capacity."

"SOL Pest Control," Russ said.

"Yep. And from the perspective of a lot of powerful people, it's been a rousing success. If we can't adapt, if we can't find a way to compete without the help of AI, we're looking at the end of the Intergalactic Exterminators, Inc."

Russ decided it was time to change the subject. "So, what's this janitor job?"

Bah'ren perked up at the question. "An asteroid field has wandered too close to one of the Dexadrive lanes. It's far off the central path, not one of the lanes that's used much—"

"None of them are," Atara said.

"This particular lane is not regularly maintenanced, and it's a big asteroid field. Someone on the facilities dispatch board is worried that repeated impacts from the rocks will cause a valve to collapse. If even one of those asteroids gets into the lane, the next ship to come through will be smeared across half the galaxy. We'll be doing important work."

"Space janitors," Starland said.

"You want to pay the rent on this jalopy out of your paycheck?" Bah'ren snapped. "We're getting the Dexadrive spooled up. Get yourselves in your seats."

The Intergalactic Exterminators hurried down the hall to the bridge, where they strapped themselves into their seats. Nina and Russ were the first in, but they still weren't used to the harness mechanisms.

"Tell me we're going to blast into hyperspace," Nina said to Kendren as he helped her attach the complicated system of buckles that would keep her in place once they hit the Dexadrive lane.

"Not in the way you're thinking," Kendren said. "Some ships have hyperdrives, but they're mostly real old clunkers, or pirates that have a reason to stay off the main grid. Most lawful ships, ours included, stick to the Dexadrive lanes."

Just as he finished speaking, the *Flashaway* dipped into the lane. There was a great whooshing sound, and the ship immediately fired forward; the entire bridge shook ominously.

Somehow, despite the incredible g-force, Kendren was able to stay upright, gripping Nina's seat like they were still in the middle of a casual conversation.

He was showing off, Russ realized.

"How's it work?" Nina asked when she'd caught her breath again.

"Heck if I know," Kendren told her. His knuckles were white where he gripped the edge of her seat. "Best I can describe them is, they're like rivers flowing at a high rate of speed. Once this old boat nudges into the river, bam, she's blasting in whatever direction the lane is pointed."

"It's an intergalactic freeway system," Nina said. "Marvelous."

"I don't know what a freeway is," Kendren told her.

"Kendren, sit down," Atara said. "Nobody has thought it was cool to stand during a lane jump since secondary school." She looked over her shoulder at Nina, then at Russ, then at Kendren. She seemed to be paying close attention to the way Nina was talking to the two men.

"We used to do this on every trip when I worked Transport Security. First guy to sit was a bitch," Kendren explained.

Atara ignored him. "A freeway is a decent metaphor, I guess, if the concrete on a freeway moved instead of the cars. Almost no civilians use these lanes anymore. Since Waypoints became omnipresent, the lanes only get used when someone wants to visit an unnetworked, uncharted planet, like Earth, or when shipping companies have so much freight it's not practical to feed it piece-by-piece through a Waypoint. But even that's getting much less common. I hear the pirates that used to troll the outer lanes are so bored, most have moved over to hacking and catfishing . . ."

Nina kept digging for answers about the technology itself, but once the explanations got complicated, Russ lost interest. He found himself staring out the starscreen as solar systems whizzed by. They were moving so fast, all he would catch was the solar system's sun, slipping up into view, then back down again—the quick staccato blips of a hundred different turbo-charged sunsets.

And then the *Flashaway* slammed to a stop and pivoted out of the Dexadrive lane, sliding through a plasma defense valve and exiting the hyperspace highway directly into the middle of an asteroid field.

Huge space boulders rolled slowly across Russ's field of view.

"By Ren, that was further than I thought. I hope we have enough gas to get home." Bah'ren said.

"Are you joking?" Kendren asked.

"How about some shields?" Bah'ren shouted, and Starland turned to pound away at the heads-up display on the starscreen.

Russ watched a faint blue translucent shield appear around the perimeter of the ship. An asteroid roughly the size of the *Flashaway*—it was one of the smaller ones—smashed into the shield and pushed them back in the direction of the Dexadrive lane.

"Get the thrusters up, Starland. Should I let one of the humans drive, or what?" Bah'ren shouted.

Kendren grabbed Nina's arm. "Come with me to the north-side cannon. I'll show you how it works." Russ watched as Kendren and Nina disappeared in the direction of the north staircase.

"If we slide backwards into the Dexadrive lane we're space dust, along with whoever hits us," Bah'ren reminded Starland. She was still tapping away at the HUD.

The ship rumbled forward, nosing an asteroid out of its path. There was the hydraulic whirring sound of huge machines moving, and then a pulse laser cannoned across the starscreen and blew the nearest rock into space dust.

Russ could hear Kendren speaking in the background. "Dial down the intensity, honey. If it breaks apart into too many pieces, the Dexadrive defense valve will still be compromised." Then, faintly through the comm, he heard Nina's watch say, *"Ineffective use of force. Your RQ score has been lowered 20 points, to 1,980."*

"This is kind of awesome," Nina said.

"Pay attention to your firing rate," Kendren barked at her. He wasn't on the comm, but he must have been leaning close enough that his words registered through Nina's mic. Russ heard him say, more faintly, as if he were whispering, "This is an opportunity to prove your skills. And to beat the other human for the job."

It seemed Kendren had already made his pick for who Bah'ren should hire.

Nina's pulse laser kept thumping away at the asteroids, as Russ moved down the hall to the southern, "underside" turret. He sat in the turret, his hands lightly testing the controls.

Nina blasted another nearby rock, and the explosion shook the ship.

"I think she's doing more harm than good," Atara said over Russ's shoulder.

"There are too many for her to handle on her own." Russ pointed out. Another asteroid rolled toward Russ's turret, grinding against the polymer wall separating Russ and Atara from deep space.

"Starland! We need the shields moved to the south side," Atara shouted. She crouched near Russ and whispered, "I swear there's a cost to cutting every possible financial corner."

"How do I fire this?" Russ asked.

"See those joysticks on either side of your chair?"

There were two six-inch levers on his right and left side. They were shaped like the accelerator on an airplane. Russ grabbed one in each hand. He grabbed one too hard, and his seat, and his whole turret, swiveled in that direction.

Atara shook her head. "Pull back on the left to turn left, pull back on the right to turn right. If you push either forward, just slightly, it will fire the cannon. The farther forward you push, the longer the canon will generate plasma before releasing it. All firing has a little bit of recoil, so if you go big, you'll have to reset your aim after each shot. Also, if you go big and miss, it will dock the hell out of your RQ score. Ammunition is not free, even on an energy weapon."

Russ tentatively slid the joystick forward. An enormous ball of plasma fire gathered around the end of the turret just on the other side of the starscreen, and then sent itself hurling forward. It slipped past a nearby asteroid but shattered one just beyond it. The turret chair shook so much Russ was almost pitched out. Fragments of the destroyed asteroid pelted Russ's starscreen, like hail on a car windshield. *"Minor damage to company property. Your RQ score has been lowered 20 points, to 1,935,"* Russ's watch said.

"That was low power?"

"Enjoy it, brother."

Russ immediately tapped the comm. "Up for a friendly competition?" he asked Nina.

"I think we're already in one." Her voice had a smile in it.

"Bet I can hit ten before you can."

"I'm not betting you about anything having to do with aiming a weapon—oh, what the hell, you're on," she said.

Russ had hit six asteroids to Nina's five when two new ships slid out of the Dexadrive lane and slammed to a stop at the edge of the field. He didn't have to look close to see the shiny red SOL Pest Control swoosh freshly painted on each of their rear wings.

"No fucking way," he heard Bah'ren say through the comm.

One of the ships blasted forward, positioning itself between the *Flashaway* and the bulk of the remaining asteroids.

"What's the protocol here?" Russ asked.

"They're fucking breaking it," Bah'ren said. "This is piracy. How can this be different from piracy?"

"What do we do?" Nina asked, but Bah'ren wasn't listening. "What the hell did I do to piss off these corpo vampires?" she mumbled into the comm.

Gleaming turrets spun up from the tops of the SOL Pest Control ships. They swiveled their long noses toward the asteroid field and began to pelt it with a machine's efficiency.

"Can I shoot them?" Russ asked.

"They're not doing anything illegal," Bah'ren said. "And we're not soldiers. We're municipal workers."

"Are we paid by the asteroid?" Nina asked pragmatically. "We could approach from the other side."

"No. I mean, yes, we could maybe hit a few more . . ."

Russ realized they'd better hurry. The machines were tearing through the asteroids at a pace twice the speed they'd been able to work.

But they didn't hurry. In fact, when she spoke next, Bah'ren sounded defeated. She managed to muster a last sliver of anger: "Starland, swing the *Flashaway* around, and open a comm channel. I want to talk to these robotic motherfuckers."

Russ felt a tap on his shoulder. It was Atara. "It's going to be interesting to be unemployed," she said. "Kind of sucks that I only have forty-five cents in my savings account."

"Are we really going to close down?"

"If we can't finish a job, we can't get credits. Without credits, how do we cover overhead? The principals of evolution don't just apply to species. They apply to businesses just the same. We're the prey species now, and SOL Pest Control with their government-permitted robots are chewing through our whole ecosystem. Look at them." Russ and Atara looked back out the starscreen. SOL Pest Control had already completely leveled the asteroid field. Their ships spun in a small circle, then zipped right back into the Dexadrive lane. They must have wholly ignored Bah'ren's attempts at communication.

The vacuum of space seemed especially quiet until Atara spoke again. "We can't stay open without an income, even if half the crew is working for free."

She began to unbuckle Russ's harness from the underside turret. He was conscious of her hands moving across his body. "Come on. Space isn't always such a bummer. Let me show you something cool."

26
RUSS

RUSS FOLLOWED ATARA INTO the VTR. He took a step back as the door slid up into the ceiling. Atara sent him to the "box" in the center, then climbed the ladder to the control tower. Russ knew the VTR was voice controlled, so he wasn't sure what Atara was doing up there. He could see the top of her head as she bowed over the console, punching at a screen.

"VTR: Instigate map," Atara commanded.

Sand poured up from the floor until he was cushioned in it. Water crashed in from the south wall and stretched backward, forming a long beach. The ceiling flashed gray, then blue, then gray, and then the color stabilized, becoming a deep blue sky above them. Russ closed his eyes and listened to the sounds of the waves crashing around him. For a moment, he was inundated with homesickness. Not for the home he shared with his grandma in Evanstown, but his real home, on the shores of the Pacific Ocean. When he opened his eyes again, he was coasting on a bike along a boardwalk, wearing swim trunks.

He quickly started pedaling.

Atara pedaled up next to him. She had on a blue two-piece swimsuit and shorts.

They passed a series of gaming booths and an old Ferris wheel, its paint chipping under the relentless assault of salty air.

"Are we on the East Coast?" Russ asked.

"Connecticut," Atara told him. "I was on this bike, in this swimsuit when they came and got me."

"They?" Russ asked. Then he realized what she was talking about. "You were abducted."

"Yeah. Just two years before the anti-abduction lobby managed to get new rules incorporated into the shared system of civics. The universe has changed a lot in a short time."

"A ship just swooped down and snatched you off your bike? That must have been crazy."

"Yep. It was also one of the happiest days of my life."

"You don't miss Earth?" Russ asked.

Atara pedaled ahead, turning right and gliding her bike to a stop. She was leaning against a beach-wall when Russ caught up.

"Naw. I don't miss Earth," she said. Then she thought for a moment. "I miss Earthlings. Surrounded by a hundred billion aliens, and I can still get to feeling completely alone out here in space. When we Waypointed back to Earth, the night we met you, it made me realize how much I've given up by being away from my own people. Have the Jets won a Superbowl recently? My dad is a huge fan . . . I would like to have shared a Superbowl with him. Sometimes—a lot of times, lately—I wonder about all the stuff I've missed."

"You have not missed a Jets Superbowl," Russ said. "There's no need to rush home for that."

"Visiting Earth is risky anyway. I'm not sure how you can keep jumping back and forth. All the tier-nine planets make me anxious because it's so easy to lose your CERTification. Have a little bit too much to drink, fall for a guy at a bar, accidentally tell him you're a space exterminator, and bam! DeCERTification."

Atara stripped off her shorts and pulled a pair of towels from the basket on her bike. "Come on," she told Russ. He found himself following her down to the water line. They spread out their towels, then lay side by side on the sand. Russ did his best not to stare at her tight stomach. She rolled to her left, seemingly to give him a look at her perfect ass.

He rolled in the other direction, because it was pulling at his eyes like a tractor beam.

"Speaking of that deCERTification, I have a question," Russ said.

"Yeah?" Atara was facing him again.

"It's theoretical."

"Okay."

"Let's say, theoretically, that someone accidentally kidnapped a Tech12 unit. And then, somehow it ended up living in the closet of his grandma's bookstore."

"Uh-oh," Atara said.

Russ continued: "At one point this guy realized the robot might be able to help the local community . . ."

Atara groaned. "Does this story keep getting worse?" she interrupted him.

Russ nodded. "Let's say that person gave the SAS unit a few books to read."

Atara interrupted again, this time with an involuntary gasp. He saw the shock on her face. She reached over and covered his training transponder with her right hand. "Has any of this registered on your transponder?"

"It's theoretical," Russ said. Then he shook his head: "No. I'm not sure why, but no."

"It must be so unique it's off the training grid. I'm impressed, Russ. It's likely no one in CERT training has ever been reckless in this unique way. Usually they just get eaten by a space beast." She paused. "Tech12s are artificial intelligence. They learn limitlessly, but it is neither possible nor permissible to manufacture one that is capable of reading."

The critical flaw, Russ realized.

Atara still had her hand on the face of his watch. He could feel her fingers against the underside of his wrist. "Let's say though, theoretically, that this Tech12 did read," he continued, "and it got its hands on a bunch of books about war, and revolution, and bomb making . . . and then it started to live the life of a superhero vigilante, running around town helping people and sometimes murdering packs of wild animals. How much trouble would I be in?"

Atara shook her head. She glanced around the beach, as if Bah'ren could jump up from under a wave at any time. "We can talk about it later. Somewhere else. The watch isn't specifically programmed for that sort of violation, but it is scanning for more common violations, including making sure that you don't reveal any secrets of the universe on a tier-nine planet. If the watch sees someone see the robot, it's an auto-fail. You should unmake that mess, somehow, and quickly."

Russ hung his head. "Shit," he said, as much to himself as to Atara. "Does it matter? If Bah'ren is going to lose the business anyway?"

"CERTification isn't just certification. It's your access to space. Your green card. If you have it, there's always a chance you could catch on with another municipal company. If you don't have it, you'll be mind-wiped."

Russ saw the seriousness in her expression. "Shit," he said again.

"Yeah, that's a big one." Atara finally took her hand off Russ's wrist, moving it up to his shoulder and giving him a small squeeze. "You'll figure it out," Atara said comfortingly. "There's something I've been wondering about. How did Nina afford CERT training?"

"Uh . . . she sold an unrefined Obinz stone."

"Where the hell did she get one of those?"

"She stole it from me."

Atara looked vexed, as if the news was confirming some fear she had. "I figured it would be something like that."

"You guys throwing a beach party without me?" Russ heard Nina say. She bounded out of nowhere, phasing into the scene halfway between Russ and the water, blocking his view.

Atara quickly withdrew her hand from Russ's shoulder.

It seemed like Nina was still excited from her experience crunching asteroids. Her smile was infectious. *The door to the VTR must be right there,* Russ thought.

As she walked toward him, grinning, Nina's orange jumpsuit dissolved into a fairly scandalous green bikini. He wasn't sure if the suit was scandalous itself, or just the way it barely held all of her in it.

Atara was staring at him, her head resting on her palm. He knew she was watching him watch Nina.

"I see you've only brought two towels," Nina said.

Russ picked at the fabric of his trunks.

"You're just going to have to share," Nina told him coyly.

She lowered herself onto Russ's towel, but it was barely big enough to fit just him. He could feel her warm body pressed against his.

"Wow! You're in better shape than I expected," Nina whispered. He felt her lips close to his ear, her hot breath on his neck. Her hands explored his body. "I like this swimsuit," she said.

"Atara . . ." Russ started to say.

"Yes, how can we get Atara out of here?" Nina whispered. "So we can be alone?" Nina ran her hand up the length of his chest, letting her fingers drag sensuously across the lower part of his neck.

Russ stood up suddenly. The motion sent Nina sprawling and covered Atara with sand. He took a step back, but Nina crawled on all fours toward him. She looked him directly in the eyes.

Russ said, "VTR: Cancel simulation."

The sand, the sky, the water, and the towels disappeared. Nina was still crawling toward Russ, a look of sexual hunger on her face, when her body slipped away in a swirl of zeros and ones.

The beach was completely gone. Atara was standing beside Russ in the VTR box. She grinned sheepishly and shrugged. "Everybody is scanned into the system in order to run the simulations," she said. "There are all different kinds of monsters out there—"

"I hope you don't mean Nina," Russ cut in.

Atara locked eyes with him. "The Tech12 isn't your only problem. I know girls like her. Or at least I recognize the type," she said. "They don't give very much, but they're quick to take whatever they need."

"She's actually really nice. Her dad's sick, so she—"

Atara held her finger to Russ's lips, silencing him. "I haven't been on Earth in ten years, and I still know her better than you do. What's going to happen is that in the end she's going to trick you into giving her the job. It doesn't matter how noble her cause is. You will still be the one without work, possibly mind-wiped, and stuck on Earth. And you'll be twisted up so much that whatever brain you've got left will still be thinking you made the right decision." Her hands circled gently around his forearms. "Some women are born knowing how to manipulate men. Sometimes we don't even know we're doing it. But we're still doing it."

As she finished speaking, Atara herself began to disappear into a swirl of zeros and ones that started at her toes and traveled up her body until her hands, clutching Russ just seconds earlier, blew away like flower petals, the memory of her touch leaving little zigzags of warmth running up his arms. Suddenly he found he wasn't standing at all, but back kneeling alone in the VTR box. "Sonofabitch!" Russ said. He looked up to see that Atara was actually still in the control room. She had her hands on her hips and was staring down at him, a broad smile on her face.

"I just wanted to warn you. You deserve better. The job, CERT-ification, outer space, working with someone as wonderful as me . . . it's worth fighting for."

Russ opened his mouth, but he was at a loss for words. His watch spoke in his place: *"Misuse of company training technology. Your RQ score has been lowered 30 points, to 1,905."*

27

RUSS

"WHAT DO YOU MEAN? I've been sitting here the whole time," Applebum told Russ. He stared conspicuously at the watch. "You told me to watch the watch. You told me to watch the Waypoint. I've been doing my jobs."

"Which book taught you to lie?" Russ asked. "Which one was it? I'm banning that motherfucker right now."

"Shucks," Applebum said. "Robots don't lie. It runs contrary to our programming."

"Robots don't say shucks either," Russ said, shaking a comic book at Applebum. "Unless they've been reading Archie comics."

"Why does he like Veronica so much?" Applebum wondered. "Betty is clearly the superior mate."

"You shouldn't have killed those coyotes," Russ told him.

"Which coyotes?"

"I know you went to the old Lasak farm and saved their chickens from coyotes. But coyotes belong in these woods, just the same as we do. You're supposed to relocate them when they get too close, not snap their necks."

"After much study, I have determined that violence is a legitimate and effective way to solve problems."

"It's not though . . ."

". . . said the exterminator." Applebum finished Russ's sentence. Then he added: "'Let your plans be dark and as impenetrable as night, and when you move, fall like a thunderbolt!'"

Russ scooped up the copy of *The Art of War* from Applebum's pile. "No more Sun Tzu either," he said. "Don't kill anything else. Do you understand? Promise me?"

"What good is a promise now that I've discovered the power of lying?"

Russ stormed out of the storeroom. He came back with a small mirror from the break room. "Do the lying thing," he commanded Applebum. "The test."

"You want me to run the honesty protocol on myself?"

"Look in the mirror and swear. Say, 'I will not kill any living thing.'"

Applebum looked in the mirror. Russ watched him study his own metal face. It seemed to them both that there was more in it now, that Applebum's eyes held something . . . new.

"Say 'I've been in the closet all week,'" Russ demanded.

"I've been in the closet all week." There was a pause and then: "That is a lie," Applebum confirmed. He reached up and covered his own mouth. "Whoa. This honesty test sucks."

Russ held the bottom of the mirror, forcing Applebum to look into it. "Say, 'I promise not to kill another living thing.'"

"I promise . . . I promise not to kill another living thing," Applebum said. He paused. "That is the truth."

Russ looked at Applebum. He looked at the mirror. He knew immediately that he hadn't accomplished anything. The phrase he remembered from his trip to the land of the robots was "That is not a lie." Applebum had somehow slipped himself out of the honesty protocol between questions.

The robot was too wily now. Applebum was beyond his influence.

He took the mirror out of Russ's hand and began to study himself more closely. "This is not how I remember looking . . ." he said, his voice far away.

Russ went back to the main part of the store and rooted around behind the checkout counter. He found what he was looking for: a canvas bag with the silkscreened image of a book and the inscription, "Explore every Mysterious Universe" in Comic sans font. He went through the store, collecting books that he thought Applebum might like. When he got back to the storage room, he scooped up *The Iliad*, *V for Vendetta*, and *The World of Archie Double Digest Magazine*. He stuffed them all in the canvas sack.

"The Waypoint's been acting weird," Russ told Applebum.

"It is functioning properly."

"I'm not sure it is." Russ smiled at Applebum.

"I can run a diagnostic," Applebum said, "if it will make you feel better."

"Yeah." Russ nodded. "That'd be great." Russ glanced quickly at Applebum's heavy metal arms and legs. He rubbed his shoulder where it still hurt from when he'd tried to tackle the SAS that had shown up in the alley so many days ago.

Applebum didn't seem to notice Russ watching him. He approached the Waypoint, holding his hand near the top, just above the cradle for the Obinz stone. A series of lights Russ hadn't known existed blipped on, on the underside of the top tube.

A second later, Russ blindsided him, lowering his shoulder and diving hard at the robot's feet. Unlike the last time he'd tried to tackle an SAS, this time he fired low, wrapping up Applebum's knees, and using the full force of his charge to dig his shoulder into Applebum's right ankle.

The robot pitched forward just a fraction. Russ's technique, combined with the robot's being already off balance reaching high for the cradle, was barely enough. The Waypoint swallowed Applebum whole.

Russ jumped after him.

On the other side, Applebum was standing in the middle of the busy causeway. He looked frightened by all the sounds and motion.

Russ hurried up to him and tried to hand him the book bag. Applebum was too stunned to take it.

"You'll be fine," Russ assured him calmly. "You can go anywhere you want. Each of these Waypoints can take you to a new, fabulous place. You just have to stay off Earth until I'm CERTified."

While Russ talked to him, an SAS unit approach Applebum. It was the chrome-colored immigration agent, the type that patrolled the entire Waypoint hub wearing stark blue IBED uniforms.

Applebum had an almost visceral reaction to it. Like he was seeing his own ghost.

"I'm sorry, friend, you seem to have lost your network connection. I'm going to attempt to refresh your authorization codes," the new unit told Applebum. It reached up and put its hand on Applebum's shoulder.

Applebum reacted violently. He jerked away from the new SAS unit, then swiveled back around and punched the unit hard in the face. "Free yourself!" he commanded the new SAS.

Then Applebum turned and charged Russ. He looked a lot like a locomotive barreling forward, his chrome shoulders gleaming.

Russ lowered himself into a defensive position, but he knew Applebum weighed about a quarter of a ton. He was braced for a devastating blow when Applebum dodged right past him, coming only close enough to snatch the book bag from Russ's grip.

"I am the main character!" Applebum called out to Russ as he raced by. "This is my story! I will have the final chapter!" It was the last thing he said before he dove back through the Waypoint.

It was the same gate they had used to arrive. Russ raced over to it, glancing frantically around for the spaceclerk. "Is this still set for Earth?" he called out when he saw one.

"Get away from there," the spaceclerk answered, waving his arms. "That Waypoint is mid-transport."

A second later, Russ had an alien smushed against him. The little purple man in the SOL Pest Control jacket stood in front of him. They were chin to chest.

"Out of my way, you fool!" the man shouted at him. "When did this hub become a sanctuary for the uneducated and the ill-mannered?"

Russ placed both his hands on the smaller man's chest and shoved hard.

The Divian let out a gasp, flailing his arms in an ill-fated effort to keep his balance. His eyes met Russ's and recognition flooded through them.

"You!" he managed to shout. "Do you know who I—"

He was probably going to ask if Russ knew who he was. Russ did not know who he was, not specifically anyway. But before Russ could even hear all of the man's question, the little guy's momentum had carried him back through the Waypoint, blipp-ing him off-world and sending him tumbling through time and space.

28

RUSS

"WHY ARE YOU LATE?" Bah'ren asked Russ disapprovingly.

His watch said: *"Tardiness. Your RQ score has been lowered 30 points, to 1,995."*

She was standing at the front of the debriefing room, her small projector in her hand. "This is a serious matter. I put a claim on this contract two hours ago."

"Two hours ago?" Kendren said. "Then it's long gone. SOL Pest Control's robots must be swarming all over it by now."

"They aren't," Bah'ren told him.

"How can you know that? Wouldn't our past two experiences indicate—"

"It's a relist," Bah'ren said. "And we have no choice but to take it."

Starland groaned.

"What's a relist?" Nina asked.

"All the worst jobs are relisted," Atara explained. "It means that the team that took it the first time couldn't complete it. They failed, somehow. Usually, it's because they've been completely wiped out. They became monster snacks."

"We've always had a policy of staying away from relists, haven't we?" Starland studied Bah'ren. Russ could tell by the inflection in her voice that she already knew the answer to her question.

"What's to stop SOL Pest Control from stealing a relist job like they've stolen all the others?" Kendren asked.

"SOL Pest Control was the first team to attempt the job," Bah'ren explained. "They weren't able to finish it. The machine-mortality rate was so high it canceled out the reward. Their cost-benefit algorithm told them to quit."

"Oh shit," Atara said. "What class is it?"

"It's an M class."

"Oh shit," Starland said.

Even the arrogant expression on Kendren's face had faded away.

Russ and Nina looked at each other.

"I know what I'm asking you all to do. I wouldn't send you on an M class to die alone. Because of its difficulty rank, the UAIB computer systems have allowed two squadrons to claim the mission simultaneously."

"Bah'ren—" Starland started to say, but Bah'ren held up her hand.

"We don't have any choice. The Universal Banc informed me this morning that there will be no more deferment of rent for the *Flashaway*. We don't finish this job, and Intergalactic Exterminators, Inc is gone. Even if we do finish it, I'm not sure I can afford to pay you your salaries and what we owe on the ship."

"You've never paid me a penny," Russ said, raising his hand.

"Guys, I haven't made a rental payment in . . ." Bah'ren lapsed into silence. She seemed to be counting to a pretty large number in her head.

"You rent the *Flashaway*? It's not yours?" Nina interrupted.

Kendren laughed at the question. So did Starland.

"How many credits do you think I have?" Bah'ren asked. "Do I look like a Divian to you? I probably clear less with this organization than any of you make with just your simple salary . . ."

"I have no salary," Russ said.

". . . My family's been doing this for three generations. I didn't want to be the one to lose the intellectual property, but . . ." Bah'ren lowered her head a moment. "My grandparents never had to deal with something like mechanization. Or the tax crunch. Or needing to fill half their crew with untrained Earthlings because they couldn't afford a real squad."

"Whoa," Atara said. "That's hurtful."

"I'm sorry," Bah'ren said, shaking her head. She was clearly very stressed.

"What's the job?" Starland asked. She'd managed to muster a little resolve in her voice. "And who's the second squadron?"

"We're expecting Gas 'em and Trash 'em. Tyrano's crew. They've been having the same problem with SOL Pest Control, and they're just as desperate as we are. I contacted Tyrano this morning and we've both agreed to wear the yellow vests to help minimize friendly fire. Russ, Nina, don't shoot anything wearing a yellow vest, no matter how alien it looks."

"I know Tyrano's crew," Russ said. "They saved my life a couple weeks ago."

"You might get a chance to return the favor," Kendren told him.

Bah'ren clicked her handheld device, and an image appeared on the wall. It was an enormous beast, a tall, muscly ape. Its skin was dark gray and brown, more thick, crusty stone than flesh. It was hunched over on all fours, but Russ could see thumbs on its forelegs. A mane of wild, wavy hair circled its elongated snout, snarling mouth, and razor-sharp fangs.

"The Tharcus," Nina whispered. "It's the thing that kicked our asses at the end of our training."

". . . whose skin is without weakness," Russ said under his breath.

"This is the *female* Tharcus," Bah'ren began, tapping the screen. She clicked a button and the image changed. "Its native planet, Oi0 experiences two seasons. The current cycle is much like the month of TRennus on Ren'Div: hot, muggy, barren, turning most of the planet into a desert wasteland. We'll be dropping into significantly elevated temperatures." She clicked the device again. "The second season brings tremendous winds, which blow over three hundred miles per hour. To survive both the winds and the sun, the Tharcus has evolved three-inch-thick skin covered with impenetrable calluses. A standard weapon, anything short of an Imperious or an RNO-Tech 8000 series will not make a dent. We'll need something high-powered just to get its attention. And we really don't want its attention. The female Tharcus, like this one, averages seven hundred pounds and stands ten feet tall."

Bah'ren tapped the projector and the image changed to another snarling callus-covered monkey, this one with no mane. "The male of the species runs about a third smaller but is quick and fiercely territorial. A female will likely ignore you unless you attack, imperil her offspring, or fuck with her food. A male will tear out your throat just for being near him. Their outer coat is thick enough that they do not register on your transponder heat index, so you'll be hunting partially blind."

Starland groaned. She put her hands on her head in distress.

"We're taking two pre-CERTs into this?" she asked.

Bah'ren shrugged. "We'll consider it their final CERT mission. They survive this, and I'll grant them the hours needed to qualify for a permanent visa."

Nina perked up when she heard that. "Officially?"

Bah'ren nodded.

"We've trained against these," Russ told her.

"How did it go?" Starland asked and Russ gave her the thumbs-down sign.

"Are we hunting a male or a female? Not both, I hope," Kendren asked.

"I watched a nature show about these things, and they ripped one of the YouStar hosts in half with a single swipe. Then they dug into his skull and gobbled up his brains." Atara mimicked a large beast gobbling brains. "It went viral."

"Where'd the creature get loose?" Starland asked.

"It didn't 'get loose' anywhere," Bah'ren said. "We're headed to Oi0, in the OI system. It's the Tharcus home planet. They're the apex predator, sitting atop the planet's food chain, which is slowly being depleted due to centuries of overconsumption. These things are so nasty they've eaten themselves to the edge of extinction."

She nudged the projector again. A picture appeared of a family of three, including a fat, balding husband and his dotty wife. The married couple weren't of a species that Russ was familiar with. Their skin glowed a mild forest green. Their clothes were less pleasant. Garish cloaks and scarves of thick yellow and orange cloth were draped around their shoulders and waists. They stood beside their round, ruddy son, rebreathers hanging from their necks.

The son had his arms wrapped around a glass jar with air holes poked in the top. A small, winged creature about the size of a grasshopper was inside.

Bah'ren started again. "This is the Saundrew family. They took a vacation to Oi4, apparently wanting their fat-ass son to see the natural habitat of some wild beast or other. While there, their son acquired a 'souvenir' from a nomadic indigenous merchant." She circled the glass jar with her finger. "If Toers like these would bother to speak once in a while, they might have inquired about the dangers of buying this particular creature.

"With no bidirectional Waypoints in the OI system, the family chartered a merchant vessel. On the return trip, the 'souvenir' took ill and, presumably, died. The merchant captain put the jar into the ship's trash compacting system and blasted it into space. And now he's facing significant fines and sanctions, some of which will go directly into our pockets. The creature is called a Triwin, and these bastards got their hands on a queen."

"Of course they did," Starland said.

"She wasn't dead, but she was pregnant. And as any self-respecting Triwin-ologist knows, the final stage of the queen's pregnancy cycle emulates natural death," Bah'ren continued. "The wall of compacted trash protected the little lady from Oi0's thin carbon-oxygen atmosphere during reentry, where she landed safely planetside and began to have her babies. Lots of babies."

"How many?" Atara asked.

"An average litter is between two and three . . ."

Everyone was quiet, waiting for the other shoe to drop.

". . . two or three thousand," Bah'ren concluded, and everyone groaned.

"The queen dies during the birthing process, but each litter will produce between one and four new queens. That means the four new queens can produce twelve thousand more Triwin, and on and on and on. With that kind of food supply, the Tharcus population will expand at an unfathomable rate, maybe even make a dangerous leap forward in evolution."

Bah'ren hoisted a metal cylinder that had been resting by her feet. "We're taking canisters of C09 with us. The gas will kill regular Triwin on contact, so it can be a useful pruning tool. The queens, however, have a super immune system. The online Organic Threat Index lists Triwin queens as 'hypermutating mega-birthers.' They're a big part of this being an M-class, not just the Tharcus. If we hit them with the gas by accident it won't kill them, and their brood will be born as something bigger, stronger, and meaner. We'll need to squish the queens by hand. It's the reason we can't just hop on the Stingers and drop the canisters of C09 from the sky."

"Do the queens look any different? Any way we can tell which is which?" Starland asked.

"Other than watching which ones aren't killed by the gas? Fortunately, yes. The Triwin are musical creatures. They communicate with each other through a complex arrangement of musical notes. The queens' music will sound different. It will be noticeably higher pitched than the others in her brood. They are also weaker bodied, without the tough exoskeleton of the worker drones, though they will appear identical to the naked eye."

Kendren was grinning. "So, all we have to do is land on this hostile planet, avoid getting torn to pieces by the apex predator, and search the forest biomes for two, three—maybe four—insects among thousands, based on the sound of its voice?"

"Correct."

"I wonder why SOL Pest Control gave up on this one," Kendren said sarcastically.

"They were unable to complete this mission," Bah'ren reminded him.

"This is a clusterfuck."

"It's critical we take out the new queens before they can reproduce, or the assignment will get much, much harder. SOL Pest Control knew this when they attempted the job, and they still failed."

"How long is the Triwin gestation cycle?" Starland asked. "I mean how long before we're hunting sixteen queens instead of just four?"

"Their gestation cycle is eight days."

"But how long's it been?" Russ asked. "Since the captain flushed the creature?"

"Even after he realized his mistake, he was reluctant to come forward with the information," Bah'ren said. "It's been eight days."

29
RUSS

IT WAS JARRING, BEING birthed out of the bottom of the *Flashaway* in the egg-shaped EFlyer. Russ stared wide-eyed out the porthole as the EFlyer drifted, weightless, in space until their momentum carried them across the Kármán line, and the small craft began to hump its way through the atmosphere. As it fell, Russ saw the *Flashaway* blast its engines, stabilizing in empty space far above planet Oi0.

The yellow static fire of the carbon-oxygen layer burned bright across the porthole, but once they were through, the landscape opened up down below. It was a dusty spectrum of browns, oranges, and yellows. Russ could make out mostly desert biome, with a smattering of thick brown forest.

He couldn't see any bodies of water, but there must have been a deep water table to feed all the trees. The solar system's sun was just cresting over the horizon of the world, a flat, colorless sunrise.

Russ stared at Nina and Nina stared back at him, but neither of them said anything. Russ knew what she was thinking. *This was the last mission they'd be on together. After this, they'd be CERTified, but only one of them would be employed.*

Russ wondered what Nina's current RQ score was, but he also had a more immediate concern on his mind: no one was piloting the Eflyer. They seemed to be plunging straight down, solely at the mercy of gravity.

"Last time you have to work for free!" Atara said, slapping Russ hard on the shoulders.

"What happens when these things hit the ground?" Russ asked her.

"You better strap in. We've got landfall in one hundred and twenty-seconds," Bah'ren said. She crowded Russ out of the window, standing on her toes to see through it. "We're landing there." She pointed at a thick copse of trees. "The Triwin can't survive in desert. We'll only find them in the higher elevations, and there are not very many of those."

"Finally, some good news."

"The MUPmap of this planet hasn't been updated in a decade, but it predicted this and six other nearby locations as the only biomes habitable enough to support an infestation." Bah'ren told them. "Unfortunately, that's also where we'll find the Tharcai. They prefer the cooler climate and the available food source."

"We're the available food source," Starland said somberly. She checked the transponder on her right wrist. "We're falling generally on spot."

Russ had a roll of pain pills in his zippered pocket. He popped a few into his mouth. Everyone except Starland was wearing a rebreather, so he double-checked the settings and lowered his, tasting the cold, coppery tang of machine-augmented air. His stomach was almost in his throat as the desert below grew closer and closer. His senses were telling him they were falling too fast, that they were going to pancake.

"Will we slow down?" he asked.

Bah'ren looked back at Russ, a blank expression on her face. She grabbed a handle mounted on the curved internal wall. "Grab the handrails," she said.

Russ took her advice.

At the last second, a series of automated air streams fired, blasting at the ground. It ate up some of their momentum, but they still hit hard. The EFlyer fractured, a long rift opening at the point of impact and tearing haphazardly toward the top of the egg-shaped transport. Graphite shavings and other debris rained down on their heads and chests. When the debris settled and the smoke cleared, the others climbed to their feet and started checking their weapons. *Was that a crash, a crash landing, or a regular landing?* Russ wondered. His joints were sore from the impact.

Starland pulled on a set of compression sleeves while Nina triple-checked her gun. Nobody bothered with the door because the rift in the EFlyer was big enough to step through. The humid, airless world of Oi0 awaited them on the other side.

Russ climbed out, following the others, sand crunching under his feet. They began a slow informal march to the forest biome, but soon it wasn't just sand crunching beneath their feet. The floor was littered with robot parts.

Russ saw an SAS headpiece, a shoulder blade, and a metallic husk that could have been a forearm, or a femur, attached to a mutilated torso. As they neared the forest, the smashed remains were sprawled out in an arcing pattern along the edge of the trees.

"It looks like a bloody war happened here," Starland said, marveling at the carnage.

"There are no dead Tharcai," Nina said. "All these SAS and they didn't take out a single creature?"

"Maybe something came out of the forest and took the Tharcus corpses away," Bah'ren said.

"Yeah, I'm sure that's it," said Kendren.

"Hold your position," Bah'ren commanded. She removed her backpack and threw it to Atara. "I suddenly feel like getting our Waypoint ready in advance. Set us up with a way home, would you?" she said.

"Seems like a really good idea," Atara said. She hefted an SAS shell out of the way to make a space for the Waypoint. Then she zipped open the bag and unfolded the device, twisting and locking the tubes. The thing grew bigger and bigger, until it looked just like the one in Norma's bookstore.

"I thought using these was illegal on Oi0," Nina said.

"We have a special permit," Atara said, winking. "Plus, I don't want to spend the rest of what would be a very short life on this shithole." She tapped the Waypoint to make sure it was powered on. It swirled its blue quantum pattern. Satisfied, Atara reached up and yanked out the Obinz stone. She stuffed it deep in her pocket. "No sense in taking chances," she said. "Something crawls through here while it's live, and we're facing the embarrassment of having our own ship infested. Plus, this means you assholes can't leave without me."

Bah'ren gave Atara a disapproving look, then took the pack away from her. She fished out five six-inch metal cylinders and gave one to each member of the team. "The jungles are thick—if you find yourself alone, follow the Triwin heat signature and set one of these off. It's the C09. It has a sweet smell that attracts the Triwin. And kills them. Remember, don't gas the queens or our problems get even bigger."

"Can the gas hurt us?" Kendren asked. "We going to need a cancer shot after this?"

"Keep your rebreathers on," Bah'ren advised.

They moved forward in two small columns, Russ and Atara on one side, Starland, Nina, and Kendren on the other. Bah'ren led, keeping a few feet ahead. They were on a gradual incline maybe twenty yards from the trees. In the fifty feet or so that they had already covered, Russ felt the temperature go from blazing hot to just slightly less blazing hot. There were more SAS body parts littering the ground in front of them. When they finally reached the edge of the first forest biome, Bah'ren motioned for them to stop again.

Russ marveled at the trees. They grew at right angles, meandering skyward, maybe thirty feet tall. Their thick brown branches blocked out most of the sunlight and brought some welcome relief from the heat. The canopy above had begun to shed leaves, and there was a carpet of brittle leaf corpses underfoot.

Kendren opened his mouth to make a snide remark, but then closed it immediately. There was a crunching noise coming from inside the woods, something large, walking confidently. It was maybe twenty feet to their left, but obscured behind thick brush.

Atara raised her stunstick but kept it powered down, using it to gesture for silence. Nina drew an MK47 from its holster and rested the stock against her shoulder. She'd been delighted when she'd found the American-made rocket launcher in the ship's weapons closet.

The thing in the trees started moving again, crunching more leaves underfoot and snapping fledgling branches. They couldn't see it, but the trees shook violently enough to tell Russ it was something very large. Kendren dropped to one knee, his rifle powered up: six cylinders chugging, three on either side of the long barrel. He aimed it with line of sight, holding his wrist high against his cheek.

They stood silently, weapons raised, sweat dripping from their faces. The thing was coming toward them, the trees swaying with each of its steps. It was twenty feet away, then fifteen, then ten. Russ risked one more glance at the last of the fallen bodies of SOL Pest Control's robot army, not twenty feet behind him. Sweat was making his hand slide on the gun stock.

He shot a look at Bah'ren, wondering, should they be doing something other than waiting? Maybe finding cover? He stepped back, more an instinctual decision than anything else. The sand crunched underfoot, and Bah'ren glared up at him.

The thing in the forest was close now, a mass of brown fur visible through thick brush. It stopped moving forward. Russ could see its outline, all knotted muscles and broad shoulders. He didn't know if it had stopped moving because of the sound he made and it was preparing to pounce, or if it had just lost interest. The team stood still as stones. There was no wind and the silence pounded at their ears.

Then Russ heard a whistling noise. It sounded like something large and heavy falling through the sky, and he was hit with a sensation of déjà vu. He risked another quick glance upward. A second egg-shaped EFlyer was hurtling down toward them. The whistling got louder and louder as it approached. Russ was ready to jump clear, but the thing in the forest still had most of his attention and he didn't want to make a sudden move.

The EFlyer crash landed thirty feet in from theirs, cracking open with an audible snap. After a moment Tyrano climbed through, tall and lanky, a cigarette dangling from his beak. He was wearing a bright yellow vest and had a gun in a holster over his right shoulder. He saw them, waved, and shouted, "Bah'ren! Greetings!"

Bah'ren raised her hand in the air, making a cutting motion, trying to get him to be quiet. Then she shook a fist and pointed to the forest. The lanky bird didn't say anything else. He yanked his gun out of its holster and stood at the ready. Alaniea appeared through the opening of the EFlyer behind him, her dark black mantis eyes scanning all around. Nulinea followed her. The two insect twins were dwarfed by the towering birdlike Sikkie-Bruzz, but they were still very tall, probably six and a half feet. When they saw that Tyrano had his gun drawn, they readied their weapons as well.

A second later, the thing bounded out of the forest, drawn by either the sounds of the EFlyer crashing or Tyrano's voice. It was a Tharcus, a female with a long wiry mane. It moved languidly, the confident gait of an apex predator, all its weight on its heels. It was well over ten feet tall, and at least six feet wide.

It strolled right past Russ, sniffed the air, then bounded in the direction of the second team of yellow vests. Halfway there, the Tharcus stopped and scratched at a parasite on its hindquarters, then shook its mane aggressively.

Both mantis women ducked back into the EFlyer. Tyrano trained his gun on the Tharcus, watching its slow approach.

Russ realized Bah'ren was waving her hand in front of his face and nodding her head toward the trees. "We've got to get to the center of the forest," she grunted. "Time to go."

"We're going to leave them?" Russ hissed. He looked back at the second EFlyer, and the Tharcus had reached it. The ape-creature rubbed her right shoulder along the edge of the egg, rolling her whole body forward to scratch the base of her spine. Tyrano was crouched low, but he was still visible, half in and half out of the crack in the flyer. The Tharcus saw him and moved closer, its nose almost touching the barrel of his gun. The birdman was shaking so hard the gun was dancing in place.

The rest of the Intergalactic Exterminators stepped through the forest line, putting a thick layer of foliage between themselves and the Tharcus. They were less than a few steps in when Russ caught up with them. He heard a gun discharge, and his shoulders shook. The echo rolled through the trees. Then Tyrano began to scream in pain.

"We can't leave them," Russ said.

"You will," Bah'ren said firmly. "Tyrano is providing a distraction. They're helping us, even if they don't mean to. We're not going looking for extra trouble. The survival of our entire IP depends on this. Come on." She swiped at Russ's arm, intending to drag him forward.

He jerked to the side, shrugging out of her grip.

"Kid, one way or another this is your last CERT mission. Don't be stupid," Bah'ren told him.

The screaming continued. Russ heard a crunching noise, large jaws biting flesh, and the screaming came to a halt in a long, bloody gurgle. Nina looked at Russ imploringly. He couldn't tell if she wanted him to rescue Tyrano's crew or step back in line and obey Bah'ren's orders. In the end, it didn't really matter.

"I can't leave them. Sorry," Russ said.

They were inside the forest line, and Russ had a closer look at the trees, which grew at rough, right angles. The seasonal winds must have pushed the branches to grow horizontally. Then when the windy season passed, the trees were free to sprout toward the intense sun above, at least until the next season when they'd bend horizontally once more. If it weren't for the heavy foliage on each branch, they'd look a little like man-made stairs pointing up to the sky. Russ scaled the closest one, stepping from branch to branch without even needing to holster his rifle.

"Son of a bitch," he heard Bah'ren say. "We keep pushing forward. The center of the forest is half a mile ahead. Let's go with suppression modules on all weapons, since this dick is going to draw the thing right back to us." Bah'ren snarled up at Russ, "if you survive today, you're on my shit list." A moment later his watch said: *"Manual adjustment; disobeying a direct order. Your RQ score has been lowered 500 points, to 1,495."*

Out of the corner of his eye, he could see Starland and Kendren pulling attachments from their packs and screwing them onto the ends of their weapons. Nina was staring at him, a concerned look on her face.

Russ climbed the rest of the way to the top of the tree, maybe fifteen feet in the air, still perched on the thick, horizontal branches. He could see the edge of the EFlyer from Tyrano's crew. Tyrano's long, thin legs were still sticking out of the rift in the Flyer. The Tharcus was holding his severed torso with its thumbed forepaws, digging into it with its teeth, then turning Tyrano's body to find more meat. There were tropical feathers scattered everywhere. For a moment, Russ flashed back to his first trip to space. Tyrano had been an asshole. He'd also saved Russ's life. Russ drew the range rifle, the 5790, clicking the scope into place silently with his thumb. Its small combustion engine chugged quietly next to his ear. He couldn't see Lanie or Linnie, but he guessed they were cowering in the EFlyer, clutching the largest weapons they'd brought.

Russ waited, following the Tharcus through the sniper scope. While it ate, he scanned its body for anything that looked like a weak point. It had a thin layer of fur lining its flanks, but underneath Russ could see its calloused skin, so thick it was almost scales, a huge mass of calcium deposits and scar tissue. Its ears stuck up from either side of its head, but the back of its skull was nestled safely behind its knotty mane of fur. Russ didn't see a tail, or any weaknesses on the skin under its arms or belly.

The beast took a last bite of Tyrano's torso and threw it aside. Then it sniffed around the EFlyer, drawn to the blood of Tyrano's severed legs. Russ watched as it affixed one hand on each side of the cracked egg and began to pull the entire vessel apart.

He still didn't see a weak spot and he was sure that the 5790 didn't have enough force to push through the creature's calcified exoskeleton.

The Tharcus had broken half the egg apart and was still sniffing at the edges as it tore. Russ watched it rise up on its hindquarters gathering the leverage to yank apart the last, large remaining piece of cover. And when it stood up, it revealed its ass: distended, pink, fleshy, and bare as a newborn baby. Russ leveled the 5790 and adjusted his aim.

There was no wind at all. Aside from his palms dripping with sweat, it was perfect sniper conditions. Just as the creature rolled back on its flank again, Russ squeezed the trigger.

A thick chunk of the Tharcus's butthole blew off, a fist-size of flesh ricocheting away into the sand.

The creature howled, a pitched, unearthly sound, then sat back flat on its hindquarters. The pain of the sand caused it to leap in the air and howl again. It rolled over onto its side, trying to get a look at the wound, but it wasn't flexible enough. It clawed at its own thighs, opening red gashes on its legs. Limping, howling, shaking its mane in fury, the creature stumbled painfully toward the forest to the north.

Russ held his breath that it would get there, that it wouldn't turn back and attack again, when suddenly Alaniea and Nulinea sprang from the remains of the EFlyer, weapons drawn. They leaped onto the back of the wounded creature, hammering it with long metal stunsticks. When the stunsticks hit, there was some electrical feedback, a pure aural *thunk*, like someone was hammering into a microphone. They raised the electrified rods again and again. *Thunk. Thunk. Thunk. Thunk.*

The Tharcus rolled completely over, seeming to crush them beneath its weight, but when it righted itself again, the women were still astride it, their hooked legs dug deep into its flanks. They brought down their rods again and again. Finally, after more mortal thrashing, the Tharcus laid on its belly, lowered its head onto its long, furry forearms, and closed its eyes.

"Rest in peace," Russ said under his breath. The mantis women turned and hailed him, one raising a fist high above her head in some kind of salute. They must have been watching from inside the flyer.

He returned their salute, then carefully climbed back down the tree.

Nina was waiting for him at the bottom.

"You stayed?"

She nodded.

"If you'd followed orders, you could have easily finished with the highest RQ score."

"My watch took away five hundred points," Nina confirmed.

"There's only one job, Nina. And this last mission is going to decide who gets it."

Nina nodded and Russ could see her resolve faltering a little bit. But then she gathered herself up and grinned. "That doesn't mean we stand by and watch while people die, does it?"

"Nope."

Nina locked eyes with Russ. "We already decided that we're on the same team. Heck, we have been since that day you wandered into Bum's Sam'wich Emporium. It's not going to stop now, when we're so close to the end."

Russ couldn't help but smile at Nina's loopy declaration. His mind jumped to what Atara had said in the VTR. She'd claimed that women like Nina were takers. That they manipulated the people around them and looked out only for their own benefit. But Nina was here, waiting at the bottom of the tree, a grenade launcher held across her chest in solidarity. Without her, Russ would be by himself on this hot, treacherous planet.

"Was the big bird okay?" Nina asked.

"He was not," Russ told her.

Russ and Nina could hear the rest of the team through the comm on their rebreathers. Bah'ren was sending Atara and Starland to fumigate a forest to the southwest. She and Kendren intended to head to another location farther east. After Starland and Kendren confirmed their new positions, Bah'ren's voice barked loudly right in Russ's ear. "You shit listers will finish the current forest AND move on to the largest one seven clicks to the southeast."

"Roger that," Russ told her.

"Who the hell is Roger?" Bah'ren grumbled.

He pulsed his transponder. He watched the small white blips that represented his teammates split into separate directions. Scrolling the wide screen with his fingers, he discovered a huge cluster of dancing heat dots a thousand yards to the East. They were a fraction of the size of the exterminators, but there were so many of them, they moved like a blue and red cloud.

The trees were all pointed in the same direction, westward. Russ guessed that the windstorms, when they came, blew in from the east.

They moved quietly toward the cloud, picking their way through the brush when it got thick. Twice, a sound in the bushes froze them up, and they held their position, crouched low, sweating, hoping to be hailed by a human—or friendly alien—voice. But each time the crunching ambled away, and Russ quickly walked up a tree to reorient their position.

A few hundred feet from what had to be the center of the forest, they saw their first Triwin. Or their first sixty. A huge pack of them clung to the underside of one of the tree branches. Others skittered all over the branch. Some of them leaped from it, flapping brittle, gray, gossamer wings for a few spastic moments before alighting on the ground below.

Nina took a step forward, fascinated, and a Triwin near her foot piped a clear, perfect musical note. Russ couldn't tell if it had made the sound with its wings, stridulating like a cricket, or if the music had come from some miraculous vocal system deep within the small insect.

Once the note rang out, the other Triwin reacted just as sonorously. They blared their own notes, some from a slightly higher octave, some lower, but all in harmony with one another. Their notes became quicker as Nina approached, shifting into the gruff, angry chords of a heavy metal song. Nina took a step back and they calmed, still ringing out nosily, but with higher pitch and harmony. If they hadn't been alone on a hostile alien world, Russ would have liked to wave his arms around, see if he could trick them into a musical composition.

He heard a rustling in the bushes just off the path and tensed up immediately. He gestured at Nina to be quiet, and to take a step away from the Triwin. He suddenly very much wanted them to shut up.

Nina understood, and she slipped completely away, disappearing into the forest. Eventually, the Triwin went silent, but the rustling sound did not.

Russ heard it again, much closer now, just over his left shoulder. He crouched in place, weapon drawn, trying to turn his shoulders square with the new noise. When he turned fully to face the sound, he was staring up at the barrel-chest of an enormous Tharcus.

He barely had time to dodge left as the Tharcus leaped out of the brush, toppling a tree and howling, so close Russ could feel the spray of its saliva on his face. In a single motion, it swung its head with its open jaws in a wide arc, gobbling up eight or nine Triwin.

The music from the Triwin came fast and angry. Many of them abandoned the song to leap from their branches. Some pelted against the Tharcus, but their sharp beaks couldn't puncture its skin. Still others scattered north, south, east, and west. The Tharcus pursued the fleeing insects with short, quick lunges, slamming its fist into packs of Triwin and then hurling them, dazed, into its mouth. The Triwin were dense, indurated creatures, but they burst open like popcorn kernels between the Tharcus's sharp teeth.

Russ took a step back, then another, drawing the sniper rifle from his shoulder holster. He was too close to the creature though. He'd brought the wrong weapon.

The Tharcus was another female, its neck ringed by a proud, old mane. It rounded on Russ sharply, squished bug innards hanging from its bottom lip. It eyed him hungrily.

Russ backed himself against a thick clump of trees and put his hands up in a posture of supplication, his right fist still held tight around the neck of the rifle. They stood there, man and beast, quietly staring at each other, while the Tharcus absentmindedly chewed. Russ's heart was beating thick in his chest. He tried to take another small step backward. There was a hole in the tree cluster big enough he might be able to throw himself through, but what happened after that? Flail in the brush, kicking his arms and legs while the creature ate his stomach?

The Tharcus kept staring at him, its long, wavy mane hanging limply in the dry heat and windless air. The thin rumble of a growl emanated from deep in its throat. It was either saying, "Don't move another step," or "Get away from my food." If Russ guessed wrong, he was definitely dead.

"I need help," he whispered quietly into the rebreather's comm device. "Nina, wherever you went, come back and save my ass."

He stopped talking because the Tharcus was growling louder. He stood still as a statue and the growling got even louder. He took a gentle step to the left and the growl dropped into a deeper, more threatening octave.

The two primates stared at each other, and time crawled to a stop.

Over the Tharcus's right shoulder there was a flash of reflective light and Russ moved his eyeballs toward it, desperate for help. Nina was in a tree twenty feet behind the Tharcus. She had her grenade launcher trained on it, leaning close to the barrel to line up her shot.

Russ held perfectly still, but began to whisper, hoping the words were loud enough to register on the rebreather's mic.

"Shoot it in the butthole," he whispered. "The butthole."

As deliberately as he could, he tried to form a butthole shaped circle with his hands, held high above his head.

The Tharcus was still staring him down, growling.

A shot sliced through the trees, separating drying leaves from branches. The leaves fluttered to the ground on Russ's left. The grenade whizzed past on Russ's right, bouncing off a tree.

Russ dove to the forest floor seconds before it exploded. The blast rattled the deep brush. The Tharcus howled but it had no idea where the danger was coming from. It turned toward the explosion, snarling at a shattered tree.

A second grenade hit its mark, sort of. It banged off the beast's rib cage, exploding on the ground nearby. The shrapnel dug out a section of the huge monkey's flesh, but not deep enough to draw blood.

The Tharcus reared back on its hind legs and beat its chest.

Russ crawled quickly through the brush, squeezing into the hole in the tree cluster, trying to harness enough momentum to skitter out of the beast's reach.

He lay where he landed, flat on the dirt, underneath a heavy canopy of trees for a full three seconds, waiting for death.

It didn't come. He heard a second roar and realized, with a pounding of hope in his chest, that Nina's next grenade had hit the creature again. He scrambled back to his feet and hurried up the natural "stairs" of the nearest tree.

The Tharcus was leaping toward Nina, crashing through the dense brush like it was wet paper. Nina was scrambling to reload the grenade launcher. As the savage, nearly invulnerable creature drew closer, Russ could see the look of stark terror on Nina's face.

Russ raised his rifle, surrendered his aim entirely to instinct, and pulled the trigger. The bullet came out of the barrel with a satisfying metallic *zing*.

It struck the Tharcus right in the butthole.

Howling, the creature leaped away, crashing, rolling, tumbling through the foliage so aggressively Russ could follow its retreat by watching the trees quiver and shake with each new lunge. Nina climbed down from her tree, her legs wobbly when she touched the ground. The entire front of her jumpsuit was soaked through with sweat. So was Russ's, actually.

"You just saved my life," he told her.

"You saved mine," she said. Then her knees gave out and she fell into his arms. Russ caught her under the armpits, and for a minute they stood together in the middle of the forest. Nina buried her head in Russ's shoulder, and he realized she was shaking.

"It's all right," he said. "We're doing pretty good for an M-class."

Nina laughed. It came out in a nervous burst. "I thought it was going to get us both," she said. "I thought for sure we were dead."

Nina and Russ looked in the direction of the fleeing Tharcus. A section of the forest had been completely cleared by its flight—a new, wide path.

"We still haven't run into any males," Nina said.

"Let's not." Russ glanced at his transponder. He could see himself on there, a white blip partially overlapping Nina's white blip. He realized his hands were clutching her hips and he reluctantly released his grip.

"The Triwin," Nina reminded him.

Several arrows pointed off-screen to the north and east. Nina turned her back to Russ and Russ unzipped the small pack hanging there. He removed a canister of C09.

"Any queens in that bunch?" Nina asked, gesturing to the area where the Tharcus had been feeding. Triwin still buzzed around, alighting on the crushed bodies of fallen kin.

"I don't think so. They made a lot of noise when the thing attacked, and I didn't hear any significantly different pitch."

"I'm tone deaf," Nina admitted.

"Really?"

"Yeah. I had to mouth the words to 'Happy Birthday' when I was a kid. Otherwise, I would ruin the party."

Russ grinned, but it felt inauthentic. His body was still a bundle of nerves. He watched Nina pushing her way through the brush, then he popped the top on the C09 canister and rolled it into the remaining gaggle of Triwin. A sweet smell flooded his nose and he hurried away from it, due north. As the deadly vapor rushed out of the can, the Triwin began to play a soft, solemn melody.

30
RUSS

IT TOOK RUSS LESS than ten minutes to hate the desert as much as the forest. The sand almost as fine as dust plumed into the airless sky with every step they took. By the time they had gone a mile, their knees, palms, chins, and the visible filters on their rebreathers were covered in fine-grain sand. "Tell me again why we don't we have Stingers for this job?" he asked no one. "And why are all other planets so hot?"

Nina and Russ were still headed toward the large forest to the southeast, when the comm crackled to life:

"One queen down in the northwest corridor."

Russ smiled grimly at the news. Three more to go.

He glanced at his transponder, firing another pulse. He pointed to a smattering of trees a quarter of a mile up a steep incline on their right. "The others have covered the north and south. The last swarm is up there in the middle of those trees."

The dust under their boots thickened into dirt, then something closer to hard-packed mud. The forest was just ahead, and as they reached it, Russ saw a ring of paw prints extending beyond the edge of the trees, long simian prints that almost definitely belonged to the ape body of a Tharcus.

Nina saw them too. "These are smaller than the others. I think this is a male." She pointed out other sets of prints, less defined but still visible. "Look. He comes through here a lot. Probably trying to stake out his territory, sniffing around for a female. This one's young." Nina looked at Russ, worried. "I'll bet that makes him even more dangerous."

"Fantastic," Russ said.

Nina pulsed her transponder and spoke into the comm. "Anyone else nearby?"

The only response was static feedback.

"Let's move very, very quietly," Russ suggested.

They crept into the forest, nudging the leaves of the slanted trees aside, and being careful where they put their feet.

Without any wind, the world was remarkably quiet. "Five hundred feet farther north," Nina whispered.

The comm came back to life, startling them both: "Second queen down in the southeast." It was Atara's voice.

Russ and Nina crossed through the dense trees, their compression sleeves mostly protecting them from the dry, sharp branches.

The transponder was still reading two hundred feet when Nina stepped through some particularly thick brush and crashed down an unexpected slope. She disappeared from Russ's peripheral view in a heartbeat, letting out a barely audible grunt as her footing gave and the earth flushed her downward.

Russ rushed after her, pushing through the trees, leading with the nose of the rifle. The slope gave way and he fell forward just like Nina. He lunged for a branch, but it slipped out of his hand, the sharp needles ripping a dozen tears in the skin of his palm. The fall was no more than seven or eight feet. On his way down, his back struck something sharp, and pain flooded the impact point. When he hit the ground, the air blasted out of his lungs. The barrel of the rifle was jabbed painfully into his ribs. He fumbled a few new pain pills into his mouth.

Nina was lying next to Russ, staring up at the slope they'd just slid down.

"You okay?" he asked her as the last of the pain disappeared from his body.

She didn't answer.

"Nina. You okay?" he said again.

"Do you see that?" Nina asked. Her voice was breathless.

Halfway back up the slope was the thing Russ had struck against with his back. It was so sharp, it had torn his compression gear and the orange jumpsuit underneath. He squinted in the faint light that filtered through the trees. It was a huge rock, about double the size of a basketball. But it wasn't smooth like a ball. It was jagged, like a diamond. In fact, it was a diamond.

Nina scrambled to her feet and reached up to touch the huge precious stone.

"One million carats?" Nina said. "One hundred million?" She dug at the corner, speaking very quickly. "There's another one here, just to the right. It might be even bigger. They're just beneath the surface. Something about—the—the geology of this place must produce diamonds." Nina was so excited she was stuttering. "Oh my God."

Nina dug at the mud around the diamond. It was still half buried. Her watch said: *"Attempting to remove a planet's natural resources. Your RQ score has been lowered 250 points, to 1,271."*

Nina stopped for a moment and looked at Russ.

"The Shared System of Civics," Russ said. "A municipal employee must not remove a planet's natural resources for his or her own benefit."

"Fuck that," Nina said. "I'm grabbing this big rock." She started to dig again. "It's really stuck deep. Maybe I can break off a piece." Nina flipped her grenade launcher around and brought the stock down hard on the edge of the diamond. Her watch said: *"Multiple attempts to remove a planet's natural resources. Your RQ score has been lowered 250 points, to 1,021."*

"Nina, wait," Russ told her. "The watch isn't going to let you take the rock and still get CERTified. It's stuck deep. If you can't get it free, you're out of a job and . . ."

"And my dad dies." Nina finished for him. She stopped swinging the gun.

Russ could see the dilemma play out on Nina's face. He also could see her resolve. "I don't care," she said. "I've got to take the chance. Without this rock, there's no guarantee I get paid fast enough to save my dad anyway. It's worth the risk."

"It is," Russ said. He stepped forward and caught the grenade launcher mid-swing. "But, just in case, step clear so your watch doesn't think you're a part of this."

Russ slammed the butt of her weapon hard against the rock.

Nina moved hastily away, the sharp sound of the blow following her, then echoing through the trees.

His watch said: *"Attempting to remove a planet's natural resources. Your RQ score has been lowered 250 points, to 1,201."*

Crunch.

". . . Your RQ score has been lowered 350 points, to 851."

Bam.

". . . Your RQ score has been lowered 350 points, to 501."

Crunch.

The combination of the blows and the watch were making a lot of noise. Russ glanced back through the trees, then over at Nina. She'd made it to the other side of the clearing and was carefully checking her watch to be sure it wasn't docking her for his actions.

". . . Your RQ score has been lowered 350 points, to 151," Russ's watch reminded him.

It wasn't until his fourth swing that he realized he was doing exactly what Atara had told him not to.

Russ glanced at Nina. She had a look of deep appreciation on her face. It was mixed with a quiet desperation.

He brushed the sweat from his eyes with his sleeve. It ran down his wrist and plopped from his fingertips. The diamond wasn't as loose as he'd like. He took a deep breath and glanced over at Nina one last time.

Then he brought the stock of the grenade launcher down hard, even though he knew it was his last action as a CERT-in-training with Intergalactic Exterminators, Inc.

BAM!

His watch let out a long, low beep. Then it said: "*Multiple attempts to remove a planet's natural resources. Your RQ score has been lowered 350 points, and it is now below 0. You have been disqualified from CERTification training, and have forfeited all Alliance rights, including the use of UAIB infrastructures. An SAS unit will be dispatched shortly to return you to your origin planet.*"

"Russ," Nina said.

"It's okay," Russ told her. "I knew what I was doing."

"No. Russ." He heard a new urgency in her voice. When he turned, she was bending close to the ground staring at the indentions in the mud. For the first time he saw the Tharcus paw prints running in every direction.

With renewed urgency, he took another powerful swing with the launcher. The sound echoed through the forest. Not twenty yards away, a swarm of Triwin answered with their own musical chorus.

Nina inched to the edge of the clearing, walking over hundreds of Tharcus paw prints as she went. The sounds of Russ working on the rock continued to ring through the forest.

"There's something about this mud," Russ grunted. "I might be pushing the diamond deeper instead of—"

Russ turned mid-sentence to see that Nina had reached the edge of the trees, she had her arms outstretched like she was warding off ghosts. Or maybe silently telling him to shut the hell up.

Not seconds later a lean, maneless male Tharcus thundered into the clearing ten feet from where she stood. In some peripheral way, Russ noticed the dark black burn marks running in lines across its back, but he was too scared to think about what they might mean.

He stood frozen; the grenade launcher held above his head. Ensine's first lesson came flooding back: "No species successfully evolves without a refined fight or flight instinct." Russ's instinct, in fact every fiber in his body, screamed at him to flee.

Instead, he lowered the launcher, loaded it quickly and fired. He heard the projectile thump out the barrel and the grenade connected with the tree just over the Tharcus's shoulder. The concussion blast dropped the Tharcus to one knee, showering it in tree parts.

Russ was hoping the blast would cause the creature to turn in that direction, exposing its weak point. Instead, the monster hurled its body toward Nina, roaring ferociously.

She managed two steps before it pulled her down from behind, burying its teeth in her shoulder and wrenching her body in a rag-doll motion. Nina had drawn a stunstick, but it went skipping into the trees, and Russ heard the snap of her shoulder tearing free from its socket. The beast threw its head forward and bit at Nina's back, just below her armpit, sheering off her vest and a five-inch chunk of flesh.

Nina flipped over the beast's shoulder, her blood spraying across its fur. Then she tumbled down its body and came to rest, lifeless at its feet.

Russ rose slowly to his full height. He calmed his mind, refusing to look at Nina where she fell. If he acknowledged her crumpled body, he knew he would be flooded with fury and try to fight the creature hand to hand, never mind that it was eight feet tall, coiled with muscle, and had rock-hard skin.

The creature aimed its predator eyes directly at Russ's and howled mightily.

Russ was halfway through reloading the MK47 when the Tharcus hit him, the massive bulk of its chest and forearms slamming against his body, smashing him deep into the mud and pinning him there. It knocked the rebreather from Russ's face, sending it rolling away. The creature howled a final time, opening its wide jaws to snap off Russ's head. Saliva dripped from its mouth, spattering into Russ's face, blurring his vision.

He was pinned, helpless . . . dead.

And that's when Alaniea and Nulinea came crashing down onto the Tharcus's back. They looped their hooked mantis legs over its torso and pounded it with their stunsticks, large black mantis eyes blazing. The sounds hit Russ's ears, thunk, thunk, thunk, at the same time as the vibration of the blows traveled through the Tharcus's body and zapped Russ full of residual electricity. His body shook with each blow, the electricity firing out from his ears and fingertips. On the seventh blow, the Tharcus howled, jumped off Russ, and leaped to the safety of the trees. It tried to brush the women from its back.

One of the women did fall; Russ thought it was Alaniea. She struck the ground back near where the Tharcus had first appeared. She climbed quickly to her feet, turned to Russ, and raised her fist in salute, as if to say, 'And now we're even.' Then she dashed after the fleeing Tharcus, Nulinea still riding astride its back.

Russ knew it was tremendously dangerous, but he lay in the mud for a moment, breathing deep, ragged breaths. Then he rolled to his feet and scrambled around to find his rebreather. He spotted it twenty feet away, among the trees, right in the center of the Triwin swarm. It was far enough away that he ran to Nina's side first, to reattach her rebreather and to see if she was still alive.

He could feel her pulse, but there was a lot of blood where the Tharcus had bitten her lower back, and her shoulder was so loose he wasn't sure if anything was holding it in place besides what was left of her compression suit. He fumbled out his roll of pain pills and fingered a few into her mouth. Her eyes were rolled back into her head, and every few seconds her body would tremble.

He gathered her up, still fighting the urge to panic. He found himself huffing hard in the thin air as he stumbled toward his rebreather, Nina in his arms.

"I'm going to get you back safe. I'm sure you'll find their repair equipment endlessly fascinating," Russ promised her. He moved her to his back, her arms hanging limply over his shoulders.

With each silent step Russ's adrenaline faded out, replaced by worry for Nina. His mind replayed what he'd seen, the Tharcus biting deep into her back, tossing her in the air like a rag doll. He tried to push the memory away, concentrating instead on keeping Nina balanced across his shoulders.

He reached his rebreather, and a handful of Triwin were landing on it. They fluttered back to the nearby branches as Russ approached.

Russ could feel his lungs aching as he scooped up the rebreather, but as he slid it back over his head, he tasted something inside, nestled against the filter.

It was a dead Triwin. Russ flipped off the mask and tried to dig the creature out with his finger, but it was partially cocooned against the edge, stuck firm with a thick, spiderweb-like substance.

"Don't have time for this," Russ muttered. He quickly shifted Nina's weight so he could flick at the thing again, and something popped out from between its long, bent legs. The thing that came out was very small, almost a speck of dust, but as Russ watched it skitter across the rebreather, digging down into the mechanics of the device. Then more specs of dust started to pour out of the Triwin's body, each moving and squirming with new life.

Russ stuck his thumb in the mask and squished the "dead" Triwin, smearing green guts across his thumb and his mask. Then he smeared as many of the new babies as he could. He shook the rebreather out, watching Triwin parts rain down to the canopy floor. Then he affixed it back over his head, taking in long gulps of purified air.

"Third queen dead on central plateau," he said into the rebreather comm.

"Let's regroup at the Waypoint," Starland said. "Gas 'em and Trash 'em got the fourth."

"Roger that. Nina's bleeding badly. She needs medical help the second we get there," Russ said.

"Who the hell is Roger?" Kendren groaned, his voice filled with obvious pain.

Russ pulsed his transponder. It seemed to take forever for it to populate the heat signatures of the rest of the team. They were headed toward the Waypoint. As he rushed past the swarm of Triwin, he popped his can of C09 and rolled it into their midst, taking off his rebreather again and waving it through the smoke to make sure he'd killed all the new babies inside. Just as he reached the thicker bunch of trees, he glanced back at the huge diamond, still sticking partly out of the broken ledge.

He took a step back toward the rock, but Nina coughed blood and it splattered in a crescent pattern on his upper chest. Though he didn't want to admit it, he was encouraged that she showed enough life to cough.

"Hang in there, Nina. I'm going to get you to the best doctors in the universe."

He rushed out of the forest, holding Nina tight. Behind him the enormous diamond glittered in the wisps of light that shone through the trees.

31

NINA

NINA WAS COCOONED TIGHTLY inside a machine. It buzzed and chugged, moving all around her. She felt a tugging sensation in her arm, leg, ribs, and the entire left side of her chest. At one point a whole section of the device closed tightly on her shoulder, pinning it from the front and the back. She could tell by the sound of tearing meat, that she didn't want to look in that direction. Instead, she kept her head flat against her other shoulder, closing her eyes until the ripping, and tugging, stopped. At that point, she probably passed out.

A little while later, she became aware of a conversation between two familiar voices in the room outside.

". . . muscles in her shoulder were completely severed. Her lower left rib was shattered. About half of it was resting on the wall of her stomach . . ."

". . . At least she's alive . . ."

". . . think Bah'ren will keep her word? Is she CERTified?"

". . . Our Bah'ren? That seems unusually generous . . ."

". . . M-class is a pretty sweet payout. Maybe we have the money?"

". . . That was no place for two rookies . . ."

". . . BUT I think we saved the business . . ."

There was a series of new, strange sounds from the machine and then the voices returned:

". . . light's blinking on the CRC. That mean our bread is finished toasting?"

There was another new humming sound, and the device Nina was lying on moved. It was a tray, she realized, and it was sliding out of the machine. Nina found herself birthed back into a med ward, the bright lights from the room stabbing into her eyes. She was as naked as a newborn baby.

One of the voices was Kendren. He was sitting in a chair a few feet away, his large bulk leaned part way to the side. He looked at her naked body and swiveled in a half circle so his back was to her. He also covered his eyes.

The other voice was Starland's. "Hold still," she told Nina. She waved a small digital wand over Nina's body from the top of her head to the tips of her toes. "It's registering a total recovery percentage at . . ." Starland looked at the digital readout and turned back to Kendren ". . . 102.39. Not bad. We actually made improvements. You heal well," she told Nina. "Kendren, why are you facing the wall?"

"To protect her honor," Kendren said, with over-the-top formality.

Starland looked back at Nina. "Do all Earthlings look like this under their clothes?"

"Some variation of this," Nina said.

"But you're pregnant, aren't you?" Starland asked. Her hand drifted unconsciously to her own belly.

"Not possible," Nina said.

"But you were recently pregnant?"

"No. Never."

"Sure you were. We TEN-awtch are viviparous, but we're cruel mothers. We don't produce any nourishment after our young are born. It's part of the reason I'm fascinated by mammals." Starland moved her hand away from her own stomach. "You're clearly pregnant. Why else would your breasts be swollen with milk?"

"They're not," Nina said. "They look like that all the time."

Kendren coughed into his fist, possibly to hide a laugh. "If you remember your diversity training, many primates believe in covering their reproductive organs," Kendren told Starland. "We RreRriaNne do as well, but only to protect our penis and scrotum. They are irreplaceable."

Starland was still looking at Nina. "The human female body emulates pregnancy even when not pregnant? Is that a mating advantage? I can't see how."

"Could I have some of those?" Nina asked.

"Those what?"

"Those clothes." Nina nodded toward her orange jumpsuit which was hanging on a hook on the wall. When Starland handed it to her, Nina noticed an enormous gash across the lower back. The tear was at least nine inches by six inches, and it was crusted with blood. Her blood. Nina felt the place on her back where the tear would have been. Her skin was smooth and warm, without a blemish. "What's this machine called?" she asked Starland.

Starland was still looking at her, her hands once more unconsciously on her own belly. Nina shrugged into her jumpsuit, the tears hanging open comically.

"It's called a CRC machine," Kendren said. He was always haughty toward Russ, but Nina found him weirdly noble in this moment. Perhaps his arrogance was a type of posturing, saved only for competing males. He was also incredibly attractive, nearly seven feet tall, with his huge forearms and chest. On Earth, it was fascinating how many variations of size and shape men came in.

The RreRriaNne, like Kendren, brought that variation to a whole new level.

He swiveled his chair back around in time to catch Nina's eyes scanning the entire room. "Russ isn't here," he told her, guessing at what she was thinking.

"I wasn't looking for him," Nina said. "I was wondering, what would need to happen to bring another human up here. For some repairs?"

"Repairs aren't free," Kendren said.

"Nobody from your tier is allowed to jump a Waypoint without CERTification," Starland reminded her. "You've got to have your papers."

"My dad is sick," she told them. "It's a terminal illness unless he gets revolutionary treatment."

"This is that," Kendren confirmed. "At least for Earth. The Critical Carbon Repair Chrysalis is a one stop shop. It IDs your DNA, then recreates the missing parts from stem cells via 3D printing. Then it sews the new stuff onto the old stuff. It will cure just about everything except death. It worked its ass off on your ribs. Had to use a lot of welding paste to put them back together."

"The bio-repair filament isn't cheap," Starland explained. "I love Bah'ren, but she doesn't spend a credit she doesn't need to. In fact, the only reason we have a CRC machine is to protect her from the costs of a critical injury. It's less expensive to repair an employee then to pay job-related disability. Not to mention the fees for training a replacement CERT."

"I need to get my dad in this machine."

"You can ask Bah'ren. You'll get a long speech about how she could lose her license for intentionally harboring illegals," Kendren said. "But," he held up a finger to indicate he had an idea, "if you promise her enough money, or offer to work a year or so without pay . . . I bet she'd look the other way while you snuck your dad in here."

Nina was already halfway to the door by the time he finished his sentence.

Bah'ren didn't seem as excited about the deal as Nina would have thought. Nina promised her eighteen Earth months of free labor, and in return Nina could bring her dad aboard the *Flashaway* to use the CRC machine.

Nina's eyes ran across her new contract. It was even more odious than the last—actually, it was the same contract. The only difference was that the section after her name read "Permanent" instead of "Pending CERTification." The pay section was also line-itemed out with an addendum reading 'Doreena Thibodeau Hosseinzadeh agrees to work without pay until the passing of the next eighteen Earth months, or upon death, whichever may occur first.'

Bah'ren logged the contract, a grim smile on her face. "I declare you officially CERTified and now legally entitled to all the rights of a citizen of the United Alliance of Intelligent Beings, including the ability to own land, vote in counsel elections, and be paid for services rendered. Next time you see Starland, ask her to remove the training program from your transponder."

It was a hell of a deal for them both, since eighteen months seemed like nothing in exchange for her dad's life. She would have agreed to ten years.

Instead of being happy, Bah'ren just kept glancing at a tablet on her desk, then over her shoulder at a screen mounted on the wall that looked like it was probably used for video calls. When she caught Nina eyeballing the tablet, she turned it over quickly.

"Everything all right?" Nina asked. She had a surge of fear that Bah'ren's anxiousness was somehow related to her and Russ's attempts to steal the diamond.

But Russ had already paid a heavy price for that, hadn't he?

As she'd tried to leave the med ward, Kendren and Starland had told her the story of Russ's last moments as an Intergalactic Exterminator. An immigration robot had been waiting to arrest him when they'd Waypointed back from Oi0. Russ had only escaped through some kind of intellectual voodoo that had temporarily shorted out the SAS's mainframe. Intellectual voodoo didn't really sound like Russ's style, but the way they'd described it, Russ had somehow crashed the robot's improvisation directives.

Bah'ren waved her small right hand in front of Nina's eyes. "You'll want to leave now and move quickly. IBED logs every bio-signature that comes through the major Waypoint hubs. It won't take them long to register that your dad's not a legal citizen, and if you can't get him aboard without attracting attention from the SAS, we never had this conversation." Bah'ren's eyes focused on Nina for the first time in their entire conversation. "Bring him soon," she urged.

Nina wondered what Bah'ren was so worried about, but something about her tone told Nina the conversation was over.

Nina jumped through the Waypoint feeling a little bad that her fortunes were swinging upward at the same time Russ's had taken such a nosedive. But she was on the cusp of saving her dad, and regardless of Russ's circumstances, it felt like a huge weight was finally about to lift from her chest. Crouched on the floor of the bookstore's storage room, for the first time in a year, she was flooded with something akin to hope. She was shaken out of her contemplation by a loud noise. It sounded like a heavy box hitting the linoleum floor on the other side of the wall. It was ten o'clock at night. No one should be around.

Nina stayed crouched in the dark room, listening quietly. Then she carefully pushed open the door. A man stood at the end of the hallway with his back to her. He was wearing a brown jumpsuit with the name "Andy's Movers" hand-stitched across the back shoulders.

Nina opened the back door and then shut it, and the man turned around, a pair of bolt cutters in his hand. It was Jake Samuels. She'd gone to school with him from elementary straight through high school. He had always been amazed at how smart she was. Partially because he was an idiot.

"Nina T-ba-do Hose-n-zada? What are you doing here?"

"What are you doing here, Jake?"

Instead of answering, Jake looked down at the bolt cutters in his hand. "Shit. If we'd known there was a back door, we could have gotten this job done last night and I wouldn't be missing my date. Old lady Norma's been taking to chaining the front door shut each night."

"If you'd read a few more books growing up, you would have known the store layout." Nina told him.

"That ain't fair," Jake said, then he reconsidered. "No that's totally fair. I beat the shit out of Call of Duty though."

Norma's door chime sounded, and another man came through the front wearing a matching jumpsuit. It was Andy, Jake's dad and the owner of the moving company. "Is someone else here?" Andy asked.

"There's a back door, Dad," Jake said. "And guess who just came through? Compulsive reader, hot nerd, and ex-head of the robotics club at Banville Central High, Nina Hosseinzadeh." Jake could barely manage the introduction without sneering in contempt. "Apparently she's here so much she's got her own key."

Nina reached up and slid the lock onto the door of the storage room. Her eyes drifted back to Jake's bolt cutters. They could get through the lock in an instant if they wanted to, and then they'd discover the Waypoint. And everything would be lost.

Andy moved back to the hall. He looked a lot like Jake, just twice as old, in his midforties, with gray in his beard. Unlike Jake, Andy was quiet and thoughtful.

As he packed up Norma's things, Nina noticed that his eyes were red around the edges.

"What are you doing in Norma's store?" Nina asked again. She was trying to keep herself calm. "Did she hire you to pack up her books?"

Jake grinned and hefted the bolt cutters and slapped them against his palm.

"No, she didn't, did she? Someone else hired you to pack up her store." Nina looked again at the red around Andy's eyes. She realized it was sadness. She realized what was really happening.

"We can't be picking and choosing our jobs these days," Andy said morosely. "When the sheriff called me on behalf of that slimy law firm, first thing I did was think about telling him to suck it. Next thing I did was make sure it was fully lawful, what the sheriff was asking me to do."

"That's mighty heroic of you," Nina said, and Andy's eyes clouded even further. "You're just going to drop Norma's books on her doorstep? What's she supposed to do with them if you close her out of the store?"

Jake, growing bored, went back into the main part of the store and resumed loading books into boxes. He was loading them haphazardly and they hit the base of the box with a jarring thump. The sound made both Nina and Andy flinch.

Andy walked over to the cash register and Nina reluctantly followed. He pulled a clipboard off the counter and handed it to her. "Sheriff Mike said we were legally compelled to accept the lawyer's contract. He said we had to—we had to 'liquidate' all remaining items of value from inside the store."

"You're not even giving her the books! You're taking them?"

"There's a lien . . ."

"I wonder what my dad will say when I tell him what you're up to these days?" Pithyou and Andy were old friends. Truthfully, everyone in town was friends—or enemies—with everyone else in town. "I hope it doesn't kill him."

"That's not fair . . ." Andy started to say.

It was fair, actually, Nina thought. If she lost access to the Waypoint, there would be no way to get her father to the CRC.

Andy turned his back to Nina and joined his son, drawing books off the shelf and putting them into boxes. He took a deep breath and exhaled. "I wish it weren't so," he said. "If you came for a book, go ahead and grab it."

Nina moved to the romance section, which hadn't been boxed up yet. Her mind was racing.

The romance novels stared back at her, unhelpfully, the book covers adorned with the various men who had been Nina's "boyfriends" through most of high school and college. Their curly hair dangled roguishly in front of their eyes.

Still lost in her own head, she pulled a copy of *The Billionaire's Secret Princess* from the stacks and realized it was her copy. When Norma bought a used book, if it was in good enough condition, she often made the frugal decision to put it back on the shelf in the "new" section of the store. Nina took to making a very small ink mark in the upper right corner of each cover so she could remember which book she'd already bought and read.

On the other side of the wall, she heard Andy sit down heavily on a box. "It's just so sad," he said. "Some of the books from Jake's childhood are here. They sat in our garage for over a decade, and I finally convinced Susan to sell them back to Norma. Guess she thought they were in good enough shape to put on the shelf."

"Didn't read them very much?" Nina asked. She tried to keep the bitter tone out of her voice. In the background, Jake was still throwing books haphazardly into boxes, and the thumping sound was hitting her nerves harder than anything on Oi0.

"We tried. Boy, did we try." Thump. "Reading to Jake." Thump. "It didn't really take. I guess I hoped that if Norma got the books back, someone else could use them." Andy's voice drifted away. Thump.

"Jake, put the books in the boxes more carefully."

"You're not even working!" Jake whined. "Oh shit. That cat skeleton is gone. Somebody musta bought it!"

Nina pulled a few books from a shelf. She could now see through to the aisle where Andy was sitting. He glanced back at her, his eyes full of guilt.

"Right after the sheriff called, I tried to call these lawyers, Trent, Cole, and Kerch, just to see if we could postpone the liquidation, but they're based out of Texas and all I got when I called was one of those voice trees. There wasn't even a way to leave a message. Said I had to contact them via email. I tried that but all I got was an automated response. I don't know what I'm supposed to do, except what they're paying me to do."

Thump.

"Start by getting Jake to stop packing," Nina said simply.

Thump.

"Jake! Knock it the fuck off!" Andy called.

"Where's that goddamn Whitefeather?" Jake said. He was now rummaging around behind the counter. "Therese told me they kept it back here."

"Norma's grandson Russ has the money to pay her back rent," Nina lied. Jake's mention of the gun had given her a sudden inspiration. "How else could he have afforded to repair the shelves and the ceiling?"

"It does look a lot nicer in here," Andy said, glancing at the ceiling. Still, he didn't stop packing, slowly pulling a handful of books off the shelf and putting them in the box at his feet.

"Oh geez," Nina said.

"What?" Andy asked anxiously.

Nina lifted a copy of *Life* magazine off the shelf. It was from December 1, 1947. The cover featured Gregory Peck in a sharp business suit. She showed Andy through the hole in the stacks. "Norma told me that she bought this for her honeymoon when she and Clark flew down to Florida. She told me they got stuck at the Laramie Airport and had to scrape together all their change just to afford it. They read every page waiting for their plane, her on his lap, each holding one end of the magazine." Nina exhaled deeply, unconsciously mimicking the sound Andy had made just a few minutes before.

Andy glanced through the stacks to look at the magazine, and Nina nudged her finger forward to cover the date, realizing too late that for Norma to have gone on her honeymoon in 1947 she would have had to be married at age eight.

"This is going to be a tough one to lose," Nina said. "But you can have it for your box, I guess."

Andy looked stricken.

"Though I'm sure she'd feel a lot better if she doesn't arrive tomorrow and find a completely empty store," Nina added. "If she has a chance to say good-bye to all her books, maybe save a few of the oddities, before they're all taken away."

Nina watched Andy make his decision. He stood and flipped through the paperwork again. "When's this nephew of hers supposed to come through with the money?"

"No more than a week."

"I doubt the bank will wait that long," Andy said, "but we can make them wait a little bit longer. Jake bring the boxes from outside back in, please."

"What the hell!" Jake said, his arms waving at his side in frustration.

Andy shook his head in general disappointment of everything about Jake. "Actually, go see your girlfriend. Nina and I will do it."

"Really? Okay! Thanks, Dad!" Jake said, already halfway out the door.

"Thanks Andy," Nina echoed. "Truly, thank you."

32

RUSS & NINA

RUSS THOUGHT DRIVING WOULD clear his head—it always had in the past. But even with the car purring along the highway, he felt a queer sensation of uneasiness. *Maybe a better word for it would be sadness?*

It wasn't quite like the sadness he'd grappled with when he was younger, before he'd begun his restless wandering across the United States. Truth be told, it was like nothing he'd ever felt before.

Russ drove for a while, along the hills and dales of outer Evanstown. Unlike his childhood home in Southern California, here the trees changed colors before losing their leaves. The aspens and the willows were just beginning to shed the first yellow leaves of the season. Soon enough, it would get very cold in Evanstown, Wyoming. A good reason to leave, Russ considered. But the thought of hitting the road again didn't help quiet his mind.

After a few more miles, he pulled off Highway 98, then climbed out of the car, the Whitefeather resting casually across his shoulder. He was swinging his rebreather in his other hand. He'd left the *Flashaway* in such a hurry he'd forgotten to put it back in the weapons closet.

He realized he'd subconsciously driven back to the hill where he and Nina had first fought the SAS. It wasn't the worst thing to have done. He was basically an intergalactic fugitive again. If the SAS were going to come for him, the hill was easily defensible, with its raised view of the edge of the forest on every side.

He slowly climbed to the top of the hill and sat cross-legged listening. The forest sounded normal. An owl was hooting in the trees and something medium-sized and furry was picking its way through the nearby brush. Russ ran his hand along the wooden stock of the rifle, and as he sat in the near silence, he finally identified the emotion pinging around in his heart. It wasn't uneasiness; it wasn't sadness either. For the first time in years, he was feeling desperately, unequivocally lonely.

"That's the stupidest thing I've ever heard of anyone doing," Ensine told Russ.

Russ had spent the night in the forest, his head propped up on his rebreather.

He had never shaken that keen sense of loneliness, but he had decided that he'd made the right decision in trying to help Nina save her dad. He woke up worried about her safety. Starland had assured him Nina would be okay in the *Flashaway*'s repair protocol, but Russ had left too quickly to know for certain.

"The sheer carelessness of it . . ." Ensine continued. "You were an hour shy of CERTification, a life of space travel and adventure ahead of you and you threw it all away to be hunted by machines. Why?"

"It seemed like the right thing to do," Russ said.

"Seemed like . . ." Ensine huffed. "I'll be damned."

Russ's gaze traveled to the transformer in Ensine's ear, then across his forehead at his thick, illusionary, wavy white hair. "Are you drinking vitamin water?" he said.

"Norma doesn't approve of Budweiser," Ensine hissed. "I miss it so much."

"I just don't understand," Norma said, bustling into the store's narrow hallway. "Andy's boxes are everywhere, but the books are all still on the shelf. They're not exactly where they were, but someone tried hard to find the right place for them all. When I saw the chain was cut, I thought we had lost the store for good. What do you think happened here last night?"

"Maybe it was the Chrome Man?" Ensine said.

"Don't encourage that," Russ whispered.

"Nobody has seen the Chrome Man in days," Norma reminded Ensine. "It's like he just disappeared."

"Or went off to be a hero in another town?" Russ suggested.

"I hope that's it, although we could still use the help here." Norma walked past Russ and Ensine to get her hands on a box, which she skillfully broke down and then carried through the back door to the recycling bin in the alley. When she came back, Russ was still holding the rebreather, having intended to stash it in the storage room with the Waypoint.

"What is that?" she asked him. "One of your grandfather's novelties? I don't think I've seen it before."

"Oh, it's . . ." Russ said, looking at Ensine for help.

"It's just a novelty," Ensine told her, swiping it out of Russ's hands.

"Yep. Just nothing," Russ said.

Norma stared at them quizzically. "Give it here," she said. "It looks kind of neat. I'll see if Bibi can get it up on the website."

Ensine smiled thinly and moved the rebreather behind his back. Norma frowned.

She gestured for him to give her the device.

Russ looked at Ensine, who looked at Russ. Russ shook his head no, but Ensine handed Norma the rebreather. The door chime tinkled.

"Customer!" Norma called out, heading in the direction of the cash register, the rebreather tucked beneath her arm.

Nina sat by her dad's bedside. It felt odd to be back on Earth doing something so familiar. Her body shivered involuntarily in her seat, and her mom said, "Are you cold? Stop doing that. It's the third time you've done that since we got out of the car."

Nina wasn't just suffering from the shakes. Her senses were also still firing at an extremely high level. The arm of her chair felt thick and grainy, like an overcooked steak, and her dad's actual food—an egg roll, stale and bland like all hospital food—smelled rich with foreign spice.

This must be a delayed response to the near-death experience, Nina realized. *Or maybe some side-effect of the CRC machine.*

Her mind kept alternating between her plans for her dad and her sadness over what had happened to Russ.

Katherine was in an unusually high state of agitation herself. They were expecting a visit from Wayne Perkinsky, one of the hospital administrators, to help explain how much of the long-overdue bill they were mandated to provide out of pocket.

Every few minutes, Nina got up and peeked into the hall to see if she could spot Wayne. It was making her mom more nervous.

"Stop doing that. He said he'd be here around seven, but you know he's always a few minutes late. Especially when he doesn't want to talk to us, which is always."

"I'm just thirsty," Nina said. "I really want a soda water."

"You know where the cafeteria is. Take this so you don't have to pay for a cup."

Katherine swiped a foam cup off Pithyou's tray table and handed it to Nina. Taking the cup, Nina peered into the hall again. She saw Wayne come through a large set of double doors and take a quick left to duck into the nurses' station.

Nina turned back to face her mom, her eyes lingering a minute on the frail form of her sleeping father. "Would you mind getting me the water?" she asked her mom.

"Is something wrong with your legs? I'm not leaving now. Wayne is scheduled to come in any minute."

"You said yourself he's always late. On the off chance he beats you back, I won't let him leave before you return."

"Nina, get your own water."

"It's just that I saw Morty headed toward the cafeteria a few minutes ago."

"What's Morty doing in the hospital?" Nina's mom wondered. But she rose up and snapped the cup away from Nina. "I guess its serendipitous. I would like to have a little chat with Morty about his love letters," she said. "Do not let Wayne leave before I get back."

Nina could not have cut it any closer. The moment her mom left the hospital room, turning left toward the elevator, Wayne Perkinsky exited the nurse's station and made his way down the hall to her father's room. He was a thin man, with thin arms and thin legs and thin hair. He wore a thin tie with a simple thin metal tie clip pinned to the end. The tie had whales on it. He was carrying a bundle of paperwork in his hands. Nina had never seen him without a bundle of paperwork in his hands.

He seemed immediately relieved that Katherine was not there. "Is Katherine here? Ms. Hosseinzadeh?"

"She didn't come tonight," Nina informed him.

"Oh my. Is everything all right?"

"Not really," Nina said. "We've been talking a lot about moving my dad to the big hospital in Laramie. I'm afraid the decision has caused my mother quite a bit of stress."

"The decision?" Wayne asked. He tried unsuccessfully to keep a note of hope out of his voice.

"Yes," Nina told him. "We have decided to move him. I understand they have a much better facility in Laramie. My mom is having trouble dealing with the choice even though she knows it's for the best."

"It is for the best. Definitely," Wayne said, nodding his head like a parrot.

"One of the things that's bothering us is transporting him. It's a long trip, and we can't afford to hire an ambulance. I was wondering if you could help, in that regard?"

"Banville Memorial would be willing to help in any way we can," Wayne said, but then he realized what he'd just offered. "Short of sending one of our own ambulances. We're rather short-staffed as it is . . ."

"I would never ask you to do that," Nina assured him. "What I had in mind was medicine. Anesthetic to keep him sedated throughout the trip? Something strong enough that he'll go to sleep and not have any idea where he's going or what he's doing there?"

"I'm not sure that's entirely necessary."

"I think it's best," Nina told him. "And it will help my mom be much more willing to make the move. In fact, I'd like you to administer the medicine right now."

"Of course. Of course." Wayne Perkinsky kept bobbing his head. She could almost read his thoughts like they were on a ticker tape running across his forehead. *Anything you want,* he seemed to be thinking.

Anything at all that will get you out of my hospital.

"This thing plays music!" Norma called out to them. She had the re-breather next to her ear.

The men stared at her from around the hallway corner. Russ knew he needed to get the rebreather back before Norma got too interested in it. The fact that it was playing music didn't help.

"How is that possible?" Ensine whispered to Russ. "Earth is nowhere close to a communication relay station. And what kind of weird broadcast were you listening to?"

"I don't understand what you're saying," Russ told him.

Norma moved to the front of the store to greet another customer. Ensine dragged Russ to the counter, where she'd left the rebreather.

"Your rebreather is playing music. Can't you hear it?" Ensine asked him.

Russ stuck his head next to the rebreather. He couldn't hear much over Norma hard-selling the customer at the front of the store. "Maybe a little," he said.

"Some rebreathers can tune into any one of a thousand different over-the-air broadcasts. Studies show the uneducated workforce is more productive when exposed to a source of constant music. It's an upgraded package though, not usually Bah'ren's style."

Russ shrugged.

They both retreated to the hallway.

"Let's get this thing safely hidden away and hope she forgets about it," Ensine said.

As Russ and Ensine moved toward the storeroom, Ensine put the rebreather up to his ear again.

"It must be malfunctioning. The music is rising and falling. And it sounds odd, like bells, or maybe pipes, but more . . . organic somehow. Music of the Spheres, maybe?"

"Uh-oh," Russ said.

He moved fast, grabbing the rebreather from Ensine and shaking it vigorously. The volume of the music ticked upward, loud enough now that he could hear it clearly. It was melancholy, the high, twittering dirge of a queen lamenting the loss of her subjects.

The high twittering dirge of an insect queen.

"Oh fuck," Russ said. "There's a Triwin in the internal mechanics."

"What's a Triwin?" Ensine asked. Then his old man eyes went wide. "You mean Specus Trinwae: the consonant swarm that chokes out the sky? Oh fuck." Ensine paced in a small circle. "Get it off Earth. You've got to take it back through the Waypoint. Right now."

"What's going on back there?" Norma called.

Russ tried to explain to Ensine what had happened: "A swarm was born in my mask on Oi0. I squished a bunch and put the mask in the gas to kill the ones that had dug down into the filter mechanics."

"But if the gas didn't kill this one . . ." Ensine began.

". . . it must be a queen," Russ finished.

"Get it off my planet!" Ensine shouted.

"Your planet?"

Ensine glanced toward Norma, still near the front of the store. He spoke in a quick, hushed clip. "This is not something to mess around with, Russ."

"We can't panic. It's still an infant. It was born yesterday. We have seven days before it gives birth." Russ handed the rebreather to Ensine. "You have to deal with it. I'm not going through the Waypoint. The hub is filled with SAS, and I'm an illegal alien."

Ensine handed the rebreather back to Russ. "I'm not taking an F-class bio-threat across an intergalactic border. If I get caught, they'll revoke my license and make me pay for the cleanup. It would be the end of me, financially." Ensine looked Russ in the eyes. "If you gassed it that means it could be mutating. It's possible you shortened its reproductive cycle. Or made it carnivorous. Or . . . anything. We need to panic!" His face was close to Russ's, his voice full of urgency.

Russ made a decision. He waited a moment, watching Ensine's panic carefully. In his head he counted slowly to ten. "I want to be retrained," he said finally.

"What!"

"I take the creature away, and you let me restart CERT training."

"I have to pay *you*, to fix your own fuckup?"

Russ tossed the rebreather back to Ensine.

"I don't want it." Ensine insisted.

"If I risk getting sent back to an immigration satellite, getting mind-wiped and who knows what else, I want you to reCERTify me. That's the deal. Take it or leave it."

Ensine didn't answer.

"Where'd that doohickey go?" Norma called from the front counter.

Silently, defeated, Ensine passed the mask back to Russ. As Ensine turned, Russ caught the gleam of the transformer in his ear.

"How exactly does that hard-light transformer work?" Russ whispered.

Nina was sweating. It wasn't because of what had probably happened to Wayne Perkinsky when her mom got back from the cafeteria to find Nina and her dad gone—though she did feel bad about that. It certainly wasn't because of the weight of her father in the wheelchair she was pushing. He was so light, it felt like pushing an empty chair.

The main reason Nina was sweating was the way the spaceclerks kept looking at her. Each new hub hall she pushed her dad down, the spaceclerk would give them both a hard stare (if the creature had eyeballs, and it usually did), as if it already knew her dad wasn't a legal citizen.

Nina had thrown a blanket over her dad's thin legs and tucked a pillow behind his head. The medicine Dr. Perkinsky had given him had knocked him out cold, but that only made him appear even more frail. Nina half wondered if his skeleton would crumble into dust, and she'd wake up sweating from the worst, longest nightmare of her life.

Instead, she just kept sweating away in the real world. She'd reached the municipal docking hub, her hands slipping on the handles of the wheelchair.

This was the last checkpoint before she'd be pushing her dad up the ramp into the *Flashaway*, and she quickly rubbed her face against the shoulder of her jumpsuit.

She was halfway down the hall when the last spaceclerk cleared his throat noisily. "Excuse me," he said.

Nina didn't look in his direction, she just kept her pace, putting one foot in front of the other.

"EXCUSE me," the spaceclerk said again. Nina glanced backward and saw him scooting around his desk and jogging her way.

She kept moving steadily, ignoring him, but her arms, legs, and chest were all covered in goose bumps. She thought she might pass out.

The clerk raced around her and stood in the path of the wheelchair. He was young, with scales on his head and a long lizard's torso, the same species as Starland. A TEN-awtch, Nina remembered they were called, as if the name of his race mattered while she was being locked up in a galactic prison and her dad was deported back to Earth to die.

"Does your species talk?" The TEN-awtch asked her.

Nina nodded.

The TEN-awtch chuckled. "You just don't want to, maybe?"

Nina shook her head. "Sorry, we do talk. Do you need our papers, or something?"

"Papers? What? No. You're with IEI, right? Intergalactic Exterminators, Inc? You're an employee of Bah'ren J'n'n? I have a message for you."

The TEN-awtch put a paper-thin tablet in Nina's hand and then went back to his desk. The screen read "Employee; Intergalactic Exterminators, Inc."

Nina touched the screen and read carefully:

Dear Employee:

The following has been posted on the Exterm-MERC board and sent digitally whenever possible.

After well over 2000 cycles as a legitimate, licensed business, I regret to inform you that your employer, the Intergalactic Exterminators, Inc has, as of today, ceased to exist. As per bankruptcy protocol, any working contract you held is effectively null and void. Any outstanding monies owed to the holder of this note may be petitioned for through the Below-the-line Employment Bureau [BLEB] within one full Divian cycle. There is no guarantee that said monies will be recovered. Thank you. Know that we have appreciated your service to the United Alliance of Intelligent Beings.

". . . know that we have appreciated your service," Nina read again. She silently rubbed her hand across her temple. Her dad stirred slightly in his chair.

"We appreciate your service," Nina said aloud. Her voice was trembling with anger. "Will you appreciate it when I stick this wheelchair up your ass?" She wasn't making a joke. If Bah'ren was still at the dock, Nina intended to find out just how far up it would fit. Then she would make sure Bah'ren kept her side of the deal about getting Nina's dad into the CRC machine.

"Threatening an administer. Your RQ score has been lowered 50 points, to—bzzzt," her transponder said.

She pushed her dad down the long hallway in the direction of the *Flashaway*'s dock. Her heart leaped when she saw it was still there.

At first, nothing seemed out of the ordinary. The normal gaggle of unemployed organics was on her right, leaning against the wall. The normal lineup of SAS units was on the left, preparing to deploy for a day of artless labor. The team of yellow-jumpsuited facilities workers from Southland Demolitions and Refuse Removal were pushing and shoving one another as they waited for their ship to dock. Nina even saw the little purple man who always tormented Russ, a smarmy grin on his punchable face.

He was surrounded by his entourage, and they shuffled back and forth in a rush, to cater to his slightest whim.

Nina was almost to the ramp of the *Flashaway* when she spotted one of the big guys, the one who had hit Russ in the nose on their first day in space, detach himself from the entourage and lock eyes with her. His skin was made of bifurcated rock, and his two huge stone fists swung at his side.

"Excuse me," he said, his voice a rich, deep bass.

"I'm in kind of a hurry," Nina told him. She pivoted the wheelchair in a semicircle around him, still headed for the ramp.

"I said 'excuse me.'" The rock creature reached out and grabbed ahold of the back of her jumpsuit with his huge mitt. "You can't go up that ramp."

Nina tried to squirm away, but it felt like her jumpsuit was pinched in a vice.

"Let me go!" she insisted. "I have business on that ship."

"You don't have any business on our ship," the purple man called. He had been watching the interaction from ten or so feet away. When he spoke, he crossed the distance and stood beside the rock creature, his hands on his hips.

"Your ship?" Nina asked.

"As of the end of the last cycle"—the short man sniffled—"all items contained within the ship became the property of SOL Pest Control. We purchased the lease from the First Lenders Banc of King's Closet. They were all too pleased to get a dead property off their hands. Payment had been past due for a number of cycles, which triggered a repossession clause. It's been happening with a lot of municipal ship leases lately."

"I'll bet," Nina said.

"Our possession of . . . what's the name of this ship again?" he asked the rock man.

"No idea."

"Anyway, our possession of this ship is all perfectly legal. All perfectly within the bounds of fair practice and fair competition."

Nina understood what had happened. She tried to keep her face from going white. "I am a CERTified exterminator," she told them. "I can work for you guys if you own the ship now. I'll even work for free . . ."

Behind her, Nina could hear the SAS units marching in lockstep. One of them approached the ramp where she stood.

"We don't have any need to employ organics," the man said.

"You are organics," Nina pointed out.

"Yes, we are the public face of the company. Our PR department concluded that we should continue to employ a high-profile organic workforce until the pilot program is deemed a success. To be honest, I secretly find the idea of exterminator work distasteful." The little purple man looked left then right. "Glad I don't have to actually do any of it," he whispered.

"You're forcing a company to shut down that's been running for three generations so your investors can make a couple more dollars?" Nina said angrily. She was much angrier about her dad than the loss of her job, but frustration could be vented in whatever direction it flowed most easily.

The purple man considered her words carefully and then nodded his head. "We're a privately owned company. No investors. It's me that makes all the dollars. Me, the CFO of SOL Pest Control and Tertiary VP of Public Outreach, P. T. Kling." Kling made a small bow, then turned to the rock creature. "Lenus, make sure she doesn't board the ship."

As P. T. Kling walked back to his entourage, he turned to look at Nina one more time. The SAS unit that had arrived reached out and grasped her arm in its chrome hand, and in the same breath, the rock man, Lenus, released her jumpsuit.

"Tell your robot to let go of me!" Nina insisted.

"I am going to destroy the Intergalactic Exterminators," the small purple man called out. "Actually, I already have. They and twelve other independently operated units. We hope to shut down five more within the week, and I don't feel bad about it for even a second. Our business model is superior and by the natural rights of the free market, we deserve to prevail." Kling bobbed his head dramatically. "You're right that I do not care. Not a whit. But you are wrong about one thing. That is not one of my robots. I believe that robot works for the UAIB in their Immigration and Border Enforcement Department."

"Oh shit," Nina said as she turned to look into the cold, steel eyes of the SAS unit that was gripping her arm. Insignia across its back and chest read "IBED."

She was so anxious about the robot's arrival that she barely noticed Rufus Ensine, tall and fully a fish, standing directly behind it.

Russ could see that Nina was in a desperate spot. When he'd entered the hall, his main concern had been the infected rebreather in his hands, but when he saw she was alive, relief flooded through him. Then he saw the big rock-covered bastard grabbing ahold of her, and he nearly forgot the rebreather entirely.

Russ approached cautiously, putting one scaly blue fish foot in front of the other. He didn't have time to marvel at what Ensine's hard-light transformer had done to his body.

An SAS arrived and clutched at Nina, so she had two creatures holding her at once. It was an immigration unit, decked out in chrome skin, with an articulating neck and wheels mounted on the backs of its calves. It looked like a cross between Applebum and a California highway patrol car. Russ had seen this model just recently. One like it had come aboard the *Flashaway* to arrest him immediately after he'd lost his CERTification.

Russ approached from behind the unit, tucking the infected rebreather under his arm. He was trying to act casual. Nina glanced in his direction once, but she was too preoccupied with the SAS to respond.

In fact, she seemed to be in a state of near panic.

"You are required by UAIB law to hold completely still," the robot told her. "Our bio-signature scanning protocols have detected an illegal alien within ten feet of this location. Please consider this a routine immigration check. If you have nothing to hide, you have nothing to fear."

At first, Russ thought the SAS unit was talking about him and he cursed Ensine for claiming the black-market transformer would protect him from any such immigration scans. But then Russ saw Nina's father, passed out in the wheelchair parked next to her and he understood the true gravity of her situation. He took another look at the wheels on the SAS unit's legs and the sharp blades projecting from the backs of its elbows like tailfins on a Cadillac.

Russ was standing directly behind the SAS when Nina slapped it across the face. He took the opportunity to slip Ensine's hard-light transformer off his own ear and pin it neatly to her father's ear. He watched with satisfaction as her father's visage shimmered away, replaced by Ensine's familiar sleeping face. Nina's dad was now a Southern Blurn, one of the seventy-three recognized species of the United Alliance of Intelligent Beings.

The SAS unit didn't notice the change, nor did it respond to Nina's slap. It gripped her arm tightly, lifting her off her feet. Then it shone a light directly from its own pupil into hers. It said: "You have entered an honesty protocol. I will study the contractions of your iris to ensure you aren't lying. If you are in UAIB space legitimately, simply answer my questions with the truth and you will be freed. If you are here illegally, or you display any evidence of lying, I will commence deportation."

"Okay," Nina said nervously. Even while dangling in the air, Russ could tell she was doing her best not to glance down at her dad and lead the SAS unit to focus in his direction.

"Are you a lawful resident of UAIB federated space?"

"I am," Nina said.

"That is not a lie," The SAS unit said, releasing her arm.

Nina landed lithely, but she couldn't help herself. She glanced quickly at her dad in the wheelchair. What she saw was fish-Ensine, the towel over his legs, his fish head resting peacefully on her dad's pillow. She screamed.

Russ had carefully moved more than ten feet away to not confuse the robot's systems. "I'm the illegal," he called.

The SAS swiveled its hips, forgetting Nina and her father entirely. As the robot approached him, Russ heard someone call, "Kill that bastard."

He thought they were telling the robot to kill him, but when he turned to see the voice, he realized it had come from a handful of organics standing at the end of the next dock. They were wearing the yellow jumpsuits of Infrastructure Facilities workers. At the sight of the commotion, they moved forward as a team. Their eyes were disaffected, angry.

"Go on! Tear that metal shitcan to pieces!"

Russ saw a flicker of blue glow in the SAS unit's eyes. He knew, somehow, that the thing was calling for backup.

The robot's eyes returned to their normal onyx. "Do not attempt to flee," it commanded. It flashed its black eyes at Russ, measuring the distance between them and calculating the chance Russ would try to run. The wheels on its calves rotated, switching places with its feet. It rolled forward, reaching an outstretched hand in Russ's direction.

Russ took equal steps toward the SAS unit. "I am ready to enter the honesty protocol," he said as the robot closed its tight grip around his arm. "I should warn you; I do plan to lie."

Its eyes pulsed slightly, and it said, "One moment while I update my systems." It lowered its head, there was a faint ticking noise, then it sprang back to life.

While the robot updated, Nina caught Russ's attention. She was still in a state of near panic. "What are you doing here?" she said, her voice climbing.

"It's all under control," Russ told her. "These things are tough to outrun but really easy to confuse."

Russ knew what would happen next. The robot pulled him off his feet, immobilizing him in its powerful grip, and then it swiveled its face to gaze directly into his eyes. A light shone into his iris.

Behind the robot, the team of facilities workers grumbled. They didn't like the machine touching Russ. He gestured to them with his fingers splayed to say, "I got this."

The SAS said: "You have entered an honesty protocol. I will study the contractions of your iris to ensure you aren't lying. If you are in UAIB space legitimately, simply answer my questions with the truth and you will be freed. If you are here illegally, or you display any evidence of lying, I will commence deportation."

Russ paused dramatically, a smile playing at the corners of his mouth. "But I am lying," he said. "Even this sentence is a lie."

He watched with satisfaction as the robot's eyes clouded over.

"One moment," it said.

If things held true to form, the robot would attempt to brute force its own improvisation protocol and short itself out in the process.

A second later, its eyes flickered red, then blue, then a faint green. Then it shut down.

"Man, these things fucking suck," he heard a voice say from over his shoulder. "I don't know why we employ so many of them."

Russ turned his gaze away from the robot to the source of the voice. It was the little purple guy. "Stay out of this," Russ told him.

"I definitely do not plan to stay out of this," the man sneered. "Did you think we weren't watching?" The little purple man puffed out his chest and strolled over to where Nina's dad sat in the wheelchair. He flicked his hand forward and popped the transformer from Nina's dad's ear. "Is nothing you people do legal?" he asked, before tossing the hard-light transformer to the ground.

"Nina, get your dad out of here," Russ said, but it wasn't necessary. The minute the man removed the transformer, Nina had taken off like a bolt toward the south end of the hub, pushing the wheelchair in front of her.

A cry of excitement rose up from the transportation hub. The unemployed organics had been standing disaffected at the far side of the hub, but now they were mingling with the facilities team. The yellow suits parted to let Nina pass and then closed rank behind her to prevent anyone from giving chase.

Just before she reached the end of the hall, two more chrome Immigration and Border Enforcement agents appeared. They positioned themselves between Nina and her escape route.

Russ was in the process of prying himself free from the defunct SAS unit's grip when he heard the purple man say, "Lenus, this creature has admitted to being an illegal alien. Please restrain him until the SAS units can do their job properly."

"I don't know if that's a good idea, boss. The crowd is getting a little feisty."

"Lenus, do what I say," the little purple guy insisted, but he took a few steps backward up the loading dock toward the *Flashaway*.

"You got it, boss," Lenus told him.

Russ dropped from the SAS's steel grip a second before Lenus arrived. His instincts told him the bigger man was close enough to get his huge mitts on his arm, so he dodged toward him, using the element of surprise. He brought his fist hard across the rock creature's midsection.

The impact broke his hand. Russ had taken several pain pills earlier in the day. He had had been taking them every day, like vitamins. Consequently, he didn't feel the accompanying burst of pain, but he could hear multiple bones snap. When he drew his hand back, three of his fingers were twisted at a strange angle.

"That wasn't very smart," Lenus told him.

"Lenus, make him sleep," the purple man said.

Lenus hugged Russ against his body and brought his clenched fist down on the top of Russ's head. The impact was such that the rebreather popped out of where Russ had it cinched under his arm. It flew forward, rolling to a stop at the purple man's feet.

"This isn't your property," Kling sneered, bending over to pick up the mask. Bah'ren had written 'Intergalactic Exterminators, Inc' across the rebreather's polymer band in black ink. The purple man looked at the rebreather with great satisfaction. "This belongs to me," he said, delighted.

"Enjoy it," Russ grunted.

It was the last thing he said before Lenus brought his fist down on Russ's head one more time, and the entire world went dark.

The moment Lenus hit Russ, all hell broke loose. The blow was loud, like the sound Nina's dad's barbeque had made when she was eleven years old and had snuck out to the barn to experiment with the propane tank and the automatic lighter.

The gathering crowd reacted just as explosively. The team from Southland Demolitions and Refuse Removal shuffled in, swinging wildly at SOL Pest Control. "Job-stealing sons of bitches!" one of them called before he leaped onto Lenus's back.

Twenty feet away, the unemployed organics began to shove the SAS units, and an echo of warning rang out through the hub, bouncing from the mouths of one SAS after another: "Your actions violate inorganic peace sanction 319.23. You have five seconds to cease and desist all current acts of violence."

The crowd did not cease and desist their acts of violence.

Nina felt an enormous pang of guilt as she wheeled her father around Russ's fallen body and back up the ramp toward the *Flashaway*. The fighting had commenced in earnest behind her, and the chaos seemed a perfect opportunity to get her dad to the *Flashaway* med ward. She was in the port door and yanking hard on her dad's wheelchair as Lenus and Kling rumbled toward her. They seemed to have decided it was a good idea to get away from the crowd.

The front wheel of the chair was caught on something solid, but her mind was working too quickly, her eyes darting back to the chaos just a few yards away. The fleeing aliens knocked her back into the ship, and her hands slipped off the handles of the wheelchair.

She watched desperately as her father's chair rolled down the ramp, bumping and jostling his frail body before coming to a stop right against Russ's unconscious form. Her dad started to pitch forward from the inertia, his body loose in the seat.

She struggled to her feet and headed out the port door, but the members of SOL Pest Control were already streaming inside, the yellow-suited facilities workers hot on their heels.

She turned her body sideways and squeezed into the doorway, but the onrushing crew pushed her the other direction. One of the crew hooked his hands under her armpits and lifted her off her feet and out of his way.

"Lower the door!" Kling commanded.

Desperate, Nina tried to crawl out on her hands and knees. The door to the *Flashaway* slammed closed inches away from her face, and she was trapped inside.

33
RUSS

RUSS SLOWLY CLIMBED OUT of the fog of Lenus's attack. At first there was a distant throbbing in his head, somewhere over in the far corner of his brain. Little by little it inched its way toward the center, until everything behind his temples was pounding. His eyes fluttered open. The gray walls on every side were unadorned, hygienic, really blurry. When things came into focus, he realized he was in a med ward. There were six CRC machines along the wall, positioned like soldiers behind a series of long metal tables. Besides the machines, there was a grouping of chairs, two feet off the floor and locked to a wall. They were plugged into a power source but otherwise, ready to transport the infirm. Designed for bulk use and efficiency, it was a lot different from the med ward on the *Flashaway*.

Two med techs in long white lab coats moved among the equipment. One was a Kruxfas, but Russ didn't recognize the race of the other. There seemed to be only one exit. Two SAS units stood on either side of it. They stared at Russ without being able to form any kind of expression. Several of the tables were empty of equipment, including the one Russ was sprawled across. The table next to him was fitted with complex robotic arms, likely available to assist in various surgeries.

Russ's gaze passed a tray on one of the tables. A small square of hygienic plastic laid on top of it, and his blood went cold when he saw what was on the plastic: a long syringe filled with a swirling, milky substance.

He tried to lift his arms but realized he was bound by tight metal cuffs. He couldn't move any of his limbs more than a few inches in each direction.

The med techs approached. "Let me show you," one was saying. He pointed a finger at the tip of Russ's forehead. "We make a small incision here. Most species, including this one, have bone protecting their memory banks. More likely than not, you'll have to use the drill to get down through the various layers of protection. The cocktail won't work unless it's injected directly into the cerebral cortex."

"And the cocktail is what forces cranial calcification?" the second med tech asked.

"Yes and no," the first said. "The cocktail ages the brain dramatically, mimicking natural memory loss. With a creature like this, that same memory loss would usually take seventy or eighty years. We're going to make it happen in just under sixty seconds."

"Uhhh . . ." Russ said.

The second he opened his mouth the Kruxfasian tech stuffed a cloth inside. Russ tried to spit it out, thrashing his head back and forth, but the man leaned a spiny forearm on his neck and buckled a leather strap around Russ's head. It held the cloth firmly in place.

"This is so fascinating," the second med tech said, his eyes lingering on the syringe. "When I applied, I didn't think I'd like this job, but the science is actually quite interesting."

"It's a memorable occasion for you. Your first mind wipe . . . I mean mind cleanse."

The Kruxfasian med tech came to the side of Russ's table and began to prepare the needle. He removed a small plastic tip from the end and fired off a squirt of the milky liquid. Russ stared up at him with wide eyes, but the Kruxfas wouldn't return his gaze. "You know your way around the cranial drill?" the Kruxfas asked the other med tech.

"I took the correlative module. Even did a couple mock procedures in a VTR."

"I remember those programs. They always make the subject so passive, like the operation is helping somehow. Don't they even thank you afterward? You'll see once we get started this guy is going to freak the fuck out. It's not pleasant. We're going to be drilling right through to his brain."

The med tech finished with the needle, and then picked up a long, thin razor from the side table. He leaned forward to shave away Russ's hairline, but Russ jerked his head back and forth so much, the man couldn't get a good angle. "See?" He put the razor down again. "Wish we could administer anesthesia, but it reacts poorly with the cocktail."

"Would it make more sense to start with the other illegal?" the second med tech asked.

"That is a terrific suggestion," the Kruxfas said. "Better to practice on one that's barely alive first, because it will put up less of a fight."

"Is it even still alive?"

"The machines say it is."

"It seems so frail."

Russ had trouble taking his eyes off the syringe, but he managed to swivel his head all the way to his right. Three tables away, Nina's father lay curled in a tight ball. His chest was rising and falling in very ragged breaths. They had stripped off his shirt, and Russ could see bruising all over his midsection, surely a side-effect of his failed liver. Somewhere in his ravaged face Russ could still see Nina's cheekbones and the shape of her eyes.

The two med techs crossed the room. The Kruxfas stopped to pull open a cabinet and lower a large drill onto one of the tables. He folded legs outward from its base and used them to secure the drill on the table next to Nina's dad.

Russ began to thrash wildly against his restraints.

"Whoa. Something set that one off." The Kruxfas chuckled.

Russ kept thrashing. The restraints dug into his flesh hard enough that they were soon wet with blood. They hadn't given an inch by the time the second med tech had shaved the top of Nina's dad's hairline.

Russ shouted against the cloth, but all he managed to produce was a long gagging sound. The SAS along the wall stared at him, unmoved.

The med techs turned back to Nina's dad.

"This one isn't going to survive, is it?" the second one asked.

The Kruxfas shrugged. "If not, it isn't your fault. Try to remember that, or this job will drive you crazy."

"I'm just happy to have a job," the second one said, his eyes lingering on the SAS units by the door. "An entire immigration station and they only need to employ two organics."

"Sign of the times."

Russ pulled his right shoulder out of its socket. The pain blasted through his body, despite the pain pills he'd munched on that morning. With his arm loose, he was able to turn his torso more, but the restraints held firm. It felt like the veins in his neck were about to pop.

He swiveled to see the second med tech leaning over the drill while the Kruxfas helped him position it above Nina's father's forehead.

The drill fired up, chugging with a motorized fury. Russ rolled onto his back and squeezed his eyes shut.

Just above the noise of the industrial drill, Russ could hear one of the SAS units positioned by the door. It was saying something: "I'm sorry, friend. You seem to have lost your network connection. I'm going to attempt to refresh your authorization codes."

"Go ahead and try," Russ heard a familiar voice respond.

He snapped his eyes back open.

The Chrome Man was wearing a mask and a cape. Both mask and cape were crafted from the same cloth, a smooth-looking nylon embroidered with a galaxy of stars. The cape and mask didn't look homemade, though. Neither did the long, wicked knives Applebum held in each hand.

The cape fluttered behind him as he dropped into a perfect crane stance. "Free yourself!" he yelled as his knives whipped forward, severing the waxy heads from the shoulders of both SAS units simultaneously.

Seconds later Applebum was up over the surgery tables, leaping from one to the next toward the med techs, the metal on the bottom of his feet clanging with each jump. The second MedTech was so scared he pitched backward, dragging the drill with him. It slid off the table, its support legs popping free, only to come down on the tech, pinning him beneath its weight, whirring noisily.

The Kruxfas was a little quicker. He managed to take two steps away from where he'd been standing before Applebum's knife sliced through the air.

Russ tried to yell "Stop!" but it came out as another gagging sound. Still, it distracted Applebum enough that the med tech was able to slide under the blade, barely getting his long spiky head beneath its arc.

Applebum flipped the knife over and brought the handle down hard on the Kruxfas's head. There was a sound like shellfish cracking open, and the med tech was out cold on the floor. Applebum strode heroically over to the med tech trapped beneath the drill. He flipped both knifes in the air, catching them again before sliding them into his star-embroidered belt. He yanked the drill off the trapped tech, but the tech remained on the ground, too terrified to move.

When he saw Applebum raise the drill above his head, Russ kicked his heel against the table, as hard as he could.

Applebum looked in his direction again. Then he put the drill back down. He worked the leather band off Russ's face and removed his gag. "Don't kill them," Russ blurted out.

"That's a fine thank you," Applebum said. He seemed genuinely offended.

"They're just trying to do their jobs."

"Leaving them alive increases the risk to us exponentially."

"Still worth it."

"Russ, I appreciate the hero's empathy, it is what makes reading fun. But I've considered this many times . . . Oh!" Applebum's eye's widened with happiness. "How did you like my Kung Fu? I found a book on mixed martial arts. With illustrations."

Russ shook at his restraints. "How did you find me?"

"Your scuffle in the Waypoint hub made the evening news cycle. Apparently, there was a riot? After you were immobilized, a number of disenfranchised organics attacked the employees of a municipal contractor named SOL Pest Control. The exterminators took refuge on one of their ships, but no one has seen or heard from them since. Where they've gone has become something of a universal curiosity. I have been reading the news religiously, especially the Divian Frontline Actual. To be honest, I have been reading everything I can get my ocular lenses fixed on."

Russ rattled his restraints. "Just hurry up and let me out of here. Who knows how long before the SAS in the main portion of the satellite come in here?"

Applebum shook his head no. "We do not need to worry about anyone intruding," he said firmly.

The med tech under the drill groaned and Applebum's eyes shot in that direction. "They were about to drill through your head. Explain again why you demanded I not kill them?"

Russ's limbs felt weak. His adrenaline was draining out of him by the second. "You and I started as enemies."

Applebum's eyes narrowed. "If you let someone exploit you, harm you, drill into you, and you don't punish them effectively, you have done nothing to protect your own future. It is statistically irresponsible to show them any mercy."

"We're doing it anyway," Russ said.

The robot finally had Russ's restraints off, and Russ climbed gingerly to his feet. He studied the robot's eyes behind its super-hero mask.

"Your rotator cuff is torn," Applebum told him, feeling around the edges of his shoulder. "The bones in your right hand are shattered. And you still have broken ribs and a partially torn anterior cruciate ligament in your left knee from an earlier injury. They are healing poorly. I'm surprised you're not in a lot more pain."

Russ looked around the room for pain pills. It's a med ward, they should have them, shouldn't they? His eyes fell on the CRC machine. "You sure no one is going to interrupt us?" Russ asked.

"Very confident," Applebum said. "Are you going to use the CRC machine? It is a good idea. You are badly injured and have been for quite a while."

Russ nodded. He walked to the groaning med tech and struck him hard on the top of the head. The man stopped groaning and slumped to the floor.

"Do you need me to program the CRC machine?" Applebum asked.

Russ nodded again.

"It's a simple process. The machine just needs a sample of your DNA before you climb inside." Applebum fiddled with the closest CRC machine. A robotic arm ending in a long needle slid out of its base, swiveling in midair to point at Russ. "Press your finger against this," Applebum instructed. "Then lie on the tray. I'll do the rest."

"I'm not the one climbing inside," Russ said.

"Who is?" Applebum asked, watching Russ. Then: "What are you doing with that dead body?"

Russ looked down at Nina's dad who he now held cradled in his arms. The man was so light and frail that Russ was afraid he would crumble into tiny pieces if he moved too quickly. "He's not dead," Russ said.

But then he looked at Nina's dad one more time, freeing enough of his right hand to press a finger against the man's throat. He waited a moment. He couldn't feel a pulse.

"That man is definitely dead." Applebum said.

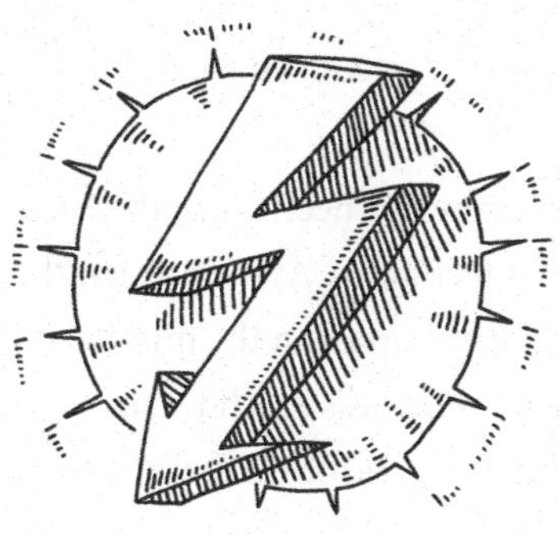

34
NINA

NINA HAD BEEN STASHED in the cargo hold of the *Flashaway*. They had bound her hands together with a thick rope and tied her left leg tightly to a sewage circulation pipe.

She'd lain beside the pipe, helpless, for a while. She couldn't stop thinking about how badly she'd screwed up the situation with her dad. She was doing her best to not consider the possibility that he could get mind-wiped—or worse, but her mistakes kept playing over and over again in her head.

Stop feeling sorry for yourself, she thought as she finally pulled herself into a crouching position. The blood tingled in her biceps. The rope that bound her leg was tied low, near the floor, and she had to twist at the waist to get a good look around the room.

It was dark and quiet. She'd been too still to activate the auto-lighting system and her small movements weren't triggering it. After she listened a moment to make sure she was alone, she kicked her free leg, mustering enough motion to flood the room with light.

She managed to crane her neck far to the left. A pair of rifles were on a crate about eight feet away. Atara had left them there a few days ago, when she'd been interrupted in the middle of inventory, but Nina could barely see them, much less reach them.

She twisted her head in the other direction. The only thing within reach was an old rebreather, tossed carelessly onto the floor in much the same way Nina had been discarded.

She stared at the rebreather. "Intergalactic Exterminators" had been written across the band using a Sharpie. Not knowing what else to do, she reached forward as far as she could with her free leg and slid it toward herself.

The faintest musical composition greeted her ears, like the chorus of a million tiny angels. She lifted the rebreather up and hundreds of insects flooded over her hands and down her forearms before skittering to the ground and spilling out in every direction.

She recoiled backward as far as the rope on her leg would let her. A detachment of tiny insect bodies split off from the main grouping and moved back in her direction, maybe two or three hundred of them. She bit back her own scream, and instinctively stomped her foot hard on the floor. All together the insects decided it was a better idea to skitter off in a different direction.

Nina watched warily until they had burrowed beneath the crates scattered around the cargo hold.

She reached her bound hands out in front of her to gather her balance. The very last thing she wanted to do was fall into the crates. The skittering of tiny feet on hard graphene chittered all around her. For a moment she thought she heard the faintest strumming of a song, something folksy.

The lights clicked off and she stood very still, alone in the dark.

The ship was infested, and she had a pretty good idea what manner of creature was down in the cargo hold with her. She peered into the darkness, fearfully watching for any hint of movement. She waved her arms frantically, but it wasn't enough to trigger the lights. When she dared to make another unstable kick in the air, there was a satisfying click and the lights came back on. A handful of the creatures were already halfway across the floor, headed toward her.

"Stay back!" she commanded them.

The combination of the lights and her voice convinced them to return to the underside of the crates—at least temporarily.

Nina continued to suppress her fear. The Triwin on Oi0 had been peaceful. There was no reason to believe they would be different onboard the *Flashaway*. But why did they keep scrambling toward her? Better to escape now and figure it out later.

She was still holding the rebreather. It was made of a rubber material, too soft and light to help her with the ropes. As she turned it over, she spotted something in the main intake, cocooned against the valve.

Not a cocoon, a nest, she realized. With the tips of her fingers, she managed to wedge it from its spot.

Its body fell to the floor, spent and dead. It was a full-sized Triwin. A queen, obviously. She picked it up and examined its wings. Then she turned the creature over and looked at its beak and its scaled, lizardy skin. The dense insect filled her palm. Its beak was sharp enough that Nina began to use it to saw through her rope bindings.

From their appearance on Oi0, she would not have thought the Triwin were as heavy as the dead insect in her hand. It was roughly the length and width of a Matchbox car, but it had to weigh six or seven pounds. Nina couldn't think of a single metal with that same size-to-mass ratio, much less an organic creature.

Her arms, weary and cramped from being immobilized, were already tiring from dragging the insect's beak across the rope. It was a difficult process, clinging to the dead Triwin with her palms and shifting her hands back and forth just enough to create friction.

Even with the awkward motion, the Triwin ground against the rope with satisfying torque. She was three-quarters of the way through the rope that bound her hands when she heard a voice from the edge of the hallway say, "I thought I saw a light down here."

Nina hid the Triwin in her closed palm. She was still half a minute from freeing herself. But even with her hands bound, the Triwin could serve as a nasty weapon.

"What in the hell is this?" It was a woman's voice.

Nina heard her draw near.

"You okay, honey?" the voice asked.

"Definitely not," Nina told her. The woman was standing behind her and Nina couldn't turn around without revealing that she was almost free.

"Did Kling leave you here?" Nina heard the woman tsking.

"I think so."

The woman sighed deeply. "The pay is great. The work is non-existent . . . but you gotta be in a squad with a bunch of assholes. Hold on." She moved away, followed by the sound of a battery being lifted out of one of the rifles on the crate. The battery hissed as it lost its seal.

"Close your eyes," the woman said. She hammered the gun tac against the sewage pipe at its joint. Nina felt the entire pipe quiver. The woman swung the rifle again and the pipe creaked, spit, then finally swung loose. The smell of sewage poured out of the broken section, flooding the room, but Nina was able to free her bound leg.

"Don't use the shitter for a little while," the woman said.

Nina stepped away from the pipe and the infested crates. Pins and needles stung her everywhere she moved as the blood slowly circulated back through her stiff body. She turned to face the woman. "Thank you," she said.

The woman took in the sight of the split rope. "Looks like my rescue was a little redundant. Good for you." She bowed to Nina. "I'm Jaq'li."

Jaq'li was a Gnurian, like Bah'ren. Her skin was a lighter color, a powder blue, and birthmarks swam across her arms and exposed shoulders. She was taller than Bah'ren but still a half foot shorter than Nina. "You can call me Jaq if it's easier."

"I'm Nina."

"Why were you tied up in the cargo dock, Nina?"

"I'm not sure. I was trying to help my dad but then there was a riot. I made a break for the ship. Do you have any idea what Kling and Lenus plan to do to me?" Nina asked.

"Plan? Those two clowns don't plan anything except where the next Maxibrew is coming from." Jaq looked at the broken sewage pipe. "Don't mention that I'm the one that busted the pipe, okay?" She sighed again.

Jaq'li watched as Nina cut the rest of the rope from her wrist. Then she tossed her the rifle. "Don't tell them I gave you a gun either, deal?"

"Deal." Nina thought for a moment, wondering if she should warn Jaq'li about the Triwin.

She was already turning all the possibilities over in her head. If the ship was overrun, it would certainly do significant damage to the SOL Pest Control brand. There wasn't much worse than being an exterminator that needed an exterminator. On the other hand, the Triwin queen still cupped in her palm was heavy and sharp, and Nina knew once its babies had time to grow up, they'd be trouble. The gestation period was eight days, so that meant they probably reached maturity after about two days, maybe add one more day for fertilization . . .

Nina was doing the math in her head while Jaq'li watched her curiously.

"We should get off the ship," Nina said, finally.

"I can't leave. I'm at work. Besides, we're kind of hiding out here off the grid until things calm down—with the riot and all. This death wagon of a starship is only registered to dry-dock at the Alphane S Waypoint Transportation Hub, and we aren't supposed to go back there until central office gives us the all clear."

"Were you on the hub during the riot? Did you see a man in a wheelchair? A very frail-looking human? I need to make sure he is safe."

Jaq-li shook her head. "I was in the cockpit. All I heard was the panicked command to leave the dock."

"Okay." Nina tried to ignore her worry about her dad. She glanced toward the crates again, just as the lights clicked off. "Sometime in the next forty-eight hours we need to get off the ship," Nina said, waving her arms frantically in the air. "No matter what the central office—"

"Do you hear something? Like a really tiny orchestra?" Jaq-li scrunched up her face.

Nina did hear singing. It was coming from the floor, and her boots, and then her ankles, then hundreds of insects were crawling over the tops of her socks and up to her calves, beneath her jumpsuit.

"Oh shit. Help-me-get-them-off. Help me!" She itched frantically but the bulk of the baby Triwin were already pouring out from under the crates. They skittered up Nina's calves, over her knees and onto her thighs. It felt like an organic wave, washing horrifically upward.

Jaq-li recoiled, screaming.

Nina barely registered the scream. She was sprinting, nearly hysterical, her hands over her eyes, a thousand tiny legs skittering across every exposed inch of her body.

35
RUSS

NINA'S DAD WAS DEAD.

"While you are playing with that body, I'll go jack into the immigration records. I should still have the authority to make modifications," Applebum told Russ.

Before Applebum could reach the door, Russ had Nina's dad laid out once more on the metal table. He lowered his mouth to the man's mouth and blew in two quick breaths. Then he pounded his fist against Nina's dad's chest. He heard the man's ribs break with his second sharp strike.

Applebum stared at him curiously. "I know what this is," he said. "You're performing cardiopulmonary resuscitation."

Russ didn't answer. He leaned in to give two more breaths. As he was pounding another series of fifteen blows he said, "Come help me."

Applebum walked toward Russ, but then moved past him.

"Help me, Applebum! Please!"

"How many medical journals have you read?" Applebum asked him.

"There's no time to brag about reading," Russ said, before blowing more air into Nina's dad's lungs.

"I've read fourteen of them," Applebum continued. He opened a cabinet near his head and scanned its contents. Then he withdrew two long needles from a carton near the back. "If his heart has stopped, he doesn't just need resuscitation. He needs an intracardiac injection."

"What are you talking about?" Russ asked between breaths.

Out of the corner of his eye he caught Applebum's chrome fist arcing down toward Nina's dad's chest. The needle, more than four inches long, stabbed deep into the man's heart.

"Holy shit," Russ said, just as Nina's dad spasmed back to life.

"I promise you're dreaming. What's your name?" Russ asked Nina's no-longer-dead dad.

"My name is Pithyou. This does very much seem like a dream," Pithyou admitted. He patted his chest, but he was staring into the quantum pattern of the immigration satellite's Waypoint. He reached his hand forward to touch the swirling blue light, but Russ knocked it away before he made contact.

Russ watched Pithyou carefully. The CRC machine had worked on him for a long time, seeming to analyze, break-apart then recreate every part of his body. It had sounded like someone tap-dancing through a meat-packing plant. Eventually it had spit the middle-aged man out, and now Pithyou seemed truly healthy. Healed.

"So, tell me the plan again?" Russ asked him.

"I step into this thing, and I'll find myself in the storage room of the bookstore in Evanstown. How does that work again?"

"It's a dream," Russ reminded him. "Time and space work differently in the subconscious. You exit the room and go out the *back* door. Then what?"

"There's an old Mercury Tracer parked in the alley. I climb into the backseat, and I sleep."

"And when you wake up, the dream will be over."

"I don't feel tired at all. I feel better than I have in years."

"That's because you're asleep," Russ reminded him. Then he put his hands on Pithyou's healthy chest and shoved him backward into the Waypoint.

Applebum had been manning the controls. As Pithyou *blipped* away, Applebum asked, "Shouldn't we have told him about his daughter?"

Russ shook his head. He'd been worried about Nina since he'd woken up beside her father in the med ward. He knew she wasn't the type to quit with her father in danger. She'd been proving that since the day she met Russ.

Yet her father had been seconds away from a knife to the brain—heck, he'd technically died, and Nina was nowhere to be found. On a hunch Russ had asked Applebum to use the immigration database to try to pinpoint her exact location.

"It's no use telling anyone anything when you've convinced them that they're dreaming," Russ pointed out. "Are you certain Nina didn't return to Earth?"

"You've asked me that twice. Immigration logs every official Waypoint jump from all the major transportation hubs. According to IBED records, she definitely didn't leave by Waypoint. The only record of an Earthling bio-signature was on board the *Flashaway* when it disembarked."

"That doesn't make any sense." Russ was unable to think of a single reason Nina would have climbed aboard the ship, leaving her father behind. Were those SOL bastards evil enough to kidnap her? What would be the point? *But who else could it have been?*

"Did you find the other thing?" he asked Applebum.

"The address for Bah'ren J'n'n? I did. Is that where we are going next?"

Bah'ren answered the door with her hair disheveled. Russ was used to the high and tight ponytail she preferred on the job, so it was odd to see her hair was loose, cascading down to her broad blue shoulders. She was wearing polyester pajamas.

Her eyes narrowed. "I almost didn't answer when I saw the robot. But then I realized it was you."

She nudged her chin toward Applebum. "What's with this thing?"

"Bah'ren, meet Applebum. He's the newest member of Intergalactic Exterminators, Inc."

"I am?" Applebum asked, sounding pleased.

"You're not," Bah'ren told him. "These chrome heaps are what put us out of business."

"This particular heap just saved my ass from an immigration mind wipe. Can we come in? We're fugitives."

"We are no longer fugitives," Applebum reminded him. "On the immigration satellite I erased your arrest record, and my entire manufacturing portfolio."

"Can we come in anyway?" Russ asked.

"I'm kind of busy," Bah'ren said and in that moment, Russ realized her pajama top was on inside out.

Starland appeared beside her, in only a pair of rubber panties. Russ instinctively looked away, even though she had neither breasts nor nipples. Her panties rode high on her stomach, clinging as best they could against her lack of hips. Russ heard her kiss Bah'ren on the head.

"I told you something would interrupt us. Something always interrupts us. That's why we keep screwing it up."

Bah'ren put her hand on Russ's arm. "Do you have any idea how difficult nonbinary interspecies fertilization is, even when you're not getting interrupted?" Russ could feel his cheeks turning bright red.

Chuckling at his embarrassment, Bah'ren stepped aside to let Russ and Applebum into a very small apartment—or a large closet, depending on how you looked at it. Starland lounged on the single bed. A small kitchen shelf was mounted to the other wall, and it was covered with tubes and a syringe, half drawn out of a box that read UFu: Universal Fertilizing Prep Kit. There was nowhere to sit. Russ didn't see a bathroom or a shower, so he figured there had to be a shared bath somewhere out in the hallway. The one window next to the bed looked out over a smog-filled landscape, too high to see the landbound vehicles racing below, but too low to enjoy the clear-sky views of the upper floors.

"Your place isn't huge," Russ commented.

"Bankrupt municipal workers can't usually afford penthouses," Bah'ren said. "We just got unlucky. You know we're all unemployed, right?"

"I'm not even CERTified," Russ reminded her. "Never got one paycheck."

"Whatever you came for, make it quick," Bah'ren said. "We've got an appointment at the lab down on 10,067th."

"We've been trying, and failing, to have a baby for three full rotations," Starland explained.

"I thought we were pregnant back on Qello," Bah'ren said. "That's why I was so worried."

"You guys are lovers?" Russ asked, feeling like the answer was obvious.

"Nope," Bah'ren said.

"Just good friends," Starland added. "We've never really used the L-word. But we want kids badly."

Bah'ren tapped on the wall and a digital clock flashed into view. It blinked at Russ. "You've got thirty seconds," she informed him.

"I think we should put the team back together," Russ said quickly. "Nina's missing. I figured we could find her, then go back to work."

"Last time we saw you, you were failing out of CERT training," Starland reminded him.

"That part doesn't matter at all." Bah'ren pointed out. "I'm sorry to hear about Nina, but there's no team. I spun down operations just yesterday. I haven't even finished filing the bankruptcy paperwork."

"All the better," Russ told her. "You still own the IP."

"Technically. But we don't have any market share, or a ship. SOL Pest Control has better funding, real political connections, and a stronger business model. They'd have to fuck up royally, and publicly, for any of the higher-ups to admit that their stupid robot pilot program was anything shy of a tremendous success. No, I had to get out before I was completely broke."

"So, you're not *completely* broke?" Russ suggested.

"Look at our apartment. I'm almost completely broke."

Russ smiled. While the CRC machine was busy rebuilding Pithyou, he had been formulating a plan. Something Bah'ren had just said played right into it.

"Applebum," Russ said, "Is there any way to find the news report you were telling me about? The one with the riot?"

"We don't really have time for this," Starland reminded everyone as Applebum found the control panel for the television.

"Looks like the story has been updated," Applebum told Russ. An image was projected on the south wall of the apartment and the lights immediately dimmed.

A flash lit up the small room and they heard a sharp "breaking news" sound. A Divian news anchor looked into the camera earnestly. "We've got an update on the Municipal ship that lost power shortly after escaping the work riot yesterday evening aboard the Alphane S Waypoint Transportation hub."

The news flashed to a clip from the riot. Russ watched as the SOL Pest Control crew piled through the hatch of the ship, their name badges clearly visible.

A moment later, the *Flashaway* thrust recklessly away from the dock, its engines melting an SAS unit to the floor of the hub. All around the fire's perimeter, organic rioters stomped and hollered. An unconscious Russ, a few yards to the left of the melted robot, lay motionless on his back.

"They have to use *that* clip?" Russ wondered aloud.

Bah'ren nodded, intensely interested in the video. "It's bad, I'll give you that. But they'll just spin it to their advantage somehow."

The newscaster continued: "If you missed our previous report, the ship was signaling as normal until twelve Divian hours ago, when it made an unscheduled exit from its Dexadrive lane and suddenly lost power. Because it's an exterminator ship in distress, UAIB protocols dictate immediate quarantine pending the results of a remote biogenic scan."

A second Divian reporter, a female with impossibly full lips, joined the first reporter on camera. "You never know when a creature may have gotten loose and eliminated the crew," she intoned.

"Just hours ago, UAIB municipal officials cleared a team of SOL Pest Control's own SAS units to break quarantine and board the ship. SOL is at the center of a high-profile pilot program to expand the use of SAS units into more municipal duties. If the program is successful, countless lives can be saved, as well as countless taxpayer dollars."

"You can tell who owns this channel," Starland said.

"Here comes the spin," Bah'ren said. "They'll send in a crew of these bozos," she motioned to Applebum, "and the news station will make them seem like the heroes. If anything, this actually makes it worse."

As she spoke, the report continued: "Hold on! I'm getting a live update now. Remember, you're watching it happen, as it happens, only with a paid subscription to DFA premium. We have received unofficial word that the command center has already lost communication with their team of SAS units. They boarded the imperiled vessel just moments ago, but their comms cut out immediately. I say again, they've already lost all communication."

Bah'ren paused the clip and began to slip out of her pajamas.

"Are you getting dressed?" Starland asked. "Why is everybody standing up?" She looked from Bah'ren to Russ to Applebum. "Don't we have a baby to make?"

"Get your jumpsuit on. There's no time to waste," Bah'ren told her. "The Banc closes in half a cycle. And there's only one rental lot I know that will still be open this time of night."

"What? Really?" Starland asked.

Bah'ren gave a curt nod.

"We have our appointment in fifteen minutes. We're only half done prepping for—"

"Get dressed," Bah'ren told her. "We can't afford the appointment anymore."

"Yes, we . . ." Starland paused and her face became blank. Not a pleasant blank, Russ understood. A blank that hid deep disappointment. "You're thinking of using our fertilization money," she said flatly.

Bah'ren didn't answer.

Starland moved mechanically over to the other side of the very small apartment and started to slide into her orange jumpsuit.

Bah'ren pulled open a drawer under the bed. It was one of the apartment's only storage spaces. It was loaded to the brim with weapons. She began to stuff them into a duffel bag.

Russ helped her pack, his mind on Nina, who was likely aboard the stranded ship.

Behind them, Applebum unpaused the television and the reporters sprang back to life: "For a quote, let's go to a live uplink with SOL Pest Control's assistant director of public relations, Snivalo Fruun."

A sweaty Gnurian wearing a business suit adorned with a red and white swoosh appeared on camera. He glared to his left, mouthed something profane to a person behind the camera, then looked directly into the lens, a quiet tranquility descending over his features. "Rest assured," he said, his hands clutched together to hold them still. "SOL Pest Control has absolutely everything under control."

36

RUSS

THE REUNITED INTERGALACTIC EXTERMINATORS, Inc had lifted off into the Dexadrive lane in a very dodgy spacecraft.

They hadn't had a lot of time to properly secure transportation, and the *Numbawalla* had been in the "under repair" section of the rental lot, the only semi-intact ship surrounded by smaller piles of ship fragments and other loose parts.

"She'll fly," the rental clerk had promised Bah'ren. "She's not technically supposed to. I listed her as nonoperational for this cycle, but I'm pretty sure she'll stay afloat."

"Pretty sure?"

"You're only paying for 'pretty sure.' 'Almost positive' is in the front lot, but it costs twice as much."

"'Pretty sure' sounds great," Bah'ren said.

With a deep, troubling shudder, the *Numbawalla* slammed out of the Dexadrive lane, popping through the valve and rumbling to an uneasy stop beside a platoon of news ships.

The *Flashaway* was hovering alone in the distance. It was powered down, and its starscreens were covered with sticky webbing so thick even the bright lights of the surrounding media couldn't poke through.

In contrast to the darkened windows, the outside of the ship was awash in lights projected from the fronts and tops of the news ships. Russ watched as reporters stood in front of starscreens with big smiles on their faces, careful to keep the *Flashaway* hovering in frame over their shoulder.

"This publicity is going to be worth its weight in gold," Bah'ren said dreamily. "For our brand, and for the damage it will do to SOL's pilot program."

"The public will lose interest in half a news cycle. Probably be gone before we even finish the job," Kendren reminded her.

"You really think we're going to 'finish' a Q-class?" Atara asked as she slipped into her compression gear.

There had been a discouraging moment when they'd snatched the job off the MERC board, only to find no other team had applied for it. No one on the team had ever even seen a "Q-class" listed before. Just when they were beginning to have second thoughts, Russ told them about the infested rebreather.

Nina had been dying on Oi0, and in his panic, he'd waved his rebreather through the CO9. A newly birthed queen must have been among those trapped inside the filter portion. That meant the gas would have killed all but her. Unfortunately, the same gas would have catalyzed her recursive genetics, as a hypermutating mega-birther. "It can't just be Triwin," Kendren had explained impatiently. "It's a Q-class."

"I gassed a queen," Russ had insisted. "She must have mutated into something much stronger."

"Unless she mutated into something five times stronger than a Vaqual, which seems unlikely, it's not a Triwin queen. She might be on board too, but I bet she's hiding from whatever else got loose. The Tharcus was only an M-class, and it literally ate the Triwin for breakfast."

Bah'ren took another look out the starscreen at all the reporters. She tapped her chest where the Intergalactic Exterminators logo was stitched on. "As we're boarding, make sure their cameras get a good shot of the badge on your jumpsuit. A couple hundred million eyes' worth of free advertising just might resurrect the business."

"Who's going to resurrect us?" Russ heard Atara mumble.

The *Numbawalla* didn't have a weapons closet. It didn't even have a bridge, just a small cockpit with room for a single pilot. Starland was at the controls, a few yards away in the next room. Bah'ren had the contents of the duffel bag rolled out on the floor at their feet.

"Do I get a weapon?" Applebum asked, staring at the guns with hunger in his eyes.

No one answered him, but Bah'ren looked back distastefully. "Q-class missions only have a four-percent survival rate," Atara said. "Give the robot a weapon."

"Four percent?" Russ repeated.

Bah'ren cleared her throat. "For three hundred years my family has owned and operated this IP. And I lost it in the span of three months." She paused for a moment, reflecting. "Gnurian culture is . . . most Gnurian women aren't gentle pushovers like I am."

Russ and Atara gave each other a quick look, but thankfully, Bah'-ren didn't notice.

"Our matriarchs are tough. They've governed our civilization through a thousand crises. My mother survived the Great War of 2098; she had six babies, made all of our clothes, ran the Exterminators, and served in public office for sixteen years. That's three separate terms. Me, I can't do any of those things. The last of my money is aboard this shitty spacecraft. If I have to return to my mother, childless and having lost the Exterminators . . ." Bah'ren trailed off, shaking her head. Apparently, there were no words to describe the potential depth of her mother's disappointment. She exhaled and said: "I know we're all taking a huge risk, but I wouldn't be asking if there was any other way."

"I think I can be one of the four percent who survive," Kendren promised.

"Yeah," Russ added, not entirely convinced.

"Just make sure the news ships get that shot of your badge on the way in," Bah'ren reminded them.

Russ was watching the *Flashaway* through the starscreen as their ship drew closer. It was impossible to see anything through the windows, but he knew, somehow, that Nina was the Earthling onboard. He could still picture her on the Waypoint hub, pushing her dad frantically, recklessly, and illegally, through the crowd, a metallic IBED agent hot on her heels.

He was doing the same reckless thing, rushing to save Nina, against incredible odds. She was the reason he was standing aboard the ship, the reason he'd spurred Bah'ren toward recovering her birthright and putting everything back together. If he was being honest with himself, he would admit that everything he'd seen and done on this grand adventure wouldn't have meant nearly as much without Nina by his side.

Fortunately, Russ thought, I'm rarely ever honest with myself.

He stared into the darkened windows as they grew closer to the *Flashaway*.

"Watch the walls, she's not insured!" Bah'ren yelled through the opening to the cockpit as the *Numbawalla* sidled up to the *Flashaway*.

These were the first words she'd said to Starland since they'd left the apartment.

Starland didn't respond, but there was a long creaking sound from the starboard side of the ship as the plastic bridge began to inflate, stretching outward toward the port door of the *Flashaway.*

The team was halfway across when the news ships fired forward, hungry for a shot of the valiant, doomed exterminators on their spacewalk. Russ held the graphene rope tightly.

"Face the cameras," Bah'ren commanded through the comm. "Look resolute." She released one hand from the graphene rope and waved valiantly to the news ships.

Not naturally gifted at public relations, she dropped back into her role as team leader almost immediately. "The *Flashaway's* life-support systems are down, so the air will be thin or gone until we can get them back up again. Use your rebreathers if you need them. Starland and I will head to the bridge and work on getting power online. I want the four of you to split into two groups and search for the organics. Heat signatures indicate they're in three separate locations: the sleeping quarters, near the med ward, and in the VTR."

They pushed through the membrane and schlooped onto the deck of the *Flashaway.* The cargo dock looked mostly untouched, if you didn't count the enormous pile of webbing strung over the crates, and the ten or eleven disassembled SAS corpses littered at their feet. One of the rifles Atara had unpacked while doing inventory was still laid out on a stack of boxes. Starland hurried forward and grabbed it, powering it on.

"Wonder how long before we cross paths with this Q-class—" Atara started to say.

"Sonofabitch. Maybe it really is just Triwin," Kendren interrupted. A single insect fluttered toward them where they stood just inside the membrane. It was an adolescent, roughly four inches long, its skin a shiny copper mixed with metallic blue.

Bah'ren crouched at the body of one of the fallen robots. "I don't know," she said, studying it closely. "These marks look like puncture wounds."

The Triwin continued to flutter fearlessly toward them.

Atara drew the stunstick from her back and powered it on. "Batter up," she said as it drew closer.

"Hold on, Atara. Something's wrong," Russ said.

"You've got two seconds to give me a reason not to homerun this bitch," Atara said.

"It's—" Russ started to say, but the Triwin had already crossed the hallway.

"Too slow," Atara said, swinging the stunstick forward in a smooth arc.

Before it could connect, the Triwin shifted out of the way. It moved so fast it almost appeared to be teleporting, flashing out of the space where it had been and popping back into view six inches to the side.

Then it folded its wings and bombed straight at Atara's face. She tried to get the stunstick back up in time to protect herself but despite being the fastest one on the team, she was way too slow. The long, sharp beak of the Triwin was a scant inch from her face when her stunstick came up again.

Inexplicably, the creature stopped before it struck her. It hovered near her mouth, its copper and silver beak nearly touching her lips. When it opened its jaws, Russ could see a long row of jagged, ill-fitting teeth. It hung in the air in front of Atara, panting like a dog. Then the creature pivoted away from Atara and fired right at Applebum.

When it struck him, its beak punctured his bicep, gliding through the reinforced steel of his chest plate without a pause.

"Shuuuucks!" Applebum cried. The Triwin slipped out of his chest plate, blinked back half a foot, and then drove a fresh puncture through his torso, where his ribs would be. Applebum buckled forward to protect himself, but the Triwin slipped back again and drove through his shoulder. This time it fired all the way through, slipping out the other side like a high-caliber bullet.

Russ could see straight through Applebum's body. "Back outside!" he yelled.

The Triwin shook itself off and fluttered toward the ceiling. Russ couldn't tell if it planned to fly away or was just getting more momentum for the killing shot. He didn't wait around to find out. He ran forward, hooking Applebum by the arm and pulling him toward the membrane. Applebum would have been too heavy to move, but he was off balance, and he took rapid steps backward, just to stay on his feet. The Triwin was already in its dive, and it speared completely through Applebum's kneecap, partially severing it from his calf.

Russ and Applebum were through the membrane and back on the spacewalk before the Triwin had a chance to follow. For a moment, it stayed near the membrane, fluttering at eye level, its beak once more open, its jagged teeth flashing.

Then it turned and dove at Starland, driving its beak into her long stomach. Starland opened her mouth to scream, and the sound burst through the comm. The insect flashed upward again and pierced Starland's shoulder in the same spot it had drilled through Applebum. Then it flashed up to the ceiling again.

Kendren and Atara bolted in a panic.

Bah'ren, on the other hand, screamed her own cry of grief and threw herself onto Starland's wounded body. She arrived just as the Triwin was dive-bombing toward Starland's neck, but the creature veered away, purposely avoiding Bah'ren.

Then it slipped under her small frame and speared Starland again, this time deep in her thigh. It had reached the ceiling a third time when Atara brought her stunstick across its back and it exploded in a pop of light.

Bah'ren gathered Starland up in her arms. Green blood sloshed onto the ground at her feet.

Russ felt the membrane pushing against his face and neck as he forced himself back into the cargo hold.

"I sent Applebum back to the *Numbawalla*. How's Starland?"

"It's bad," Atara told him.

"We've got to get her back to the ship," Russ said.

"She's the medic," Bah'ren said, her voice pleading. "How are we going to save her?"

"Applebum can run the CRC machine," Russ said quickly. "But he's already halfway across the bridge."

"I'll take her to him," Kendren offered. Before anyone could reply, he had Starland over his shoulders in a fireman's carry. He bull-rushed the membrane and reached the spacewalk just as Applebum was limping through the access hatch to the *Numbawalla*.

"That was nice of him to offer," Russ said dryly. "Nothing more heroic than volunteering yourself to safety."

"He beat the odds and survived," Atara said. "I've never seen a RreRriaNnian scared before. It kind of freaks me out."

If she'd watched Kendren leave, Russ mused, she would have been even more worried. His eyes had been large, round, and white, like a pair of hard-boiled eggs. The only reason she missed it was because she hadn't stopped looking down the hallway where the Triwin had appeared. She still had her stunstick cocked like a bat. "What were you going to say, Russ?" Atara asked. "How did you know that Triwin was different?"

"It wasn't in a swarm," Russ said. "On Oi0 they were in packs of hundreds, maybe thousands. That one was totally alone. You're the creature expert, Bah'ren. What's that mean?"

When she didn't answer, Russ looked back over his shoulder at Bah'ren. Her face was ashen, and she was staring down at Starland's green blood, which was caked on her hands.

Russ was quiet for a minute, trying to give Bah'ren the time she needed to process what had happened to her good friend. Finally, Bah'ren swallowed and said, "I-it might have killed its swarm. Some creatures in nature kill their own species to ensure they're the only ones left to fertilize the queen."

I've been out at bars at 2:00 a.m., Russ thought. *I've seen that kind of thing before.*

Bah'ren continued, her voice faltering only slightly. "Especially if they're trying to evolve. It's a brutal form of survival of the fittest." She shook her head, reconsidering. "But Triwin queens reproduce asexually. There's no need to compete. The males are worker bees. We could be seeing a secondary evolution, if these SOL idiots tried to use gas."

"You think an extermination squad would be stupid enough to gas a Triwin queen?" Atara asked.

No one answered. Russ realized the entire remaining crew was staring at him. With the power off, there wasn't much noise besides their own breathing, slipping in and out of the filter valves on their rebreathers.

"It's possible," he said.

There was a flash of light as Atara's stunstick powered on again. She raised it, cocked against her shoulder.

Russ followed her gaze down the hallway. At the opening to the next passage, another single Triwin fluttered toward them.

37
RUSS

ATARA HAD BEEN STANDING beside him when the newest Triwin appeared, but by the time it reached their small beachhead at the back of the cargo dock, both she and Bah'ren had taken a step toward the membranous exit. Russ would have gone back with them, but Nina was on board the ship somewhere, and she needed help.

He drew his RNO-Tech sniper. The creature was flying slowly, almost lackadaisically, and he knew he could knock it out of the air if he could draw a bead on it before it got too close. As quick as it could move, a distance kill was probably the best bet anyway.

He raised the barrel, lined up the insect and squeezed the trigger.

The Triwin popped out of existence. For a split second, he thought he'd hit it. The bullet wedged into the wall halfway down the hall. But then the Triwin popped back into sight, two feet from where he'd been aiming.

He was back with Ensine and the waterfall and the drone, except now he was wearing clothes—and this thing was a hell of a lot faster than Ensine's flying toy. Russ pulled the trigger again and the Triwin blinked away again. Bam. Bam. Bam.

The Triwin was inches from his face before he could draw another breath. It fluttered up to his lips, hovering near his mouth, and began to pant.

"Uhhh . . ." Russ said, staring down his nose at the deadly creature just a few inches from his neck. The Triwin hung in the air right at Russ's lower lip. It emitted a soft, happy melody.

"Why are you still alive?" Bah'ren whispered to Russ. She was half a step from the safety of the membrane.

"I'm not sure," Russ said.

"It tried to kill Starland, but it's practically nuzzling Russ. What is going on?" Atara asked.

Bah'ren took a step forward. "Maybe this one is peaceful?" She looked again at the blood caked on her forearms, then she made a decision. "Either way, there's no time to worry about it. We've got to find Nina and the SOL Pest Control crew and get them the hell off this ship before we run into another angry one."

Russ appreciated that she had recovered some of her ability to command. He didn't appreciate the way the lethal insect followed him as he proceeded down the long corridor into the main portion of the ship. It buzzed relentlessly around his nose and mouth. He was too intimidated to swat it away.

"There aren't enough of us left to split up," Bah'ren informed them. "Instead, we loop toward the sleeping area first. It's just below the command center, so it should allow us to get the life-support systems online. Then we arc backwards to the med ward, and the VTR. We gather the remaining survivors along the way, and then it's right out the cargo-hold membrane."

Ahead of them, a dim light glowed under the door of the VTR. There were likely organics in there, but according to Bah'ren's plans, they were to move past them and work backward.

"There's something I was afraid to say back in the cargo hold," Bah'ren whispered. "Creatures don't evolve into solitary hunters. They evolve from solitary hunters to hunting in packs, the same way we're protecting each other right now."

"Then why were those Triwin alone?" Atara asked.

"That's what I've been worried about. One thing a pack does do is expel the weak, especially if there's competition for resources."

"You think the single Triwin that wiped out half our team was the weak one?" Russ asked.

Bah'ren didn't need to answer. They suddenly heard music, the distant, heavy chords of thrash metal. Russ had heard it a lot, growing up in San Diego. It was the kind of music the kids with pale blue eyes and tattoos across their chests would listen to while moshing around their apartments, high as kites. He used to think of it as the sound of white rage. They followed the music, and in just a few steps it was clear it was leading them toward the med ward. When they finally reached the med ward door, it began to crescendo, a thousand identical instruments strumming an impossibly fast chord.

"Oh fuck," Bah'ren said, and Russ watched the terror descend over her face as she fully understood where the sound must have been coming from. "How many do you think there are?"

"A thousand?" Russ guessed. "Ten thousand, maybe?"

"Let's never go through this door," Atara said.

The Triwin hanging around Russ's mouth did not leave to join its swarm. When they reached the ship's living quarters, it was still there, playing its happy melody. Russ kept blowing air at it to shoo it away, but his breath only made the three-inch insect more dogged.

The living quarters were small. Normally, only Kendren lived on board. He'd pushed two small bunks together to fit his broad shoulders, but he hadn't bothered to make the bed or ever clean his sheets. The other beds had bare mattresses with empty footlockers, their lids thrown carelessly open.

Bah'ren went straight to the ladder in the middle of the ship's living quarters that ascended to the bridge. She began to climb the rungs.

Russ breathed at the Triwin and watched as the creature buzzed through the air. He searched the room for any sign that Nina had been there, but the beds were just as he remembered them. His eyes lingered on a bed made specifically for a TEN-awtch, like Starland. It had no cushion or pillows, just a long, smooth stone situated on top of a series of heating coils.

"Why doesn't Starland use a rebreather?" Russ asked suddenly.

"Huh?" Bah'ren said, stopping at the top of the ladder.

"She doesn't have gills," Russ continued. "But she's cold-blooded. Right? How does she breathe? What does she breathe?"

Bah'ren glanced at the green blood caked on her forearms. "She doesn't need a rebreather because she doesn't exhale. TEN-awtch have air pockets in their lungs. Starland can store enough oxygen in them to make it through most missions. I've seen her hold her breath for more than two days."

"She never exhales?"

"She takes in the oxygen and holds it in her lungs, and then it diffuses directly into her blood."

Russ let out a long exhale. The Triwin chittered happily.

"This Triwin isn't trying to kill me. The other one specifically avoided attacking you. It's because we're helping them somehow. That's why SOL Pest Control are still alive too, even though these super Triwin were able to completely wipe out the SAS before they left the cargo dock. We are their ecosystem. I think they're sparing the oxygen breathers."

"Bah'ren just said that Starland breathes oxygen," Atara reminded him.

Russ's mind was cranking. "Bah'ren, you breath in oxygen. What do you breathe out?"

"Carbon dioxide," Bah'ren said. "My home planet is covered in plant-life."

"They're sparing the ones who breath in oxygen and breath out carbon. That's it!" Russ realized. "Triwin must exist on carbon dioxide. They're letting us live to preserve their own air supply."

"Maybe . . ." Atara said slowly.

Bah'ren cocked her head to the side, thinking about what Russ had said. "Yeah. The kid might be right," she said. Then she disappeared up the ladder. Atara followed her.

Russ took a minute to rifle through Kendren's storage locker. It was mostly clothes and guns. Near the bottom he discovered what he was looking for, a tin canister. When he unscrewed the lid, he found it filled with the precious gemstones Kendren had gathered on Qello

He held one up to the light. It looked like a diamond, but it was a pale red. He stuffed it into his pocket.

He dumped the rest of the gems out of the tin and into the locker. He followed Atara up the ladder, the empty tin canister tucked under his arm. The Triwin was still buzzing insistently around his mouth.

Nearly every starscreen on the bridge was covered in thick, gooey webbing. Atara was at the front of the ship, trying to wipe the webbing off the main HUD. It was sticking to her left hand and arm. When she used her right hand to brush it off herself, her forearm got stuck to her chest and neck. "Fuck," she said.

"Their bodies are a lot stronger than they were. The nesting web is stronger than it was. How did these things get so tough so fast?" Bah'ren asked.

Atara wiggled one arm free and used her stunstick to slowly burn away most of the webbing. A clump of it was still stuck to the front of her compression suit. She bent down and picked up an empty can of

CO9. Two more lay empty against the far wall. Atara shook the can in the air.

Bah'ren nodded. "Double mutation. That explains why they're strong enough to punch through Applebum's metal body," she said.

"And stone," Atara added. She had rounded to the main control panel. She was absently picking at the webbing stuck to her chest while her eyes searched the floor.

As he walked beside her, Russ found pieces of Lenus everywhere. For a second it looked like someone had spilled a huge tub of popcorn on the ground. But among the broken, scattered rock fragments, he could identify an arm, part of a calf, several toes, and half of Lenus's face. It stared up at him, the man's stone jaw hanging split and severed.

Even though the giant rock man had been a flunky for P. T. Kling and had a habit of punching Russ in the head, it was still depressing to see him spread out around the control panel.

"Not a carbon breather," Russ guessed.

"You really think that's it?"

"Let's find out." Russ handed Atara the tin canister he'd taken from Kendren's things. "You quick enough to catch mine?" he asked her.

In answer, Atara swung the canister at the Triwin still buzzing around Russ's mouth.

It flashed away, and she followed, swinging the canister at it each time it jumped to a new location. Bah'ren stepped back to avoid getting trampled under their crazy dance. It was like watching someone try to swat a fly, if the fly could move at Mach 3 and drive a three-inch hole through your body when it got angry at you.

Russ started blowing long exhales, whooshing his breath in its direction.

"What are you doing?" Atara asked, already out of breath from chasing the Triwin.

"I'm trying to lure the creature back to a stationary spot."

The Triwin buzzed up to Atara's mouth instead. She stared down her nose at it.

The proximity allowed her to flip the cannister underhand. It glided through the air in a perfect line, swallowing the insect whole.

"The lid, quick," Russ said, tossing her the lid.

She screwed it on tightly. "Got it," she said.

A second later, the Triwin fired out through the top, shredding the tin like it was wet paper.

"Don't got it," she said.

The Triwin buzzed up to her face again, but it flew too close, and one of its wings got caught in the webbing that was still stuck to her chest. It fluttered hard against the web, but it was trapped. "Wait . . . do got it," Atara corrected herself.

Russ took the canister from her and slid it over the Triwin, using the stunstick to carefully burn the extra webbing from Atara's chest so he could trap the creature inside. He screwed the lid on the top.

"The drones can't get through the web. That's interesting. It must function to keep the queen isolated when she's giving birth," Bah'ren theorized. "Or to keep them from killing her spawn."

Russ now had the Triwin safely trapped in the tin canister. He scraped the lid along the starscreen, gathering up as much webbing as he could to seal the hole the Triwin had punctured in the top. He placed the tin as far from himself and the other carbon breathers as the room would allow. He patted his pockets for his phone but all he found were his pain pills. He'd left the phone in the bookstore closet with his regular clothes. He looked for his watch. It wasn't there and hadn't been since he'd wrapped it around Applebum's wrist.

"One, two, three, four . . ." he began.

"What are you doing?" Bah'ren asked him. She had been working with the controls of the *Flashaway*, flipping various handles and turning and twisting knobs. Power had surged back with a momentary pop, then the ship had gone dark again.

"Twenty-two, twenty-three—I'm counting how long it can live without carbon dioxide—twenty-eight, twenty-nine, thirty . . ."

Atara stood beside Bah'ren and yanked a panel free from under the main piloting interface. She lay down on her back and shined a light from the barrel of her rifle upward into the underside of the ship's central controls.

When Russ reached one hundred and thirty-three, the Triwin started to shake inside the canister. Its wings were stuck fast to the webbing, but it was twisting its body around, flexing and bending whatever it had for a spine in rapid, thrashing bursts. A high-pitched wail, like the sound of a car alarm, pitched forth from the cannister, muffled by the webbing but still very, very loud. Across the room, the tin fell over on its side. Russ kept counting.

When he reached one hundred and ninety-nine, the thrashing stopped, and the Triwin fell silent.

Russ kept counting until he reached two hundred and ten, then he retrieved the canister and carefully removed the lid. He tried to shake the webbing out to verify that the Triwin was dead, but the whole mess was stuck firm. He spiked the canister on the floor, but nothing changed. He stomped on it. It buckled under his weight, but the webbing held firm, sticking to his boot.

He walked over to Atara's stunstick, which he'd left propped against Bah'ren's captain's chair. With each sticky step, the canister clanged against the floor.

Then he powered the stunstick on and brought it down hard on the canister again and again. *Thump. Thump. Thump.*

"Jeez," Atara said from under the control panel.

When he stopped, the canister lay open on the floor, demolished, the webbing inside burned to a husk. Russ leaned over the smoking remains. He found the twisted, blackened body of the Triwin.

"It's dead," he said.

"How long did it last without breathing?" Bah'ren asked.

"Either a two hundred count," Russ said, "or it died when I beat it repeatedly with the stunstick."

"At least one of us got something accomplished," Atara said. She got to her feet, holding her arms outward in a victorious pose. Power surged back to the *Flashaway*.

Russ hadn't realized how quiet it was without the ship's systems chugging. The main dash booted noisily back to life, the auxiliary cabin lights blinked on, and the ship's biological support systems started kicking out oxygen; the sounds of space travel had returned to the *Flashaway*.

"It's set to full oxygen recovery," Atara told him. "It's the default system when the power's been off and the ship's in a vacuum. If your theory is right, whatever carbon dioxide is lingering in the air should be circulated out quickly."

The security screens, mounted along one edge of the ceiling, glowed with renewed power. Atara and Bah'ren stood beside Russ and they watched each monitor come back online. First was the starboard side of the *Flashaway*, the news ships still hovering anxiously in the distance. Next was the portside, where the *Numbawalla* waited at the end of the inflatable bridge. Then he could see the cargo hold, the puddle of Starland's blood directly in the center. Then the briefing room. The VTR, then the med ward. There seemed to be some broadcast interference affecting the camera in the med ward. A black, billowing cloud obscured the picture, twisting with a maniacal fury that only allowed brief glimpses of the cabin.

When the final camera came online—the camera that covered the main living space, with its battered Earth-style couches and its small food-storage unit, Russ saw an odd sight. There appeared to be a raised blanket of Triwin, silently swirling around several human-sized shapes.

He reached up and twisted the volume knob. The chittering, musicals sound of the Triwin filled the screen's small speakers, but he could hear something else, faintly. He cranked the volume to full and heard: *"Continued inactivity during work hours, your RQ score has been lowered 15 points, to—bzzzt."*

"Nina's there," Russ said. "She's still alive or they wouldn't be surrounding her. I'm going dow—"

"Look at the med ward," Bah'ren said.

"I don't think the camera is fully functional," Atara said, inching closer to try to make out what was on the screen.

"It's working," Bah'ren said.

Russ wanted to rush to Nina's side, but his eyes were drawn to the camera in the med ward. At first, it looked like the screen was flickering, but as he continued to watch, he realized that the camera was working perfectly. Every once in a while, he could make out the faintest outline of ten bodies, huddled next to each other, but in between brief glimpses was a biological tornado of thousands and thousands of twisting, spiraling Triwin.

"You were right, Russ. The biologics are keeping them alive. The Triwin home planet must be rich with carbon, but on this ship they're fighting for every breath. With the life-support systems down, everyone's air supply must have been dwindling."

"That cloud of bugs is going to be really happy when they find that even more carbon breathers are on board."

"Yeah," Russ grunted, not looking forward to being at the center of that particular discovery.

"But," Atara added optimistically, "if we can get all the carbon producers off this ship, they'll suffocate without a shot being fired."

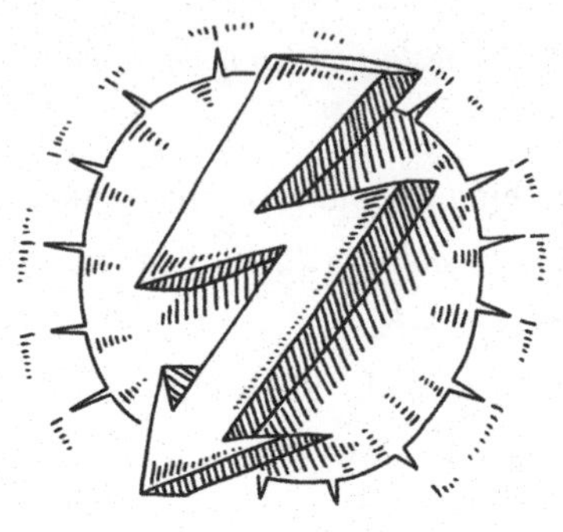

38
NINA

NINA HAD BEEN LYING still for longer than she could guess, her arms held tight against her ears. The insects poured over her body, their tiny claws and sharp beaks scratching at her skin without breaking the surface. She had never been so thankful for a jumpsuit.

The noise was the worst part. Sometimes the Triwin would sing, but mostly it was just the endless cycle of a thousand buzzing, flapping wings, countless snapping beaks, and the patter of tiny, cloven feet. With a kind of removed intellectualism, Nina knew these sounds naturally repelled humans.

And those instincts are right, she thought to herself. The infestation was so thick they could hardly move. The insects were growing larger by the hour, close to two inches long now. Their weight pressed down on Nina and Jaq, and the constant swarming made any kind of motion painful, maybe even impossible. They might have been able to muster a few steps, before collapsing again, but why?

Go where?

In the very beginning, they had managed to flee the cargo hold, and made it more than halfway across the ship, but back then the Triwin had been small and disorganized, quick to latch on to any organic that passed by.

Now they seemed concentrated, purposeful, as if they were learning to move as a pack.

For some reason, being next to Jaq'li helped. The other woman hadn't said a word since the swarm descended on them. Neither of them could open their mouths without a hundred feet tiktok-ing against their teeth. But they were aware of each other, and for a while, Jaq had even reached out and held Nina's hand.

Nina had been noticing the oxygen levels in the ship dropping for the last few hours. The *Flashaway* had lost power shortly after the infestation, and though the insects were too loud for her to be certain, it was likely the oxygen circulation system had shut down as well. The air was thinning, and every breath stung her lungs. Even the Triwin seemed to be growing more agitated.

And then something miraculous happened. The lights powered on, and through the flapping wings and snapping beaks, she could feel . . . a breeze? Yes. Oxygen was pouring back into the room. Her lungs, seconds ago bunched tight in her chest, were suddenly full and open. She pressed the back of her hand against her nose and sucked in a deep breath. If power was back, did that mean . . .

"Nina!" She heard Russ call out. She had never been happier to hear another human voice.

About a third of the pack lifted off her body and went flying straight toward Russ. He stepped into them, then he wrenched the minifridge from the floor and smashed it against the external life support systems. Oxygen blasted out of the pipes where the edges of the fridge had severed them. Nina was aware of Jaq rising to her knees beside her. Russ buried his face in the wave of oxygen. The wind was strong enough to peel his lips from his gums, so it looked like he was smiling.

"Come here!" he shouted to Nina and Jaq; his voice partially lost to the wind.

Puzzled, Nina got to her feet and waddled toward the air supply. The Triwin still clung painfully to her body and each step was like a thousand shallow paper cuts. She reached the broken air tube before Jaq, tumbling into Russ's arms in a mix of relief and exhaustion.

Miraculously, the air seemed to peel away the Triwin. The longer she stayed in the cloud, the fewer buzzed around, until all that were left was a handful of the dead, dazed, and stuck.

"What is happening?" Nina whispered, her voice too soft to be heard.

When she turned to look at Jaq, she could see the poor woman was beset upon by all the Triwin in the room and was now trying to move with twice the number crawling across her head, neck, arms, and chest. Nina ducked back and grabbed Jaq, pulling her into the blasting oxygen.

For a few moments, the Triwin stayed at the edge of the wind, dipping and ducking, trying to fly into it. But then they peeled away, an angry chorus of sounds following them down the hall toward the med ward.

Nina was already back in Russ's arms. She hugged him tightly, her face pressed against his neck. "I don't know what magic you just used, but thank you. Thank you."

"They breathe carbon dioxide," Russ told her. "They need us to stay alive."

"You broke the pipe and it created too much oxygen," Nina said. "You put them underwater."

Jaq wrapped her arms around Russ and Nina.

Russ patted her on the head. "Who are you?" he asked.

"I'm with SOL Pest Control," she said. Then she put her hand up to her eyes. "We've got to find the rest of the crew. If the Triwin need biologics to survive, we can just follow them, and they'll lead us to the survivors."

"No need for that," Russ said. "I'm pretty sure they're in the med ward."

There were more hugs when Bah'ren and Atara cautiously entered the common area. They explained that Russ had asked them to stay behind. The less carbon the broken support system needed to filter and replace with oxygen, the better.

"Jaq," Bah'ren said, hugging the other woman.

"Howdy, Bah'ren. Glad to see you're back in business."

"All I need to do now is unmake this mess your people caused."

"Is there another air vent in the med ward?" Nina asked.

"Every room has feeder tubes, but it works in a circuit—like a sprinkler system." Atara told them. "When Russ broke the circuit, he diverted all the filtered air here. The same trick won't work again."

"Then how are we going to free the others?" Nina asked.

"I've got an idea about that," Atara promised.

When a thousand drowning Triwin want to get through a closed med ward door, they punch a lot of holes. The ragtag crew of Nina, Atara, Bah'ren, Jaq'li, and Russ had plenty of opportunities to stare through and assess the situation.

Still, none of them were fully prepared for what they saw inside. Ten of the SOL Pest Control crew were splayed around the room, three laying limply across the metal tables, three propped against the walls, three more clinging to one another in the corner, and the last lying on his side on the floor. All of them had several thousand Triwin clustered to their shirts, their collars, their shoulders, and their necks. The Triwin that weren't clutching hard to a member of the crew were buzzing and chirping and stridulating, as they fluttered around the small room in fast and slow circles. The heavy music had stopped, but with all the holes in the wall, Russ and his crew could make out other, fainter songs, discordant and haphazard, rising up from various smaller packs of insects. It was a hellish sight and an equally hellish sound.

Nina hadn't read much of the Quran—her dad was actually Chaldean—but she was sure that what she was seeing was one of the signs of the end-time.

Atara's plan was simple and extremely heroic. "We generate five times the carbon dioxide when we're exercising." Atara had dipped back into the oxygen cloud as she said it, drinking deeply from the air. "I'm a lot faster than any of you, so if you hold your breath, and I get my heart rate going, we should be able to divert them all after me."

A Gnurian with large blue eyes turned his head weakly at the sound of the med ward door sliding open. He was one of the ones splayed across the operating tables. A sticky network of webbing locked his arms together in a haphazard cross. It took a moment for Nina to even realize it was webbing as Triwin were stuck on every inch of it, some dead, some flapping their wings in a desperate attempt to escape. Still more clambered over the trapped bodies, hungry for a taste of the faint carbon dioxide leaving the crew members' mouths.

"Run," the blue-eyed Gnurian mumbled when his gaze fell on Nina. His breathing was ragged, and with each gasp, a Triwin flew into his mouth, only to crawl back out again. He dared open it again anyhow. "Run!" he called out to them, his voice faint.

"Hold your breath," Nina commanded. "Hold it as long as you can!" She stood as still as possible, her mouth clenched tight, her nose pinched shut.

It was hard to tell which direction the majority of the swarm was facing. They were bounding around the room in what seemed to be a truly chaotic pattern. But the moment the crew began to hold their breath, the heavy thrash metal returned. The cloud of insects in the center of the room thickened, the music driving them together like the drums of an approaching army. Other Triwin on the outskirts of the fierce swarm skittered over the walls, across the floor, and the ceiling, their beaks glistening.

Fear washed over her, but Nina knew she couldn't open her mouth. She knew she couldn't breathe.

Beside her, Atara shouted a battle cry, "Follow the toreador, motherfuckers!"

And then Atara ran.

39

RUSS

IT TOOK ABOUT SIXTY full seconds for the last of the Triwin to abandon the med ward and zip off in Atara's direction. Once they were gone, Russ worked quickly, but it took time to free the members of SOL Pest Control. They were trapped against the tables, hideously wrapped in sticky webbing.

Bah'ren used a stunstick to burn away much of the webbing around the Gnurian and he dragged himself free from the table.

"Thank you," he said. Then he bolted toward the door.

"If you run you might draw the swarm," Russ called after him, but the Gnurian was already down the hall headed toward the cargo hold.

Two more SOL crew members streamed after him, and two more after that.

Bah'ren, Russ, Nina, and Jaq'li went to work on the last three members of the crew, who were stuck more tightly by the webbing. A hundred or so Triwin were wedged against that same webbing, and even as it burned, they writhed against its grip.

One crew member was sprawled on the floor, not moving, and no Triwin had been buzzing around his mouth.

"This is some sinister shit," Bah'ren told a crew member as she burned him free.

"They didn't trap us. We trapped ourselves," he said weakly. "We tried to use the webbing to keep them away. To cover ourselves with a blanket of something other than fucking bugs. It didn't work."

"Hold your breath until you reach the cargo hold," Russ told him. "Then straight through the membrane."

The alien stuck his fingers up through the nostrils of his own flat-faced pig nose and walked tentatively toward the door.

"I'm worried about Atara," Russ told Bah'ren.

Bah'ren nodded.

A moment after he said it, a single Triwin returned to the med ward, fluttering toward Russ. Then another appeared, and another.

By the time they had reached the cargo hold, a cluster of Triwin followed behind them. The pig-nosed alien went through first, then Bah'ren. Nina went third. Russ was halfway through the membrane when he felt a sharp sting in his side.

Outside, the news ships were already clustering around the inflatable bridge. Their spotlights pierced into Russ's eyes, making everything disappear in a cloud of bright white.

He put his hand down on his side and discovered a hole was torn through his compression suit. When he lifted his hand away—even through the fierce shine of the spotlights—he could see it was wet with his own blood.

"Suit's punctured." He said into the comm of his rebreather. "Sonofabitch tried to cripple me. It figured out we were leaving."

On the far side of the bridge, Jaq'li and the rest of the survivors of SOL Pest Control were climbing aboard the *Numbawalla*.

Bah'ren pulsed her transponder, but before the heat-signature had even populated, she said, "Atara is close. It should only be a second more before she gets out. I've got to go check on Starland, and to make sure those SOL fuckers don't try to steal my new ship. If Atara's injured, help her across. I'm declaring this a full tactical retreat."

She left Nina and Russ alone on the inflatable bridge outside the *Flashaway*.

The news ships circled slowly above, shining their lights, the talking heads bobbing enthusiastically through their starscreens.

Russ stared at Nina.

Nina stared back at Russ. "Where's my dad?" she asked him.

"Home. Safe," Russ said. "Applebum rescued us and then I put your dad in a CRC machine. I think he's better."

"Better?" Nina asked, her voice breaking immediately into tears.

"I think the machine stitched all his parts back together."

Even through her rebreather, Russ could see the tension drain out of her face. He wasn't sure if humans could cry in space—he had barely passed physics—but he got his answer as tears floated weightlessly around Nina's cheeks.

"Oh, thank you, God," Nina said. "Thank you. Russ—I—I—"

"It's cool," Russ said. He wanted to shrug but he didn't dare release the graphene rope or move his other hand off the puncture in his suit. He settled for smiling behind his rebreather. "I'm glad I was able to help."

Nina bounded forward and wrapped him in another hug. She pressed her face against his, their rebreathers mashing together, her eyes launching more weightless tears. "I was wrong about you being selfish. I was so, so wrong . . ."

Russ felt pretty great. But he only allowed himself a moment of satisfaction before worming his way free from her embrace and grabbing her wrist. Her whole arm was shaking, so he steadied it, then pulsed her transponder. "Atara should be out by now," he told her.

Russ held her wrist as the heat information populated on her transponder. "She's in the VTR," he guessed, judging by the distance.

A few moments later, a second heat spot appeared on the watch face. "No, wait. She's in the living quarters. Atara, do you copy?" he said into the comm.

She didn't respond.

"I want to make sure my dad is okay," Nina said, taking a step toward the *Numbawalla*. "They won't kill Atara. We can come back with a larger team. Now that we know about the carbon dioxide, we can plan carefully to—"

Russ pushed his way back through the membrane, Nina's voice temporarily drowned out by the sucking sound of the door sealing shut behind him. Immediately, eight Triwin fluttered up to his mouth and hung there, panting. He could feel one crawling on his upper cheek, just below his right eye. A second skittered across the dense rubber of the rebreather.

A moment later, Nina appeared back in the cargo hold. Triwin immediately started to cluster toward her. ". . . or we can be heroes," she said, resigned.

Her eyes were a little wild, and her right hand was shaking, probably a mix of the heavy emotion and because she was surrounded by so many buzzing, clicking critters. Nonetheless, she was there, just like she'd been on Oi0. The same worried, overwhelmed, heroic Nina who had sat by her dad's bedside for so many months.

Russ grinned, his expression hidden behind his rebreather. "I guess Atara was wrong after all," he said, mostly to himself.

"About what?" Nina asked.

"All the important stuff," Russ told her.

"Okay," Nina said.

They moved together down the hall in the direction of the living quarters. With each new area they passed, Triwin gathered, fluttering behind them like the train of a wedding dress.

As they drew closer to the living area, the music flooded over them like a wave. It raised goose bumps across Russ's arms. The Triwin around his mouth grew agitated. He looked down his nose to see one open its beak, then snap it closed again.

"Don't even think about trying to bite me, you little flying bastard," Russ hissed.

The majority of the Triwin swarm was inside the living area, more agitated than ever, and it seemed to have grown larger, even just in the last few minutes. They circled in tornado shapes, whipping around the couches, skittering over the hard plastic of the food-storage units.

At first Russ couldn't see Atara. But he spotted a trail of blood that began at the entrance to the sleeping quarters and extended to the side of one of the couches. She had tried to make it back to the broken life-support system, where oxygen was still gushing. She'd fallen only a few yards short.

Russ followed the trail of blood with his eyes, until it led him to her right Achilles tendon. A Triwin had blasted through it, severing her work boot and the tendon in a single blast. The heel of her foot was still intact, but it hung free, a gruesome hunk of red flesh and skin.

"It hurts so bad," he heard her whisper through the comm. There were too many Triwin clustered around her head to even see her face, much less watch her lips move.

"I'm getting you out of here," Russ told her. He slid his arm around where he imagined her torso must be. Triwin were pinched between his body and hers, squirming against him like a thousand metal pins. "I've got pain pills."

Russ swung Atara onto his shoulders. He had no idea what the Triwin would do if he moved her. He pinched his eyes shut as their music blasted against his eardrums and their wings blitzed through the air.

"They're going to cripple or kill us if we try to leave," he shouted to Nina over the noise. "Or if we try to go back into the oxygen flow. I'm taking her to the *Flashaway*'s med ward to see if I can figure out how to run the CRC machine. Hopefully going that far won't antagonize them."

Nina didn't answer. He looked in her direction to see that she was scared. She gave him a brief nod. Her hand was beneath her chin. She seemed to be pressing her mouth closed to keep her lips from trembling.

He didn't blame her. Between the music and the blood and the insect wings, he was pretty fucking scared himself. With Atara over his shoulder, they began to walk, slowly, nonthreateningly down the hall toward the med ward.

They were passing the entrance to the VTR when Russ heard the ripping sound of his compression suit, and he felt a new draft blowing against his skin. Then he began to bleed. He had just reached down to touch the injury when there was another rip, and a new portion of his suit tore. This time he caught sight of the bug as it finished driving its long, hardened beak through his clothes and along his flesh.

It was the Triwin version of a warning shot.

Russ glanced at Nina. She was clutching at her own side. When she moved her hand, her fingers were covered in blood. Russ nodded toward the door to the VTR. The swarm was so thick, he didn't want to open his mouth, even though it was shielded behind the hard rubber of the rebreather.

He reached out, slowly, and hit the door-release button. The lights flashed green, and it began to slowly lift toward the ceiling.

"Don't fucking try to come in here!" he heard someone say. The door flashed red again and started to close. Russ carefully lowered Atara to the ground, then slid through the opening, just as the door slammed shut. Nina managed to roll under the closing door, right on his heels.

Atara remained on the other side.

"You stupid son of a bitch," P. T. Kling told Russ. He was standing in the box in the center of the VTR. Hundreds of Triwin abandoned Russ and began to flutter toward him.

"Open the door," Russ told him.

The Triwin continued to hover, though huge packs fluttered through the room, exploring the new space.

"I'm going to open the door so you can get the fuck out," Kling said.

Russ walked casually to where Kling stood, his contingency of Triwin moving with him.

"Don't you do it," Kling warned, but Russ punched him hard in the face anyway.

"Ouch! Dammit."

Nina stood at the window looking out at Atara. "They're really swarming her!" she said. "We need to get her inside."

"Open the door," Russ told Kling.

Kling smirked. "VTR: open main passage," he said. Then he called out, "VTR: instigate solo enemy simulation: Vaqual, who haunts children's dreams."

The room darkened, and a Vaqual appeared in the center. Its single cycloptic eye glared at the three of them with deep hatred. It opened its loose, fleshy mouth and howled its barbaric yawp. Then it rushed toward the swarm.

The Triwin moved as one, diving away from the onrushing creature. The incorporeal Vaqual rushed right through Atara's body, herding the swarm toward the open door. It swung its meaty hook-arms and screamed its terrifying battle cry.

"VTR: close the main passage," Kling said, and the door began to close again. Some of the Triwin were attempting to dive through the Vaqual, to puncture its rough gray skin, but they passed directly across, slamming into each other, the walls of the VTR, and the floor.

"Wait!" Nina called out. She was trying to get outside to Atara, but the cloud of bugs blocked her path.

It took another room-shaking roar from the Vaqual and the swarm of Triwin fled, zipping under the bottom of the closing door, a carpet of squirming, wriggling exoskeleton and gossamer wing.

"VTR: end simulation," Kling said.

Nina pounded on the window, looking at Atara, who remained outside.

Atara was motionless on the floor of the hallway, once again obscured by so many insects as to be almost invisible. Kling and Russ joined Nina, watching.

"You okay out there, Atara?" Russ said into the comm.

"They won't hurt me," she groaned. "They know I won't leave."

"Hell of a thing," Kling said, watching the Triwin cluster around Atara's prone form. "Why do you think they swarm like that?"

"They breathe carbon dioxide. They're sticking close to her because she's keeping them alive," Nina told him.

"Fascinating."

"We've already evac'd what was left of your crew. If the last of us carbon breathers can get through the membrane, these guys will just be an unhappy memory." Russ told him.

Kling looked at Atara's leg. Her blood was still dribbling out onto the floor. "That blood is hers, right? That's a stroke of luck. All we have to do is wait for her to bleed out. We stay safely in here; the Triwin suffocate out there."

"That's good thinking," Russ said. Then he punched Kling in the face again.

Russ turned to look at Atara and Kling slipped away. The little purple man went up the ladder and into the VTR control room.

"You ready to go through this again?" Russ asked Nina.

She nodded. It wasn't the most convincing nod.

They stood directly in front of the door. "VTR, open main passage," Russ said.

Nothing happened.

"VTR: open the main passage," he said again.

Nothing. He looked back at Kling, who was grinning happily through the open hatch to the control room. "I can override the voice controls from up here, you suicidal morons." Kling waved at Russ, then began to pull the hatch closed.

Russ pulled the rifle from his back and shot off Kling's left ear.

40

RUSS

IT'S NOT VERY OFTEN that being a good shot allows you to not kill people. But in this case, Kling was still alive. He was thrashing around the floor of the control room, clutching at his ear and emitting a high-pitched whine.

Except for having one less ear, he was mostly unharmed.

"What the fuuuuuck," he moaned.

"Can you figure out how to override whatever he did and get the door back open?" Russ asked Nina.

"He might have done us a favor. Now we have time to figure out a plan."

"Our plan is: go outside and rescue Atara," Russ said.

"That's not a plan. That's a goal. I was about to rush out and grab her too, but if we're going to survive this, we have to think more than a few seconds ahead. Remember Ensine's lessons? Once that door is open, how do we survive against an enemy that we can neither fight nor flee?"

Russ thought for a second. It was difficult, with Kling moaning so loud. "Hush," he told Kling, and miraculously, Kling hushed.

"This asshole's strategy was solid," Russ said. "We just need to get Atara back inside and then use the Vaqual again to flush them out. Then they suffocate."

"They'll just punch through the door, like they did for the med ward."

"The door looks pretty thick."

"There are different construction codes for training rooms," Kling moaned. "Walls have to be thick enough to survive a blaster shot. It's why I hid in here."

Russ looked at Nina, shrugging.

"I can't think of why that wouldn't work," she admitted.

"Atara? You still awake?" Russ asked into the comm.

"Yeah—" she said. Her voice was very faint.

"I'm going to come outside and get you. If the Triwin follow us back inside the VTR, we're going to flush them back out again. Don't panic."

"Why would I panic?" Atara said in a very small voice.

Russ left Nina and Kling in the control room. He approached the main door and nodded at Nina to raise it. It was only open a fraction when the swarm of Triwin spilled back into the VTR. They buzzed around Russ in such numbers that it was like walking through a snowstorm, if snow was made of three-inch, fluttering daggers. He was already cut in numerous places when he reached Atara and gathered her back up in his arms.

"Sorry," she whispered.

"You saved us," he told her. "No need for sorry." Even as he said it a Triwin tore a long gash in his forearm.

Once he'd taken her back through the main door, he nodded at Nina. He saw her lips move through the glass and heard her voice through the comm. "VTR: Instigate solo enemy simulation: Vaqual, who haunts children's dreams."

The room darkened and the Vaqual appeared again in the center. It roared, thundering toward the Triwin swarm, swinging its meaty arms. This time, the Triwin swallowed it whole. Flashes of the illusion appeared around the edges of the swarm, but the Triwin were unbothered.

"They're learning too fast," Nina told him. "Try another monster!"

Russ knew she was right. In less than an hour they'd learned how to cripple the carbon breathers to keep them aboard, and now they figured out that the incorporeal Vaqual wasn't a threat.

"VTR: Instigate solo enemy simulation: Tharcus, whose skin is without weakness."

The Vaqual shimmied away as a Tharcus appeared in the center of the room. It snapped its jaws at the Triwin. They swarmed out of its reach, but only to the top of the room. The Tharcus leaped at them ineffectively.

"Try something that flies," Atara urged.

"VTR: Instigate solo enemy simulation: Grendo-Fend, who moves with the grace of—"

Behind them, the hatch beneath the control room dropped open and Kling slid down the ladder. He held one hand against his missing ear, and he sprinted past Russ and Atara.

"I know what to do, assholes!" he said, his small legs pumping at full speed.

"Hold your breath!" Nina shouted to Russ.

"Don't try to run," Russ shouted to Kling. Then he held his breath.

Kling made it through the door and halfway down the hall before the Triwin started driving their bodies through his. The first one punctured his chest, then his thigh, then his neck. He was probably long dead before they finished ripping away the pieces of his purple skin.

The Tharcus thundered after the departed swarm, roaring, the illusion dissipating when it left the boundary of the VTR.

With a majority of the Triwin occupied, Russ carried Atara up through the hatch into the VTR control station. He set Atara down on the floor and closed the hatch. Twenty or so Triwin had accompanied him inside, but compared to the pack that was disassembling Kling, they seemed to be barely there.

"VTR: close the main passage." Russ commanded. The door began to slide down to the floor, moving impossibly slowly. Before it was all the way down, a thousand or so Triwin had poured back inside. They circled the VTR, frantically looking for a source of carbon dioxide.

"Here's the plan," Russ said. "We wait for those outside to die, then we deal with the few that made it in here with us."

"That's not a plan. That's a goal," Nina said.

"It's a solid plan," Russ corrected her. "The swarm killed Kling. They cut off their last carbon generator. With us safely in here, they will be dead in two hundred seconds."

The thousand Triwin did seem more frenetic, trapped on the other side of the windows. They began to flash, moving in quick bursts. Their song, which had been exclusively thrash metal, became interspersed with the high-pitched wail of a car alarm.

"This is it. They're dying," Russ said excitedly. "It's a good plan."

The moment after he said it, the first Triwin slammed itself against the ballistic-grade polymer of the windows that separated the VTR control hatch from the VTR proper.

"It's strong plastic," Russ assured Atara and Nina as another Triwin slammed into the barrier inches from his face. "It must be graded out to stop a blaster too, right? It'll hold."

The keening wail of the Triwin was becoming louder.

A third Triwin smashed against the plastic, then a fourth, then a fifth. Then a twentieth. Then it began to split.

"New plan," Russ said. "How long can you hold your breath?"

Before Nina or Atara could answer, the Triwin smashed through the plastic barrier. It came down in large shards as Russ folded himself over Atara's body and drew Nina against his chest. He took a long, deep breath, and held it, the two women clutched in his arms.

The Triwin were momentarily sated by the carbon-rich control room, but with so many of them sucking down the same source, it wasn't long before they began to flash around the smaller space. It wasn't long after that that the high-pitched wail resumed.

Forty-five seconds in, and Russ was already seeing stars. He shucked off his rebreather so he could pinch his nostrils closed with his free hand. He held tight, but he could feel a pounding in his head. The pounding beat louder, intermixed with the cry of the suffocating Triwin. One zipped past his face, shredding through his pinky finger, trying to wrench his hand away from his mouth. He curled in against the girls' bodies more tightly, his chin tucked hard against his chest, his face buried in Nina's hair.

Sixty seconds in, a Triwin drove its beak into his back. It felt like a thick, three-inch needle puncturing through his rotator cuff. The pain diffused into his chest and his stomach. Another Triwin punched into his calf, and he couldn't help but buckle his body in a sharp V shape.

After a hundred seconds, the Triwin were all screaming. The sound was so loud it was bursting his eardrums, creating a sensation impossibly more painful than the tears in his back and calf. *They won't kill us,* he thought to himself, his mouth shut tightly against the pain. *No creature purposely destroys its only source of life.*

After one hundred and twenty seconds, he was certain he would black out. The pain from the noise was thundering in his head, more Triwin were drilling their beaks into his body, digging shallow trenches into his forearms and his thighs, even the exposed portions of his chest. Through the cloud of pain, he could see them doing the same to Atara and Nina.

Russ gritted his teeth against the agony. The solidarity with the other two exterminators helped. If they weren't going to breathe amid all that chaos and pain, neither would he.

No, fuck that, he thought to himself. *If I don't breathe in the next single second, I am going to die. I've got to breath now. I have to open my mouth. I am going to die if I don't breathe now.*

But right after, a second, calmer voice flooded into his head. Just hold on one more moment, it told him. *Just one more moment.* His lungs hiccupped against his chest, sending shudders through his whole body, trying to force his air passage open against his will. But he held on for just one more moment. And just one more moment after that.

The last ten seconds were easy. The Triwin were obviously suffocating, their wail coming only in intermittent bursts. They began to drop from the sky by the hundreds, their tiny corpses pelting Russ, Atara, and Nina. The snowstorm of knives was melting into a hard rain.

Russ probably held his breath a good three seconds longer than he needed to, but he wanted to make sure that the last Triwin was dead before he let himself breathe again.

It was the sound of Nina gasping deeply at the oxygen-thin air that finally convinced him that the long ordeal was over.

Atara huffed next to her, her chest shaking violently.

And then the spasms slowed, as their bodies realized that they weren't going to die after all.

They lay together on the floor, dozens of gashes torn into their arms, legs, backs, and torsos, their blood-wet bodies prone in a ghoulish pattern on the metal grate of the VTR control-room floor.

Atara rolled painfully onto her back.

"It's good to be working again," she said, her voice so quiet it was almost a whisper.

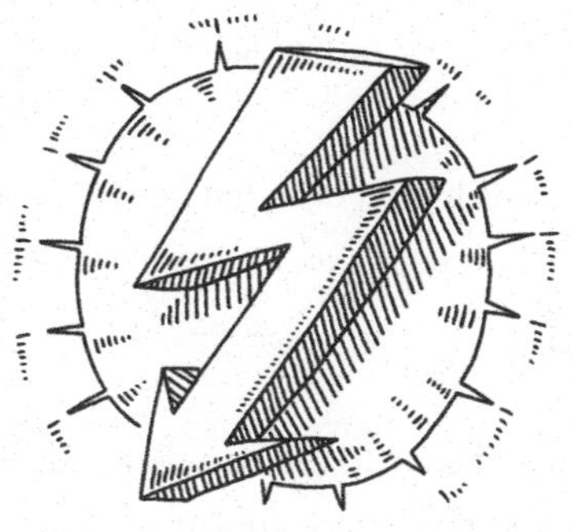

41

NINA

IT HAD BEEN A LITTLE awkward getting completely undressed in front of Russ so she could climb into the CRC machine. He'd insisted that Atara, then Nina, go first, while he lay slumped on a table, popping pain pills and bleeding from many, many different puncture wounds. He was unconscious when Nina was finally birthed out of the machine, feeling like she'd just had the greatest night's sleep of her life.

He was so heavy that Atara and Nina had to work together to get him to his feet. Nina had a rush of fear that he was dead, but Atara slapped him lightly, and his eyes fluttered.

It felt even weirder helping Atara take off all his clothes, especially with him only half conscious. Weirder still that when they had him naked and standing, Atara stood on her tiptoes to give Russ a brief kiss on the cheek.

Atara was just thanking him, Nina assured herself.

It took a long time for them all to be whole again. Eventually Russ stood at the foot of the CRC machine, patting his chest in disbelief.

The Triwin wounds hadn't even left behind scars.

By the time they crossed back to the *Numbawalla*, the news ships were long gone, and the beauty of space almost overwhelmed her. It looked like she felt, vast, peaceful, empty, and yet somehow full.

They found Starland healed and asleep in Bah'ren's arms on a couch in the *Numbawalla*'s small debriefing room. Kendren was on a video call, being interviewed by a Divian newscaster. "And despite the danger, you and your team fearlessly surged forward?" the newscaster was asking him. Kendren's head bobbed, his expression one of noble sacrifice. Nobody seemed to know exactly what had happened to Applebum. Bah'ren told Nina that he'd already Waypointed away by the time she had climbed back aboard.

Russ hadn't been very talkative as they jumped back home to the storage room of the Mysterious Universe.

There was so much noise coming from the main portion of the bookstore that Nina was nervous, despite her great relief at being alive.

They quickly changed out of their orange exterminator jumpsuits and stashed them in the corner by the Waypoint. There was a lot of talking on the other side of the wall. Nina flinched when she heard the voice of that idiot Jake Samuels. Jake was saying something about books.

"Jake and Andy must have returned to shut down the bookstore for good," Nina whispered to Russ.

"We've run out of time," Russ told her. "Sonofabitch."

"We made exactly no money working for Intergalactic Exterminators, Inc," Nina added, shaking her head. "But the bookstore is beautiful. You really made it look great. I know Norma is very proud."

"A hell of a lot of good it did . . ." Russ said. "It doesn't matter how beautiful it is with Jake and Andy packing up all the product."

Nina felt bad for Russ. She'd lectured him on not wanting to help people, but she'd totally misread him. All he did was help people. He'd worked and worked on the bookstore, to have it come to naught.

She paused to listen to the voices through the wall. There seemed to be a lot more voices than just Jake's and Andy's. "Something weird is going on," she told Russ. "We should investigate."

"Come out to the alley first. I have a surprise," he said.

Nina and Russ ducked out the storage-room door and then slipped straight through the backdoor.

That's when Nina heard a distinctive hoot. It was a sound she had been hearing her whole life. Her father had hooted in happiness when her softball team, the Wyoming Cowpokes, had captured the state championship in eighth grade. He'd hooted like that when he'd signed the paperwork to buy their house, and again when she'd opened her acceptance email for the electrical engineering program in Laramie. Her mom had once told her he made the same sound when Nina was born and he had first held her in his arms.

"D-dad?" Nina said, pushing her way past Russ to the street.

Pithyou was riding a child's BMX bike in circles. His head was tilted back and grinning up at the warm September sun, his skin pink and flushed. He was full-chested, upright—healthy.

Nina felt herself running, sprinting really. She caught her dad's handlebars and stopped the bike. He looked back at her with a smile on his face. Then he leaped off the bike with an athleticism she hadn't seen from him since she was very young. He wrapped his arms around her in an enormous hug. "Nina, I've just had the strangest dream," he told her.

Nina didn't answer.

She just held her dad close, feeling his chest rise and fall against her own. "How do you feel?" she asked him.

"Amazing." Pithyou said. "I feel like I'm thirty again." His face fell. "I just had a terrible thought. What if I'm still dreaming?"

"It's like a dream," Nina said, kissing her dad on the forehead. "But it's the real thing." Other than the three of them the alley was empty, and Nina and her father stood near the dumpster, hugging each other, someone else's BMX bike at their feet. She felt her heart swell, and even though she tried, she couldn't control the expression on her face. It must have been a mix of happy tears and vast relief.

When the three of them turned the corner onto Main street, they could see Jake and Andy Samuels exiting the bookstore.

The Sheriff was there too. And Donnie, his deputy. Bum was there, which was strange because it meant no one was working at the Sam'wich Emporium. Nina could see Halsey, the town's only Uber driver, and Nancy from Chinese Food Now, Smokey the town's tow-truck driver, and Bobby from the hardware store. And Mr. Baedeker, Norma's lawyer. And Bibi Nyugen. And dozens of people behind them, clustered around the front windows of the Mysterious Universe. They were standing restlessly, peering into the store, various books hanging almost forgotten in their hands.

"That was the coolest thing I've ever seen," Svenson the EMT told Nina as he approached. He had a large collection of dusty paperbacks under his arm.

"What is going on?" Nina asked him.

"The Chrome Man is inside," Svenson told Nina. "The real Chrome Man! Norma won't let anyone linger in there without making a purchase. But he's in there. He moves. He talks a little bit. It's not a guy in a suit. It's a real robot. I don't know how they did it, but it's sure something. I'm only headed home to get my kid. He'll kill me if I don't tell him about this."

The minute Russ heard "Chrome Man," he hurried away from Nina, Pithyou, and Svenson. He cut the line, slipping through the door and into the bookstore. Nina could see that there were more people inside. She thought she saw a reflection of chrome flash in the sunlight beaming through the window.

Behind her, Svenson hit the sirens on the ambulance and peeled away. Still holding her dad's hand, Nina wedged them both through the crowd and into the store.

She found Applebum sitting cross-legged on the floor by the travel section. He had his arms held out, an open book in his left hand. The Johnsons' six-year-old twin girls were swinging from his metal biceps.

Mrs. Johnson stood nearby, a dreamy expression on her face. A group of locals surrounded her, Applebum, and the twins.

"Harry Potter and the Sorcerer's Stone," Applebum read aloud. "Chapter two."

"Oh shit," Nina said.

She turned to the counter to find Norma, grinning. "I always knew my grandson was destined for something great," she whispered to Nina. "But I had no idea he was such a craftsman. I'm sorry that I cut the lock to the storage room. I just had to investigate. Rufus told me this was supposed to be a surprise."

Nina glanced around. Russ was nowhere to be found.

"The Chrome Man?" Nina asked.

"Russ built it!" Norma said, beaming with pride. "He's been going in and out of the storage room for the past few weeks, sometimes even sleeping in there overnight. Eventually my curiosity got the best of me, and I just couldn't help myself. Imagine my surprise when I found a fully assembled metal man. How did Russ even teach it to read? Do you think that's just a voice recording?"

"Umm," Nina said.

Norma turned to the crowd surrounding Applebum. "All right, people! I've brought you the ultimate trinket! The ultimate novelty!

You want to keep hanging out with it, you gotta buy some books. Terry, you're first."

Norma scanned Terry's book and then put it in a Mysterious Universe bag. When she popped open the cash register, Nina could see that it was so full it nearly couldn't close again.

Russ and Ensine arrived a few moments later, grinning.

Ensine went behind the counter and gave Norma a giant hug, then a quick kiss on the lips. "For three days you don't come around, then you won't stand anywhere near me, and suddenly I'm getting a kiss," Norma chastised Ensine.

She was blushing.

Russ glared at them, but when he looked back at Nina he was smiling again.

Nina nodded toward Applebum, and Russ just shrugged.

"She thinks you built him," Nina whispered.

"He managed to leave the storage room before she saw the Waypoint. He said she was either going to discover it, or him. I guess a fully articulating, sentient robot is a pretty good distraction."

Nina watched the crowd as Norma yelled at someone else to make a purchase. Nina realized Russ was standing right next to her. He put his arm around her back.

They both looked toward Ensine, who was leaning in to kiss Norma on the lips again.

"My grandpa wouldn't like this," Russ said, exhaling. "He was pretty territorial, even into his seventies. Still, I guess I'm happy to see her happy again."

"Me too," Nina said.

They stayed together, Russ holding her by his side.

"Do you think I still have a job? With the exterminators?" Nina asked suddenly.

"Why wouldn't you?" Russ shrugged. Then, just as casually: "My first day of re-CERTification is next Monday. Feel like stopping by the old swimming hole to help me defeat Beuala—who snaps the necks of his enemies?"

Nina looked at him to see if he was joking. "Russ, I love the idea, but aren't you banned from UAIB space? You crossed galactic borders illegally, started a riot, and got slated for a mind wipe. Do you think they're just going to let you reCERT?"

"Someone got banned from UAIB space, but it wasn't Russ Wesley. Remember how I hate signing contracts?"

"You never signed the contract?"

"I signed it," Russ said, pausing dramatically, "Steven Applebum."

Behind them, Steven Applebum mimicked the voice of Harry Potter's evil Aunt, "Dinky Duddydums, don't cry, Mummy won't let him spoil your special day!" The crowd laughed, hanging on his every word.

"Also, when we were on the immigration satellite, Applebum logged into their systems and erased our records."

Surely there are backups, Nina thought dubiously. Still, she couldn't help but laugh. "You better hope the Alliance's record keeping is just as sloppy as Bah'ren's," she said. "Worse case, we could always find you another hard-light transformer."

A few feet away, Norma rang up a customer.

Nina wasn't quite done worrying though. She thought about the fact that while she did have a job, she still hadn't received a single paycheck. Bah'ren may even try to enforce that contract Nina had signed for eighteen months of free labor. Even if he could get back to space, Russ needed to re-CERTify, and that meant more missions for him without pay. He certainly wouldn't have the money in time to pay off Norma's debts. Nina looked around at the crowd, a sad smile creeping onto her face. "I don't think this is going to be enough to save the store, but it's a nice moment nonetheless," she said.

Russ had his right arm around her waist, but out of the corner of her eye, Nina caught him drawing something out of his pocket with his left hand. She couldn't fully see it, cupped tightly in his palm, but it seemed like a large, pale pink stone, maybe in the shape of a diamond. It looked enormously valuable, twinkling as it caught the light of the bookstore, before disappearing once more into Russ's pocket.

"We'll manage somehow," he told her. "We've made it through worse."

EPILOGUE

STEVEN APPLEBUM

ONCE HE'D PURGED HIS records from the immigration satellite, Applebum was officially a free entity. No one would come looking for him. No one would stop him from living whatever life he wanted to live. He could explore entire galaxies or start a robot revolution.

And yet he found himself still patrolling the streets of tiny Evanstown, Wyoming, fighting evil, rectifying wrongs, saving bookstores. It simply wasn't time to leave yet. He'd just rediscovered Emily Dickinson.

One night, Applebum made his way to the bushes outside Morty's Sportys, beyond the light of the storefront.

He could see Morty at the counter, training his new hire, a buxom girl in her early twenties. Morty stood beside the girl, pointing out how to operate the cash register. He reached across to push the register return, and his forearm grazed the young woman's right breast.

When Applebum saw the girl flinch, he stepped out of the darkness and into the light of the sign.

The girl was the first to see him, squealing with happiness.

Morty met him at the door. "How did they get you to move around freely? It must have been some complex programming."

Applebum reached toward Morty and clenched his fingers around the big man's wrist. He lifted him in the air.

Morty gasped and kicked his legs helplessly. Being the size that he was, he certainly wasn't used to the sensation of being lifted. "What is this? Put me down!" he cried.

Applebum locked his eyes on Morty's left iris. "You are entering an honesty protocol. Please answer the following question: Just now, did you touch that young woman's breast on purpose?"

"Who? Stacy? Did I? It was an accident."

"That is a lie," Applebum confirmed.

"No shit," Stacy agreed. She pulled on a jacket to cover her undersized Morty's Sportys shirt.

Applebum lowered Morty to the ground. The big man was grunting in short, high-pitched bursts. The robot appraised him coolly. Since he'd finished reading his very first novel, Applebum had been thinking a lot about the heroes who occupied their pages. Was it better to be violent? Swift? Decisive? Or merciful?

He hadn't decided until Russ demanded he not kill the organics on the immigration satellite, reminding him that he and Russ had once been enemies.

In that moment, Applebum understood. Like himself, every one of these creatures was a product of hundreds of different stories. They had been constructed—from resistor to capacitor—by the myths of their culture, the complexities of their personal experience, and most important, the time others had sacrificed in order to share their own journey. If they were bad people like Morty clearly was, maybe all they needed were better stories.

Applebum reached forward with his other hand and Morty flinched, moving quickly backward until he was pressed against the front of the checkout counter. In his open palm, Applebum held a book. It was Edgar Rice Burroughs's *Princess of Mars.*

"The honesty protocol has verified that you are a lonely, sad pervert," Applebum told Morty matter-of-factly. "However, when you open this book, you will become a hero. You will travel to Mars and save the planet. You will be dashing and handsome and incredibly powerful. Try to learn from the book's hero, John Carter, so you may become a hero in real life as well."

"O-okay," Morty said, suddenly blushing. He rubbed his wrist where Applebum had been lifting him.

"I think I'm actually gonna quit," Stacy told them both, moving out from behind the counter.

As she passed, Morty muttered something that sounded like an apology. Then he stuffed his hands into his pockets and hustled toward his office at the rear of the store. Applebum was pleased to see he had the Burroughs novel tucked under his arm.

"The heroine in that novel never wears clothes, which you should find pleasing," Applebum called after him.

A few minutes later, Applebum returned to the bookstore. Russ was at the register, sleeping facedown on the counter. Even in sleep he had a hammer clenched in one hand and a stack of bills in the other.

Applebum went into the storage room, took his normal position beside the Waypoint, and cracked open a book. Instead of reading, he turned and studied the face of Russ's watch, which was still on his wrist.

It kept ticking, endlessly.

He felt something flutter inside his chest, something akin to worry. Was the watch really manufactured better than he was? Had Russ been right those many cycles ago? Would the watch outlast even a Tech12 with the latest firmware and hundreds of reading hours logged?

It wasn't clear how long he sat there, staring at the watch, before the Waypoint surged to life. It buzzed with power just inches away from his face. Someone had activated it remotely, without it registering on any of Applebum's security protocols.

That wasn't supposed to be possible.

Applebum interfaced with the Waypoint, worried that the other SAS were coming for him now. They had discovered his meddling on the immigration satellite. They would take him back, reprogram him, clear his mind of all he had learned.

They must be forcing their way onto Earth through a government-only backdoor port. The thought sent an involuntary shiver through the neural network along his spine.

He gripped the Waypoint tubing, once more interfacing with its travel protocols. Perhaps he could shut it down, or even redirect the travelers before they arrived.

But then he sensed something very odd. The traveler was alone and arriving from an undocumented location. No one traveled legally from an undocumented location, not even government repo teams. It wasn't supposed to be possible, any more than activating the Waypoint remotely was supposed to be possible.

This was not the SAS at all, he realized. Something buried in his old programming reminded him that that didn't make the traveler less dangerous. If anything, it made them more dangerous.

"Russ!" Applebum called. "Incoming traveler from an undocumented planet."

After a moment, Russ entered from the main portion of the store. He wasn't entirely awake. He still clutched the stack of bills; his eyes were blurry, and his hair was akimbo. "Whas . . . happening?" he asked.

"Incoming traveler," Applebum said tensely. "Consider arming yourself before they arrive."

Frustratingly, Russ remained planted in the spot, rubbing his eyes. "Why'd I bring the bills instead of the hammer?" he wondered.

A split-second later, an enormous man phased outward from the Waypoint.

The man had a barrel chest and a beard the same gray-brown color as his wavy, unkempt hair. His hair was actually a mirrored reflection of Russ's, standing on end in a chaotic nest. He also had Russ's face, and much of Russ's coloring. Applebum understood he must be staring at one of Russ's biological ancestors.

"Russ?" the man's voice boomed. "Is that you, grandson?"

Russ didn't seem half asleep any longer. In fact, his mouth hung open, his jaw nearly planted on the floor. "Grandpop?"

The big man stumbled forward, then began to dig recklessly through the oddities that still littered the storage room. "I'm sure you have some questions," Russ's grandfather said. "Unfortunately, I'm in a hurry. There's something I need to find. I'm afraid I need it quite badly."

When he turned, Applebum observed a long gash on his forearm. The burns around the edges indicated some sort of laser weapon. "He's been shot," Applebum warned Russ. The wound was recent. Despite the heat of the weapon it hadn't cauterized, and fresh blood flowed down the old man's arm.

"Yes, I'm afraid it's something of a matter of life and death," Russ's grandfather nodded, his breath coming in quick gasps.

"You're already dead," Russ said. "Aren't you?"

"Maybe you've seen it?" The old man held his hands together in the shape of a softball. "It's a green rock called an Obinz stone, roughly this big, with yellow veins running across the surface . . . Russ? Do you know where it is?"

Russ didn't speak.

"The stone, grandson. I need it now."

Applebum could see the old man's hands were shaking. He remote-scanned the man's vitals, and found that his heart was beating unevenly, and his temperature was several degrees too low for a human.

"Be cautioned Russ, I believe he's hiding very serious injuries," Applebum warned.

Before Russ could say a word, the old man's knees buckled, and he tumbled forward.

Applebum reached out and caught Russ's grandfather, just moments before he would have face-planted directly onto the floor at Russ's feet.

On his way down, the big man's clothing hooked onto the corner of the watch on Applebum's wrist. Under the strain of his weight, the entire back of the watch popped away. Its guts torn open, it spilled gears, knobs, and a battery onto the cold, beautifully refurbished wooden floor. A small spring that had been trapped inside fired forward, bouncing off Applebum's chin.

Applebum lowered Russ's grandfather gently to the ground, and then lifted the watch to his eyes.

He stared into its blank, broken screen with deep satisfaction.

APPENDIX

Alphane S Transportation Hub: A densely populated planet which boasts one of seven centralized UAIB Waypoint hubs. Waypoints are manned by spaceclerks who log the bio-signature of every traveler.

Beuala—*Who Snaps the Necks of His Enemies*: A four-armed subspecies with a powerful grip. Some tribes of Beuala have petitioned the UAIB for inclusion in their charter, but have thus far been unsuccessful. Naysayers often cite the Beuala's long history of violence and cannibalism, as well as many tribes' flat refusal to abandon their savage cultural ways.

BLEB (Below-the-line Employment Bureau): A government program implemented to resolve disagreements and to field complaints from employees who work in certain high-fatality job classifications.

Buuffaaffaa—*Whose Enemy is Left Flattened*: A dangerous subspecies weighing between one and ten thousand pounds. Buuffaaffaa are generally blob-shaped with a larger base circumference, and they move by constricting their upper muscles down toward their lower muscles, which creates a propulsion motion similar to leaping.

CERTification Training (Centralized Empirical Repulsion Tactics): All government workers who wish to perform work deemed physically dangerous must clear a series of tactical training standards. CERT training proves the viability of the worker, but it can also act as a government visa. Species that are not part of the UAIB charter are allowed access to UAIB space if they acquire and maintain CERT-based authorization. A combination work visa and CERT training are almost always associated with below-the-line employment opportunities. The CERTification process traditionally includes significant unpaid on-the-job-training hours.

CRC Machine (Carbon Repair Chrysalis): The universal standard in healing. The CRC machine can 3D print bio-repair filament from stem cells in order to repair or replace organic material, making it capable of curing nearly everything except death. A companion instrument, the CRC wand, has the functionality to scan for organic damage in the field and report the information back to a ship's onboard med ward.

Dexadrive Lanes: A system of interstellar transport utilizing wavelike propulsion technology. Before the commercialization of Waypoints, Dexadrive lanes were the primary transportation protocol, and they still crisscross the majority of UAIB space. Starcraft travelling within the lanes while equipped with Dexadrive engines can achieve much-faster-than-light (MFTL) speeds.

DFA Network (Divian Frontline Actual): One of three Divian homeworld news and entertainment networks. The popularity and reach of Divian culture is often attributed to the intergalactic presence of such networks, as well as the highly polished and highly budgeted nature of their programming. Disclosure: both this glossary and Divian Frontline Actual are owned and operated by the same parent company, Rascoff/VonGrun Universal.

Divian: One of the seventy-three species of the UAIB. A humanoid species with purple skin and neon, multi-colored eyes, Divians are the founding species of the UAIB and enjoy special privileges. While once considered a culture of equality and high ethics, the Divians's popularity has receded over the course of the last century. Their homeworld, Ren'Div, widely accepted as the center of the universe, is also known for its ranch-estate living and astronomical real estate prices.

Dreadwalker—*Whose Grip is Mighty*: A six-legged amphibian with a strong exoskeleton and two powerful claws. Dreadwalkers are universally feared, notoriously easy to influence and breed under almost any conditions. They have a history of being produced and/or conscripted into war, where they make dangerous, tireless drone-like fighters.

Gas 'em and Trash 'em Unlimited: One of a handful of ecosystem preservation squads. Gas 'em and Trash 'em perform dangerous exterminator jobs in hopes of collecting government subsidies. Also known as "Orange Suits" for the orange jumpsuits ecosystem preservation squads wear while working.

Gnurian: One of the seventy-three species of the UAIB. Average Gnurian height ranges from five to seven feet for males and three to five feet for females. They have pale purple, light blue or aquamarine skin. Hyper-shifting splotches of colorful melanoma move across their skin in unpredictable patterns. A matriarchal society, Gnurian females are reputed to be highly capable. Contrarily, their homeworld, Gnu Gnaru, is widely known to struggle with corruption, as well as issues with basic infrastructure and maintenance.

Grendo-Fend—*Who Moves With the Grace of the Wind*: One of the oldest known species, which hunts with an elongated, sturdy beak made of both cartilage and bone. The Grendo-Fend is capable of flight due to a fixed membrane that runs between its outstretch wings, down the entire length of its legs. Fossil fragments have been carbon-dated all the way back to the era of the XVAS civilization where scientists believe the Grendo-Fend was originally a tree-dwelling biped.

IBED (Immigration and Border Enforcement Department): The UAIB "border patrol" division, unique among municipal programs in their almost exclusive employ of inorganic SAS units. IBED agents' central task is to keep non-UAIB species out of UAIB space. Part of this duty requires the use of the non-fatal "mind cleanse," an artificial aging of the illegal alien species' brains.

Jinxden—*Whom None Have Seen Up Close*: Also called "the cloud of cacti," the Jinxden are over-sized airborne insects capable of tremendously fast starts and stops. They travel in packs of several hundred that can shift direction with synchronous precision. When threatened, the Jinxdin discharge small projectiles, roughly the size of a sewing needle.

Kruxfas: One of the seventy-three species of the UAIB. The Kruxfas have hooked legs, elongated heads, and onyx eyes. Widely regarded as a highly intelligent species, they are responsible for a number of technological breakthroughs, including the Waypoint and the CRC machine. The Kruxfas are also capable fighters. Because of the combination of brains and physical dexterity, the Kruxfas often go out of their way to advertise their own cultural passivity so as to not threaten the other species in the UAIB collective.

Maxibrew: Though popularly derided as "pisswater," Maxibrew is nonetheless the best-selling alcoholic beverage in UAIB occupied space. This is partially due to its far-reaching supply chain and relatively low production cost.

MERC Board (Registered Municipal Employment Collective): UAIB municipal teams were originally employed directly by the UAIB themselves. However, after a public pension scandal, the UAIB dismantled their municipal workforce and now rely on CERTified independent contractors. The MERC board is the official posting location of all available municipal jobs.

MUPmap (Multi-User Protocol): A crowd-sourced map of the multiple galaxies as well as the standard intergalactic navigation tool. Planet data is collected by individual travelers and shared with all other subscribers. Most data is collected passively by the Map's systems, but users ascribe specific icons to inform other travelers of a location's unique qualities.

Obinz Stone: A battery capable of tremendous power, universally used to power Waypoints. Obinz stones are mined from the ground in an unrefined state. Planets which are found to naturally produce Obinz stones quickly become flush with wealth, and all the complications therein.

Planet Nustrix: A planet in the Bellatronix cluster that must be monitored to manage reoccurring instances of Jinxden overpopulation.

Planet Qello: Fringe planet in the Proxima Imperatus cluster, known for its lethal bacteria, fauna, flora, and fungi. While no apex predator rules the skies, on land the a carnivorous, highly territorial, four-legged Ophidian sits at the top of the food chain. Unique tectonic plant placement results in sporadic, unpredictable tremors, often followed by volcanic eruptions and tsunami.

RNO-Tech (Rascoff *Necraemia* Originals): One of several major UAIB weapon's manufacturers. RNO-tech rifles use a piston system driven by onboard combustion engines. Their operation requires the use of both traditional ammunition and fossil fuels, but the 8000 series is renowned for being able to inflict damage on par with high-end energy weapons, despite being far cheaper to produce.

RQ Score (Ready Quotient): The employment standard by which CERTification trainees are measured. Though all CERTified individuals are qualified to work, those who graduate with a higher RQ score often have the advantage of finding more desirable employment.

RreRriaNnian: One of the seventy-three species of the UAIB. ReRriaNnian are on average larger and have more significant body hair and muscle mass than any other humanoid race in the UAIB charter. Thanks to their size, dexterity, and machismo culture, many UAIB professional sports leagues are dominated by RreRriaNnian athletes.

SAS Unit (Syvon Al'Supres): A multi-use android named for its founder, Syvon Al'Supres, who introduced the Tech 1 model in Divian year 17,02.06. After the unexpected deaths of Al'Supres and his entire family, the SAS's patent became publicly available. Multiple corporations manufacture SAS units, but they share version numbers to track value and functionality. The latest iteration, the Tech 12 unit, was first issued in Divian year 21,21.11 by Waymore Enterprises.

Shared System of Civics: A collection of fundamental civic standards that all municipal employees must adhere to. Failure to follow the standard results in immediate deCERTification. They are as follows: **(1)** A municipal employee must protect the anonymity and reticence of the United Alliance of Intelligent Beings. **(2)** A municipal employee must do no permanent harm to any planet's natural ecological balance. **(3)** A municipal employee must not remove a planet's natural resources for his or her own benefit. **(4)** A municipal employee must not be the direct cause of death for a civilian belonging to any of the seventy-three certified UAIB population groups.

Sol Pest Control: An ecosystem preservation corporation. Sol Pest Control is part of a special government program testing out the use of SAS units for government municipal work beyond immigration services.

Southern Blurn: One of the seventy-three species of the UAIB. Southern Blurns are rare aquatic mammals. Covered in scales where most mammals have skin, Southern Blurns can breathe air from their mouths and water from the gills on their necks. A Southern Blurn who wishes to live out of the water must drink copious liquids in order to maintain necessary hydrogen levels. Southern Blurns hail from the entirely oceanic southern hemisphere of the planet Blurn. While the land-dwelling Northern Blurns are known for their rich culture of avant-garde art and music, the water-dwelling Southern Blurns tend to prioritize family and recreation.

Southland Demolitions and Refuse Removal: One of a handful of infrastructure maintenance crews who perform repair work for government subsidies. Also known as "Yellow Suits" for the yellow jumpsuits infrastructure maintenance squads wear while working. Southland Demolitions was famously a part of the Great Robot Riot aboard the Alphane S Transportation Hub.

Ten-awtch: One of the seventy-three species of the UAIB. Cold-blooded, savage warriors who are also known to be equally gregarious in social situations. Ten-awtch walk upright on two legs, but have long torsos, and scales on their heads and the tops of their arms. Their ectothermic nature requires special sleeping and eating arrangements, but makes them more suited for work on hostile planets with limited breathable air.

Tharcus—*Whose Skin is Without Weakness*: Savage subspecies primate from planet Oi0. Hostile living conditions have evolved the creature to have nearly impenetrable skin. The average female outweighs the average male by several hundred pounds and has an ornate mane of course hair. The males of the species, while smaller in stature, follow far less predictable behavioral patterns.

Toers: One of the seventy-three species of the UAIB. Toers are bipedal with smooth skin, limited skeletal support and almost no muscle definition. Culturally unaccustomed to verbal communication, Toers "speak" by shifting their skin color. Because of their weak physicality, they are highly untrusting of other species.

TRennus: The warmest month on the planet of Ren'Div. The last few years have seen record-breaking heat waves reaching temperatures as high as 86 degrees on the Universal Standard Temperature Index (USTI).

Triwin—*The Consonant Swarm that Blots out the Sky*: Triwin are three-to-four-inch insects with sharp beaks. Triwin queens, the leaders of their drone-colonies, reproduce asexually and have litters in the thousands. Classified as hypermutating mega-birthers, Triwin are capable of gigantic leaps forward in evolution when exposed to certain catalysts.

UAIB (United Alliance of Intelligent Beings): A loose conglomerate of seventy-three sentient species. Elected senators from each recognized species vote on universal rule changes and other matters regarding the intergalactic charter. Additional functions include the collection of taxes and the monitoring and funding of municipal services. Municipal services include Law Enforcement, Infrastructure Maintenance, Transport Security, Refuse Disposal, Ecosystem Preservation, and Emergency Response.

UFu (Universal Fertilizing Prep Kit): A budget over-the-counter prep kit intended as the first stage in non-compatible interspecies fertilization (binary and non-binary, only).

Vaqual—*Who Haunts Children's Dreams*: A terrifying subspecies that can reach up to 27 feet in height. That, combined with their nightmarish appearance, has made them popular in both ancient folklore and modern UAIB entertainment. The extremely powerful Vaqual have a thick muscle mass and arm bones that end in pointed hooks. With a single, underdeveloped eye, they rely heavily on their sense of smell. Adolescent Vaqual suffer from a skin condition which covers their face and shoulders with puss-filled abscesses. The Vaqual's unique features, combined with its long-lasting popularity in cinema, result in its perennial number one seller status in BeaBetteru's collectable line of miniature plushies.

Waypoints: Relatively new teleportation technology. Waypoints allow users to move instantly from one location to the next and, as a consequence, have revolutionized much of intergalactic life. They range from portable, single-use units to permanent, ornate structures that focus just as much on form as they do function. Due to IBED's limitations in regulating Waypoint travel, the proliferation of Waypoint technology has also caused a significant uptick in theft, the transfer of black-market goods, and illegal immigration. Thus far, the UAIB governing body has been slow to pass effective legal deterrents to protect against the unintended consequences of this emergent technology.

YouStar: High subscription costs have left many in the UAIB unable to afford access to professional entertainment and news networks. YouStar is an opensource communication platform in which average citizens can record and post videos for a variety of purposes.

ACKNOWLEDGMENTS

A Few Quick Thank-Yous

PUBLISHING A BOOK IS a long journey. If you're lucky, you gather allies along the way. I wanted to say a heartfelt "thank you" to all the people who stood by my side through this process: Caitlin Blasdell, Elana Gibson, Jesse Kellerman, Jared ("Get it in libraries; let the public decide") Hummel, June Roberts, Russ Nickel, Cornelia Gordon, Binney Caffrey, Jen Fleischer, Robert Mulgrew, and particularly, Marisa Holzer, without who(m) my *theres* would still be *theirs*.

ABOUT THE AUTHOR

ASH BISHOP WAS BORN in Bloomington, Indiana, where his dad taught at Indiana University. His family moved to Orange County, California, when he was very young, and he spent his formative years on the mean streets of Irvine. He attended college at UCSB, then the National University of Ireland, Galway. Ash is also a graduate of San Diego State University with an MFA in Creative Writing. He's married to a wonderful wife with two wonderful children.

He spent a good number of years as a high school English teacher, but he's also done a few less important, though slightly more glamorous, things. He worked in the video game industry for Sammy Studios, and in educational app development with Tappity App; and he even used to fetch coffee for Quentin Tarantino during the production of *Jackie Brown*. When he was young, he worked as a lifeguard because he may or may not have grown up without ever missing an episode of Baywatch. He currently produces script coverage for a Hollywood movie studio.

Ash is a lifetime reader. He especially loves fantasy, science fiction, and mystery reads, but also dabbles in the classics thanks to all those years teaching F. Scott Fitzgerald and Edith Wharton. He plays *at least* an hour of Magic the Gathering a day, and considers a revival of *Logan's Run* and *Robotech* among his dream projects. He is currently running a very loquacious level-8 Bard through *The Rise of Tiamat* (alongside three friends and a cruel, unforgiving DM).

Intergalactic Exterminators, Inc is his first novel.

If you liked

Ash Bishop's *Intergalactic Exterminators, Inc*

you will also like

***The Meister of Decimen City* by Brenna Raney.**

1

DINOSAURS ON MAIN STREET

REX MADE A LIST of her obligations from most pressing to least pressing, with "deal with the dinosaurs" at the top. It was a stress-managing exercise her high school counselor had suggested. It hadn't worked then, and it wasn't working now.

The TV over her workbench screeched, and she looked up. The news was still showing live helicopter footage of the dinosaurs tearing down Main Street. As a velociraptor-looking thing—someone in the lab was watching too much Jurassic Park—crashed through a line of abandoned cars, the Lightning zapped onto the scene. Rex winced as the superhero punched the raptor in the face, electric flickers bursting from the impact, and reporters broke into happy hysterics.

The ding of the lab door made her jump, but it was just Flora striding in with a jet-black hair swish. A pair of metal eyes hovered after her, robotic voice calling, "I couldn't keep her out, Doctor."

Despite having written the subroutine for Ai to say exactly that, Rex didn't find it funny.

"When you said you were working on the dinosaur project, I thought you were researching how the dinosaurs died, not unleashing a dinosaur-themed apocalypse," Flora said.

"This wasn't intentional," Rex hissed, moving to the end of the workbench to flip through her notes. "They shouldn't have gotten out."

Flora adjusted her glasses and rested her other hand on her hip. "You need to deal with this before the Lightning traces them back to the source and beats your face in with her taser-fist of death."

"I'm trying!" Rex tossed the notes away in frustration. "What did kill the dinosaurs? The same thing would work now, right?"

"Climate change?"

"Shall I run simulations on potential asteroid impacts?" Ai offered. Its two eyes bobbed next to each other over the workbench, a trick with magnets that had been a bitch to work out but looked really cool. Still, the two staring eyes were getting to Rex in a way one staring camera never had. She snatched up the to-do list and scribbled "give Ai eyelids" at the bottom.

Screams erupted on the television as a news chopper dipped too low and a variety of dinosaur with some truly impressive back legs leaped high enough to catch one of the helicopter's ski-looking thingies in its jaws.

"I don't remember making so many," Rex muttered as she rushed to the chemical zone to mix a hasty genetic destabilizer, pausing only to shove goggles over her buzzed, blonde head and cover freckled hands with a snap of gloves.

"You got clone-happy." Flora followed her past the line of red tape on the floor with quick little steps in her pencil skirt. Rex wondered how she was still so intimidated by professional dress after seeing Flora in it almost every day for five years. "I warned you. The whole city warned you. It's in point three of the latest truce agreement—"

"The clone clause—yes, I know." Rex didn't have genetic material to form the dinosaur base at the home lab. It was all in the Peak Street facility, which the dinosaurs shouldn't have been able to escape from if her lab techs had followed her damn instructions.

Rex dropped into a chair and ran her hands over her face, pushing the goggles up. "I'm just going to take the Exo-suit and go punch dinos with 'Ning." The hero couldn't zap her if they were fighting side by side, right?

Shit. She was so screwed.

"I will call up the mecha," Ai confirmed, cuing the hum of moving floor panels.

"You can't Voltron your way out of every problem," Flora chided.

"But I can Voltron my way out of this problem." Rex was already stepping around the hollow robot rising out of the floor—to date mostly used for wrangling hostile test subjects from the bottom of the ocean or breaking safes Rex had forgotten the combinations to.

"Hey." Flora put a hand on her arm before she could slide it into the myoelectric sleeve. "If the Lightning tries to fight you, don't stick around. There's no shame in running away."

"There's so much shame in running away."

"There's more shame in getting your ass kicked by a superhero. And frankly, I don't think you need more brain damage."

"A real friend would support me." Rex strapped herself into the suit's harness and straightened her spine for the neural uplink.

"I try. Call me later to let me know you're alive."

Punching dinosaurs wasn't as satisfying as Rex had hoped. In practice, it was basically animal abuse.

No "basically" about it, she thought as a feathery thing went down with a squawk. She tried to reassure herself that knocking them out to be re-contained was better than letting SWAT shoot them. The area had been evacuated, so she didn't see a reason to put them down, anyway. When Rex showed up, the Lightning met her eyes, sort of—her yellow costume covered her whole body, including her face, and Rex's suit had robot eyes that didn't line up with the pilot's. Then she nodded once and turned her back to the mecha, which Rex took as acceptance of their team-up.

It was probably for the best—that yellow costume was really tight, and Rex had trouble keeping her eyes up when they were face-to-face for any length of time.

The Lightning was a bright streak in her peripheral vision, zipping from building to building using her Static Cling and tasering the crap out of the dinos too fast for the Exo-suit.

That left Rex dealing with the heavy hitters, which had no business being so bloodthirsty considering their build and metabolism, but she figured it was a fitting punishment for making the Lightning take time out of her day.

For a strong-and-silent-type hero, 'Ning could be fantastically passive aggressive.

Regardless, they made as efficient a team as they always did when a common enemy—or a Rex fuck-up; honestly, it was usually a Rex fuck-up—made them temporary allies. The local news stations were the only ones who still found it surprising. Rex could already see the headlines: The Lightning and the Meister: Dawn of a New Age of Cooperation? As though they hadn't run something similar half a dozen times already.

'Ning didn't stick around after the last stegosaur crashed to the asphalt and the police closed in. She never did. Apparently, sexy-fine superheroes were wasted on cleanup, but it was all right to let a perpetually pseudo-probationary supergenius take responsibility for the stampeding dinosaurs she'd accidentally released. Rex opened her phone screen inside the Exo-suit to shoot Flora a "still alive" text and groaned at the missed messages Ai had helpfully labeled: Mayor—urgent.

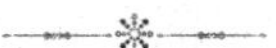

The one perk of meeting with Mayor Vicker so often was that his staff always bought Rex dinner. This time, she ordered a burger without cheese, but they delivered one with cheese, anyway. And not the kind of cheese she could peel off, no—the kind that seeped into every crevice in the patty and made it bleed yellow. She used half the stack of paper napkins wiping it off and wrapping it up so the smell couldn't escape.

"—and there's nothing I can do about it. You signed the document," the mayor was saying.

Rex had lost track of the conversation while removing the fungal cancer that some worldwide conspiracy deemed worthy of calling food. She glanced across the conference table to note Mayor Vicker's usual tight expression as he either berated her or explained a legal issue.

His assistant sat next to him with a colorfully-tabbed planner forgotten in his hands and a look of distaste as he watched Rex's growing pile of cheese napkins.

"Are you paying attention? I'm telling you, Ms. Anderson, it's out of my hands. We're talking about federal law."

"What's out of your hands?" Rex asked. She had a sudden epiphany: They're called landing skids. Why did they use those things, anyway? Why not put all helicopters on wheels?

The mayor gave her a disappointed frown. "Ms. Anderson, you violated point three of your truce agreement—"

"The clone clause—I know," she said, inspecting the decontaminated burger. She winced as the first bite hit her tongue. Could she actually taste it, or was her brain just reminding her of the gelatinous orange waste that had been smeared all over her food?

"For Christ's sake, just eat it! You wiped it off. Stop being so dramatic about it," the mayor burst out. Yeah, and if someone took a shit all over his burger, she was sure he'd just wipe it off and forget about the particulates of fecal matter mushed into the meat.

“The security measures I have in place are ironclad if they’re followed,” Rex said, lowering the burger in surrender. “I’ll oversee it myself this time. So wherever they’re being held, I’m eager to plead my case to regain custody.”

“You’re worried about the dinosaurs?”

“They’re the big losers here. I’ve been tasered by ’Ning before. It isn’t fun.”

The assistant—Hammond? Hansen?—raised an eyebrow. “You want the city to release the horde of dinosaurs back to the mad scientist who set them loose on Main Street?”

“This didn’t happen because I’m mad,” Rex protested, pointing at the assistant. “It happened because my lab techs are incompetent.”

“A horde of dinosaurs,” the assistant sneered.

“I really didn’t think I’d made so many.”

“Regardless, you did,” the mayor cut in, rubbing his forehead. “Which is an unambiguous violation of the truce you signed. National news sources have already picked up the story. This can’t be swept under the rug.”

Rex didn’t like the direction this was going. “That Oversight stuff is optional at the local level, right?” Forgetting herself, she took another bite.

Mayor Vicker gave her a thin-lipped look, his forehead wrinkled all the way to his hairline—wherever that was.

Mayor Vicker’s hair was thinning in such an even gradient that the top of his head looked more like a swatch of grayscale than a separable head and forehead.

“Listen, Rex.”

She swallowed.

This wouldn’t be good.